HOLLY OAK
PRESS

RON JAMES

QUANTUM DECEPTION

A LUKE PAYNE THRILLER

QUANTUM DECEPTION

Published by Holly Oak Press

www.hollyoakpress.com

Cover & book design: Ron James

ISBN (Paperback): [979-8-218-80544-9]

ISBN (eBook): [979-8-9998895-0-8]

ISBN (Hardcover): [979-8-9998895-1-5]

Printed in the United States of America

First Edition: August 2025

5

FOR MARY

MY PARTNER IN ALL ADVENTURES

THANKS TOO FOR THEIR HELP AND
ENCOURAGEMENT

JOHN MUNCIE

MICHAEL HELLMAN

AUTHOR'S NOTE

While this novel may reference real-world locations, events, and general political climates, all characters and situations are fictional. Any similarities to actual persons, living or dead—including public figures—are coincidental or the result of creative dramatization. Nothing in this work is intended to represent actual facts.

"Nearly all men can stand adversity,
but if you want to test a man's
character, give him power."

— ABRAHAM LINCOLN

PROLOGUE: THE MISSION

SHANGHAI, CHINA

The room was dark—deliberately so. Every nonessential detail had been stripped away, leaving only the soft glow of a monitor casting a cold blue light over a polished desk. Beyond the tinted glass, Shanghai sprawled in steel and neon, its rhythm distant and disinterested.

A secure line crackled to life. The voice was calm, unhurried. "Are you ready to begin?"

Chandra Sochi adjusted his cuff with slow precision—a ritual more than a habit. "Yes. As instructed. We've identified Lee. Ambitious, cautious. Paranoid about surveillance—which makes him controllable. Once he sees the money, he'll sign on."

"Good. Lee's team is ideal. You've reviewed the assignments?"

"Finance. Defense infrastructure. Energy grid. All confirmed."

He hesitated. Then, "And the arts foundation? It has no strategic relevance."

"It's not about value," the voice replied. "It's personal. Old ties, old debts. Execute as instructed."

He nodded, understanding the implication. It was much more than a regular operation. It was a web of secrets, old loyalties, and hidden agendas all intertwined.

"Understood."

"Timing is everything."

Click.

Sochi replaced the receiver and let the silence settle. He turned to the mirror, smoothing his hair and adjusting his tie with meticulous care. His reflection showed a man composed and in control—at least on the surface. But beneath, something tugged at him. A faint feeling of unease. Kahn had brought it up three times in two weeks—too often to dismiss as coincidence.

He understood men like him. When they fixated on something, it wasn't random. And it wasn't wise to ask why. You didn't pull at threads unless you were prepared to be part of the unraveling.

He held the stare in the mirror a moment longer, then let it go.

He opened a matte-black briefcase, revealing stacks of crisp U.S.. hundred-dollar bills. They felt heavier tonight—symbols of the stakes at play.

Outside, the city pulsed beneath a haze-heavy sky—horns blaring, mopeds weaving through puddles of pink and gold. The vibrant chaos of Shanghai thrived, oblivious to the shadows cast by unseen wars.

He slowly opened the door and stepped into the corridor, leaving the room in darkness.

The game had begun. Some of the pieces didn't even know they were in play.

CHAPTER 1: NOT TODAY

Shangri-La Estate, Point Loma, San Diego — Two Weeks Later

Luke Payne stood barefoot on the cool flagstones beside the pool, palette knife in hand. Sunrise spilled softly over his hillside refuge, casting golden hues across the bay—the hazy shimmer blurring edges, the Coronado Bridge reaching toward the sky. The view was meant for peace. Today, it mocked him.

At the easel, an abstract sky—the first tentative strokes of hope—began to take form. Sunflower yellow tried to crack the heaviness pressing on his chest. It held, then bled into the blue beneath, softening into grayish washes. Still no joy—only hollow. Savannah's smile haunted him—her voice telling him, It's beautiful.

Behind him, the Beach Boys played from a speaker. A curated cheerfulness, a lie, masking the ache. The warm beer sitting near his feet tasted bitter—nothing more than a tether to the moment. He took a sip, bitter and sharp, grounding himself.

He stared past the pool toward the shimmering bay, then saw it—the cracked pavement, the blast radius, the dust and blood. Afghanistan. The boy's breath, the final blink. Dust on lashes. Blood rushing beneath ribs. Luke had cradled him, helpless. Not fast enough.

Not Savannah. Not the boy. No.

His breath caught.

He turned back to the painting, trembling. A drop of paint fell—spattering concrete like a warning flare.

"Damn it," he muttered, wiping the mess. A yellow smear lingered. He whispered her name—Savannah.

The sun on the bay deepened. In his mind, she was there—barefoot, laughing, twirling—a breeze lifting her scent of citrus shampoo. She'd have pulled him away from the canvas, smiling. *Come on, Lukey. It's beautiful.*

But she wasn't here. Only her absence. Two years of it.

Dark thoughts pressed—silence thickening. The urge to end it—quietly, finally—whispered again.

A voice, soft but certain, broke the moment: "Alexa, stop." The music died.

"Hi, Luke."

Peter Manning stepped into view, sleeves rolled, calm as always. He never judged, never questioned—only presence, steady and sure. He glanced where Luke's hand trembled near the bottle, eyes clouded with understanding.

"She wouldn't want you like this," Peter said gently.

Luke said nothing, only looked down at the canvas.

Peter stepped closer, his voice soft yet firm: "You're not done. You know that, right?"

"I don't think I have anything left," Luke admitted, voice cracking.

Peter placed a warm hand on his shoulder. "So borrow some of mine. Just for today."

Luke's shoulders sagged slightly—small enough to miss but enough to breathe. They stood in shared silence, the tide whispering between them.

Peter exhaled, glancing toward the house. "Maggie's rattled. Something about the foundation this morning. She asked for you— said you'd understand."

Luke looked down. "So it wasn't about the auction."

Peter offered a faint smile. "That too. But mostly it's you she needs."

Luke nodded slowly. "I'll come up... just need to clean up first."

Peter squeezed his shoulder briefly. "We'll be waiting." He

turned and walked the path toward the house, disappearing into the shade.

The stillness returned, but it felt different—thicker, heavier with unspoken truths.

Luke crouched beside the easel, pulling the wooden paint box into his lap. His fingers traced Savannah's carving—a heart, rough but hers. Imperfect but real.

Inside, among the brushes and tubes of paint, lay the revolver—a.38 Special. His father had carried it through Vietnam. His grandfather—on Iwo Jima. Three wars, three generations. Now, it was in the hands of a man fighting a quieter war.

It didn't belong here. Neither did the memories.

He lifted it, thumbed the cylinder release, and swung it open. One brass cartridge gleamed—reminding him of what was… and what could be. He'd planned to use it, not for drama or spectacle, but to escape it all.

He raised the revolver, holding it loosely. No music. No Savannah. Just silence—except for the faint, cold click of metal settling.

Suddenly, Peter's words echoed—not from his lips, but from memory: "We'll be waiting."

He set the gun back into the box, closed his eyes. Savannah's face flickered—her laughter, her trust—then the boy's, etched with pure faith. Gone now. But he remained.

He reached for the silver chain around his neck—the pendant cool against his skin, etched with the words "Last Call." He unscrewed the cap, placed the bullet inside, and twisted it shut, feeling the thread bite into flesh, blood welling at his fingertip. A small wound, a quiet wound—but one that matched the weight he was carrying inside.

He returned the revolver to the box, sliding it beneath the easel. Out of sight, but never out of mind.

The pendant thumped softly against his chest.

Luke wiped at his eyes. The sun had climbed higher, the light brutal and honest.

The painting remained unfinished. So did he. But for today, he made one final, deliberate choice.

Not today.

He wiped his hands, grabbed the rag, and turned toward the house.

The haze had burned away—the sky sharp and clear. The day was waiting. The storm, too. But not today.

CHAPTER 2: THE RECKONING

A half hour later, Maggie Manning poured fresh lemonade into two glasses, the ice clinking as she watched her husband walk up the path. Peter Manning still moved with the quiet confidence of a man used to getting things done. The silver in his hair and the lines around his eyes hadn't slowed him down—if anything, they'd sharpened him.

She handed him a glass as he stepped onto the deck. "Thought lemonade might hit the spot."

"Perfect timing," Peter said, wiping his brow with the napkin she offered. "It's a scorcher. Too bad we had to scrap the sail."

Maggie hesitated, fingers tightening slightly around her glass. "I know. But honestly, I wouldn't have enjoyed it—not with the foundation's accounts in chaos. We're staring at a loss of over a million dollars. After everything we risked on last year's expansion, this couldn't have come at a worse time."

Peter drank, and for a moment his expression stiffened. "We can't absorb that hit. Not with how fast we're burning through reserves. You'll have to tap into that well of goodwill again, Maggie."

Her smile flickered—measured, automatic. "Oh, I'll squeeze them—believe me. You know I have the magic touch. Next auction, I'll make sure no one leaves with a full wallet." She looked out toward the bay, her voice lower. "But it isn't solely about the money. This made us feel... exposed. And the only person I trust to help? Luke."

Peter nodded slowly. "He's been in a tough place. Today's the anniversary—Savannah's accident. That shadow still follows him."

Maggie set her glass down. She remembered the look in Luke's eyes after the funeral. Not grief exactly—something quieter, more dangerous. The kind of loss that rearranges you.

Footsteps on the deck pulled her from the thought. Peter turned and lifted his glass. "There he is."

Luke Payne stepped onto the redwood deck, the sun behind him, casting long shadows across the planks. His posture was easy, but his gaze swept the space, slow and practiced—checking corners, exits, the space between things. Not nerves. Just muscle memory.

Maggie noticed it right away. She'd seen it before—after Savannah died, when sleep was rare and his reflexes were still in charge.

He accepted the lemonade she offered with a nod. "Thanks, Maggie. I'm sorry I didn't make the function last night. I just wasn't up to it. I'll make it up to you."

Maggie glanced toward the garden, as if searching for the right words. "You were missed, Luke. But I know what..." Well, I understand. So don't worry about it."

His eyes landed on the massive stone fireplace and the abstract painting above it—his own work, catching the light in strange, shifting ways. He'd painted it before everything fell apart, back when the Foundation—his mother's legacy—still felt untouchable. It looked like something left behind by someone else.

Maggie followed his eyes. "I still love that piece. It was my first Payne." She smiled. "You were the talk of the auction. All three of your works went fast. Transcendence set a record—sixty-five thousand. A woman from Santa Fe bought it. She wanted to meet you."

Luke's expression softened—faint but real. "Glad it helped the foundation."

He met her eyes. "But that's not why you called me up here, is it?"

Maggie's fingers brushed condensation from her glass. "Clearwater Financial called this morning. A breach—one of our accounts was hit. They think it was a phishing scam."

Luke straightened. The relaxed tone dropped. "How much?"

"Over a million. They're still investigating."

He turned, looking out toward the water, then back. "Why target an art foundation? And won't the bank make it good?"

Peter stepped in. "We don't think so. Our accountant, Joe Bailey, fell for a spoofed email that looked like it came from Maggie. He clicked a link—downloaded malware. That gave the attackers access to our accounts. They initiated multiple wire transfers before the bank's system flagged anything. It's with the FBI now, but they've got bigger fish. We're just a line on a backlog."

"We think it was only the funds," Maggie added. "We don't know what else might've been compromised. Maybe the donor list. That list is a who's who of Western philanthropists. If this leaks, it could shake our biggest supporters."

A breeze rattled the umbrella above them. Luke's voice stayed calm. "Let's not get ahead of it. Unless your donor database was linked to the same network your accountant used, it's unlikely that information was exposed. Right now, we need to follow the money. I might have someone—ex-military, cyber warfare background. If anyone can trace it, it's him. I'll see him soon."

Maggie pressed her lips together, her expression sharpening—not from fear, but from resolve. "If he can give us anything—even a direction—we'll take it."

Luke met her eyes. "I'll do what I can."

She nodded, then hesitated. "This didn't feel random, Luke. It felt... targeted."

He didn't answer. But something behind his eyes shifted.

The storm wasn't coming. It was already here.

CHAPTER 3: THE DISRUPTOR

Kowloon, Hong Kong

Nature had been unkind to nineteen-year-old Zhang Zhilan. Frail from birth, his life unfolded as a series of silent rejections. His parents, weighed down by poverty, even tried to give him away once, but no one wanted him. Not the relatives. Not the neighbors. Not even the orphanages. No one took in the boy with the over-sized head and hollow frame.

He grew up crammed inside a sweltering Hong Kong apartment with his parents, grandparents, and two older siblings. The thin walls seemed to amplify every cough, every murmur. Each morning, his parents sent him to hawk counterfeit bottled water in the ancient district. The cheap plastic bottles grew slick in his sweating hands under the relentless sun. The streets reeked of dried fish and diesel. His acne-ridden face and gap-toothed grin inspired more pity than persuasion. People looked past him, and when they didn't, it was to hurry away.

He wasn't strong. He wasn't charming. But he was brilliant.

His father—a janitor at a British bank—insisted his children speak English at home. "It's the language of survival," he'd say. Zhilan absorbed it like air. While his family clung to hope in soap operas, he vanished into the internet. Their ancient Dell, held together with electrical tape and a hijacked Wi-Fi signal from the bar downstairs, was all he needed. The keyboard clacked loudly, a rhythmic pulse in the quiet hours. Night after night, while the city slept, Zhilan devoured everything he could—coding forums, security blogs, encryption protocols. He taught himself to bypass the Great Firewall with a pirated VPN. He didn't just browse the web—

he cracked it open.

At first, he stayed under the radar. But curiosity gave way to experimentation. He didn't touch malware—no viruses, no ransomware. He didn't need them. His approach was cleaner, more elegant. He'd slip quietly into servers just to see if he could, leaving no trace—or sometimes the wrong one. Once, during the 2016 election, he hacked into the New York Times' online archive just long enough to swap a headline: "Hillary Wins by a Landslide." The glitch lasted less than a minute, but screenshots exploded across Reddit. No one ever traced it back to him. That was the moment he knew he could shape perception—not through brute force, but by rewriting the story before anyone realized it had changed.

Then everything unraveled at home. His sister, who despised him, emptied the family piggy bank to buy a pair of jeans. When their mother discovered the money missing, she pointed the finger at Zhilan. He protested, pleaded—but it didn't matter. There were no arguments, no shouting. Just a plastic bag of clothes left by the door and a quiet order to leave.

He waited outside until dark, hoping someone would open the door. No one did.

He didn't go back.

He wandered the edges of Kowloon until he found a hole-in-the-wall internet cafe run by an ex-gamer with poor eyesight and no interest in background checks. Zhilan kept the systems running and got paid in access—unlimited screen time, his own key, and a back room with a mattress on the floor. The stale air hummed with the constant drone of computers, a smell of hot plastic and cheap coffee.

That was when Rusty was born.

Rusty was tall, tan, and American. He surfed and vlogged and smiled through every post. At first, he tried to fit in online—forums, group chats, social servers. But he was always the outsider, always a little off.

Eventually, the need to belong hardened into something else. Rusty became a ghost in the machine. A disruptor. A provocateur. Not a typical hacker—but something more dangerous. He could steer conversations, inject chaos, and fracture communities from the inside. His comments weren't loud—they were loaded. He spotted insecurities, played to tribal instincts, and escalated debates until no one remembered what started them. He didn't just provoke. He dismantled.

On a dating forum, he pushed a moderator into meltdown with five posts spaced over two days. They banned each other, then dissolved the group.

And when he wanted to make a point, he still knew how to get inside locked systems and leave a calling card.

One humid morning during typhoon season, Zhilan unlocked the cafe as usual. The air hung thick and stale. After wiping down the counters and rebooting the routers, he slumped into his corner chair and refreshed his inbox. He blinked the sleep from his eyes, cracked his knuckles, and refreshed his inbox. Just another morning trying to stay fed.

There it was. A direct message. Subject: High-Paying Job Offer for Rusty—Expert Disruptor

He clicked.

Dear Mr. Rusty,

I've been observing your online activities and am impressed by your ability to manipulate narratives, bypass security, and create strategic disruption. Your talents are exactly what we need.

I am the president of a private contracting firm based in Shanghai. We're working with a client who requires precision digital engagement—someone fluent in chaos, confident in misdirection, and capable of real-world influence through social engineering.

Our offer: $5,000 signing bonus $50 per hour, with advancement based

on performance; full relocation to Shanghai, all expenses paid

If interested, reply by noon today. Otherwise, we'll assume you're not who we thought.

Sincerely, Chen Lee President, Chen Lee Enterprises, Inc.

Zhilan watched the message. Fifty dollars an hour? A signing bonus? Shanghai? It felt too good to be real, but it was also unnervingly specific. It used "Rusty." It referenced skills only someone truly watching would know. This wasn't spam. Someone had seen him. Wanted him.

He hovered over the keyboard, hesitation in his gut. Maybe it was a trap. But maybe it wasn't. He imagined the Shanghai skyline—him at the top, finally seen. Finally respected.

CHAPTER 4: NO WAY OUT

Lee leaned against the sleek glass railing of his penthouse balcony, a cold Tiger Beer in hand. Below him, the Bund shimmered, the Huangpu River winding like molten silver through the neon sprawl of Shanghai. His gaze lingered on Huangpu Park—just a quiet patch of green now. No speeches. No signs. Only memory and pride.

Normally, the view calmed him. Tonight, it felt staged. Success had painted a target on his back. His social media intelligence firm had brought wealth, prestige, this penthouse—but also attention from people he couldn't afford to cross.

The doorbell cut through the quiet. Sharp. Uninvited.

Setting down the bottle, Lee crossed the marble floor and checked the peephole. A short, balding man with sharp cheekbones, a weak chin, and cold, beady eyes stood alone, gripping an blackj briefcase.

Lee's instincts screamed: Don't open it.

He opened it.

"Who is it?" he asked, keeping the door latched.

The man's voice was calm. Professional. Icy. "Good evening, Mr. Lee. I bring an opportunity you'll find lucrative. May I come in?"

Lee hesitated. Ten seconds. Then twenty.

Curiosity—and greed—won out.

"Ten minutes," he said, unlatching the door.

The man stepped inside with practiced ease. Tailored suit. Watchful eyes. Politeness masking something colder.

Lee gestured toward the balcony. "We'll talk outside. It's a nice night."

As they stepped into the humid air, heavy and still with the city's breath, the man produced a black wallet and opened it to his Ministry credentials with mechanical precision. "Colonel Zhou Shaozeng. Ministry of State Security. Sixth Bureau—Counterintelligence."

Lee's stomach dipped. He forced a smile. "An honor, Colonel. Beer?"

"Gladly."

In the kitchen, Lee's hands trembled as he reached for two bottles. The cold glass sweated in his grip. By the time he returned, his expression was composed again.

The Colonel took a sip, surveying the skyline. "You have a spectacular view, Mr. Lee. Huangpu Park. The river. A testament to how far we've come."

Lee nodded cautiously. "The city's changed."

The Colonel turned to him, all pleasantry vanishing from his expression. "And change requires sacrifice."

A beat. Then, flatly: "We need your help."

Lee tensed. "Help with what?"

"A cyber operation targeting American tech firms—Qualcomm among them. We need access. Passwords. Vulnerabilities. You've gathered social intelligence. Now we need deeper cuts."

Lee's tongue felt dry. Metallic. "That's... risky."

Zhou showed a flicker of cold amusement. "Of course. But with great risk comes great reward."

He flicked open the aluminum case. Inside: neat stacks of U.S.. hundred-dollar bills, crisp and gleaming. "One million dollars. Down payment. More to follow."

Lee watched the cash. Temptation and dread twisted through him like a rope. "And if I refuse?" The question came out barely above a whisper.

The Colonel's face hardened completely. "You won't. We know your partnerships. Your debts. Your family. You've worked with the PLA before. This is simply an extension." There was no bluff in his voice. Only finality.

Lee said nothing. But his breath grew shallow, his chest tight. A pressure without motion.

"I understand."

The Colonel smoothed an invisible wrinkle from his lapel. "You'll report directly to me. We'll supply the tools—keyloggers, RATs, phishing kits. Your job is to infiltrate, extract, and destabilize."

Another sip of beer. Then: "Start with the financial elite. Turn them on each other. Hollow them out from within."

Lee set his bottle down. His hand had steadied. His gut hadn't.

"You'll get what you need."

The Colonel stood. "Failure is costly, Mr. Lee. For you. For your family."

Without another word, he left.

The click of the door echoed like a verdict. Lee watched the elevator doors close—silent, smooth, final. He stepped back onto the balcony. The skyline—once a symbol of how far he'd risen—felt like the edge of a cage. The Monument to the People's Heroes loomed in the distance, lit hard and sterile.

A reminder: some sacrifices aren't chosen. They're demanded.

He raised the bottle again. The rim trembled slightly against his lip.

The money was real. So was the threat.

The line was behind him now. And there was no way out.

CHAPTER 5: A WOMAN WITH A MISSION

Carol Chan, Maggie Manning's long-time assistant, knocked twice and peeked through the office door. "Maggie," she said, "Vanessa Griffin is here to see you. She didn't have an appointment but said it was important. I think she's the woman who bought Luke's painting last week."

Maggie glanced up, surprised. "Let's hope she's not here with regrets. Returning that much money would be... complicated. But yes, send her in."

Maggie took in the woman as she crossed the room—tall, poised, with an athlete's posture and quiet confidence. Mid-forties, maybe. Her auburn hair framed her face in a chic, chin-length cut, and her gray linen pantsuit managed to look both sharp and effortless. Elegant, but unpretentious.

Maggie gestured to a chair. "Of course. Please, sit."

Vanessa settled in. "As you may know, I recently moved here from Santa Fe. I'm trying to find something meaningful to do—something more than just decorating my new condo in Little Italy."

Maggie offered a polite nod. "I imagine there are plenty of opportunities in San Diego right now. If you'd like to send me a resume, I'm happy to circulate it among my network. Might take a little time, but something could open up."

"That's very generous of you," Vanessa replied, "but I have a specific role in mind. One I think I'd be perfect for."

"You do?" Maggie looked puzzled

Vanessa leaned forward slightly. "I read The Nonprofit Times. I'm sure you're familiar."

Maggie gave a slow nod. "I've used it for years. In fact, we ran an ad there recently, but most of the promising applicants disappeared once they heard the salary."

"You ran it last month," Vanessa said, smiling. "That's how I found it."

Maggie narrowed her eyes slightly, studying her. "Are you telling me you're here for that position?"

Vanessa nodded. "Yes. I probably should have gone through formal channels, but when I saw the listing, I couldn't wait."

Maggie chuckled despite herself. The woman radiated a kind of energy that was hard to resist. "Miss Griffin—Vanessa—this isn't an easy job. I'm looking for someone who can not only help carry the load but eventually take over. That means long hours, high expectations, and plenty of setbacks. It's rewarding, yes, but it's not for the faint of heart."

Vanessa's voice didn't waver. "I understand. I ran a successful business in Santa Fe for over a decade. I also served on several boards, chaired fundraising campaigns, and worked directly with arts nonprofits. Supporting artists has been part of my life since childhood. This isn't a whim—it's a calling."

Maggie sat back. "That's good to hear. But we're only offering thirty-eight thousand to start. It comes with healthcare and—"

"The salary doesn't matter," Vanessa interrupted. "I don't need the money. In fact, I'd donate my salary back to the foundation. What I need is purpose. And I believe in what you've built here."

She reached into her purse and handed Maggie a sealed envelope. "These are references—people I've worked with and for. Call them. Ask anything. If you're satisfied, I'm ready to start tomorrow."

Maggie turned the envelope in her hands. The handwriting was neat, confident. She looked back up, meeting Vanessa's gaze. A steady gaze. Eager. Genuine. Maybe even a little vulnerable beneath the polish.

Still, a voice whispered in Maggie's head—soft, cautious.

Be careful. Even dreams come with strings.

CHAPTER 6: REFERENCES

The next morning, Peter and Maggie Manning sat on Shangri-La's patio, coffee in hand. Luke Payne's rhythmic splashes drifted up from the pool, but Maggie's thoughts were elsewhere. Vanessa Griffin's visit still clung to her mind, raising more questions than answers.

"No wonder he's in such good shape," Peter said, nodding toward the water. "Better than last week. Looks like he made it through the anniversary better than I feared."

"I think you're right." Maggie's gaze stayed on the pool. "He's been spending more time at the foundation—working with the kids, judging entries for the West Coast abstract show. Twelve hundred submissions, only eighty-five spots. Brutal." She hesitated. "Oh—I may have found someone to replace Carol."

Peter arched a brow. "Thought no one would bite at the salary?"

"Until now. Remember the woman who bought one of Luke's paintings last week?"

"The one with perfect timing and a big check? Sure. Why?"

"She asked for the job. Gave me a list of references—Georgia O'Keeffe Museum, New Mexico Museum of Art, the Santa Fe Symphony. I called three. They couldn't praise her enough. One was in tears. Brilliant, warm, relentless at fundraising."

Peter leaned back. "Sounds like a dream hire. Where's the catch?"

"She's wealthy," Maggie said quietly. "Messy divorce. Owns several properties on Canyon Road. And—" she let it hang "—she owns The Atchison."

Peter blinked. "The Atchison? The hotel we stay at in Santa Fe?"

She nodded. "One of the oldest, most prestigious in New Mexico. Practically an art museum."

Peter let out a low whistle. "So she doesn't need the job."

"Exactly." Maggie's tone cooled. "And that's what worries me—

people with nothing to gain often have the most to hide."

Peter took a thoughtful sip of coffee. "Maybe she's chasing something more meaningful after the divorce. You said it was messy?"

"It was," Maggie said with a sigh. "According to my source, her ex made her life miserable. Showed up at events with younger women. Humiliated her. She stopped going out completely."

"Sounds like a real piece of work."

"She came here to start fresh," Maggie said. "But…" She trailed off, staring into the steam rising from her cup.

"But what?"

"When she toured the foundation after buying Luke's painting, she stayed longer than expected," Maggie said. "Listened to Luke's whole lecture on abstract art. She's asked about him a few times since."

"You think she's interested in Luke?"

Maggie shrugged. "Maybe she's just interested in the art. But… call it intuition."

Peter chuckled. "Can you blame her? Luke's a handsome man. But you know how he's been—no interest in anyone since Savannah."

Maggie's gaze drifted back toward the pool. "I know. He's been through so much. But maybe someone like Vanessa could help him move forward."

Peter crossed his arms. "So—are you going to hire her?"

Maggie hesitated, then nodded. "I think so. I'll call her this morning. But I'm laying all the cards on the table first. She needs to know exactly what she's getting into."

Peter nodded. "Good plan. Especially with the missing funds hanging over us."

CHAPTER 7: HUMAN RESOURCES

The Peninsula Arts Foundation Campus, Liberty Station

Outside Maggie's office Vanessa's fingers tightened on her bag strap until the leather creaked. Purpose—that's what she told herself this was about. Helping others. Building something new. But beneath the noble reasons, a quieter truth whispered—the one that always moved in her shadow.

The life she'd left in Santa Fe might not be done with her. Her ex-husband had reach, charm, and a knack for appearing where he wasn't wanted. She doubted he'd follow her here, yet the doubt never really left—it rode in her shadow.

This place—the art, the children, the mission—felt untouched by all that. Untouched… for now.

But shadows have long memories, and she knew better than to think they wouldn't follow. She only hoped the people here wouldn't notice when hers finally caught up.

Carol Chan, Maggie Manning's assistant, opened the door and nodded to Vanessa. "She's ready for you."

Vanessa stepped inside.

She shook Maggie's hand, managing a smile. Her palm was damp—nerves she hadn't quite shaken. "My pleasure, Maggie. I've been hoping you'd call."

Maggie glanced at Carol and sighed softly. "It's a sad day at the foundation."

Vanessa's smile faltered. "Oh no. I hope it's nothing serious. If you'd prefer to reschedule…"

Maggie's expression softened. "No, not that kind of sadness. Carol's leaving us—she found love and is starting a new chapter."

"She's been with me for almost two decades. Feels like losing a sister."

Carol's eyes welled up. "You're going to make me cry again, Maggie." She turned to Vanessa with a laugh. "I wish we'd had more time to get to know each other—I think we would've been wonderful friends. But I've got to run. They're throwing me a farewell party, and I need to make sure they don't mess it up." She winked, then pointed playfully at Maggie. "And you better make your speech as good as the ones I've written for you."

With a wave, Carol slipped out, leaving Maggie chuckling.

"Please, sit," she said, gesturing to the chair across from her desk. "Let's talk about the position."

Vanessa sat, hands clenched lightly around the strap of her bag.

Maggie looked out toward the sunlit courtyard, the distant sound of students drifting in through the open window. Then she turned, her gaze sharp but not unkind. "What do you know about the foundation, Vanessa?"

Vanessa straightened. "I've only had a brief look around, but I like what I see. The campus covers five acres, with eight main buildings including a library, a dining facility, and a fully equipped ceramics workshop with six kilns. One of the buildings houses over sixty individual artist studios. There's also a black-box theater, an outdoor performance space, and multiple galleries open to the public. It's a world-class campus."

Maggie's expression didn't change, but there was a flicker of amusement behind her eyes. "That's fine. You did your homework. But what do you see beyond the buildings and fixtures?"

Vanessa was surprised for a moment. Then she softened, as if something truer rose to the surface.

"I see a community," she said. "A rare one. Not just artists and instructors passing through, but something interwoven—people from all backgrounds, all ages, engaging with each other through creation. It feels democratic… accessible. The kind of place where a retired engineer can take up watercolor next to a high school student sculpting her first figure. I've never seen anything like it."

She leaned forward, her voice gaining quiet momentum.

"And I see what it could be. This campus is the heart, yes—but I see satellite studios in underserved communities, mobile workshops visiting schools, partnerships with hospitals, veterans' centers, even correctional facilities. I see this place becoming a national model. A blueprint for what the arts can do when they're not locked behind glass but placed directly into people's hands."

She stopped herself, smiled a little. "I'm sorry. I got carried away."

Maggie studied her for a long beat, then slowly shook her head.

"No, you didn't get carried away, Vanessa. You had a vision. Just like we did when we started this place. And I think it's brilliant. But I'm too old to see that kind of expansion through. If we're going to grow into the next chapter, we need someone who has the knowledge, the skill, and—maybe most important—the fire to make it happen."

She didn't hesitate.

"The job is yours if you want it."

Vanessa's breath hitched, then broke into a radiant smile. "That's wonderful, Maggie!"

Maggie smiled but held up a hand. "Before you accept, I want you to fully understand what you're stepping into—no surprises."

Vanessa nodded. "Of course."

"At first, I was looking for someone to take over Carol's role—operations, logistics, the administrative grind," Maggie said, her voice even. "But after meeting you—and after talking to people who've worked with you, who, by the way, absolutely adore you—I had to reconsider."

"Reconsider how?"

Maggie took a breath. "Well, we'll start by hiring you as my assistant, but I want you to eventually take over my role as director of the foundation. And when I say 'eventually,' I mean soon."

Vanessa blinked. "I'm not sure I'm ready to take the helm. I'll need time to ramp up."

"Oh, I understand that. But I know you have what it takes. I'll stay on as director until you're comfortable—until you're ready. Once you take the reins, I'll still be around as chair of the board and a resource. I've already picked out a nice office upstairs with a view of the bay." She smiled. "And Luke knows the foundation inside and out—he'll be a great support. You'd need to hire someone for the day-to-day admin work, but the vision, the leadership, the responsibility? That would be yours."

Vanessa sat back, stunned. She had expected a challenge—

But this felt like a calling.

Maggie watched her closely. "I know it's a lot. But I believe in you. And I'll be here to support you every step of the way."

"I wanted a challenge," Vanessa said. "This definitely fits the bill. But before I commit, I need to know everything—the good, the bad, and the ugly. And I'd like to talk with Luke—see how he feels about this."

"Deal," said Maggie, her smile returning. "I'll arrange a meeting with Luke. And if you've got an hour, I can walk you through the foundation's history. Then we'll join Carol's farewell party, meet the staff, and have a proper lunch. How does that sound?"

Vanessa's nerves had shifted into excitement. "That sounds perfect. I'd love to meet everyone."

Maggie grabbed her purse and keys. "Great. Let's start with lunch at Old Venice—it's a cozy little Italian place just a few blocks away."

"I love Italian," Vanessa said, standing. "And honestly? I'm starving."

They stepped out into the soft buzz of the San Diego streets, their conversation drifting to food, travel, and art. Vanessa didn't say it aloud, but something settled inside her.

Like—for the first time in a long while—she fit.

CHAPTER 8: BRIEF ENCOUNTER

The Next Day – The Peninsula Arts Foundation Campus, Liberty Station

Vanessa moved through the foundation's main courtyard portico, her footsteps soft on the warm Spanish tile. A light breeze stirred her hair, carrying the scent of roses and oil paint. She touched the turquoise bracelet for luck—a childhood gift from Georgia O'Keeffe, a dear friend of her father's who had once showcased her work at the hotel.

She'd been exploring the foundation's facilities for over an hour and was more than impressed. Not just by the five acres of classrooms, workshops, galleries, and performance venues—but by the eclectic mix of students and instructors. Talented. Engaged. Joyfully immersed in their craft. The creative energy here pulsed with authenticity—more alive, she thought, than anything she'd felt on Canyon Road in Santa Fe.

"Excuse me," she said, stopping a young woman balancing a precarious stack of canvases. "Could you point me to Luke Payne's studio?"

The woman shifted her load with practiced ease and smiled. "Luke's studio? Last door on the right. If the door's open, he's probably in. Are you a new student?"

Vanessa hesitated, then returned the smile. "Something like that. Thanks."

"Good luck!" the woman called as she disappeared down the hall.

Vanessa approached the last door. An oversized ceramic mug propped it open. From inside came the rhythmic pop of a staple gun. She peeked in.

Luke Payne leaned over a large canvas, stretching the fabric taut with the practiced ease of someone who'd done it a thousand times. Worn cargo pants. Faded navy T-shirt. The lettering—PROPERTY OF UCSD SWIM TEAM—a quiet echo of a past life, maybe one with more structure and less paint.

Vanessa stepped inside, brushing her hand along the doorframe. "Admiring the work of a master canvas stretcher?"

Luke's voice broke through the quiet, dry and amused. "Hard to compete with Pollock's drip techniques, but I do what I can."

Startled, she turned and smiled. "I didn't mean to interrupt. How did you know I was here?"

"Good ears," he said, straightening and wiping his hands on a paint-stained rag. "And the door creaked."

He turned fully, scanning her face, puzzled at first, then familiar. "Wait… you were at my talk last week. Abstract expressionism, right?"

"Guilty," she said, stepping closer. "I caught the tail end of your take on Pollock. I liked it… though I'm not sure I agree."

Luke held up his staple gun. "Pollock? Some days he's a genius. Other days, he's just finger-painting on adrenaline. What's your take?"

Vanessa looked around, eyeing the rows of easels and paint-splattered stools. "I once saw a blank sheet of paper at an exhibit. The artist claimed to have stared at it for a thousand hours." She grinned. "I appreciate Pollock's chaos more than that kind of performance art. At least he gave us something to look at."

Luke chuckled, his shoulders easing. "Fair point. I've always leaned more toward Rothko or Kandinsky—guys who challenged the rules without making you wonder if they were just messing with you."

Vanessa tilted her head, studying him. "And Luke Payne? Where does he fall on that spectrum?"

He grinned. "Somewhere between wrestling with the rules and pretending I never read them."

She smiled. Her voice softened. "That's the space where real art lives—in the figuring it out."

Luke glanced at his watch. "I'd love to keep this going, but I've got a meeting with the boss and a new hire."

Vanessa stepped toward the door, her smile playful. "Then I'll let you go. Thanks for indulging my art talk, Mr. Payne."

"Wait. What's your name?" he asked.

Her eyes meeting his. "I'm sure we'll bump into each other again."

Luke stood for a beat, her voice still hanging in the air. He looked at the canvas, then the open door.

"Well... that was unexpected."

He checked his watch. "Damn. I'm late."

He swung the studio door shut and locked it, then ducked into the supply closet. A clean shirt, slacks, and a blazer hung behind the door—part of his emergency stash for foundation meetings. Two minutes later, he emerged paint-free, presentable, and still slightly breathless as he headed down the corridor toward the main office.

Luke let the studio door swing shut behind him, the scent of gesso and raw canvas still clinging to his hands. He rubbed a thumb along a rough patch on his palm—he'd been stretching frames all morning. Meditative, almost. Still, the woman who had wandered in and out like a breeze had left more of a mark than he expected.

He shook his head as he approached the office. Maggie had said they were bringing someone new on board. An assistant director. "Someone you'll want to meet," she'd said. He was five minutes late.

Carol had been irreplaceable—organized, grounded, always ten steps ahead. Whoever this new person was, they had some seriously high standards to live up to.

He knocked once on Maggie's office door.

"Come in," she called.

He stepped in—and froze.

Sitting across from Maggie, legs crossed, calm as could be, was the woman from the studio.

She turned toward him with the same relaxed confidence and just the hint of a grin. "Hey again."

Luke blinked. "You've got to be kidding me."

Maggie looked up, amused. "Luke, meet Vanessa Griffin. She's our new assistant director."

"I met her," he said, eyes still on Vanessa. "In the studio. You... let me ramble about Rothko."

"You looked like you needed the warm-up," she said, standing and offering her hand.

He took it, smiling now. "So that was a setup."

"Just a soft opening," she said.

Maggie laughed lightly. "Looks like you two are already acquainted."

Luke nodded, still half-shaking his head. "I think we're off to a very interesting start."

CHAPTER 9: THE ALCHEMIST'S APPRENTICE

From his 23rd-floor corner office, Rusty Zhilan looked out at the Huangpu River, shimmering like liquid chrome. The skyline stared back—polished, powerful, unreal. Not bad for a gap-toothed kid who once hawked fake bottled water in Kowloon. Chen Lee had kept his word. The apartment was high-end. The salary more than generous. Designer suits filled the closet—costume armor for a man he was still learning to play.

And Lee… Lee had become more than an employer. He was a father figure. One Rusty didn't know he'd been missing.

Their bond formed in the pre-dawn quiet, moving through martial forms near the Bund. Tai Chi. Xing Yi Quan. They looked slow. Graceful. Almost easy—until you tried them. "Softness overcomes hardness, Rusty," Lee would say, adjusting his elbow with a gentle touch. "Yield, then strike. Find the opening." He guided Rusty's arms through Peng energy—circular, expansive—then into Lu, redirecting invisible force. "Lu isn't just defense," Lee said. "It's listening. Sensing the imbalance."

At first, Rusty resisted. He was clunky, tense. Fast with code, but stiff in the real world. He tried to muscle through the movements. Failed. Often. But Lee never scolded. "Don't chase the form," he said. "Feel the ground. Root yourself. The tree that bends in the wind doesn't break." And over time, Rusty began to bend. He practiced zhan zhuang—standing like a tree. Letting tension drain away. Feeling the ground beneath him, the stillness humming. Tai Chi wasn't just exercise. It was rewiring his nervous system. And it worked.

Away from the training ground, he noticed a change. His

thoughts were clearer. His movements more precise. There was calm in him now—measured and quiet. Like a tide that came in slow but steady.

But something still felt off.

His job had changed, too. He wasn't sowing chaos in online forums anymore. Now, he was gathering real intelligence. On-screen, stolen conversations scrolled past. Rusty, posing as "Rusty Chong," cybersecurity contractor, had embedded himself into email chains at Qualcomm. They trusted him. Engineers shared confidential updates. Performance flaws. Temporary workarounds. No hacks. No brute force. Just rapport—and betrayal. He reclined in his chair, pressing a thumb into the bridge of his nose.

Tai Chi had showed him how to interpret shifts in balance—how to feel when your footing was wrong. And tonight, he felt it.

Outside, the river gleamed like a mirror. It used to look like freedom. Now, it looked like a warning.

CHAPTER 10: GHOST CITIES, LIVING GHOSTS

Bullet Train to Beijing

Chen Lee never tired of traveling at 217 mph. Savoring his pre-ferred salt soda water—sweet, with hints of lemon and mint, a taste of old Shanghai—he watched the Chinese countryside blur into streaks of green and gray. But his thoughts weren't on the view. She had summoned him, and his mind had already drifted else-where. Deeper. Older. The world's fastest passenger train carried him from Shanghai to Beijing in under four and a half hours. Every fifteen minutes, it rocketed past a second- or third-tier city—former farm towns now transformed into sprawling urban complexes, their gleaming skylines clawing at a hazy horizon.

He grinned. Those towers? Empty. A forest of hollow ambition. Built for show, never for shelter. Ghost cities—monuments to greed, erected by status-hungry officials chasing quotas and illusions.

But they had made him rich. The oversupply of luxury offices meant he'd acquired a penthouse for a fraction of its value. His team lived well too—spacious apartments near the Bund, more than they ever imagined possible. A perfect arrangement. Clients happy. Staff loyal. Results undeniable.

So why the sudden summons to Beijing? What did she want? Did she know about his work for the Colonel?

He knew better than to trust what cities promised. Skylines could lie. So could progress. He'd seen stranger turns. Survived them.

Born in Nanjing in 1975, son of privilege. His father chaired the history department at Nanjing University. His mother's English was flawless—an echo from her missionary grandmother, un-touched by purges or shame. Their campus home was filled with books, laughter, and the scent of possibility.

Then came the Anti-Spiritual Pollution Campaign. He remembered the shift. The sudden tightening. Fear on every corner. His father's lectures were labeled subversive. His Western readings—suspicious. Students turned on professors overnight. His father was denounced in an anonymous bulletin. Before the authorities arrived, he hanged himself in the basement. The family was exiled to the outskirts of Anhui province. Work camps. Menial labor. Hunger became routine. Fear, constant. One wrong word—one glance too long—could end you.

Lee turned toward his reflection in the train window. Past and present blurred in the glass. He remembered his mother's quiet resistance—teaching them by candlelight, feeding their minds when the state starved everything else. Her will had kept them alive.

And he remembered the girl. Yang Yue. Beaten. Filthy. Half-starved. They found her sorting plastic behind a fertilizer plant, bruised by enforcers. She flinched when he approached, arms wrapped tight around herself. But he'd spoken gently. Promised she was safe. She never left them after that. She became a sister. Studied English and science beside them, hunched over notebooks by dim lantern light. Endured the same backbreaking shifts. Survived.

An automated voice crackled over the intercom, snapping him back. "Next stop: Beijing."

Lee straightened in his seat, drained the last of his soda, and set the bottle aside. His pulse was steady. His mind sharp.

Waiting for him at 14 Dongchangan Avenue—adjacent to Tiananmen Square—was General Yang Yue. No longer a bruised girl. Now one of the most powerful women in Chinese intelligence. The bond they'd forged in hell still held. But bonds could become shackles. Or nooses. And in the capital, no one summoned you without a reason. He would find out soon enough.

CHAPTER 11: FAMILY SECRETS

General Yang Yue rose smoothly as Lieutenant Jin Yong ushered Lee into her expansive office. "Mr. Lee, thank you for coming. I trust your journey was comfortable. Please—sit."

With a curt nod, she dismissed her aide. "Lieutenant, confirm our lunch reservation—Mr. Lee will need time to recover from his travels. And close the door on your way out."

The soft click echoed like a cue. Lee took in the woman before him, imposing and elegant. Only Yang Yue could make iron look graceful. She rounded the desk, her movements fluid, precise.

"Stand up, Chen Lee," she said. His pulse stuttered. A prickle of sweat touched his brow. She knows. Then she beamed and pulled him into a hug. "It's wonderful to see you again, brother. Still as stiff as ever, I see."

Relief hit like cool water. No firing squads today. "It's always a pleasure, little sister. And congratulations on your second star. You must be proud."

She smoothed the front of her uniform before easing back into her chair. "Thank you. You played a part in that, you know. The intelligence your team delivered exceeded every expectation. Some of my superiors doubted the value of raw data from Facebook and Twitter—but your work proved... persuasive, politically and militarily."

Lee gave a slight nod. "I'm honored. The credit belongs to my team. Their commitment matches my own."

"Please extend my regards," she said. "I hope to meet them someday. Though, as always, the clock is unkind."

She slid a stack of manila folders across the desk. Lee hesitated.

Like being handed a sealed verdict. The urge to confess rose. Surely she would understand. But Zhou's warning whispered through his mind: Failure is costly. A flash of Zhou's unblinking eyes, a chilling promise of consequences.

Yue watched him closely. "Something wrong? You look… off."

He cleared his throat. "No, just the dumplings on the train. Too much vinegar, perhaps."

"Then lunch might be a mistake." The heat pressed in. His palms were slick.

"You're right," he said. "A fine meal would be wasted today." She let the silence hover before continuing.

"Let's finish, then. I'll have Lieutenant Jin drive you back to Shanghai." She tapped the folders. "Inside: your next targets. A few are outside the U.S.. You'll need to recruit new operatives—people with cultural and linguistic reach. Your compensation will adjust accordingly." She indicated the top folder. "There's seed money for staffing. More payments as each phase rolls out."

Her tone sharpened, just enough to register. "I expect the same results as before."

Lee reached for the folders, fingers unsteady. "Thank you for your trust," he said. "You won't be disappointed."

Her smile returned—brilliant, bladed. "I trust not. Now go home and rest."

As Lee followed Lieutenant Jin out, Yue remained seated, her expression cooling. A cold knot tightened in her gut. Something didn't add up. She keyed her intercom. "Surveillance. Sergeant Chan, connect me with Major Liu. I have a task for him." She leaned back, eyes fixed on the door Lee had just exited. The color in his face, the strain—it wasn't just exhaustion. She had seen him pale before. But not like this. Not even in Anhui. Not even when the cadres came for his mother. What are you hiding, brother?

CHAPTER 12: THE DEVIL'S WORK

Shanghai, China

Lee threw himself into the mission, but the unease from his sister's visit clung to him like grit under the skin—always there, impossible to ignore. The morning after meeting with the Colonel, a package arrived: seven thumb drives, each preloaded with encryption tools, malware payloads, and precise, unambiguous instructions. Every day since had brought new assignments—riskier, more invasive. Password cracking. System breaches. Laundering stolen funds. Orders delivered without explanation, only deadlines.

He parceled out the drives himself, meeting each team member face to face. He watched their eyes as he handed over the tasks, studied their reactions. At first, the double paychecks lit up the room. But within two weeks, the energy had turned. Excitement gave way to doubt. These weren't black hats. They were trust builders—social engineers, fluent in digital rapport, not digital war. What they were doing now wasn't just illegal. It was corrosive.

By the third week, when Lee dropped by Rusty's place, the change in the young man stopped him cold. Rusty slumped at his desk, skin pale, dark crescents under his eyes. The screen in front of him was blank, cursor blinking like a metronome for a breakdown.

"Rusty," Lee said quietly, "you look like hell. What's going on?"

He rubbed his face with the sleeve of his hoodie. "I can't keep doing this, Mr. Lee," he said. "It's like I'm split in half. There's me, and there's the guy doing this crap. And I don't know who I am anymore."

Lee sat beside him, a knot already forming in his chest.

Rusty's voice cracked. "Yesterday I emptied the account of a non-profit. In San Diego. A million dollars—gone."

Lee didn't speak. Couldn't.

"It's called the Peninsula Arts Foundation. I looked it up. I know we're not supposed to, but I had to. They run programs for under-privileged kids—like me, back then." He swallowed hard. "I stole from them."

Lee felt his composure falter. He'd seen the target list. At the time, it was just another box to tick. But hearing it in Rusty's voice made it real—too real.

Rusty pressed on. "They help kids get off the streets. Give them something to care about. I ripped that out from under them." He looked up, hollow. "I'm not okay with that."

Lee laid a supportive hand on his shoulder. "You're right to feel that. This isn't what we were meant to be doing."

Rusty nodded, blinking hard. "I don't want the extra pay. I'd go back to normal salary. I just want to get out of this."

Lee glanced toward the windows—where the lights of the city twinkled like nothing was wrong. But something was. Everything was. "Give me two weeks," he said. "Can you do that?"

Rusty hesitated. "Two weeks. That's it."

"Two weeks," Lee repeated. The promise tasted bitter in his mouth. "Then it ends. I'll make sure of it."

He left the apartment quietly. Outside, the Bund was packed with tourists—laughing, taking selfies, chasing moments they'd re-member fondly. Lee walked among them like a ghost, trapped be-tween duty and regret. The Colonel's presence still pressed against him, silent but oppressive. And Rusty wasn't the only one fraying at the seams.

Something had to give. And it would. Very soon.

CHAPTER 13: THE BOARD GAME

Balboa Park, San Diego

It was a quintessential San Diego spring morning—perfect weather for Luke Payne's red '82 Fiat Spider. Top down, engine humming, he sped north on the 163 Freeway, passing beneath the historic Cabrillo Bridge—built for the 1913 Panama-California Exposition. Today, he was off to fulfill his corporate duties.

Coronado Seafood's monthly board meetings were unusual affairs. Every member actually looked forward to them. They usually took place in a remote corner of Balboa Park, tucked between a swimming pool and baseball fields, down an unnamed road.

Luke turned off Morley Field Drive onto a narrow lane and parked behind a white Mercedes Sprinter van plastered with a colorful logo: a giant clam shell circled by the words Coronado Seafood Catering. He couldn't help the smile tugging at his mouth. "Time to suffer through another grueling lunch with millionaires and war heroes."

Inside the San Diego Club de Pétanque compound, his fellow board members were already gathered around a long cloth-covered table, set with silverware and Riedel stemware. There were hugs and handshakes all around—a camaraderie rare in corporate boardrooms.

These men and women weren't just shareholders. They were veterans. Shipmates. Survivors of missions no civilian would ever hear about. They had risked their lives for each other more than once—and now, thanks to a $10,000 investment years ago in one of their own, they prospered.

Owen Cooper, the former SEAL mess cook turned seafood

mogul, sat presiding over the table, with a broad grin.

A young server in a Tommy Bahama shirt approached Luke. "Your usual Dos Equis, Mr. Payne? Or we've got a chilled Château La Monde Rosé—beautifully balanced."

"Beer for the game. Rosé at lunch."

He glanced at the pétanque courts. "Have we picked teams yet? I'm itching to win back my five bucks after last month's drubbing."

Cooper laughed, pulling a sleeve of boules from his backpack. "Helen and Hank had the misfortune of drawing you. Moises and Mark are stuck with me."

"Helen and Hank play like they've got tungsten nerves—and actual steel balls," Luke said, earning a round of laughter. "You're going down, Coop."

The game was on. Pétanque—like bocce's tougher French cousin—was a tradition they had picked up during their Navy days. Anywhere there was dirt, there was a game.

After a fierce match, Luke collected three crisp five-dollar bills from Cooper. "Luke, you have one incredible eye," Cooper said, shaking his head. "Three of our balls went sailing, and yours stuck for the win."

"Just luck," Luke said, though the glint in his eye told another story.

By the time they sat back down, bowls of steaming clam chowder were already being served—a house tradition. Cooper's chowder had built an empire, after all.

Cooper tapped his glass. "The Coronado Seafood Corporation is now in session. Bar's open: Oregon Pinot Gris, French rosé, or Coronado Amber Lager on tap. Carl, bring the chowder."

Steam curled above the tables. Bread broke. Wine flowed. Laughter rippled across the table as wine glasses clinked and stories spilled freely. They were a board of warriors and chefs, not suits and ties.

Cooper stood, serious now. "We've weathered tariffs, bottlenecks, fuel costs—hell, even a pandemic. And we adapted. Years ago, when all you had were GI paychecks, you believed in the dream of a third-class mess cook. I'll never stop thanking you for that. Now, let's get rolling."

One by one, the board members stood and gave updates. Hank, the explosives expert turned restaurateur, reported soaring sales. "Our seafood markets, catering, and home delivery kept us alive. Now they're fueling our biggest growth yet."

Jenny, the rescue swimmer turned Internet sales boss, shared a sharp report. "Our frozen chowder's killing it. Amazon, Whole Foods, Cerberus Capital grocery chains—contracts across the board. Internet sales up twenty-five percent year-over-year."

Moises, the pilot Luke had once dragged from a burning Chinook, lifted his pant leg to reveal a sleek new prosthetic. "Bionic wheel's working fine. VA's finally getting it right."

He smiled. "Our air fleet's up to fifteen aircraft. Gulfstreams, Mi-38 choppers. Seafood's flying fresher than ever. And we're halfway through electrifying the truck fleet. Eight million in savings projected next year."

Cheers, laughter, more glasses raised.

But when the final Dungeness crabs hit the tables—still steaming from the pot—the meeting faded into silence. There was only the sound of cracking shells and sighs of satisfaction.

As the others laughed and drifted back toward the courts, the day's warmth couldn't shake the unease pressing on Luke's mind. He stepped to a shaded corner where Admiral Mark Patton nursed a second glass of rosé.

"Got a minute?"

The two-star admiral looked up, reading Luke in one glance. "Still can't turn it off, can you?"

The words landed harder than they should have.

Luke's mind flashed to the Florida sun and the Aviation Rescue

Swimmer School.

The concrete deck radiated heat, but the water in the survival pool was a different story—deep, cold, and unforgiving. Luke stood next in line, fins tucked under his arm, chest still heaving from the last evolution. Across the pool, the Shallow Water Egress Trainer—nicknamed the Dunker—bobbed gently. Simulating a helicopter crash, it was designed to flip, seal shut, and trap trainees inside. Only skill and calm under pressure would get them out.

Inside, Jenny and her partner strapped in. The cage flipped. Bubbles surged up—then nothing.

Luke frowned, something wasn't right. "Come on, com on Jen..." he whispered to himself.

The bubbles should've cleared. Heads should've surfaced by now. He stepped forward, eyes locked on the simulator's small windowasn'tw. A flash of movement—Jenny's hand pounding against the interior. Her partner's mask floated free, drifting toward the surface.

Luke walked over to the instructor, with his clipboard, looking at his watch."Sir, there something's wrong. They're not surfacing."

The chief instructor didn't look up. "Then they fail. Lesson's in managing panic."

"No," Luke said, louder. "The latch isn't releasing. I saw her signal."

Another instructor turned. "Quiet, candidate. Watch and learn."

Luke hesitated—just long enough to know he'd get written up.

Then dove.

The water closed over his head as he swam hard toward the simulator. The emergency release was jammed. He slammed his heel against it—once, twice. The mechanism gave with a crack, and the hatch sprang open.

He pulled Jenny's partner out first—barely conscious. Then Jenny, coughing and gasping but alert. She clung to his arm as he guided them both to the surface.

Medics rushed forward. Instructors shouted. The drill was blown.

Luke ignored them all.

Across the pool deck, a senior officer stood watching from the shade—arms folded, white cover tucked under one arm.

Captain Mark Patton, commanding officer of the Aviation Rescue Swimmer School, stood near the edge of the pool, arms folded.

"You're still doing it," Patton said now, the San Diego sun warming his face. "Assess. Adapt. Execute."

Luke let the silence stretch. "My gut says something's off."

Patton studied him. "Talk to me."

"Maggie and Peter's foundation got hit. Account drained. Over a million gone."

Patton's face tightened. "How clean was the job?"

"Very. No trails. Whoever did it knew what they were after. They asked me to find someone who could help," Luke said. "I told them I'd ask around."

Patton gave a single nod, slow and deliberate. "I may know someone... private sector. Quiet operator. Used to run cyber-ops."

"You trust them?"

"With what matters."

Patton finished his wine and stood. "I'll make a call. If they're willing, I'll connect you. If not—you'll never hear about it again."

Luke met his gaze. "Thanks, Mark."

Patton offered a parting nod and stepped into the light.

Luke stood alone as the admiral disappeared into the sun-drenched haze of Balboa Park. The game of pétanque would go on. Laughter would echo. The rosé would keep flowing. But somewhere else, the real game had already begun.

CHAPTER 14: WINE AND INTRODUCTIONS

Shangri-La, Point Loma, San Diego

Three weeks later, Maggie and Peter stood at the edge of the crowd gathered across the Shangri-La grounds. The cream of Southern California society was out in full force. Music floated beneath the rise of conversation and the occasional clink of glass.

"I love it when a party finds its rhythm," Maggie said, watching couples sway by the pool.

Peter followed her gaze. "It's coming together. Vanessa's done a phenomenal job."

Vanessa stood among a knot of donors near the pergola, mid-laugh, drawing a small circle of guests around her.

"She's a natural," Maggie said. "Poised, smart, and she makes people feel seen. That alone is worth gold in this role."

Peter sipped his wine. "She suspects anything yet?"

Maggie shook her head. "No. But I plan to tell her tonight. She deserves to know."

Peter's brow lifted. "Now?"

"We're about to raise serious money. I won't let her be blindsided if the press or board hears it first."

Vanessa broke from the crowd and approached, her heels crunching softly over the gravel path. "You two hiding over here?" she teased.

"Just catching our breath," Maggie said, smiling. "How are you holding up?"

Vanessa exhaled with a grin. "Still vertical. And the pasta bar saved me."

Peter chuckled. "That's the secret to fundraising: feed them first."

Maggie took a breath. "Vanessa, there's something I want to share with you. Before the night gets away from us."

Vanessa's smile dimmed just slightly. "Okay."

They moved toward a quieter edge of the patio near the bougainvillea, candles flickering inside hurricane glass.

Maggie folded her arms. "Three weeks ago, we discovered that funds had been siphoned from the foundation's endowment. A sophisticated breach."

Vanessa's eyes widened. "How much?"

"Over a million," Peter said softly.

Vanessa blinked. "My God. Why didn't you tell me?"

"I wanted to," Maggie said. "But we needed time to understand the scope—and whether it might be ongoing. We're working with law enforcement and a private cybersecurity team to trace it, but we're not out of the woods."

Vanessa was quiet a moment. "Is that why you arranged this event so quickly?"

Maggie nodded. "It is. And fortunately, we're on track to put a big dent in that loss tonight. But you needed to know."

"I appreciate the honesty," Vanessa said. "Truly. If I'm stepping into this, I'd rather see it clearly."

Peter added, "Luke's helping with the investigation—off the books. He has a contact from his military days, someone who knows how to dig."

Vanessa arched an eyebrow. "He's more involved than I thought."

"He always is," Maggie said, a wry smile tugging at her lips. "Just doesn't like taking credit for it."

Vanessa looked toward the house, where lights flickered against glass. "I won't let this derail us," she said. "This place matters too much."

Maggie's eyes met hers. "That's why you're here."

Back near the pool, the music swelled again under the string lights. Peter raised his glass. "To new beginnings."

Maggie touched hers to his. "And before they drain the wine bar, let's move."

Vanessa slipped away from the crowd, the hum of voices fading behind her. She found a quiet spot behind the pool house, leaning against the rough trunk of a cedar. The scent of roses and salt air gave her something to breathe in—something real.

The party was going well—donors happy, smiles easy—but she felt worn thin. Too many names. Too many curated conversations.

A burst of laughter drew her eye. She turned and spotted Luke standing near the pool house with a small group, drink in hand, relaxed in a way she hadn't seen before. He looked up. Caught her eye. Gave a crooked smile.

Her breath hitched. She smiled back, turned to leave—

"Vanessa, wait!"

She stopped as he threaded his way through the crowd. "I tried to find you earlier," he said, catching his breath. "But your fan club had you pinned down."

She laughed softly. "Yes, they were great. But Maggie and Peter pulled me out just in time."

"Well, while you're catching your breath, come meet some friends."

"I don't want to intrude."

"You won't. They'll like you. Come on."

She hesitated, then smiled. "All right. Lead the way."

Luke introduced her to his old Navy teammates, now the board of the Coronado Seafood Company. Their camaraderie was easy, worn-in. Vanessa found herself laughing more than she expected, surprised by how natural it all felt. Among them was one a women, poised, quiet, watching her with the careful measure of someone taking stock.

Eventually, Owen Cooper stood and stretched. "We'd better get going before someone drags me into a karaoke duet."

Mark Patton chuckled. "Good luck with that. I promised my wife I'd only stay an hour."

Luke got up and said goodbye to his friends and returned to Vanessa, who was taking it all in. "Would you like a nightcap, beer, wine, cocktail?"

Vanessa smiled and shook her head. "Thanks, Luke. But I should mingle a bit more. Maggie might revoke my privileges if I hide out."

Luke grinned. "Fair enough. Another time."

He melted back into the crowd. Vanessa stopped, watching him for a moment, then turned to go.

A voice stopped her. "He's quite a guy, isn't he?"

She turned. The quiet woman stood nearby, expression unreadable. "Yes," Vanessa said. "He is."

Jenny's smile was faint. "I've known Luke a long time. If you're thinking of getting close... there are some things you should know."

Before Vanessa could respond, Jenny turned sharply and walked off. Something in her tone clung like mist. Vanessa's pulse kicked. "Jenny—wait."

Jenny hesitated. Vanessa caught up, voice even but firm. "I'm not trying to intrude. But if there's something I should know, I'd appreciate it."

Jenny studied her, then nodded toward a bench beneath the magnolia tree. They sat.

"Luke's a good man," Jenny said. "One of the best. But he's been through hell. And he doesn't open up easily."

"I've noticed," Vanessa said.

Jenny nodded. "He lost his wife," she said.

Vanessa felt something tighten in her chest. "He was a Navy rescue swimmer," Jenny continued. "They dropped him into combat zones. He pulled people out. Saved lives. A lot of them. But when Savannah died... it broke something."

Vanessa looked toward the patio. Luke stood laughing with Peter and Hank, but even now, behind the smile, there was distance. Not cold. Just... careful.

"He seems strong," she said.

"He is," Jenny replied. "But strength like that doesn't come free. If you're thinking about getting close, make sure you're ready for all that comes with it."

She hesitated. Then added, softer, "He didn't save her. And even though no one blames him—not really—he blames himself. Still."

Vanessa nodded, something quiet and fierce in her expression. "I'm not here to fix anyone. But I don't scare easy."

Jenny gave a small nod. "Good. He doesn't need fixing. He needs someone who'll stay with him through the hard stuff."

They stood, brushing leaves from their clothes.

The music pulsed beneath the soft lantern light, mingling with laughter and the crisp clink of bottles. Jenny stood with the Coronado Seafoods team, her beer cold in her hand, listening to Hank recount his latest near-disaster with a catering van and a cliffside driveway.

She laughed along—honestly, too—but part of her attention kept drifting across the patio.

Luke stood under the edge of a hanging paper lantern, speaking with Vanessa Griffin. The light caught his profile—clean lines, unreadable expression—and something in the way Vanessa leaned in, fingers brushing his sleeve, caught Jenny off guard.

Not jealousy. Not quite. More like static. A shift in the atmosphere. The casual rhythm of the party felt suddenly jarring, out of sync.

She took a sip. Too long. The beer went flat on her tongue.

Vanessa laughed at something Luke said. Luke smiled back, polite but soft.

Then, without warning, the cold returned. Not from the drink. Not from the breeze off the bluffs. From memory.

Warner Springs, Years Earlier

Snow flurried sideways through the trees. Jenny's gloves were soaked, useless. Her breath rasped, slow and ragged, barely warming the air inside her hood. Her teeth clacked hard enough to bruise.

She crouched behind a downed pine, trying to stay hidden. But that didn't matter anymore. The instructors weren't chasing her. Not now. They'd written her off already.

Her shelter had collapsed hours ago. Her compass lost somewhere in the underbrush after a bad fall. The emergency ration bar she'd saved was soaked with creek water.

It was SERE training. Survival. Evasion. Resistance. Escape. But mostly—it was cold. So cold it crawled into her bones and made her wonder if it would just be easier to stop. Just for a while. Just sit down and—

The wind hissed through the pines like a warning. Her knees ached. Her fingertips stung. The kind of pain that no longer felt sharp, but distant—the kind you didn't come back from.

"Hey."

The voice cut through the dark. Soft. Focused.

Jenny turned, blinking snowflakes from her lashes.

Luke knelt beside her—no instructor vest, no clipboard. Just the same steady calm that had carried them both through swim qualifications and cold-water conditioning.

"Easy," he said, already pulling a silver thermal blanket from his pack. "You're not done. We didn't even expect a freak snowstorm in the Springs. They should have postponed the test— not in this shit."

She shook her head. "You're not supposed to talk to me."

"I'm not," he said. "I'm just a hallucination with great gear."

The blanket crackled as he wrapped it over her shoulders. The foil caught her breath, held it close.

"I lost everything," she whispered.

"You didn't lose your will. That's the only thing that matters out here."

"I can't feel my hands."

"Good," he said, smiling just enough. "That means they're still there."

She barked a laugh, more out of shock than humor. "You're going to get dropped for this."

"Probably. But better that than finding you frozen solid like a training dummy."

His hand pressed briefly to her shoulder. Solid. Real.

"You've got this," he said, voice low. "Stay still. Stay small. Dawn's not far."

She turned toward him."Luke—"But he was already gone. The trees shifted, a shadow vanished, and she was alone again. Only now, there was warmth. Real and stubborn.

She curled deeper into the blanket. And when she moved again, it was forward.

She exhaled and blinked hard. The music returned. Glasses clinked. Laughter floated.

Luke glanced over again, just briefly. A nod. Nothing more. But it was enough.

She turned and walked back toward the party lights, the still warming her from the inside.

CHAPTER 15: BEGINNINGS

A week later at Shangri-La, the lingering warmth of the sun filtered through the olive trees on the garden terrace, casting soft shadows across the table where Maggie Manning sat with a glass of iced tea in hand. Across from her, Vanessa McGowen adjusted the folder on the table—blueprints, budgets, and construction timelines neatly tucked inside. But what caught Maggie's eye wasn't the paperwork. It was the quiet intensity on Vanessa's face.

"Don't be shy," Maggie said with a smile. "You've earned your seat at this table. So tell me—what's driving all this?"

"When I first came here... I didn't expect to feel anything," she said. "I'd built walls. After Santa Fe, after my marriage—I thought I was done with foundations and causes. But this place... it's different."

Maggie nodded. "It is. But it wasn't just Peter and me. The Foundation's soul came from someone else. Luke's mother."

Vanessa turned, surprised. "I didn't know that."

"Kathleen Payne. She started it all," Maggie said. "A young widow with a son and a gift for painting. Her husband died in Vietnam. Grief drove her to art. She rented a tiny gallery space in Ocean Beach. Luke was just a boy—always nearby, trailing her like a shadow, paint on his hands."

Vanessa leaned in, listening. "Kathleen didn't have much. Just her insurance payout and a stubborn spirit. That gallery became a haven. She taught classes. Let people paint for free if they couldn't afford supplies. Eventually, she ran out of room. That's when I met her."

"You were friends?"

"Fast. Deep," Maggie said. "She gave me a place to belong when I didn't even know I needed one. And Luke? He called me Aunty Maggie. That boy was always covered in paint."

Her voice turned wistful. "When the gallery was threatened—rent hikes, new developers—she nearly walked away."

"But she didn't," Vanessa said quietly.

Maggie shook her head. "No. Because Peter bought the building next door. Gave her the space. She cried when he handed her the keys. That was the beginning. The Peninsula Arts Foundation grew from her hands and her heart. When she died... COVID took her fast. Luke was overseas. He barely made it back."

Vanessa looked down at the folder. "So it's in his blood."

Maggie nodded. "He keeps it alive—even when he doesn't realize it. Every brushstroke. Every student he mentors. It's all her."

She reached into the side drawer and pulled out a small framed photo. "Here," she said, sliding it across. "The Ocean Beach gallery. That's Kathleen in the doorway. And the little one with the paintbrush—that's Luke."

Vanessa leaned in. The building was modest—sun-faded, a little weathered—but full of life. Kathleen beamed from the doorway. Young Luke grinned at the camera, streaks of red and blue paint across his face.

"She made something out of almost nothing," Vanessa said. "That... reminds me of where I started."

Maggie glanced at her, curious. "I had a hotel once," Vanessa said. "Still do, technically. The Atchison, in Santa Fe. But after everything—my ex, the divorce, the mess he left behind—I figured that chapter was done. Coming here..."

Her fingers brushed the edge of the photo. "Maybe it wasn't the end. Maybe it was the beginning I never saw coming."

She looked up, eyes steady. "Let's build something worthy of what she started."

Maggie smiled, sunlight catching the rim of her glass. "Then let's get to work."

CHAPTER 16: NO SAFE PLACE

Subic Bay, Philippines

They called him Tiger Boy—king of the darknet, ghost of Olongapo. Tonight, he sat bathed in the glow of a 30-inch monitor, grinning at the code on his screen. Twenty-six-year-old Michael Perez had just finished programming his most sophisticated ransomware virus yet—Scorpion. It was supposed to slip into American computers disguised as a routine security update. Once inside, it would lock down their files, holding them hostage for a hefty Bitcoin ransom.

Growing up in the slums of Olongapo City, Perez had learned the value of survival. His mother did what she could, but their home had always been full of shadowy figures Perez knew better than to question. It showed him how to interpret people—how to stay invisible when necessary, and how to take control when the moment was right.

Now, he was close to something big. With Scorpion, he wouldn't just be feared—he'd be legendary. He would sit with the royalty of hackers.

But a lingering unease gnawed at him. Two weeks ago, something strange had happened. Late one night, while coding, his monitor flickered and went black. At first, he thought it was a power surge. Then an image appeared—a grinning Guy Fawkes mask, floating in the darkness. Perez had laughed, thinking it a prank from a rival hacker. But what followed wasn't funny. "Hello, Michael. Listen carefully. Your life depends on it. We've been watching you. Stop your activities now—or there will be consequences." Then the screen went dark again.

He had hurled his mouse across the room, cursing. Who the hell thought they could threaten him? He was Tiger Boy, soon to be the most feared name online. "Screw you!" he'd shouted into the dark. "You don't know who you're messing with!"

He had no intention of stopping. After thoroughly scrubbing his system for malware, Perez resumed work. His sextortion scams raked in cash. His scams were profitable—and real. Hacked webcams. Compromising footage. Shame paid well. If a few victims couldn't live with it, that wasn't his concern.

Two weeks passed without another warning. Perez dismissed the intrusion as a bluff.

Then one night, as he sipped a beer and drafted a new extortion threat, the screen went black again. "Hello again, Michael."

The same mask. The same voice.

Perez tensed, fingers tightening around the bottle. This wasn't a prank. But he wouldn't let them see fear. "You don't scare me," he said, though his heart hammered in his chest.

The mask tilted, mechanical laughter echoing from the speakers. "Before you make more threats, check your system logs. You'll find proof we're already inside. Understand?"

Perez said nothing, his mind racing. Whoever this was, they had been inside his system—and left something behind. "You've hurt a lot of people. We've been patient. No longer."

Perez sneered. "I pick my targets carefully. Nobody important."

The mask leaned closer. "You should have been more careful. You targeted someone who will make you regret every decision. Ever heard the name Paul Le Forge?"

Perez's blood ran cold. He knew the name—whispered in the darkest corners of the underground. Paul DesForges wasn't just a crime boss—he was a shadow ruling Manila's underworld, feared by cops and politicians alike. Rumor had it he controlled half the cyber racket in Luzon.

Perez remembered the story: a coder skimmed crypto from one of DesForges's fronts. Days later, a video surfaced on the darknet—grainy footage showing the coder's lifeless body, dumped in an alley. No explanation. No mercy. Just a warning: Don't cross DesForges.

Perez's throat tensed. "You're bluffing."

The mask said nothing for a long moment. Then: "We helped him find you. He's already coming."

The screen went black.

Perez sat frozen, mind spinning. DesForges. If that monster was involved, it was only a matter of time. He had to run. Now.

Perez shot to his feet, adrenaline surging.

Then—a knock at the door.

A knock.

One rap. Calm. Final.

CHAPTER 17: A NEW GAME

CyberWatch HQ, La Jolla

Jason Edwards leaned back, then slowly swiveled away from the bank of monitors, tension finally slipping from his face. "That's a wrap," he said, meeting Helen Shepard's gaze.

Helen stood with arms crossed, eyes still on the now-dark screens. "I don't think we'll hear from Perez again," Jason added.

Helen nodded, the tightness in her shoulders loosening slightly. "I think you're right," she said, exhaling slowly. "DesForges… well, Perez picked the wrong man to mess with."

Jason gave a humorless chuckle. His eyes drifted toward the Guy Fawkes mask hanging over the console—their quiet warning to hackers like Perez. It dangled in the soft blue glow, its hollow eyes unblinking. He sighed and reached over to power down the final camera feed. "Three suicides we know of—two teenagers and that professor in Lyon," he murmured. "Perez didn't just breach fire-walls. He tore people apart."

Helen watched the mask. "I wish—just once—we could scare one of them completely straight. Before they go too far."

"Yeah, me too. But it's never that simple." Jason's voice filled with regret. "Feels like we're always cleaning up the mess after it's too late."

Helen gave a tired, half-smile. "Next time," she said.

Jason looked up at the mask that seemed to be mocking him. "Yeah. Next time."

Helen pushed off the desk and started toward the door and stopped. "Before I forget—something's coming up. My dad needs a favor. I need you involved with the meeting."

Jason looked up, curiosity sharpening his tired features. "Your dad? What kind of favor?"

Helen crossed her arms, a shadow of a smile rising. "An old Navy buddy of his, some kind of hero he said—Luke Payne. Runs an arts foundation now. They got hit with a major hack."

Jason frowned. "A hit on an arts foundation? That's not usually our turf. Those cases typically go to the feds—although they're pretty overwhelmed these days."

Helen shrugged. "No. But my dad doesn't call in favors lightly. And from what I hear, it's serious." She hesitated, then added, voice softening just a notch: "Besides… maybe it'll be good for us. Something different."

"You just want to meet a hero," said Jason with a sly smile.

Helen grinned wider. "Guilty." She jabbed a finger toward her office. "Which is why you'll be sitting next to me when Luke Payne shows up."

Jason stood and stretched. "Wait a second," he said, feigning offense. "I thought I was your hero."

Helen laughed, tossing him a look over her shoulder as she walked away. "You are. Now move your ass—we've got work to do."

CHAPTER 18: JASON'S REDEMPTION

Jason Edwards watched Helen Shepard leave the ops center, leaving him alone with his thoughts. His fingers hovered over the keyboard, but his mind drifted—back to a time when lines of code meant something else entirely.

Yeah, I'm a bad man doing bad things to bad people, he mused. But sometimes that's the only way to stop worse things from happening.

He wasn't always proud of the work he did at CyberWatch. But every time he stared down a ransomware ring or watched a hospital's network come back online, he remembered why he stayed.

Because he knew the other side too well.

Jason's story started like a thousand others—brilliant kid, Stanford fast-track, fingers always on a keyboard. His first taste of power came from pirating video games. Then it was streaming sites. Then micro-skimming—shaving pennies off thousands of credit card accounts so subtly, no one ever noticed. He stole millions before he was old enough to rent a car.

And then, someone outsmarted him. A rival in the hacking forums—jealous, slick, and just a little faster—doxxed him and dropped a full trace to the feds.

The arrest was swift. The courtroom, clinical. "You've committed serious crimes, Mr. Edwards," the judge intoned. "Your actions have consequences."

Jason barely heard her. He just stared at the cuffs around his wrists, knowing the life he'd built—however recklessly—was over.

His father pulled strings, hired the best lawyers, begged the judge for leniency. But Jason's digital trail was too deep. The deal was clear: repay the money, plead guilty, serve two years at FCI Lompoc.

He expected hell. Instead, he got low-security beige: hedge fund criminals, white-collar grifters, tax cheats who still spoke in IPOs and earnings calls. There were a few tough guys too.

His bunkmate was a former Wall Street shark who narrated his dreams in ticker symbols. But most inmates left Jason alone—until a dustup in the library over access to the sole working computer put him on the radar of Red Torres, a former cartel accountant with a chip on his shoulder.

"You think you're smarter than us?" Red had growled. "Let's see how smart you are without your precious computer."

Jason didn't back down. He didn't fight either. He adapted.

Instead of fists, he offered favors—legal help, financial advice, research tricks. And in time, even Red came around. It wasn't friendship. It was mutual utility. That was enough.

Then the warden had an idea: "You're teaching a class."

Jason scoffed. "On what?"

"Programming. Coding. Something useful."

At first, it felt absurd—teaching tech to inmates. But slowly, it became real. Purposeful. He watched inmates lean into terminal prompts like they were decoding the matrix. Watched former scammers reinvent themselves with HTML.

He taught. They learned. And in those hours, he wasn't a convict. He was someone who could still offer something to the world.

Six months in, a guard interrupted his class.

"You've got a visitor."

Jason raised a brow. He didn't get many visitors. His parents had visited just last week.

When he walked into the visitation room, she was already seated—jeans, white sneakers, jean jacket. Sharp eyes. Calm confidence.

"Jason Edwards?" she asked.

"Yeah…"

"I'm Helen Shepard." She extended a hand. "And I'm going to break you out of here."

Jason blinked. "What?"

Helen smiled. "Not literally. But I want to offer you a job."

He laughed, unsure if it was a joke. "Doing what?"

"I run CyberWatch. We go after the worst actors in the cyber-crime world—ransomware groups, blackmail rings, human traffickers hiding behind layers of encryption. You know how they think. I need someone like you."

Jason hesitated. "And if I say no?"

"You'll finish your sentence. Get out with a felony record. No prospects. No security clearance. No second chance. Or… you walk out now and start over. This is your shot, Jason. Take it."

And he had.

It wasn't easy. Helen didn't give him the easy cases. But she gave him purpose. Redemption didn't come with applause—but it came with clarity.

He still didn't feel like a hero. But the kid who once siphoned money from strangers' accounts was now unmasking the monsters who preyed on families and hospitals.

Tonight, as he sat alone in the darkened CyberWatch bay, he thought about the man he'd meet tomorrow.

Luke Payne. A warrior. A ghost. Another man chasing something like redemption.

Jason leaned back in his chair, the blue glow of the monitors painting his face in code.

Maybe they weren't so different.

Maybe none of them were.

CHAPTER 19: THE INSTITUTE

Prospect Street in La Jolla bustled with tourists and well-heeled locals. He didn't visit the community very often, mostly for gallery openings. Parking spots were rare. After circling twice through the narrow streets of the Village —the locals' name for San Diego's most exclusive and expensive enclave—Luke Payne gave up and handed the keys to a restaurant valet. He hadn't heard of the CyberWatch Institute. Worse—he couldn't find anything about it online. That alone set off alarms.

The email from Mark Patton had been cryptic:

Hi Luke, I made you an appointment tomorrow at 1 p. m. at the CyberWatch Institute in La Jolla. They might help with the foundation situation. Address: 7723 Prospect, Suite B303. Ask for Helen when you get there.

Weaving his way down the crowded sidewalk, Luke passed boutiques, galleries, and oceanfront cafes. An odd place for a cybersecurity firm.

The address led him to a sleek office tower climbing toward the bluffs—retail shops and law offices filled the lower floors, their polished glass reflecting the Pacific coast. Luke checked the directory for Suite B303. Nothing.

He asked a security guard standing nearby, who eyed him cautiously before nodding toward a dimly lit service stairwell tucked behind a side entrance. He descended three flights below street level. The air grew cooler and heavier with each step until he reached a plain steel door marked with a faded sign: B303. The door was locked.

He pressed the intercom button, his thumb brushing away rust.

A tinny voice crackled, "Suite B303."

"Luke Payne. Appointment with Helen."

A pause.

"Yes, Mr. Payne. We've been expecting you."

The door buzzed open.

The reception area was sterile. A Danish modern couch. A silent receptionist tapping on a screen. No logos. No brochures. No clue what this place was.

Luke sat, eyes sharp, body still. The overhead light hummed faintly.

A second door buzzed.

A petite woman stepped through—blonde pixie cut, bright smile, energy sharp as glass. "Hello, Mr. Payne. I'm Dr. Helen Shepard, director of the institute. My father tells me that you have a problem. It's a pleasure to meet you."

Luke blinked, surprised. "You're Mark Patton daughter? I didn't know he even had a child."

Helen's smile deepened. "He didn't know he had one, until I showed up on his doorstep. Surprised?"

"Not even a whisper."

"It's a long story," she said softly—but something behind her eyes told him not to push. "Right now, let's focus on you. My associate, Jason Edwards, is waiting in the conference room."

She led him through a secured door into a minimalist meeting space—one table, a few chairs, a black-and-white photo on the wall. Two soldiers in combat gear. Faces obscured.

A tall broad-shouldered man in his thirties stood and offered a firm handshake. "Jason Edwards. Good to meet you, Mr. Payne."

Luke noted the sharp eyes behind the casual tone—curious, calculating, like someone who mapped every variable before making a move.

"We don't get many visitors," Jason said. "Hence the charming decor."

Luke grinned. "Yeah, it crossed my mind. And the exterior? Not exactly screaming 'startup.'"Helen and Jason exchanged a glance—mutual understanding, this wasn't a typical cyber company.

"CyberWatch operates under the radar. We don't advertise," Helen began.

Jason leaned back. "Technically, we don't exist."

Luke tapped a finger against the polished tabletop. "So discretion is the product."

Helen smiled. "Exactly. But first—let's talk about why you're here."

Luke nodded and laid it all out—the breach at the foundation, the siphoned funds. The fear of losing the one thing tethering him to life after Savannah.

Helen listened. Jason didn't interrupt. Both absorbed every word.

When Luke finished, silence settled in. Helen tapped the table, eyes narrowed. "This wasn't random. It was surgical."

Jason nodded. "They knew exactly what to look for. Which means it wasn't just about money."

Helen rose and paced. "Give us a moment."

They left, and Luke waited with a knot in his stomach.

Five minutes passed.

They returned. Helen sat down, eyes direct. "Luke, we don't usually take cases like this. But we're making an exception."

Luke exhaled, the mix of relief and caution tightening in his chest.

"Why?"

Helen didn't blink. "Because we believe in what the foundation does. And because Mark trusts you."

She leaned forward, voice low but clear. "Now it's time you understand what CyberWatch really does."

CHAPTER 20: THE BROKEN

Helen led Luke Payne through a heavy security door triggered by a retinal scanner. It clicked open into a bright, sterile corridor.

Both white walls were lined with black-and-white mugshots—mostly young, mostly male. "These aren't employees of the month," Luke said dryly.

Helen laughed. "Correct. International rogue's gallery. These were the 'unreachables'—until we got to them."

Luke let out a low whistle. "I'll bet you're very good at what you do."

They reached another thick steel door. Helen leaned in for a second retinal scan. The four-inch-thick panel slid silently into the wall.

What Luke saw next made him stop. It looked like the lobby of a luxury resort. Three towering palm trees rose from a central planter. A glass wall stretched to the ceiling, revealing a sprawling patio with red umbrella tables and a lap pool gleaming just beyond. The Pacific sparkled on the horizon. A soft ocean breeze drifted through sliding doors, carrying salt and sunlight.

Helen caught his look and grinned. "The rec room. We like our people to be happy. Private elevator to the beach—surfing, kayaking, paddle boarding, snorkeling. Private gym. Gear storage. Six bedrooms for the all-nighters."

Luke chuckled. "Where do I sign up?"

She led him down a new corridor lined with glass-walled offices. "Admin and media studio on the left. On the right—team rooms. Each handles a different part of the world, or

Luke peered into one room. A dozen specialists, diverse in every way, hunched over glowing monitors. Focused. Intense. Dangerous. "Where do you find these people?" he asked.

Helen's voice held quiet pride. "Each of them was a hacker. A few of the greatest in the world. Now they work for something better. Most never get that chance."

They stopped at a final black door. Another retina scanner. Luke nodded toward it. "And behind door number three?"

Helen's smile faded. "Our newest division. The ones even we can barely reach. The true unreachables." Her tone told him not to ask more.

Before he could, she pivoted. "This way. My office."

CHAPTER 21: BENEATH THE SURFACE

Helen's office reflected the rest of CyberWatch—understated, precise. A cherry wood desk. A matching conference table. Four sleek swivel chairs. The far wall was dominated by a massive eight-foot monitor flanked by smaller side screens.

She gestured toward the table. "Have a seat. Coffee? Water?"

"I'm good," Luke said, scanning the setup. "You must love your TV."

Helen chuckled as she sat across from him. "Video conferencing. Government partners, field teams, and overseas clients. The big screen's for shared intel. The side panels handle faces, chatter, and real-time feeds."

Luke leaned back, half-smiling. "No wonder you stay off the radar. No one's stumbling across this place."

"Exactly," she said. Her tone shifted—sharper now. The ease dropped away.

She folded her hands on the table. "Let's get to it." She leaned forward, her voice tightening. "The internet changed everything. Every day, more than six thousand new hackers go after Americans."

Luke blinked. "That many?"

Helen nodded. "It's a firehose. And it's only getting worse. The government's underwater—too many agencies, too little coordination. Everyone's stepping on each other's wires."

Luke raised an eyebrow. "Sounds like a cluster—"

"*—fuck," she finished. "Exactly.*"

She stood and began pacing methodically. "The FBI focuses on the president's latest immigration boondoggle, billion-dollar breaches and foreign actors. They don't have the bandwidth to chase down every ransomware infection, every hijacked nonprofit, every compromised server at a community art center."

Luke leaned forward. "So what happens to those?"

She stopped, facing him. "They get screwed."

She didn't blink. "That's where we come in. We find what falls through the cracks. Not for the money. Not for the press. For the people who get hurt."

Luke let the words land. Then gave a smile. "Digital vigilantes."

Helen smiled back, faint but proud. "Exactly."

The door opened quietly. Jason entered and took a seat beside her.

Helen's tone dropped. "We may not get your foundation's money back, Luke. I hope we do. But I'll tell you what—we'll bust some balls along the way."

Luke sat back, relief slipping into his eyes. "Rodger that."

CHAPTER 22: THE SHANGHAI SIGNATURE

CyberWatch, La Jolla – Next Day

Jason Edwards slid behind his triple-monitor rig, fingers already in motion as the quiet hum of processors filled the room. Cool blue light reflected across his face.

Helen Shepard leaned against a nearby table, arms crossed, the faint scent of coffee lingering between them. Lines of code scrolled across the central display.

"I'm starting with the basics," Jason said. "Looking at traffic in and out of the foundation's servers. Whoever hit you went in fast and quiet, but they left footprints. Everyone does."

A few more keystrokes. "Here."

He zoomed in on a dense cluster of outbound data. "Time-stamped the night the money vanished. Bounced through Sweden, Thailand… a few familiar blind spots."

He tapped the final hop. "But the exit node? Shanghai."

Helen straightened. "Shanghai," she repeated, the word. "that's a hotbed of cyber bad guys, including the military. There's been a lot of chatter from that region lately. Not just noise—strategic mischief. And not always the usual suspects."

Jason dug deeper. "Yep. This doesn't look military, they don't go after back accounts that I know of. Whoever it was used the account's actual credentials. Spoofed email. Classic phishing op. Once inside, they triggered a quick-transfer protocol. But here's the thing—they didn't touch anything else. No donor records, no back-end systems. Just in and out."

Helen frowned. "So it was targeted. Surgical."

Jason nodded. "Exactly. Whoever did this wasn't some kid looking to make a name. This was military-precise. Could be state-sponsored—or someone who learned their playbook."

He launched a trace visualization. A digital constellation unfolded across the screen, pulsing with data nodes. One node pulsed brighter than the rest.

"There." He leaned in. "The source node is anchored in the Bund. And it's got PLA fingerprints all over it."

Helen's eyes narrowed. "Too clean?"

Jason hesitated. "Almost like they wanted us to find it."

He glanced back at the screen, fingers hovering. "They didn't even try to bury the trail—not really. That's not just arrogance. That's a tactic. Plant a signature someone's trained to recognize, then let them follow it straight into the wrong conclusion."

Helen absorbed that in silence.

Jason continued, quieter now. "It's either sloppy... or it's misdirection. Could be a false flag. And if it is—then the real source isn't PLA. It's someone framing them."

Helen's voice sliced the air. "Which means this wasn't just about money."

Jason nodded. "No. This was a message. We just haven't decoded it yet."

Helen reached for her phone, already typing."I'll let Luke know we've found the location. Why would someone in China pull this off? Still more questions than answers I'm afraid."

Jason nodded, eyes still locked on the constellation of nodes. "Yep, this hacker is an odd duck for sure. I'll push this pattern to a few federal contacts—see if anyone else is seeing hits like this. If it's part of something bigger, we won't be the only target."

CHAPTER 23: A HACKER'S REMORSE

*Later That Night – Shanghai

Rusty Zhilan sat in darkness, his mood no brighter. The windows behind him framed Shanghai's glow—too bright, too distant. He hadn't moved in hours.

Lines Lines of code trickled across the screen. Scripts. Ghost commands. Intrusions dressed as elegance. He had written them. Perfected them. But they were wrong.

He opened his browser. The cursor blinked. Almost against his will, his fingers betrayed him, spelling out the site he swore he'd never open again: the Peninsula Arts Foundation homepage.

Children. Paint-stained smocks. A boy smiling with a violin tucked beneath his chin. A girl guiding her fingers through wet clay. Underneath: "Creativity is a refuge."

He scrolled deeper into the site, past the summer workshops and testimonials. A short biography caught his eye. Margaret Manning, it read. Founder. Artist. Visionary. Tireless advocate for underserved communities. There was a photo—gray curls, smart jacket, a hand resting gently on a student's shoulder. Not posed. Just real. Warmth radiated from her eyes like someone who saw the best in people and believed it mattered.

He kept reading. The Foundation wasn't just for kids. There were dance classes for children in wheelchairs, art therapy for those struggling with speech or trauma, and music ensembles blending beginners with the blind. Seniors weren't left behind—volunteers who once felt invisible were now mentoring young artists, teaching forgotten skills, or simply showing up so the kids knew someone cared.

Rusty stared at the screen. This wasn't just a community center. It was a refuge.

He couldn't remember the last time anyone had looked at him like that. Not his mother. Not his father. Not even his grandmother.

Maybe if he'd had someone like her—someone who saw potential, not threat—he wouldn't be sitting here, trying to scrub his conscience clean with crypto.

Back at the desk, he opened the encrypted wallet interface. The numbers glared. He transferred the full amount—everything from the Foundation job. And then more. Funds from the same account.

He bounced the money transfer through a half-dozen scramblers. Washed it until even he wouldn't be able to follow the trail.

He sat still, breathing shallowly, then reached for his phone.

He opened a new message. Stared at the blinking prompt and typed.

TO: no one yet

MESSAGE:

"I made a mistake. I'm trying to fix it. If this reaches someone who still believes in second chances... I'm listening."

He didn't send it. Not yet.

Instead, he powered everything down. For the first time in weeks, he let the silence settle without trying to outrun it.

CHAPTER 24: HOOK-UP

Jason Edwards leaned forward. One signal blinked. "Got him."

Helen stepped beside him, arms folded. "He opened it?"

Jason shook his head. "Didn't open it—just brushed it. That was enough. A partial load leaked metadata. An old IP pinged off a residential block in Pudong district."

Helen's expression sharpened. "Shanghai."

Jason nodded. "We're not in his room, but we're in his neighborhood. Wait… transfer initiated."

Helen leaned in. "Where's it going?"

Jason tracked the digital trail. "Outflow—$1.7 million. Scrubbed through layers, but I've got the direction."

He pulled up a separate window, fingers moving fast. The foundation's account refreshed. The numbers shifted, the balance climbing. Jason let out a low breath. "It's back."

Helen blinked. "What's back? You mean he returned it?"

"All of it. Plus half a mil. Incredible."

"No note?"

"Nothing. Just a silent apology, I think."

Jason clicked through a final string of commands. "He thinks he disappeared clean. But he left us a breadcrumb."

"Can we reach him?"

"Maybe. But gently. No pressure. No chase."

Helen nodded slowly. "Then we offer him a choice."

Jason's fingers hovered over the keyboard. "Better than a cell."

"Or a grave," Helen said softly.

She studied the screen for another moment, then turned toward the door.

"Let's see if we can find out who he works for. Right now, I'm going to call Luke and give him the good news."

CHAPTER 25: RETURN TO SENDER

Luke ended the call with Helen and sat in silence, letting the news settle. The money was back. More than back. That extra half-million sat like a loaded weapon—maybe a gift, maybe a warning. Maybe bait dressed up to look like a blessing.

He tapped Maggie Manning's number and lifted the phone to his ear. She picked up on the second ring. "Luke? Everything okay?"

He got right to it. "Maggie, the missing money—it's back. Plus an extra half-million."

A sharp inhale. "Are you serious?" Her voice cracked. "Luke, that's… that's incredible."

He let her have the moment. The relief in her voice pulled a smile from him—his first in days.

Then his tone shifted. "Maggie… listen carefully."

Her joy vanished. "I'm listening."

"This isn't over," Luke said. "Whoever returned the money didn't do it out of generosity. That extra five hundred grand? It came from somewhere. And whoever lost it might not be the forgiving type."

"You think it's a threat?"

"I think it's a message," he said. "Or a mistake. Either way, it's dangerous."

Maggie exhaled slowly. "What should we do?"

"Nothing public. Just let it sit. Be grateful. Look distracted. Meanwhile, I've got people still looking into it. Quietly."

Her voice steadied. "Alright. We'll keep it quiet. But Luke…"

"Thank you. For everything."

Luke closed his eyes. "I'm not doing this alone, Maggie. We're in it together."

They hung up.

Luke settled into his seat, gaze drifting past the pool at Shangri-La to the glittering sprawl of San Diego Bay. Postcard-perfect. The kind of view people dreamed about.

But even paradise had shadows.

The foundation was safe—for now. The money was back. But somewhere out there, someone was watching. Calculating.

Luke's instincts had saved lives more than once. And this time they told him the storm wasn't gone—it was only circling back.

CHAPTER 26: MR. LEE'S RECKONING

Rusty's voice cracked over the secure channel cell phone, raw with something close to fear and remorse.

Lee's grip locked around the phone. "Extra?"

Lee closed his eyes. He knew the accounts Rusty tapped weren't just buffer zones. They were assets Lee wasn't cleared to touch.

And now Rusty had touched them.

Shanghai — Present

Lee stood by the window of his office, staring at the rain-slicked streets below. His thoughts circled the same dead ends. Every path led to risk.

Rusty's confession gnawed at him. This job hadn't just gone sideways—it had detonated every line he thought couldn't be crossed. And now, they were teetering on the edge of something volatile.

The Colonel never needed to issue threats. His presence alone changed the air. Orders were orders. Lee had always believed they came from higher up. From the Ministry. From China itself. Questioning them had never felt like an option.

His team wasn't built for conflict. They were shadows—quiet, precise. Experts at mapping human and corporate networks. No hacks. No takedowns. Just clean extractions.

When his adopted sister, General Yang Yue, had begun steering military intelligence contracts his way, it felt like a win—for her, for the state, for him. Smarter work. Cleaner hands.

Then the Colonel arrived. Demanding more. Deeper breaches. Blackmail. Sabotage. Lee told himself it was still service. Still duty.

But the Peninsula Arts Foundation? That never sat right. It didn't feel strategic. It felt personal. Like someone settling a score.

Still, he hadn't refused. You didn't refuse the Colonel.

And now Rusty had gone rogue—stepped out of the shadows and into the spotlight.

Those accounts weren't just padding—they were tied to operations Lee had never been cleared to even ask about. Rusty had no idea what he'd touched. And truthfully, neither did Lee.

He still believed the state had his back. But the cracks were widening. If this was truly sanctioned work, why all the backdoors? The shell companies? Why target an obscure American arts foundation?

He turned from the window and began to pace. He couldn't go to the Colonel with this. If he found out that Rusty had skimmed half a million from the dark pool? The Colonel didn't forgive mistakes. Not ever.

His phone buzzed on the desk. A secure message pulsed on the screen.

Colonel: Status?

Lee wiped his palms on his pants.

Lee: Encountered obstacles. Job will be completed. Request ten days.

The reply came instantly.

Colonel: No delays. No failures.

Lee gently placed the phone down. His hand trembled.

He returned to the window, the skyline blurred behind rain and neon.

The pretense of control was unraveling. If they couldn't clean this up quietly, he knew how it would go.

Rusty would vanish first. Then the others. Eventually, him.

He had thought he was serving China. Thought loyalty would protect him.

But loyalty wouldn't save him now. He wasn't sure what would.

CHAPTER 27: THE KILL CHAIN

Elsewhere in Shanghai.

The Colonel sat in a windowless concrete safe house, hands folded as encrypted data scrolled across his monitor. John Kang stood nearby—silent, unmoving.

"They're unraveling faster than I expected," the Colonel said, watching the screen.

Kang gave a slight nod.

The Colonel allowed himself a smile. "The moment Rusty touched Kahn's reserve," he murmured, "he signed his death warrant."

Kang didn't speak. He didn't need to.

"Two weeks," the Colonel said. "Let them believe they still have a chance. Then clean up."

Kang smiled. Cold as ice. "It will be my pleasure."

First Rusty. Then Lee.

The Colonel leaned back into the gloom, his face swallowed by shadow. The pawns had served their purpose.

Soon, the board would be cleared.

CHAPTER 28: THE LAST FAVOR

Lee sat in the kitchen of his apartment, his leg bouncing beneath the glass and steel dining table. His phone felt slick in his grip—too light to carry what he was about to do. The Colonel's voice still echoed in his head—calm, deliberate, terrifying in its restraint. And now, he had failed.

His fingers hovered over the keypad. Rusty had delivered the decisive blow. He didn't blame him. Rusty acted from his heart. The funds were traced. Lee had delayed the fallout as long as possible, but it was over. The walls were closing in.

He wanted to believe the Colonel might understand. Might allow for nuance. But he knew better. He didn't deal in forgiveness. Only outcomes.

With a shaky breath, he dialed.

Two rings.

"Lee." The voice was smooth. Controlled. Deadly.

Lee swallowed. "Sir... It's not going well."

"Go on."

Lee's throat stiffened. He forced the words out. "Rusty's blown. The money was traced. If I push any further, they'll connect it to us. I—I can't keep this up."

Another pause. Longer this time.

Lee braced for the cut.

Instead, the Colonel's voice remained steady. "I see."

No blame. No anger. Just that quiet edge that always felt one syllable away from judgment.

"I'll finish the two weeks you asked for," Lee said quickly. "I'll hand over everything—hardware, drives. I'll clean it up."

"You've done excellent work, Lee," the Colonel replied, smooth as silk. "There's no need for concern. I anticipated complications."

Lee's pulse jumped. Anticipated?

"I'll reward your loyalty, Chen Lee. There will be… a gesture."

The line went dead.

Lee sat frozen, the phone still in his hand. A reward?

Now? It didn't add up.

Across the city, in a dimly lit office above the Bund, the Colonel set his phone down with care. A thin smile touched his lips. "Just as expected," he murmured.

John Kang stood near the window, hands clasped behind his back.

"Lee's losing his nerve," the Colonel said. "But he'll finish the job. Fear's a powerful motivator."

Kang didn't respond. "What are your orders?" he asked finally.

"Tell Mumbai: Phase One is nearly complete. In two weeks, we shut it all down."

Kang grinned. "Starting with Lee?"

The Colonel grinned. "No. We finish with Lee. Let him believe he's in the clear. Then… remove him."

"And the others?"

"Rusty first. Then the rest. I want eyes on all of them. Patterns. Routines. Exit points. When the time comes, make it clean."

Kang gave a short nod and turned to go.

The Colonel stopped him at the door. "We're nearly finished here, Kang. Soon, we return to Mumbai."

Kang nodded once, then slipped into the hallway. The Colonel moved to the window, watching the sprawl of city lights flicker beneath the haze. The cleanup would begin soon.

And as far as the Colonel was concerned, Chen Lee was already gone.

CHAPTER 29: SHADOWS OVER SHANGHAI

Rusty Zhilan pulled his hoodie tight against the wind as he wove through Pudong's alleys. His shift at the internet cafe had ended hours ago, but the unease clung to him like static, like something unfinished. He zigzagged through side streets, avoiding cameras and crowds. The deeper lanes reeked of oil and wet concrete, but he pushed forward, chasing motion to outrun the fear.

Still, his gut twisted. Something was off.

At a busy intersection, he ducked into a convenience store and loitered near the instant noodles, scanning the glass door's reflection—movement, shapes, a black cap. Nothing. Just scooters. Vendors. A pair of tourists drifting past.

But outside, that same prickling sensation crept up his spine. Watched.

He crossed the street.

A man in a black cap crossed too.

Rusty stopped, pretending to tie his shoe. The man slowed.

His pulse kicked. He turned down a narrow alley. Grease-slick walls. Overflowing bins. Concrete gleaming with rain. Halfway through, he slipped into a darkened doorway and held his breath. Footsteps followed. Measured. Closer.

He bolted. One turn, then another. Over a trash can. Through a side gate jammed open by a rusted chain. He didn't stop until the hum of a fluorescent-lit market snapped into view. Only then did he look back.

No one.

Lee.

Should he call? Warn him? No. That would drag him deeper. He'd returned the money. That had to count for something.

What Rusty didn't know:

John Kang had seen everything. His route. His building. His hours.

Rusty thought he'd bought time. He hadn't.

He'd just started the clock.

CHAPTER 30: THE BOSS'S FURY

Chandra Sochi—known to Lee as the Colonel—stood before a wall-sized map of Shanghai, charting operational routes when his secure phone buzzed. He saw the number and tensed. The Boss. Now?

He answered, voice steady. "Yes, sir."

The Boss didn't waste time. "Sochi, what the hell is happening with my money?"

Sochi braced. "There's been a complication, sir. One of our junior assets—an unsupervised hacker—went off-script. He returned the siphoned funds… and the five hundred thousand we staged for Phase Two."

A long pause followed. Just air, crackling in the silence.

Then: "Returned it? And the half million?"

"Yes, sir." Sochi swallowed. "And he left a message: 'Don't screw with the Foundation.'"

He waited. Nothing but breathing.

Then the Boss spoke again, quieter now. "This isn't about the money, Sochi. It's about respect. Someone thought they could humiliate us."

"We're already moving, sir," Sochi said, keeping his tone measured. "We traced the breach to a hacker inside Lee's team. He's being dealt with."

"Not enough," the Boss said. He didn't raise his voice—but the intent in it was unmistakable. "I want all of them wiped out. No survivors. Make it look like Beijing. Leave trails. False flags. Do whatever it takes."

Sochi hesitated. He remembered Beijing. What the Boss meant by it. Blood in the stairwells. A city block collapsed to hide a body count. This wasn't containment. It was spectacle. But he knew better than to push back.

"I understand."

"And the foundation?" the Boss's tone sharpened. "Maggie Manning and her husband—I want them gone. Make it loud. Make it echo across the Pacific."

Sochi frowned. They'd never hit U.S.. soil before—not like this. This wasn't just retaliation. It was escalation.

"The team is already positioned," he said. "It'll be done."

"Failure is not an option," the Boss said. "We lose face once, they test us. We lose it twice—we're gone."

Click. Just like that, the call ended.

Sochi lowered the phone and stood still. Behind him, Kang adjusted his stance.

"The Boss is angry," Kang said.

Sochi nodded. "Beyond angry. He wants scorched earth."

Kang gave a tight grin. "Then we don't wait. Clean work is for cowards."

Sochi turned back to the map, eyes scanning routes, targets, fallback zones. First: eliminate the weak link—Rusty. Then the rest of Lee's team. Quiet. Surgical. Then San Diego. Loud. Public.

. The Boss wanted more than cleanup. He wanted a message no one would survive. And Sochi would deliver it.

CHAPTER 31: THE PAST NEVER STAYS BURIED

The sun dipped low over Balboa Island, staining the harbor in copper and flame. Jimmy Wei's eyes narrowed as he scanned the bustling patio of The Dragon's Den. The bistro he and Edward Song had built from scratch had become a haven—a quiet life carved out of noise and regret. Laughter and silverware clinked in the background, blending with the soft thrum of passing boats.

This was the life Jimmy had dreamed of—peaceful, nameless, unmarked by who he used to be. But ghosts had a way of finding you—even in daylight.

Jimmy had never fit the mold of a gangster. Even as a kid running through San Francisco's Chinatown alleys, he'd known he didn't belong. His father, one of the old guard in the notorious Wah Ching Tongs, had pressed Jimmy into the life under the guise of protection. "The only way to keep you safe, son," he used to say.

Jimmy obeyed—out of fear, out of family obligation. But while the others reveled in collecting dues and bruises, Jimmy found solace in the kitchen. He preferred the scent of flour to the stink of fear. Baking, not beatings.

Edward Song had been the same. Sons of the Tongs, but dreamers at heart. Late nights at the Golden Dragon restaurant's back kitchen, scheming about a life that didn't end in a prison cell—or a coffin. "We'll open our own place someday," Edward had said, flicking a cigarette into the gutter. "Real food. Real peace."

Their dream nearly died on September 4, 1977. The Joe Boys gang stormed into the Golden Dragon that night, guns blazing. Bullets meant for others tore through the dining room. Five dead. Eleven wounded. Chinatown changed forever in minutes. In the chaos that followed—the cops, the blood feuds, the revenge killings—Jimmy and Edward disappeared. No goodbyes. No second chances. South, to Orange County. South, to a second life.

Balboa Island was their salvation. A derelict diner transformed by grit and sweat into The Dragon's Den—a fusion of Chinese flavors and American comfort. Locals embraced them. They became part of the community: sponsoring Little League teams, hosting charity dinners, teaching kids how to fold dumplings. They had outrun the shadows.

So they thought.

The phone vibrated next to Jimmy's iced tea. Unknown number. He hesitated, thumb hovering over Decline. Something cold crawled up his spine.

He answered.

"Jimmy."

The voice—smooth, but edged like broken glass.

Jimmy lowered his voice. "What do you want?"

A low chuckle. "Come on. Can't family stay in touch?"

Jimmy's eyes drifted to the kitchen. Edward was laughing with the staff. He gripped the phone tighter. "Cut the bullshit, Sochi. Why are you really calling?"

The tone shifted. Colder now. "I need a favor."

Jimmy's pulse kicked. "I'm not that guy anymore."

"It's not a request," Sochi said, voice low and blade-sharp. "You think the Tongs ever let anyone walk away clean? You owe me. You're alive because of me."

Jimmy gritted his teeth. The memories surged—bloody, fast, and ugly. After the Golden Dragon massacre, it was Sochi who pulled strings, bought them time, kept them breathing while others were buried or locked away.

"What do you want?" Jimmy asked.

"There's a woman in San Diego. Maggie Manning. She and her

people need a scare. No questions. No mercy. Instructions will follow."

Jimmy's hands curled into fists. "And if I say no?"

Silence. The kind that makes your skin crawl. "You won't say no, cousin. I know where you sleep. I know where Edward's grandchildren play. One call—and everything you built goes up in smoke."

Jimmy's breath caught. He spoke quietly. "After this... we're done."

Sochi laughed, low and cruel. "You're done when I say you're done."

Jimmy watched the phone, heart pounding. And just like that, the past had a pulse again.

CHAPTER 32: THE LUNCH MEETING

The line outside Hodad's wrapped halfway down Newport Avenue. Surfboards lined the walls, the windows pulsed with neon, and the sound of sizzling burgers mingled with the rumble of beach traffic. Ocean Beach moved at its own rhythm—loud, unbothered, and unapologetically real.

Vanessa walked tentatively through the door. This was not what she pictured when Luke said lunch. Not a place where the walls were covered in license plates, skateboards, Sharpie graffiti, and laminated newspaper clippings. Not a place where the tables looked like they'd hosted generations of locals and hamburger aficionados from around the globe. Her eyes fell on a painting; abstract and raw—deep cobalt blue crashing into streaks of burnt orange. Something about it made her pause in front of it.

"That one hits people," said the hostess beside her. "Local guy painted it. Luke Payne."

Vanessa smiled. "I figured as much. I'm here to meet him."

The hostess grinned. "You're Vanessa. He's in the back booth. Right under the van seat."

She led Vanessa past a line of people waiting for booths, past a cracked mirror with Sharpie messages from five different decades, to a corner seat where Luke sat with a vanilla shake and a pencil in his hand. He was sketching something on a napkin.

He stood when he saw her. "Didn't think you'd find it," he said.

"I didn't think this is where we were meeting."

Luke shrugged. "It's where my story started."

She slid into the booth, eyeing the painting. "That's yours?"

"Yeah. One of the first I did after Afghanistan. Mike Harden—he owned the place—traded me a month of burgers for it."

She smiled. "Solid deal."

"My mom used to bring me here," he said. "Her art studio was right here on Newport. She taught classes—had kids from all over OB stopping in. My stepdad taught at San Diego State—printmaking and mixed media. Hodad's was our family reset button."

Vanessa raised a brow. "You had artist parents and still joined the Navy?"

He paused, glancing toward the window. "I know it seems strange. But after I got my MFA, 9/11 happened. There wasn't much opportunity, so I enlisted in the Navy like my dad. Then, I stayed, I liked my job."

A server arrived—clipboard menu and a permanent grin. Luke ordered a Guido with onion rings. Vanessa did the same, with a vanilla shake.

When the server left, Vanessa glanced toward the entrance. "That mural photo by the door—is that Mike and Rich?"

Luke nodded. "Yeah. Hodad's sponsored the mural project for the fireworks street fair every year. Rich James would grid out these giant panels, and the kids would fill them in. Total chaos. Pure joy." He smiled at the memory. "I was just a kid when I met Rich. He was a character. Drove an old Chevy convertible covered in hand-painted dolphins—every panel, even the dash. It looked like something Poseidon would ride into a surf contest."

Vanessa laughed softly. "And Mike?"

"Mike Harden ran Hodad's like it was a church—only with bacon and skateboards. He fed half the neighborhood, no questions asked. When I started painting, he gave me a booth and a shake and said, 'Don't waste it.'"

"They're legends around here."

Luke smiled. "Still are. Four of the James brothers are still around, still part of OB. Rich passed, and Mike Harden too. But yeah, their fingerprints are everywhere. Mike gave me burgers. Rich gave me paint. That's more than most people ever get."

Their food came—massive burgers, onion rings stacked like building blocks. The shake was thick enough to slow a straw.

Vanessa laughed when she took her first bite. "This is insane."

Luke grinned. "Told you."

As they ate, the conversation turned to the Foundation. Vanessa talked about walking away from a life that had collapsed under politics and pressure. Maggie and Peter saw something in her, she said. Something worth saving.

Luke nodded. "They do that."

"And for you?"

"They gave me a reason to come back. The painting helped. Teaching helped. They saw something I didn't know how to name yet."

Vanessa finished her shake and leaned in. "You trust people easily?"

"No," Luke said. "But you haven't given me a reason not to."

She stood, brushing crumbs from her hands. "Then let's make something good out of all this."

Luke walked her outside. The air smelled like salt and fryer grease. The breeze off the ocean was just cool enough to carry some clarity with it.

At her car, she turned. "Thanks for lunch, Luke. And the surprise."

He smiled. "See you Thursday?"

"I'll be there."

He watched her pull away. Across the street, a busker strummed slow, steady chords on a weather-beaten guitar. A seagull drifted low over the street, banking toward the pier.

Luke lingered a moment, then patted his pockets. Hoodie. He'd left it on the back of the booth.

He stepped back into Hodad's. The place was louder now—more crowded, more alive. The smell of grilled onions hit him the moment he crossed the threshold. As he passed the register, he slowed.

The photo was still there—Mike Harden with a teenage Luke beside him, both grinning. Luke's arms were crossed, a streak of blue paint on his cheek, like he'd just come from helping Rich James at the fireworks mural and stopped in for fries. Rich and Mike's eyes seemed to reach out to him from a time long ago, as if to say: *Don't worry. Everything's going to be alright.*

He nodded toward it once, not quite ready to let it go.

CHAPTER 33: DRIVE WITH THE DEVIL

Just north of San Diego, a black SUV took the Rancho Bernardo exit and headed east, winding through the back roads skirting the San Pasqual Agricultural Preserve. The hills glowed amber in the afternoon sun, and neat rows of avocado trees lined the slopes like a well-tended orchard fortress.

"There," Sochi said, pointing to a utility truck parked on the shoulder. The Spectrum logo gleamed under the sun. "Pull over. A hundred yards back."

Edward hesitated. "What are we doing?"

"Just follow directions," Sochi said, already opening the door.

He walked calmly up the road, stopping near the truck. One of the techs stood on the ground, sipping from a thermos, while the other worked in the bucket lift overhead. "What's going on?" Sochi asked casually.

"Maintenance," the tech said, barely glancing his way. "Nothing major."

Sochi stepped closer, then struck hard and fast, his elbow smashing into the man's temple. The tech collapsed without a sound.

"Hey!" Sochi called up. "Your partner's sick. You better come down."

The man in the lift—a tall, muscled guy covered in tattoos—grumbled and lowered the basket. "What the hell? He better not have eaten my lunch again," he muttered, stepping out and bending over the fallen tech.

Sochi looped a length of cable around his neck and yanked hard. The man thrashed violently, but Sochi held firm, twisting until the body went limp. When it was over, he dragged both bodies behind the truck.

Back at the SUV, he flung open the door. "Out. Now."

Jimmy's face went white at the sight. "Jesus, Sochi—you killed them!"

Sochi pulled his jacket aside, revealing the pistol under his arm. "Take off the shirts. Put on the hard hats. Now."

Edward took a shaky step back. "We didn't sign up for this."

"You signed up when you picked up the phone," Sochi snapped. He popped the rear hatch and tossed a black duffle bag onto the dirt. "There are your weapons. Load up while we drive."

Shaking, Jimmy and Edward stripped the dead techs' uniforms and suited up. Moments later, they were back on the road—the utility truck now leading, the black SUV trailing at a distance.

At the San Diego airport, they abandoned the SUV in long-term parking and piled into the truck. Sochi slammed the door. "Next stop, Point Loma."

The sun hung low as they wound through the quiet streets of Point Loma, closing in on Shangri-La—a modern Craftsman estate tucked within a walled compound that spanned nearly an entire block. A high stone wall surrounded the property, its clean lines broken only by an ornate wrought-iron gate—open now, as if inviting them in.

Sochi maneuvered the truck to a stop a few houses down, then climbed into the hydraulic bucket. "I'll be working the pole across the street," he said. "You two walk up, claim you're troubleshooting interference. Once you're inside—do it fast."

Jimmy and Edward gripped the heavy tool bags at their feet—each one packed tight with silenced pistols, duct tape, and industrial zip ties. No mistaking what they were walking into.

They stepped out onto the sidewalk. Jimmy hesitated, staring at the open gate ahead. It stood wide, like someone had forgotten to close it—or worse, left it open on purpose. Beyond it, the house sat quiet under the early afternoon sun. Cedar shingles, broad overhangs, stonework tucked into the landscaping—orderly, serene.

It looked calm. But Jimmy felt anything but. He glanced at Edward, who gave a shallow nod. No turning back.

They moved up the long, curved drive toward the front door. Jimmy rang the bell.

No sound from inside. Just the faint rustle of leaves and the distant hum of a passing car. Somewhere in the house, someone was talking on the phone—unaware that violence had already reached the gate.

The stained-glass front door swung open. Maggie Manning stood there—warm, welcoming, smiling. No idea what waited behind those "technicians'" polite expressions.

Jimmy hesitated. Just for a second. And that was all it took for everything to start unraveling.

CHAPTER 34: COUNTDOWN

Luke weaved down Harbor Drive past Lindbergh Field, heading back to Shangri-La, keeping an eye on confused tourists late for their flights. Despite the chaos, he felt pretty good. Vanessa's voice echoed in his head.

But something gnawed at him. The Foundation's money showing up so cleanly didn't sit right. Too neat. Too timed. His instincts—sharpened in places where loose ends got people killed—refused to let it go.

The buzz of his phone snapped him out of it.

"This is Payne."

"Luke, it's Helen Shepard at CyberWatch. Hate to cut into your Sunday, but this couldn't wait." Her voice carried an edge—urgent, clipped.

"Go ahead," he said, focus sharpening.

"A few minutes ago, we intercepted a message on one of the hacker forums. It's disguised as trash talk, but it might be a warning, a threat… or just cyber BS." She hesitated. "It said: 'Old roots run deep at the Foundation. Better prune before sunset, or there'll be nothing left to save.'"

Luke's hands contracted on the wheel. "Sounds like a veiled threat, Helen. You think it's about Maggie?"

"Could be. Maggie's the public face of the Foundation," Helen said. "If they blame her for the traced money, she's the likely target."

Luke exhaled sharply. "This isn't just a warning. It's a countdown."

"We're still tracing the IP hops, but it's masked well. Luke, you need to check on her. Now."

"I'm already on my way."

"Be careful. This one's different."

Luke hung up and immediately dialed Peter Nicolas. The phone rang. Once. Twice.

Each ring twisted in his gut, tighter than the last.

"This is Peter Nicolas."

"Pete, it's Luke. Listen carefully."

"What is it? You sound—"

"Just listen." Luke's voice cut through. "We intercepted a credible threat targeting Maggie. It's happening before sundown. That's four hours away. Has anything seemed off today?"

Peter hesitated. "Well... there was a cable guy on the pole outside the west wall earlier. Looked like a Spectrum truck."

"Now that you mention it... that struck me as odd. Spectrum doesn't usually service our area. But from a distance, it looked routine."

Cold dread hit Luke like a gut punch. "Peter," he said, voice low and tight, "Spectrum doesn't service Point Loma. That truck isn't real." "You and Maggie are in danger. That cable crew? They're not techs. They're cover for a hit team."

"Luke, what the hell—?"

"No time. Get Maggie. Lock yourselves in the wine cellar. Hit the panic alarm. I'm ten minutes out. Move. Now."

Luke heard Peter start to respond—then a muffled sound, like a door creaking open. Peter's voice, sharp and hoarse: "Oh God— Maggie's opening the front door—"

Then silence.

Peter's voice vanished mid-sentence.

Luke floored the gas, weaving through traffic, adrenaline surging. Stop signs blurred. Horns blared. He didn't care. All he could think was: Don't be too late.

CHAPTER 35: BAD DAY AT SHANGRI-LA

Luke's Fiat tore into the circular driveway of Shangri-La, tires whispering against the pavement. The estate basked in golden afternoon light—lawns crisp, palms swaying, everything too calm.

His gut clenched. Something was wrong. "No weapon," he muttered, scanning the glove compartment. Just a sleeve of pétanque balls. He grabbed two—heavy, smooth, brutal if used right.

The front door was cracked open, a throw rug bunched awkwardly at the threshold like someone had tripped. Luke flattened against the stone wall, peering in.

Inside, Peter and Maggie sat frozen on the living room couch, hands raised. Two men in white utility shirts and hard hats stood near the foyer, each holding a sleek black pistol. Luke's eye narrowed on the weapons—Chinese standard issue. One of the men shifted, and Luke spotted it—a twin-dragon tattoo coiled up his neck.

This wasn't random.

Luke weighed the pétanque balls in his hands. No time for doubt. He stepped inside and snapped the first ball low and hard. It hit the nearest man's forearm with a dull crack. The pistol clattered to the tile. "OWW!" the man shrieked, cradling his arm.

The second froze, wide-eyed. "Whoa, whoa! Don't hurt us!" he gasped, dropping to his knees. "We didn't want to do this! The guns—they're not even loaded! We were just supposed to scare them, leave a warning!"

Luke's voice was ice. "Face down. Now."

They obeyed, shaking.

Luke crouched, scooping up both pistols. He popped the magazines—empty. Just props.

He fixed a glare on the man with the tattoo, who groaned, "We're not here to kill anyone! It's the guy outside—he forced us into this!"

"Who's outside?"

"He's got an Uzi, man! He's serious. Said we go first or he shoots us."

Luke didn't wait. He grabbed Maggie and Peter, dragging them toward the kitchen.

"Wine cellar. Move!"

They stumbled down the narrow stairs. Luke slammed the door shut and rammed a heavy wine barrel in front of it. In the dark, he tore open two crates and shoved bottles into Peter's hands. "Peter—these are our weapons now. When he comes in, aim for the head. Fast, hard. No clean shots."

Peter nodded, adrenaline burning off the haze.

Above them, footsteps thundered across the porch. Then the pounding. One hit. Two. On the third strike, the door cracked—splinters flying as the barrel gave way.

Darkness swallowed the cellar. A black-clad figure surged through the breach, Uzi barking short bursts. Glass exploded. Wine sprayed. Smoke curled between the racks. Luke threw himself over Maggie and Peter as bottles shattered around them. Glass sliced his scalp. Blood leaked into his eyes.

He tracked the strobing muzzle flashes and hurled a bottle of Screaming Eagle. It struck the intruder's head with a dull thud, staggering him.

Peter grabbed a bottle from the other box, then shouted through the noise: "Not the Screaming Eagle—just throw this one.!"

Luke grabbed blindly. A Silver Oak Cabernet caught the light in his hand. He flung it fast—it smashed into the attacker's shoulder with a meaty crack.

Peter followed with another bottle. It burst against the doorframe, shards catching the attacker full in the face.

Sochi reeled back, bleeding. His head rang. Vision blurred.

Wine bottles. They were fighting him with wine bottles.

Outside, sirens wailed—closer.

Sochi cursed. No time.

He spun and sprinted up the stairs, boots crunching over glass. At the top, he turned and fired a final blind burst into the cellar.

A bullet skimmed Luke's temple. He dropped, blood pouring into his eye. The world tilted. Sound collapsed. Then—nothing.

Later

Police swarmed Shangri-La, sweeping the estate with weapons raised. Paramedics rushed to Maggie and Peter first—shaken, bleeding, but alive. A medic dropped beside Luke, working fast to bandage his head.

Luke blinked through the blur. "Are they...?"

"They're alive," the medic said. "You did good, sir. Stay with me."

Luke tried to nod, but the night folded around him. Sirens faded. Then silence.

CHAPTER 36: BROKEN AND WAITING

Naval Medical Center San Diego – Two Days Later

The sharp bite of antiseptic filled Luke Payne's nose as consciousness crept in. His skull throbbed. When he stirred, the IV yanked against his arm, halting him. Overhead lights flared in a sterile halo, forcing him to blink until the blur settled. Machines beeped—slow, steady, like a metronome.

He was alive. The doctor told him he's luck to be that way.

Memories flickered—gunfire. Maggie. Peter. The wine cellar. A voice shouting his name.

"Luke?"

That voice.

He turned his head. Vanessa McGowen sat beside his bed, curled into a cheap plastic chair. Her hair was arranged into a loose braid, eyes red-rimmed, fingers twitching against her jeans.

"You're awake," she whispered. "God, you scared the hell out of us."

He managed a smile. "Been a rough couple days?"

"You have no idea." She leaned forward and took his hand, gently. Her voice shook. "Peter's still in ICU. He's not breathing on his own. Maggie's stable, but... it was close. Too close."

Luke closed his eyes. The guilt surged. "Vanessa, I'm so—"

"Don't. Don't you dare." Her grip tensed. "You saved them."

She exhaled, voice fraying. Her hands wouldn't stop moving—folding and unfolding in her lap. "I've been running the Foundation. Board meetings. Crisis management. But my heart's been here. With them. With you." A tear slipped down her cheek.

Luke squeezed her hand. He held back more than words.

"They're fighters," he said. "And they're not alone."

She gave a soft, shaky laugh. "Guess the rumors were true. You really are stubborn."

"Takes one to know one."

They sat in silence, bound by breath and pain.

The door creaked open. A man in a dark suit stepped in, flanked by a uniformed officer. "Mr. Payne?" the man said. "I'm Special Agent George Gregson, FBI. If you're up for it, we have a few questions."

Vanessa stood, brushing a hand along Luke's arm. "I'll be just outside."

He watched her go. Then turned to face the next storm.

CHAPTER 37: COLD QUESTIONS

Gregson pulled up a chair and sat, the legs scraping tile. He took out a pocket-sized spiral notebook, a pen, and a manila folder already creased at the edges.

"Glad you're still breathing," he said. "Could've gone a lot worse."

Luke didn't look at him. "Feels like it did," he muttered, voice dry as dust.

Gregson gave a tight nod. "Mind if I ask a few questions while it's fresh?"

Luke shrugged, then winced as the motion tugged at his stitches. "Go ahead."

Gregson opened the folder and clicked his pen. "Start from the top. What happened at Shangri-La?"

"Two men," Luke said. "Dressed like cable techs. Chinese weapon. Suppression tactics, not an execution order."

"You're sure it's Chinese?"

"I've seen enough of them. I'm sure."

Gregson jotted something down. His handwriting was slow, deliberate. "And the third?"

"Uzi. Tactical entry. Blew the cellar door. He didn't hesitate. That one came to finish the job."

Outside the door, a cart wheeled past. The muffled beeping of a monitor chirped from the next room over. Luke's heart matched its rhythm, too fast, too loud.

Gregson slid a stack of photos from the folder and fanned them out on the tray. Black-and-white stills. Luke scanned them.

At first, nothing.

Then—there it was. The edge of a tattoo peeking from his collar. Twin dragons. Familiar. Intimate. A ghost from the worst chapter of his life.

Luke's pulse kicked. But he stayed stone.

You name it, you own it.

"Don't recognize them," he said, voice even.

Gregson's eyes didn't leave him. He tapped the corner of the photo once. Twice. Then stopped, as if catching himself.

"Right," he said finally, and snapped the folder shut.

Luke said nothing.

Gregson stood, the chair legs groaning beneath him. "Off the record? Whoever did this wanted it to scream Beijing. But I've seen cleaner work from real state actors. This felt... dressed up."

Luke frowned. "Meaning?"

Gregson hesitated just long enough to register.

"Meaning your enemies might not be the ones you think."

He started toward the door, then turned back.

"If anything else comes to you—anything at all—you know where to find me. Not that I expect a call."

A pause.

Then, more softly: "Just... be careful who you trust."

The door clicked shut behind him.

Luke stared at the ceiling. The antiseptic sting in the air, the thin light buzzing overhead, the dull weight of gauze across his ribs— all of it felt far away.

His heart thudded in his chest like a war drum.

Someone had sent a message. He'd heard it loud and clear.

War had come to his doorstep. And he was done playing defense.

CHAPTER 38: NO TIME TO HEAL

Naval Medical Center San Diego – Four Days Later

They told him to rest. To take it slow. To heal.

Four days. That's how long they'd kept him.

Luke peeled back the hospital blanket and swung his legs over the edge of the bed. Pain lit him up—some sharp, some buried deep—but he bit down and kept going. He tugged at the IV taped to his arm. Blood tracked the needle as he yanked it free. It hit the tile. He didn't notice.

Every step reminded him how close he'd come to never walking again. But someone was still coming after the people he cared about. And he wasn't waiting around for round two.

He had just gotten one leg into his jeans when the door creaked open.

"You trying to get yourself killed for real this time?"

Luke froze.

Vanessa stood in the doorway—eyes blazing, arms locked tight. Her hair was pulled into a quick, uneven knot. Her sweatshirt looked like it had been slept in. She wore exhaustion like a second skin, buried under defiance.

"You look like hell," she said.

"Thanks. Feel like it too."

She stepped inside and shut the door with a soft click. "Then maybe sit your ass back down before you rip something open you'll regret."

He gave a crooked grin but didn't move. "I have to go."

Vanessa's disbelief hit hard. "You're bleeding. You can't stand straight. What's the plan—hero mode on half a pint of blood?"

Luke met her eyes. "If I don't move, someone else gets hurt."

"They didn't finish the job," he added. "They'll come for the others."

She didn't back down. "Peter's in ICU. Maggie's barely stable. You think this helps them—collapsing in the street because your ego can't stay in bed?"

He looked away.

Vanessa stepped closer, the edge softening in her voice. "Then don't make it easier for them."

He paused. Long enough to see what was really there. The fear behind her fury. The fire beneath both.

She added, quieter now, "You don't have to carry it alone. Let me help."

Luke stood still.

He wanted to say yes. But wanting meant trusting. And trust had gotten people hurt.

He let out a long breath. "... Alright. But we move smart. Not desperate."

Vanessa exhaled too. "I'll take that."

He shrugged into his shirt with a wince. Vanessa grabbed his jacket, helped him ease into it, then held onto his hand a second longer.

"Thank you," he said.

"Get used to it," she replied. "You're going to need me."

They stepped into the corridor together—him barely standing, held together by grit and stitches. And she wasn't going to let him fall apart.

Outside, the world waited. They didn't look back.

CHAPTER 39: A DIGITAL LEAD

Back at the Shangri-La pool house, Luke sat at his desk. A mug of coffee cooled beside him, untouched. The search bar waited, blank and expectant.

He typed: double dragon tattoo gang. Enter.

Most hits were noise—conspiracy threads, dead police blogs, faded headlines about Chinatown turf wars. But one link caught his eye: a grainy photo buried in a 2012 article on San Francisco gang violence. There. Same narrow jawline. Same dragon tattoo curling from the collar.

Jimmy Wei.

Low-level Tong associate. Petty arrests. Suspected in bigger crimes. No convictions. Slippery.

Luke's pulse ticked upward.

He dropped the image into a reverse photo search. Another match appeared. This one didn't fit the profile. A glossy Orange County food magazine. A lifestyle feature on Dragon's Den, a trendy Balboa Island bistro known for bao buns and cult-favorite sourdough.

Luke opened it. The photo showed two men outside the restaurant. Jimmy Wei—clean-cut, smiling in a tailored suit. Next to him, flour-dusted and grinning, stood Edward Song, co-owner and executive chef.

Luke zoomed in on Jimmy's collar. The dragons were still there.

His gut hardened. This wasn't a coincidence. Whether Dragon's Den was a front or a safe house, he couldn't afford to assume anything.

He grabbed his jacket, slid his phone into his pocket. His mind was already mapping the next move. Balboa Island was ninety minutes away—less if he didn't stop.

Outside, the sun dipped behind Point Loma. A chill was in the air.

This time, he wasn't walking in blind. And he wasn't asking nicely.

CHAPTER 40: THE DRAGON'S DEN

The lunch crowd was gone. Inside, the dining room sat mostly empty, caught in that quiet lull before the dinner rush. Perfect for what Luke had in mind.

Jazz floated low through the air, mingling with the scent of ginger, garlic, and baked bao. A few diners lingered by the windows, murmuring over half-finished drinks. Behind the bar, Jimmy Wei polished glassware. From the kitchen, Edward Song emerged, drying his hands, eyes narrowing the moment he spotted Luke.

Jimmy noticed a second later. "Afternoon. Can I help you?"

Luke approached the bar, slow and measured, gaze locked. Shoulders relaxed. "We should talk. Privately."

Jimmy hesitated. His eyes darted to Edward, who stiffened but said nothing. Then Jimmy called over his shoulder, "Hey, Bob! Cover the front."

"Sure thing, boss!" came a voice from the kitchen.

Jimmy nodded toward the back. "Follow me."

He led Luke past the dining room into a private space at the rear. Oxblood-red lacquered walls, warm lighting, understated elegance. Edward followed and closed the door—hard.

Jimmy motioned to a chair, but Luke stayed standing. He didn't need height to take control—his silence did it for him. Jimmy sat, uneasy. Edward leaned against the wall, arms crossed.

Luke's voice came low and cold. "You were at Shangri-La. Start talking."

Jimmy flinched. His polished calm cracked. "We didn't want to be there," he said quickly. "We were forced."

"By who?"

Jimmy looked at Edward.

Edward sighed. "Sochi... Chandra Sochi. Family, kind of. Distant cousin.

Dangerous as hell. Said he came from someone high up in Shang-hai."

"Our uncle used to run with the Tongs," Jimmy added. "Sochi said he owed him. Dropped our names. Said it was time to pay up."

Luke didn't blink. "What was the job?"

Jimmy hesitated.

Edward stepped in. "We were told to hit a house in San Diego. No names. Just said we'd know it when we saw it. We pushed back —he opened his coat, showed us a gun. Said if we didn't help, we'd end up like others who crossed him."

Luke tensed. "He's the one with the Uzi. At Shangri-La."

Jimmy nodded. "Yeah. After you got the couple downstairs, he showed up—furious. Screaming that we'd screwed it up."

Edward's voice dropped. "Then he opened fire. Glass every-where. We thought we were dead."

Luke stared.

Edward looked away. "After that, he dragged us out. Drove us straight to the airport. No explanation. Told us to rent a car and dis-appear. Called us idiots. Said we blew the op."

Luke let the silence stretch. "You didn't even know their names, did you?"

Jimmy shook his head. "He just said, 'the old couple in the big house.' That's all we had."

Luke studied them both—tight, pale, still shaken. "And now?"

Jimmy exhaled. "We've been laying low. Waiting. For cops. Or for him."

Edward nodded. "He doesn't leave loose ends. We've been scared out of our minds."

Jimmy leaned in. "You're not turning us in, right?"

Luke didn't answer right away.

They'd stood in Maggie and Peter's home with guns. That was enough to bury them. But Luke saw the truth in their faces. They were cornered. Not killers. Just men used and thrown away.

He spoke quietly. "No. I believe you. You were set up. Disposable muscle. People like Sochi always let someone else take the fall. But it ends here."

Jimmy frowned. "What do you mean?"

"You disappear," Luke said. "Somewhere far. Stay quiet. I'll tell you when it's safe."

Jimmy hesitated. "How long?"

"As long as it takes. If Sochi contacts you, don't run. Call me."

Edward shifted. "And Sochi?"

Luke's voice dropped. "We'll take care of him."

Luke reached into his coat and pulled out a folded sheet and a short pencil stub. "Edward," he said. "Describe Sochi. I need to know exactly what he looks like."

Edward blinked. Then nodded. "Asian, like us. Sharp cheekbones. short, ferret-like. Weak chin, thin lips, beady eyes. Hair's thinning, but trimmed close. "

Luke began to draw—quick, clean strokes. His hand moved steadily, muscle memory overriding the throb at his temple. A face emerged.

Jimmy leaned over. "That's him. Dead on."

Edward's voice was tight. "Yeah. That's Sochi."

Luke folded the sketch and slipped it into his coat. "This helps. He won't be out there much longer."

He stood slowly, wincing as the stitches at his temple pulled. He wasn't close to healed. But waiting wasn't an option.

He turned for the door. Jimmy called out, "Hey, Mister?"

Luke stopped.

"Thanks," Jimmy mumbled.

Luke didn't smile. "Don't screw it up."

He sat in his Fiat reflecting on the meeting. Sochi wasn't merely a shadow with an Uzi anymore.

Now he had a face.

CHAPTER 41: THE CLEARINGHOUSE CONNECTION

Lance Benton hunched over his desk at DC3—the Department of Defense Cyber Crime Cente. He scrolled through the latest cyber incident reports from the Homeland Security Technology Clearinghouse, a knot tightening in his gut. Something felt fundamentally wrong.

Cyberattacks had spiked across Southern California, but the targets were baffling. Not the usual suspects—no major financial institutions or federal agencies. Instead, they were hitting municipal infrastructure, mid-sized businesses, even a private arts foundation. Too scattered for standard cybercrime. Too patterned to be coincidence.

It felt like a predator testing fences—looking for the weakest point.

One flagged alert flashed red on his screen: Breach Report: Shangri-La – San Diego

Benton frowned. He remembered the case. That wasn't just a breach. It had escalated—violently. Cybercrime didn't end in a shootout.

His phone buzzed. A new notification from the Clearinghouse cut through the silence.

Information Request: Cybersecurity Incident Trends in Southern California Requester: Jason Wells – CyberWatch Operations

Benton straightened, his chair creaking. CyberWatch.

The name wasn't splashed across headlines, but inside the intelligence community, Helen Shepard's outfit was known—unofficial, unregulated, and damn effective. They didn't just monitor threats. They neutralized them.

He opened the request. Jason Wells was tracking the same regional anomalies—and linking them to physical violence. That wasn't routine. That was urgent.

A voice from the doorway broke his focus. "Something interesting?"

Benton looked up. Harry Worthington stood there, coffee mug in hand. Grace Peterson followed, dropping a printed call log onto Benton's desk.

"Morning summaries," she said. "Also, Harry—your DHS briefing got bumped to 11:45."

"Thanks, Grace," Worthington replied with a nod, dismissing her with a glance.

He'd seen decades of cyber warfare, and his instincts—honed by a career as a bird colonel in Marine Intelligence, often embedded with CIA spooks—were rarely wrong.

"We've got a request from CyberWatch," Benton said, rotating the monitor. "Jason Wells flagged the same pattern we're tracking. Including Shangri-La."

Worthington's face darkened. His easy morning calm vanished, replaced by a hard edge. "That's not a coincidence."

"No," Benton agreed. "And if they're looking, they've got reason to believe it's bigger than it looks."

Worthington took a long sip, his eyes distant. "What's your gut say?"

"That we reach out," Benton said. "They work off the books, sure—but they know what they're doing. We stay close, we might learn more than we give away."

Worthington gave a short nod. "Do it. Let them know we're watching. And if this escalates, we're in—quietly."

Benton pulled up a secure line, dialing the number from Jason's request.

After a few rings: "Wells."

"Jason Wells, this is Lance Benton—DC3. You submitted an inquiry through the Clearinghouse about cyber intrusions in SoCal."

"That's right," Jason said.

"We're tracking the same thing," Benton said, skipping pleasantries. "And your request wasn't subtle. What do you know that we don't?"

Jason exhaled softly. "Enough to know this isn't random cybercrime. Someone's probing for weaknesses—systematically. It feels less like an attack and more like a logic bomb. Something set to go off on schedule. And they're moving fast."

Benton glanced at Worthington, eyebrows raised. "We're seeing it too. Mostly San Diego. But it doesn't match traditional state-sponsored playbooks. Too erratic. Too... careless."

Jason's voice sharpened. "You think they want us to think it's China?"

"Could be," Benton said. "Or they're using cutouts—contractors who don't care about being traced. Either way, the Point Loma incident wasn't some isolated event. Whoever's behind this has real backing."

There was a pause on Jason's end, punctuated by faint clicks of a keyboard.

"We may have one of the hackers," Jason said finally. "Shanghai-based. We're confirming his role, but the trail is still hot."

Worthington leaned in, his voice calm but direct. "Keep us looped in. If you need resources—off the record—we can assist."

Jason gave a dry chuckle. "That's how we operate anyway."

Benton's tone dropped, more warning than invitation. "This isn't cybercrime anymore. This is something else."

Jason ended the call without another word.

Then he turned, walking deeper into the CyberWatch war room. Helen needed to hear this—now.

CHAPTER 42: THE CALL FROM CYBERWATCH

Jason Wells stood on the balcony of his CyberWatch's La Jolla office, watching the morning light glance off the Pacific. Far below, kayakers cut across the calm waters of the cove. The breeze was crisp, but his thoughts stayed locked on the call with DC3.

Inside, Helen Shepard didn't look up as he entered. "Tell me."

Jason shut the door behind him. "DC3's officially watching. Lance Benton reached out directly."

Helen's eyes widened. "And?"

"They flagged Shangri-La as a pattern breaker. Too violent. Too sloppy. Doesn't track with China's usual fingerprint."

"False flag?" she asked, eyes narrowing.

"Possibly. Benton floated third-party contractors. Someone trying to pin it on Beijing—or hiding behind their signature."

Helen leaned back. "Sounds like they're as unsure as we are."

Jason nodded. "But they're sharing what they've got—quietly. Behavioral flags. Network sniffers. They'll keep hands off, unless something tips."

"And the funds?"

Jason gave a dry smile. "Still sitting where they were returned. That part spooked Benton more than the breach."

Helen nodded. "It was a signal. Someone's watching us watch them."

He dropped into the chair across from her. "DC3 isn't moving yet, but they're listening. That buys us time."

Helen glanced at her screen, then at him. "We both know it's not just a hack anymore."

Jason exhaled. "No. It's escalation."

Helen reached for her phone. "Luke needs to be briefed."

Jason met her gaze. "You think he's ready?"

"No," she said, dialing. "But he's already in it. Ready or not."

CHAPTER 43: MEETING OF MINDS

Luke's Fiat hugged the curve of I-5, the city's skyline rising ahead in the warm fade of daylight.

The meeting at Dragon's Den still rattled him. Jimmy Wei and Edward Song hadn't been lying—their fear was real. And the name they gave him? Chandra Sochi. Luke didn't know much, only that Sochi was the kind of man you called when you wanted someone gone. Permanently.

Someone had sent him to Shangri-La.

This wasn't about hacking or stolen money anymore. It was bigger. Deadlier.

His phone buzzed.

Helen Shepard.

He hit the hands-free. "Shepard."

"Luke, we need to talk."

His grip on the wheel tightened. "What's happening?"

"It's not just your problem anymore," she said. "It's mine too."

"Talk to me."

"Jason just got a call from DC3—Lance Benton. They've been watching a pattern of cyber intrusions across Southern California. Municipal systems, nonprofits, mid-sized businesses. At first, it looked random. But after Shangri-La? They're starting to connect the dots."

"What's DC3?" Luke asked.

"Department of Defense Cyber Crime Center," Helen replied. "They track hostile digital activity that crosses into real-world threat levels. Quiet, sharp, and very well-funded. If they're calling us, it means the problem's grown teeth."

Luke frowned. "So… hackers become hitmen?"

"Exactly. When digital attacks turn physical, DC3 starts paying attention. They're not acting yet—but they're circling."

Luke gave a tight nod. DC3 didn't posture. If they were sniffing around, this wasn't fringe anymore.

Helen's voice shifted. "Now tell me what you found."

He hesitated. She was already in deep. But saying it aloud made it more real.

"I met with Jimmy Wei and Edward Song. They're scared, Helen. And they gave me a name: Chandra Sochi."

A pause.

"Who?"

"Some kind of freelance enforcer. Jimmy says Sochi ran the attack—called the shots."

"And you believe him?"

Luke sighed. "Yeah. These guys have been clean for years. Running a legit business. They wouldn't blow it up now—not like this. And they don't have the stomach for murder."

Helen exhaled. "So someone sent Sochi."

"Exactly."

Silence stretched between them.

Then Helen said, "If Sochi's already gone to ground—or worse, slipped back to Shanghai—it means the people behind him are still active. This isn't over."

Luke nodded slowly. That's what he'd felt since the hospital. The antiseptic. The blood. The helplessness.

It hadn't ended there.

"Helen…" His voice dropped. "I'm not sure I'm the guy you need for this."

She didn't answer right away.

And somehow, the silence hit harder than anything she could've said.

"I was there," he said quietly. "I let it happen. I couldn't stop it."

"You didn't let it happen," she cut in. "They did. If you want to make sure it doesn't happen again—stop looking backward."

Luke squeezed the wheel hard. He wanted to believe that. But what if he got someone else hurt?

He wasn't sure what he had left to give—but Helen wasn't giving him much room to say no.

"Alright, Shepard. I'll hear you out."

"Good. Drive safe, Payne."

The call ended.

And Luke was alone again—with the road, the skyline, and the gnawing certainty that he was already in too deep.

CHAPTER 44: A PLAN TAKES SHAPE

Next Day – La Jolla, CyberWatch Headquarters

The room buzzed with quiet energy—laptops open, data streams scrolling across wall monitors, hushed conversations at the edges. Helen Shepard sat behind her desk, papers and a laptop spread in front of her. Jason Wells stood near a display, pointing to a satellite map of Shanghai.

Luke knocked and walked through the open door, still looking like he'd been in a street fight. "I'm back."

"Glad you could make it," Helen said, motioning to the seat opposite her. Her tone was brisk, but her eyes took a careful read of him. "You're looking better... kind of."

Helen glanced at Jason, who turned from the screen. "We've been tracking Sochi's network in Shanghai," he said, tapping the monitor to zoom in on a high-rise complex in Pudong. "Luxury residential, discreet. Fits his profile."

Luke leaned forward. "You think he's there?"

Helen nodded. "Shell companies are tied to that address. Wire transfers. Leasing agents. It's not conclusive, but it's the best lead we've got."

"And the plan?"

Helen steepled her fingers. "We use Coronado Seafood's logistics footprint. Your planes already fly into Shanghai. We go in as sales consultants—passports and paperwork are being finalized."

Jason added, "No drones—too risky. We've built recon kits disguised as consumer tech. Local assembly only. Optical modules, short-range encrypted comms. No long-range signals to tip them off."

Luke gave a tight nod, a beat too late. "Weapons?"

Helen's expression hardened. "We can't bring any in. I'll talk to DC3—if they've got someone on the ground, we might be able to access gear already in-country."

Jason raised a brow. "Hopefully someone who won't flip us to the Ministry of State Security."

Helen ignored him. "We'll vet anyone they give us. Meanwhile, your team needs to be tight. Surgical."

Jason leaned forward. "Four, maybe five max. We stay dark until we confirm Sochi's presence. We know the hacker's operating out of that building. Chances are he's there—or someone who knows who runs the op and who greenlit the hit on Peter and Maggie."

Luke nodded again, more automatically this time. "I'll pick the team. Eyes, hands, backup plans."

But his mind wasn't charging ahead like it used to. It lingered. In the gaps. In the silence after gunfire. In Maggie's scream. In Peter's blood. The pendant around his neck felt heavier than usual. A weight. A reminder of the night he almost gave up—and the reason he didn't.

Helen tapped a key, switching screens. "One more thing. The money trail runs deep. Funds tied to Sochi bounce through Hong Kong, Singapore, and Dubai. Whoever's backing this isn't just rich—they're protected."

Luke's fingers drummed the chair arm, the rhythm uneven. "We're not taking on a gang. We're taking on a machine."

Helen met his gaze. "Exactly. And if we fail, it doesn't just survive—it expands."

Jason folded his arms. "The Shangri-La hit was brutal, but sloppy. Not classic state work. If this is political, someone's winging it. If it's personal, they're escalating."

Luke considered that. "Sochi's the hinge. Take him alive, and we might finally see who's pulling the strings."

Helen's face darkened. "He's slippery, paranoid, and protected. If he senses pressure, he'll vanish."

Jason nodded. "Which is why recon comes first. Once we confirm he's there, we go in fast. One shot."

Luke didn't speak for a moment. Then: "Alright. I'll start assembling the team." But as he stood, something chilled him deep in the chest. He'd led men into storms before—but this felt different. He wasn't just afraid of the mission. He was afraid of himself. Afraid the next hesitation would cost someone their life.

Helen gave a tight nod. "I'll push DC3. If they've got someone there, I'll get a name."

Jason arched an eyebrow. "And hope they're not on someone else's payroll."

Helen stood. "We don't get hope, Jason. Just chances."

Luke didn't argue. But as he walked out, he admitted something he hadn't before—not even to himself. It wasn't just the danger that unnerved him.

It was the fear that next time, he might freeze.

And someone else would pay the price.

CHAPTER 45: FEAR OF COMMAND

Shangri-La, San Diego – The Day After

The cool metal of the balcony railing pressed against Luke Payne's forearms as he stared out over San Diego Bay. The city shimmered beyond the darkness, a scatter of lights against the night. The Coronado Bridge curved into the distance like a spine of steel and resolve.

The view hadn't changed.

But the rest of the world had.

Peter was still in a hospital bed. Unconscious. Motionless. Maggie, still recovering herself, had entrusted Vanessa to keep watch—and to let her know the moment anything changed.

He ran his thumb along the edge of his pendant. The bullet. Cold against his skin. Heavy in a way that had nothing to do with its weight.

Behind him, the balcony door slid open with a quiet whisper.

"I figured I'd find you out here," Vanessa said.

Luke didn't turn. "Couldn't sleep."

She came to stand beside him, not too close. Not pushing. Just there.

"The hospital called," she said softly. "No change."

Luke nodded once.

They stood in silence for a while. The breeze shifted. A cargo ship crept across the bay, its lights flickering like a trail of second thoughts.

"You thinking about leaving again?" she asked gently.

He didn't answer right away.

"I told myself I was done," he finally said. "Too much damage. Too many close calls."

Vanessa didn't respond. Just waited.

"I used to be sure," he continued. "About what was right. About the line between helping and harming. Lately… it all feels blurred."

He turned slightly, watching her face in the dim light. "Peter always had clarity. Even when I didn't agree with him."

Vanessa's voice was quiet. "So what would he tell you now?"

Luke looked down. "Probably call me a stubborn ass and tell me to stop feeling sorry for myself."

She smiled faintly. "Sounds like him."

Luke exhaled through his nose. "The truth is, I'm scared. Not of dying. Of leading someone into a fight they don't come back from."

Vanessa's eyes didn't waver. "You've led before."

"I was a rescue swimmer. I pulled people out. I didn't send them in."

"Maybe now it's about both."

He leaned on the railing again, shoulders tight. "You really think I'm the right one for this?"

"I think you're the only one who won't let it happen without a fight."

Luke didn't reply. The bay stretched before him, endless and dark. Somewhere in that horizon was the answer. Or maybe just the next step.

Vanessa touched his arm briefly. "When you're ready," she said. "We'll be here."

She slipped back inside.

Luke stayed, fingers still on the pendant.

He didn't make the decision easily. But in the end, he didn't have to make it alone.

Peter couldn't speak, but Luke knew what he'd say: Don't run from the hard thing.

And Vanessa—quietly steady, fiercely loyal—had reminded him, without pressure, who he still was beneath the grief.

So he said yes. Not because he was ready. But because it was time.

CHAPTER 46: TEAM BUILDING

Shangri-La, Point Loma – Afternoon

Sunlight dappled the area around the Shangri-La pool as palm trees swayed gently. Luke Payne sat on a lounger, his face and neck bearing an assortment of stitches and bandages. Though he held himself upright to address his friends, the dark rings under his eyes and the way he slumped slightly revealed his lingering exhaustion. Even with the fatigue, his eyes were sharp as he looked over the faces of his closest friends.

Cooper Marshall, ever the charismatic leader, stood by the pool's edge, tapping a spoon against his glass. "Alright, everyone," he announced, his grin as sly as ever, "time to call this meeting to order. The Coronado Seafood special board meeting is now in session. And yes, the bar is open, courtesy of Chef Carl—even if it's just lemonade for the boss."

The group chuckled, the light humor lowering the tension of recent events. Carl, the company's executive chef, stood nearby, holding a tray of snacks.

"No chowder this time," he quipped. "But give me a reason, and I'll bring the portable stove out here."

"Save it for the victory dinner," Luke said, his voice clear. He gestured toward the group. "Take a seat, everyone. Let's talk."

As friends settled in chairs around the pool, Hank Kobayashi adjusted the brim of his baseball cap, his sharp eyes scanning the horizon. "You look like hell, Chief, but I've seen you bounce back from worse," he said with a wry grin.

Luke exhaled. He hadn't been sure if he'd go through with this. Maybe he wasn't the man he used to be, but he wasn't going to sit on the sidelines either. Not while the people he cared about were still in the line of fire.

He'd sat alone, turning over every doubt, every failure. The pendant he always wore had felt like an anchor—reminding him of the night he nearly quit for good, and why he never would.

"Appreciate the vote of confidence," Luke replied. "I wasn't sure about this at first. But I am now. We've got work to do."

Jenny Lewis, perched on the corner of a chair, her aviators catching the sunlight, leaned forward. "Alright, Master Chief. You've got us. What's the plan?"

Luke's gaze swept over his friends, gratitude crossing his face. "Thanks, all of you. This isn't just about me. Shangri-La's under attack, and whoever's behind it won't stop unless we make them."

He briefed them on the hacker location and what they knew about Chandra Sochi. "We don't know for sure he's there," Luke said, "but it's our best lead."

The air grew heavier as his words sank in. Cooper broke the silence, his tone steady. "You know we're not just friends—we're a team. Tell us what's up, Luke. Let us help."

Luke nodded, the determination in his eyes unwavering. "It started with the hack on the foundation's accounts, but it's bigger than that. These people have the resources to send armed hitmen after me, Maggie, and Peter. This isn't just about money—it's about something else. Like it's personal."

Jenny frowned. "What's their endgame? Money? Power?"

"Both, maybe," Luke said. "But until we figure out who's pulling the strings, we're fighting blind. That's why I'm working with Helen Shepard. We're planning an infiltration of their hub in Shanghai. If we can shut it down and capture Sochi, we'll get the answers we need."

Moises Alvarez straightened, his expression resolute. "You're not doing this alone. Coronado's got resources—planes, contacts, whatever you need. Coop said anything you need. And I'm coming with you."

Luke hesitated, then nodded. "Alright. I'll need you in the field, Moises. You know how to move quietly, and you're solid under fire."

Jenny interjected, her tone light but her expression serious. "And I'm thinking aerial recon. Small drones, quick drop options. I'll loop in with Moises on the logistics."

"Done," Moises said, tipping an imaginary hat toward her.

Hank leaned forward, his voice serious. "What about arms and tech? Shanghai's not a forgiving place if you get caught."

Luke nodded. "Coronado's cover as a seafood company gives us a legitimate way in. Once we're there, we'll rely on local contacts Helen's team is working on. Jason Edwards is managing comms and drone surveillance from the States."

Hank crossed his arms. "You're gonna need more than resolve out there. Are we talking comms gear, smuggled sidearms, or what?"

"We adapt," Luke said firmly. "And we stay invisible as long as possible."

Jenny cocked her head. "Does this thing have a name?"

Luke gave a small nod. "Yeah. Helen's calling it Operation Silent Dagger."

Jenny smiled. "A little dramatic, but, fitting."

"It better be," Luke said. "If we do this right, no one sees it coming."

Jenny's expression darkened. "And the bigger picture? Are you sure this is just the Tongs? This feels… off."

Luke nodded grimly. "It's been on my mind too. The hit on Maggie doesn't align with typical Tong methods. Whoever's behind this, Sochi is the key to finding out."

The table went quiet. Each of them knew what it meant to go

dark in a foreign city with no backup.

Cooper raised his glass of lemonade, his voice firm. "Then here's to success. To finding the truth and shutting them down for good."

The group raised their glasses in unison, a silent promise binding them together.

As the glasses clinked, Luke felt the familiar warmth of camaraderie and resolve. This wasn't just his fight anymore—it was theirs. And they would see it through together.

CHAPTER 47: SILENT PARTNERS

Lance Benton stepped into the dimly lit office. Behind the massive oak desk, Harry Worthington didn't look up. "What've you got for me?"

Benton dropped the folder on the desk and opened it. "Cyber-Watch is moving. Shepard's team is prepping for Shanghai. They're targeting what they believe is the central hub—money, weapons, people."

Worthington leaned back, fingers tapping slowly. "Chandra Sochi?"

"Primary target. If they get him, we might finally get a clear line to whoever's running this show."

Worthington nodded just once. "Green light. Quietly. No fingerprints."

Benton frowned. "You want Sochi taken out?"

Worthington didn't flinch. "Keep surveillance on him. And if CyberWatch slips—someone else finishes the job."

Worthington leaned forward, voice lowering. "I'll activate a back channel through Gus at Langley. If he's got someone in Shanghai, I want them warming up."

"I'll make the call."

Worthington tapped his fingers on the desk. "And keep your ears open. The walls aren't clean."

Benton's face hardened. "You think someone's leaking?"

"I know it," Worthington said. "Since POTUS gutted our funding, they watch everything we do. If they don't like what we're doing, they won't just pull the plug—they'll pretend we never existed."

Benton hesitated, a trace of unease in his eyes. "You think they planted someone?"

Worthington didn't blink. "I think he reads our reports before I do. So move quiet, move smart. And if you smell anything, I want to know first."

He tapped the folder. "If CyberWatch pulls this off, I want names—no more ghosts."

"You'll have them," Benton said, closing the file.

As he reached the door, Worthington's voice followed. "And tell Gus—no second chances."

Benton stepped out into the corridor, the chill of the hallway seeping under his collar. The storm wasn't coming. It was already inside the house.

CHAPTER 48: LOOSE ENDS

The pale light of dawn seeped through the curtains of Luke Payne's pool house at Shangri-La. His body still ached with a dull throb, a lingering reminder of the chaos that had nearly claimed his life. Yet, as his eyes opened to the stillness of the room, rare clarity—a sense of purpose that had been missing for too long.

Pushing himself upright, Luke winced as the pain from his stitched wounds flared. The doctors had been thorough, but recovery was slow. The scars, physical and otherwise, served as constant reminders of how narrowly he'd avoided the edge.

A soft knock interrupted his thoughts. "Come in," he called, his voice rough but steady.

The door opened, revealing Vanessa McGowen with a tray in her hands. The smell of fresh coffee and toast wafted into the room. She gave him a small, tired smile.

"Thought you could use a proper breakfast."

Luke nodded, motioning for her to set the tray down on the table beside him. "Thanks. You didn't have to."

Vanessa shrugged, and sat on the chair beside his bed. "After everything that's happened, feeding you seems like the least I can do."

He studied her face, noting the faint lines of exhaustion beneath her eyes, and the smudge of mascara at the corner of one eye she hadn't had time to fix. "You've been running yourself ragged."

She sighed, brushing her hair back. "Running the Foundation from my phone, taking care of Maggie, trying to hold everything together... It's been a lot. But we're managing."

"Maggie?" Luke asked, his voice softening.

Vanessa's expression grew somber. "She's stable. Her leg is in pretty bad shape, they're not sure she can walk again, and her eyesight..." She hesitated. "No guarantees. She's trying to stay strong. You know how Maggie is."

Luke nodded, the tightness in his chest returning. "And Peter?"

Vanessa's lips pressed into a thin line. "Still critical. The doctors are doing everything they can, but..." Her voice broke, and she blinked quickly, fighting for composure.

Luke reached out, covering her hand with his. "He's tough. He'll pull through."

She smiled weakly, blinking back tears. "I hope you're right."

They sat in silence briefly before Vanessa said, with a faint note of optimism, "I thought you'd want to know—I rehired Carol Chan."

Luke tilted his head. "Carol? She left when her husband got transferred, right?"

Vanessa nodded. "Yeah. But he's got two months left on his WestPac duty, and when I reached out, she jumped at the chance. She knows the Foundation better than anyone except Maggie. We're covering her travel and accommodations to be here."

Luke smiled. "Good call. Maggie always said Carol could run the place blindfolded."

"She's already hit the ground running," Vanessa said. "Honestly, I couldn't do this without her."

Luke studied her genuine gratitude flickering in his eyes. "You're doing more than anyone could ask, Vanessa. Maggie and Peter are lucky to have you."

Vanessa's throat worked silently before she spoke. "You're lucky too, Luke."

She looked away, then back again—her voice catching just slightly. "The EMTs said another few minutes..." She shook her head. "You gave us a terrible fright."

He tried to grin, but it was faint and fleeting. "I'll try not to make a habit of it."

Later that morning, cane in hand, Luke made his way slowly to Maggie's room. He found her propped up in bed with her cell phone, listening to an Arts Foundation podcast, her face pale but unbowed. She turned her head slightly at the sound of his steps, her sharp ears compensating for her weakened sight.

"Luke," she said, closing the book with a smile. "You shouldn't be out of bed."

He chuckled softly, easing himself into the chair beside her. "Neither should you. But here we are."

Maggie grinned. "They've patched me up better than a B-17," she muttered. "But I wouldn't trust me on a flight of stairs yet."

Luke smiled. "How are you holding up?"

"I'm breathing," she replied. "Which is more than some expected. But I've been thinking about the Foundation. If Peter doesn't wake up..."

Luke reached out and squeezed her hand. "He will. But just in case, Vanessa's stepped up. And she rehired Carol Chan. Between the two of them, things will hold."

Maggie exhaled slowly. "You've been thinking ahead."

"I've also been thinking about your leg," Luke said. "I know the doctors here are good, but Moises has connections—some of the best orthopedic specialists, guys who've been fixing wounded warriors since Vietnam."

"Luke, what are you getting at?"

"I'm going to have Moises reach out to his contacts in the Navy," Luke said. "Let them look at your case. If anyone can help you heal better than expected, it's them."

Maggie's eyes glistened. She swallowed hard. "Luke, you don't have to do that."

"Yes, I do," he said simply. "You've done everything for the people around you. It's time someone looked out for you."

She reached out and squeezed his hand tightly. "Thank you, Luke."

"Just say you'll let them try," he said. "That's all I need."

"Alright. I'll do it."

Luke leaned back in the chair, letting out a breath he hadn't realized he was holding. Small steps, but steps forward. The fight to put things back together had begun.

CHAPTER 49: AWAKENING

The late afternoon sky stretched pale and cloudless over the deck at Shangri-La. A soft breeze stirred the palms, carrying the scent of sea and jasmine. Maggie sat comfortably in a cushioned chair, her face tilted toward the warmth of the sun. Her hair, silvered with age, shimmered faintly as she traced the rim of her teacup. Vanessa, seated beside her, couldn't help but admire the peacefulness of the moment—a fleeting calm amid the storm they'd survived.

"You know," Maggie began, her voice soft but steady, "I think I'm starting to see something. It's not clear, just blurred movement and colors, but it's more than before."

Vanessa turned toward her, eyes wide. "Maggie, that's incredible! Have you told the doctor?"

Maggie shook her head slightly, a gentle smile playing on her lips. "Not yet. I wanted to enjoy it first, just for myself. The world has been so dark for so long... even the hint of light feels like a blessing."

For a short while, they sat in silence, the quiet interrupted only by a plane going overhead. Finally, Vanessa spoke.

"Carol Chan has been amazing. She's jumped right into her role at the Foundation, and honestly, it's like she's breathed new life into the place. Everyone feels steadier, more hopeful."

Maggie's smile deepened. "I knew she was perfect. It's beyond skill; Carol has always had that."

Vanessa nodded. "She's made it clear she's not just filling in for you. She's honoring everything you built."

Before Maggie could respond, a phone vibrated. Vanessa grabbed it, heart quickening when she saw the caller ID. "It's the hospital," she said, answering immediately. "Hello?"

A calm but urgent voice came through the line. "Ms. McGowen? This is Dr. Patel. I'm calling to inform you that Peter has come out of his coma. He's stable and responsive. We'll need your help with his memory and rehabilitation."

Vanessa gasped, breath catching in her throat. "That's... that's incredible. Thank you, Doctor. I'll be there right away."

As she hung up, her eyes met Maggie's. The older woman was already leaning forward, hope etched in every line of her face.

"He's awake?" Maggie whispered, voice trembling.

Vanessa nodded, tears brimming. "He's awake. The doctor said they'll need me to help jog his memory."

Maggie covered her mouth, her tears spilling over. "Oh, thank God. Oh, thank God."

She pressed her palms together, steeling herself. "I'm coming too."

Vanessa hesitated. "Are you sure? It could be overwhelming."

Maggie's eyes flared with determination. "I've waited too long for this moment. I need to see him."

Vanessa stepped over and helped Maggie gently to her feet. The older woman rose slowly, one hand bracing against the chair, the other gripping Vanessa's arm. She wavered for only a breath, then straightened with resolve.

As they left the deck, Vanessa stopped at the threshold. She glanced toward the corner of the room where Luke's jacket hung. The silver chain that always rested around his neck peeked out— quiet and familiar. A reminder, not just of what they'd been through, but of what still lay ahead.

Together, they stepped into a future that—just hours ago—had seemed almost lost.

CHAPTER 50: CHANGE OF COMMAND

Shanghai — 2 Days Before the Wheels Up

Lee didn't notice the time. He'd been digging through data for hours, each line heavier than the last, when a sharp knock at the door broke the silence and froze him in place.

His heart kicked hard. He rose slowly, crossed the room, and checked the peephole.

The Colonel. And someone else—a tall man in a tailored suit.

Lee cursed under his breath. He thought they were finished. That the plan had run its course. He'd done everything asked—bent every rule, ignored every instinct. Now he knew he'd miscalculated.

With a hand that barely held steady, he unlatched the chain and opened the door.

"Mr. Lee," the Colonel said, unusually cheerful. The forced smile only deepened Lee's unease. "Apologies for the unannounced visit, but circumstances have changed. I've been reassigned. I'm here to introduce your new handler."

He stepped aside.

"This is Captain Kang."

Kang gave a curt nod, posture stiff with military precision. He produced a black wallet and flicked it open—an official-looking military ID flashed briefly before disappearing back into his coat. From beneath the edge of his white cuff, a cobra-head tattoo curled into view—barely visible, but unmistakable.

"A pleasure, Mr. Lee," Kang said. His voice was flat, deliberate. "We'll see this mission through. Together."

Lee returned the nod with a slight bow. The suit was expensive, but the man inside it radiated quiet violence. Kang's eyes didn't wander. They locked and held, like a predator gauging when to strike.

The Colonel continued, tone smooth, almost rehearsed. "Captain Kang will oversee the debriefing of your team and arrange final payment. The bonus will be… generous. Your team has executed its duties with precision, and the Bureau is grateful. However, recent irregularities require a full and uncompromised audit."

Lee swallowed. "Yes, of course."

The Colonel's smile thinned to nothing.

"The debriefing will be comprehensive. In three days. All team members are to remain in their apartments that day. Every piece of Bureau-issued equipment must be present and accounted for. We will inspect each workstation and erase all sensitive materials. Captain Kang—or one of his lieutenants—will explain the consequences of… breaching confidentiality."

Lee nodded quickly. "Understood."

"You'll be the last to be debriefed," the Colonel added, stepping slightly into the apartment. "Here. In this room."

His tone sharpened. "Do you understand, Mr. Lee?"

"Yes, sir," Lee said, forcing a mask of resolve. "Everything will be ready."

The Colonel studied him for a long beat, then nodded. "Good. The Bureau thanks you for your service. Goodbye, Mr. Lee."

They turned and disappeared down the hallway.

Lee closed the door behind them and leaned against it, knees weak. Relief flickered for a moment—then vanished. The danger hadn't passed. It had only changed uniforms.

CHAPTER 51: SHANGHAI INTERCEPTS

Beijing — 0400, Day Before wheels up

General Yang Yue's office was silent but for the faint buzz of overhead lights. She leaned forward at her desk, scanning a fresh stack of intelligence reports. Despite reassurances from one of Lee's most trusted men, her instincts refused to settle. Something in Lee's tone during their last call had raised flags she couldn't ignore.

The secure phone buzzed. "Major Liu reporting, General," came the clipped voice of her top surveillance officer.

"Proceed," Yue said, already bracing for confirmation.

"We've flagged two men in dark suits entering Lee's apartment about twenty minutes ago. Appear to be businessmen. Connection to Lee is still speculative."

"Current surveillance?"

"Passive. Secondary unit is tracking from an adjacent building. Subjects remain inside."

"Maintain distance," Yue ordered. "I want full background packets—military, civilian, financial. If official channels come up dry, scrape the public streams. Social feeds, security leaks, traffic cams. Use AI-assisted OSINT to build complete behavioral profiles."

"Yes, General." A beat. "We've also intercepted fragments of encrypted outbound traffic. Pattern suggests tactical burst transmission. Short. Scrambled."

"Prioritize decryption," Yue said coldly. "If Lee's transmitting, I want origin, destination, and content. Keep surveillance on his apartment. If anything changes—anything—I want to be the first to know."

"Understood."

The line went dead. Yue crossed to the window. The courtyard below was still and gray, offering no clarity. Her thoughts remained fixed on that Bund apartment—and on Lee.

She remembered the moment clearly. Decades ago, in the chaos of Guangdong, he'd pulled her from a collapsed building—bleeding, half-starved, and ready to give up. That single act had shaped her life. She owed him everything.

But now... Lee was hiding something. Whether out of pride, guilt, or some misplaced loyalty—she couldn't yet tell. But she would soon find out.

CHAPTER 52: SIGNALS IN THE DARK

CyberWatch Command Center, La Jolla — Night Before Wheels Up

The buzz of Helen Shepard's phone pierced the low hum of the CyberWatch command center. She answered instantly—Lance Benton. DC3. He didn't call unless it mattered.

"Helen," he said, skipping formalities. "We've zeroed in on a command node—top-floor apartment on the Bund. Heavy outbound traffic. Private terrace. Civilian on paper, but the behavior doesn't match. We traced the breach signature through local ISP leasing and access point logs. It leads there."

Helen's fingers flew across the keyboard, pulling up a satellite feed. A single dot blinked to life over Shanghai's glittering skyline. "How solid?"

"Very. Signature's an exact match. But no PLA routing. No military encryption. Feels rogue."

Helen's eyes narrowed. "Sochi?"

"Possibly. Or one of his people. Whoever it is—they're good. And here's the kicker: we're not the only ones watching. Somebody else is sniffing around. If you're going to move, you move now."

The line went dead.

Helen turned back to the room. "We've got an active signal on the Bund—top-floor apartment. No visible military, no confirmed armed threat, but the traffic's off the charts. Whoever's inside is reaching out. This doesn't match the known pattern. Someone's freelancing—and it could get messy fast."

"If they're reaching out, they could be a defector," she said, "or bait." She looked to Jason. "Either way, we need eyes on it."

Jason frowned. "What's your play?"

She tapped her tablet, pulling up the building schematics. "Flag it for recon as soon as we land. Luke needs this the second we hit the ground."

Jason nodded. "I'll map remote access. Scrub anything we can reach before you're in-country."

Helen kept her eyes on the blinking node. "If someone in that apartment is trying to make contact, we need to be there before someone shuts them down."

She turned to go. "Keep watch. If that signal goes dark, we waited too long. I'm heading to brief Luke and the team. Ping me the moment it shifts."

Jason's fingers flew back to the keys. "That confirms our earlier probe. We caught the spike—just didn't have the floor. Now we've got something actionable."

The blinking node pulsed once. Then held steady—waiting.

CHAPTER 53: REHEARSAL IN PROGRESS

Point Loma – Evening Before Wheels Up

Two weeks later, the Peninsula Arts Foundation meeting room was sealed tight. A handwritten sign on the door—REHEARSAL IN PROGRESS—kept wandering staff at bay.

Inside, shadows slanted across rows of empty chairs. Still. Watchful.

At the front, a satellite image of Shanghai shimmered on a mounted screen. Steel blue. Alive with heat signatures and high-rises.

Luke Payne, now stitch- and bandage-free, stood at the center, hands braced on the table. His posture was loose. His eyes weren't. They scanned, mapped—locked in.

In front of him sat Helen, Hank, Jenny, and Moises. Not just colleagues. His circle.

"This isn't Helmand," Luke said. "But it's just as lethal. Shanghai's one giant surveillance net—cameras, drones, facial rec. State. Corporate. Criminal. You blink wrong, you're flagged."

No one spoke. The warning landed.

"No tactical kit. No visible hardware. We move civilian. Blend. Disappear."

He stepped to the side and flipped open a hard case.

"Dart guns," he said, holding one up—compact black polymer, no larger than a phone. "Low-profile. Near-silent. Six-meter effective range. Aim for shoulder or thigh."

He passed one to Hank, who turned it over slowly in his hand.

"The payload's a fast-acting neuro-sedative," Luke continued. "Takes effect in six to eight seconds. Full drop in under thirty. One shot. Then reload."

Jenny raised an eyebrow. "Any side effects?"

"Disorientation. Nausea. No long-term damage—unless they've got a weak heart or fall off a high floor."

Moises grunted. "Rules of engagement?"

Luke's tone hardened. "Non-lethal unless our lives are at risk. If someone draws, that changes. But if we can't bring Sochi in alive, we lose more than we gain."

They nodded. Grim, but agreed.

Luke tapped the screen. The image zoomed to a gray stone building beside a waterfront park.

"Target's here—top floor penthouse. Helen's team cross-checked tenants. Only residential unit in the building. The lower floors are retail and storage—no random neighbors to trip alarms."

He zoomed again. "Four-story Greystone on East Zhongshan Road. On The Bund. Right on the Huangpu River. Immediately next to Huangpu Park. Water access is ideal for extraction—but it's a historic district, always busy. Tourists thin out between four and six, just before dinner. That's our window. We breach then."

Helen added, "DC3 spoofed the local grid. Facial scramblers are injecting synthetic IDs. No known security on-site, but internal cameras and motion sensors are active. We'll jam them. You've got ninety minutes if the tech holds."

"I'll be in the lead van," she continued. "Running comms and drone intel. Eyes on the Huangpu River, Lujiazui across the water, and anything moving through the park."

Jenny didn't look up at first. Then she lifted her gaze—focused, cold.

"Shanghai's AI grid flags anomalies—wrong gait, wrong face, wrong posture. But we injected a feedback loop. You'll read as background noise. For thirty minutes after breach… you're invisible."

Luke scanned the room, making eye contact with each of them.

"We get thirty minutes. Make them count. Five to breach. Twenty to locate and extract. Sochi, if he's there. Hackers, if he's not. Either way, we pull intel. Then head to the dock. DC3's got a container ship standing by—Singapore bound."

Hank leaned forward. "Fallback?"

Luke pointed to a marker on the map. "If the dock's blown, we divert to the South Bund Ferry Terminal. If it all goes sideways—we split. Hank runs interference. Jenny scrubs the feeds. Helen coordinates pickup. Moises handles Van Two—exfil or distraction."

Moises gave a half-smile. "Clean and quiet, right?"

Luke offered a dry grin. "Cleaner than Kandahar."

Helen stepped in again. "The hacker's not the enemy. He gave the money back. Closed the door behind him. Left a trail. He wants to be found."

Luke's voice dropped. "This isn't revenge. Or justice. It's cleanup. We neutralize Sochi. Secure the source. And we get out without lighting up the city."

Hank gave a grim smile. "Let's make it count."

CHAPTER 54: GHOSTS IN THE DUST

Point Loma-Night Before Wheels Up

The night was calm, city lights shimmering below like distant constellations. On the patio, Maggie, Peter, Vanessa, and Luke sat in quiet companionship. It had been six weeks since the attack—long enough to heal wounds, but not forget them.

Luke leaned against the stone railing, outlined by the bay's glow. Across the water, helicopters lifted from Naval Air Station North Island, the low thrum pulling his gaze skyward. Red navigation lights blinked like warnings.

Vanessa noticed the look in his eyes. "You all right?"

Peter and Maggie exchanged glances. They recognized the silence—the way Luke folded into himself when memories surged.

"Time to hit the sack," Luke said. "Big day tomorrow. Long flight ahead."

Maggie rose and hugged him. "You take care of yourself. We'll be here when you get back."

Peter shook his hand. "You've got this. You've been through worse."

Vanessa stepped forward, watched his. "Be careful out there. Promise me you'll come back."

Luke didn't speak. He just gave a faint nod—enough.

He turned, paused once at the steps to the pool house, then disappeared into the shadows. The silence returned, broken only by ocean wind and swaying palms.

Peter watched the pool house, then glanced at Vanessa. She was still staring after Luke.

"He'll be all right," Peter said. "But there's more to him than most see."

Vanessa turned. "I want to understand."

Peter nodded slowly. "Nine years ago—Afghanistan. Bad mission. He shouldn't have been there, he was ready to ship out. But they needed someone qualified who could handle chaos. Luke went in on a Chinook. Landing zone was hot. RPG hit the tail rotor."

Vanessa's breath caught.

Peter's voice lowered. "He woke up in wreckage. Rivera, his teammate, was pinned—dying. Luke tried, but he couldn't save him. Rivera made him promise to get the others out.

So he did. Carried Moises—the pilot—through enemy territory. Hid in a cave. Flares. Rescue came. Luke got the Navy Cross. Purple Heart. But it left a scar no medal could cover."

Vanessa blinked back tears.

"He doesn't talk about it. Doesn't need to. That's the part of Luke you're seeing now. The man who keeps going because someone once asked him to."

Maggie reached for Vanessa's hand. "Be patient with him. He's more than just carrying out a mission. He's carrying ghosts, too."

Peter slumped into his seat. "He'll do what needs doing. He always has."

No one spoke after that. The night settled in around them—quiet, heavy, unfinished. Across the water, the helicopters were gone. But the echo remained.

CHAPTER 55: DANCING ON GLASS

Department of Defense Cyber Crime Center (DC3), Linthicum Heights, Maryland – Night Before Wheels Up

Lance Benton stepped into Harry Worthington's office just after dusk, a folder tucked under his arm. The lights were low, the air close. Just silence—and the sense that lines had already been crossed.

Worthington didn't look up. His eyes were fixed on the glowing thermal overlays cycling across his monitor—each hotspot pulsing like a warning.

"Satellite feed's coming online," he said. "Full sweep over central Shanghai within the hour."

Benton laid the folder on his desk. "Updated grid of the Pudong complex. Jason tapped a slice of the municipal surveillance net—traffic cams, building feeds, posture analytics. No clean hit on Sochi yet, but there's movement. And we've got anomalies near the Bund."

Worthington stroked his chin. "Same signature we tracked from San Diego?"

"Nearly identical. Packet behavior, masking techniques—it's high grade. Source is a top-floor apartment. Private terrace. Civilian on paper, but everything below that floor's dead space. Helen thinks it's their node."

"Sochi?"

"Could be. Or one of his people. No PLA signals. No formal routing. Feels freelance." Benton hesitated. "CyberWatch is already on it. Shepard's briefing Payne now."

Worthington leaned back, rubbing his neck—more fatigue than

thought. "If they pull him out, maybe we get answers. If they don't…"

"We're blind," Benton said. "And whatever's behind this stays buried."

A knock. Grace Peterson entered with a folder. "Updated satellite window. DHS briefing moved to 0430." She placed the file on his desk and slipped out without another word.

Worthington slid the file across to Benton. "Prep the uplink. Tight channel only."

Benton glanced up. "You still trust Shepard's team?"

"I trust them to do what we can't." A pause. "Stay off the radar. Make noise only when it matters."

"Any pattern yet?"

"Not enough to call. A few anomalies in and out of that penthouse. Synthetic IDs. Digital masking. It's where I'd be."

Worthington finally turned from the screen, his voice low. "You feel it too, don't you?"

"Sir?"

"That itch. Like someone's shadowing us. Someone inside."

"You think we're compromised?"

"I think we've been dancing on glass since the President gutted half our budget." Worthington drew a sharp, controlled breath. "If Ward thinks this op undermines his narrative, he'll bury us before morning."

"What do you need from me?"

"Eyes open. Quiet conversations. If someone at DC3 is feeding the West Wing, I want a name."

Benton nodded. "I'll keep it low. Deep trail."

Worthington tapped the glowing map again. "Payne's wheels up at 2230. CyberWatch is handling insertion, surveillance, comms—full net. Our contact in Shanghai has prepped the drop cache."

Benton nodded. "Tranquilizers, comms, facial scramblers?"

"Everything they'll need. Jenny's gear's coming in through diplomatic pouch. Helen gets a scrambled satellite link. They'll blend."

"Non-lethal rules?"

"Unless it goes loud. Then fallback protocol—hard extraction."

Benton leaned in. "And if they find Sochi?"

"Then Operation Silent Dagger gets teeth. They neutralize and extract. He's packed in a disguised med container, loaded at night through South Bund Terminal, rerouted on a flagged freighter bound for Singapore. No customs. No alerts."

"And if it burns?"

"Then we burn the site and pray we didn't start a war."

Benton lowered his voice. "You still want to keep it dark?"

"If we go public, it dies. If it leaks, it dies. If Ward smells smoke, he'll bring fire." Worthington's eyes hardened. "This stays sealed until it's done. Operation Silent Dagger doesn't exist unless it succeeds."

"If Sochi flips, we frame it as rogue intel. Blame the black market. Local gangs. Keep the Foundation out of it."

"Maybe that keeps them from getting hit again," Benton said.

"Or puts a bigger target on their back."

Worthington tapped the folder once more, then looked up. "Good work. Stay off-grid until they land. And Lance—"

"If I even sniff a leak, I contain it. Whatever it takes."

Benton gave a single nod and left. The door whispered shut behind him.

Worthington remained still, eyes on the map. In the digital dust, someone was watching.

CHAPTER 56: SIGNALS OF BETRAYAL

CyberWatch HQ – 1300 PST, Day of Operation

Back in his office, Lance Benton didn't waste time. He dialed. "Edwards."

"Jason, it's Benton. I need you in Maryland. Tonight."

Jason's voice stayed flat. "What's going on?"

"Your Shanghai lead just lit up. The penthouse in Pudong. I want your eyes on it. Could be Sochi. If not, someone just as critical. Heavy data movement. Same packet structure. It's not random."

Jason exhaled. "You want me running digital."

"Exactly. DC3's covering satellite and thermal. But I need someone in the chair who can read the flow in real time. You know how they move."

"I'm not field."

"That's why you're perfect. You won't improvise. You'll analyze."

A pause, then: "I'll need full access—satellite streams, intercept logs, everything."

"You'll have a direct pipe. Front seat in the control room."

Jason nodded to himself. "Fine. I'll grab the next flight out—"

"No flights," Benton cut in. "Head to Miramar. The Marines are wheels up in ninety."

Jason let out a dry laugh. "Classy ride."

"Best we've got," Benton said. "Get moving."

Jason grabbed his go-bag and walked out. Field or not, this was as close as it got.

DC3 Operations Room – 2000 EST, Day of Operation

The DC3 operations center hummed with low urgency. Screens blinked with satellite sweeps, signal intercepts, and Shanghai's skyline bathed in infrared.

Harry Worthington stood in the heart of everything, arms crossed, watching the feed from Pudong.

Benton entered, tablet in hand. "Sir, Jason Edwards is en route. Should be here within about four hours."

Worthington gave a brief nod. "Good. We'll need him."

The main screen zoomed on the target building. The windows glowed faintly. No motion. No heat signatures. Too quiet.

"Something on your mind?" Worthington asked without turning.

Benton hesitated. "Sir... I think we've got a breach. Internal. Every time we move, someone gets there first. Feels like Ward's fingerprints."

Worthington's face darkened. "You think he's got a source inside DC3?"

"I don't know yet. But it's too clean. And it matches his style—quiet pressure, long game, total deniability."

Worthington turned slowly. "Ward's idea of oversight is starving the agencies he doesn't control. POTUS gave him the axe and the budget. Now we're running lean, and blind."

Benton nodded. "That's why I'm raising it now. If we lose this one, we may not get another shot."

"Keep it off the books. You, me, and Jason. Anyone else asks? Tell them it's a satellite calibration."

"If Ward's watching," he said, "let him. He won't realize what he's looking at until it's too late."

The room shifted into motion—screens updating, relays syncing, the feed from Shanghai coming into focus. The digital war had begun. And this time, they weren't blinking first.

CHAPTER 57: UNDER HER WATCH

Beijing- wheels up day

General Yue sat in her office, the faint sound of the city muffled by thick concrete and discipline. She moved through the reports quickly, eyes skimming, decisions forming as she read. She didn't underline or annotate—just absorbed, discarded, and filed away.

A soft ping interrupted her rhythm. She glanced at her laptop. It rarely drew her attention.

The subject line made her pause:

Subject: Important Message from Your Brother

Her eyes narrowed as she clicked it open.

Dearest Sister,

I must finally tell you something that has haunted me for months.

I wasn't honest with you the last time we met in Beijing.

I had just taken on a client I should've refused—but I didn't.

The price was high, the risk higher, and I was too afraid to say no.

A week before that meeting, Colonel Zhou Shaozeng from the Sixth Bureau approached me. His credentials seemed legitimate.

He knew about you—our relationship. It didn't feel like an offer. It felt like a trap.

He paid me generously.

My team was forced to carry out operations I now believe targeted innocent people. Everything focused on Southern California.

We weren't told why. The fear kept us quiet, but I can't live with that silence anymore.

Captain Kang has now replaced Zhou. A final debrief is scheduled.

They plan to inspect our equipment and erase all evidence of our work.

Something feels wrong.

I fear for my team—and for myself.

I know I've failed you. I've failed them. And I've failed myself.

Your shameful brother,

Lee

She read it again. Slower this time.

A hollow feeling pressed in beneath her breastbone. For a moment, she saw the boy Lee had been—skinny, stubborn, protective—dragging her from the rice paddies, shielding her with his own body from the Red Guards. Then the vision faded, replaced by steel.

The Sixth Bureau's covert use of her brother's company wasn't just a betrayal of trust. It was a breach of national protocol. And if Lee was right about a pending cover-up, then someone had lied to her. Directly. Under her watch.

"Surveillance, this is Sergeant Chan."

"Sergeant, inform Major Liu to call me immediately," Yue ordered, her tone cool and precise. *"And have my driver ready. I'm going to Shanghai."*

Minutes later, her phone buzzed. Liu.

"General," he said.

"Have you noticed anything unusual in Lee's surveillance?" she asked.

Liu hesitated. "His team is quiet. They mostly stay inside. Comms are heavily encrypted—standard for a unit like his. There's been a recent uptick in volume, but nothing that triggered alerts."

"Any visitors?"

"Two. Yesterday. Business suits, professional demeanor. No attempt at disguise. We're running facial recognition now."

"Were they carrying anything? Did they take anything out?"

"Arrived and left empty-handed. Routine body language. But we'll run a secondary review."

"Do that," Yue said. *"And prioritize identifying those men. Cross-*

check for Bureau ties."

She hesitated. "Liu, do you know anyone in the Sixth Bureau?"

"A classmate. He's a major now—adjutant to their commanding officer."

"Call him. Find out everything you can about Zhou Shaozeng. If they're running operations inside our borders without clearance, I want answers. Today. You'll report back within two hours."

Yue set the phone down, her thoughts racing.

Lee's confession. The Sixth Bureau's meddling. Foreign targets. Ghost visitors. If Liu couldn't bring answers, she would find them herself.

Uncertainty was weakness. And weakness was something she refused to allow—on her watch.

CHAPTER 58: WHEELS UP

Private Hangar, Brown Field, San Diego – 2230 Hours

Cool night air rolled across the tarmac, laced with the distant roar of departing jets, as Luke Payne and Helen Shepard led the team toward the waiting Gulfstream G700. The jet gleamed under the floodlights—a sleek machine built for stealth and speed. Tonight, it would take them into hostile territory.

Moises Alvarez stood at the base of the stairs, calm and ready. "Flight time's under fifteen hours. We're wheels up in five."

The team moved with quiet precision, double-checking cover IDs, stowing gear, and syncing secure comms. At the foot of the steps, Helen handed Luke a slim, encrypted flash drive.

"Insurance," she said. "If I go down—or Silent Dagger does—get that to Benton at DC3. No one else."

Luke nodded and slipped it into an inner pocket without a word.

Onboard, Hank strapped down a canvas pack filled with unmarked hardware. Jenny unfolded a digital map of Shanghai. Moises handed out burner phones.

"Nothing says 'legit' like a seafood guy with calloused hands," he muttered.

Luke took his seat near the front. Helen slid in beside him, Diet Cokes in hand. "You look uneasy," she said.

Luke watched the dark tarmac. "The hit on Maggie and Peter—it wasn't just a breach. It was personal."

Helen nodded. "Then we're not tracking hackers. We're tracking a purge."

"Or a warning," Luke said, voice flat.

The jet lifted off, slicing into the night sky.

Wheels down, Shanghai Hongqiao Airport – 1745 Local Time

The Gulfstream touched down smoothly. Moises taxied to a secluded strip beyond the terminal. As the cabin door opened, thick heat and jet fuel rolled in.

They cleared immigration in staggered pairs. At the exit, a woman in jeans and a plain black tee held a simple placard: PAYNE.

Luke approached. She didn't smile. "Name's Evans. I'm your contact." Her voice was flat, clipped. "I work with the Embassy. Sort of."

Helen grinned. "Sort of?"

"You don't need the details," Evans said. "Just know I'm your ghost. Your gear's already loaded. You're guests here. Don't act like anything else."

She led them to a black van idling at the curb. In the rear compartment, hard-sided cases sat beneath a tarp marked WATER FILTRATION PROTOTYPES—the label stenciled in Mandarin.

Evans pulled Luke aside as the rest climbed in. "No embassy help. No extraction. Not if you're arrested, not if you're bleeding out in the street. This operation doesn't exist. If it fails—it fails quietly."

Luke didn't flinch. "We clean up our own mess."

She nodded once. "Then don't make me regret this. This is Joe— your driver and maybe your guardian angel. Listen to him. If he likes you, you might survive this mess—or whatever it is you're doing. I don't want to know."

Joe looked them over through mirrored sunglasses, chewing the end of a toothpick like he'd been waiting his whole life for this moment.

"I drive. You sit."

They piled into the van.

Evans pointed toward the tarp-covered crates. "There's your gear. I don't know what's in them, and I don't want to. Joe will get you to the hotel's back entrance—he's arranged a blind spot for the transfer. Don't make me regret this. No—too late. I already do."

As the van pulled away from the terminal, Joe offered a thin smile. "She's actually a real sweetheart."

A few chuckles from the back.

The city blurred past in a haze of neon, exhaust, and ambition. Skyscrapers flashed like circuit boards. Street hawkers shouted under overpasses. Joe kept one hand on the wheel, the other casually gesturing at streets and buildings as they passed.

"Shanghai wears makeup for the tourists," he said. "You want the truth? Look in the shadows."

He took a curve down a lesser-known route and added, "You want dumplings, go left. You want contraband, go right. Usually, they share a kitchen."

As they neared the hotel, Luke leaned forward. "Can you give us a recon run tomorrow morning? Eyes on the building. Get the lay of the land."

Joe didn't answer right away. Then, with a shrug, "Sure. I'm sure they'll pay me overtime. Day's better anyway—tourists all over the place. I'll pick you up at 0930. Back entrance. Wear your best tourist outfits."

The van pulled into a dimly lit loading bay behind the hotel. Joe killed the engine and turned in his seat. Reaching into a leather pouch beside him, he pulled out two large manila envelopes and handed them to Luke.

"Room key cards are in the first one—your names are on them. No need to check in. Don't use room service, but the minibar and snacks are on the house. The other envelope's got your proof of accommodation and tour company details. If anyone stops you, play dumb American and show them that. You'll be fine. There's also enough local cash—best not to flash U.S.. dollars."

He gestured toward the rear of the van. "Use the freight elevator for your gear. My guy's on break—conveniently. Go through the back, stay quiet, and he won't see a thing. You didn't meet me. I don't exist."

Luke nodded. "Hit the bunks early. Final Silent Dagger briefing at 0700. Daylight recon and positioning at 0900. We break for lunch and prep. By 1600, we're in position. We breach as soon as we see targets."

Joe opened the door. "Sleep light. I'll see you in the morning."

CHAPTER 59: THE RIDGE

Shanghai – 2300, Night Before the Operation

Luke Payne lay on the stiff hotel bed, eyes tracing the slow, hypnotic rhythm of the rattan ceiling fan. Outside, Shanghai murmured—people, traffic, a thousand lives in motion. The air conditioner spilled cold air into the room, its chill at odds with the heat climbing through his chest.

The Shanghai skyline stretched beyond the glass—alive, sprawling, watching. He should've been asleep. The mission was hours away. The team was ready. The plan was solid.

Still, something gnawed at him. It wasn't the op itself. It was what it meant—his first without the shield of uniform or rank. No protocol. No chain of command.

Just instinct.

And ghosts.

He reached for the pendant around his neck and closed his fingers around it—Last Call. Cool metal against his palm. The reminder was enough.

And just like that, he was back at Roberts' Ridge.

Rotors screamed through the Afghan night as the MH-47 Chinook descended toward Takur Ghar. Snow whipped through the open ramp, misting the black sky. Luke adjusted his headset, voice calm through the turbulence.

"Eagle One, this is Viper Two. Coming in hot. Confirm clear for landing."

A burst of static. "Negative, Viper Two. Heavy enemy fire at the LZ. Roberts' Ridge is compromised."

No reaction. No surprise. Just focus.

SEALs checked gear around him—calm, controlled. He wasn't one of them. But he'd trained with them. Trusted them.

He wasn't even supposed to be here. He'd submitted his papers.

His last deployment. Savannah had circled the date—plans made, life waiting.

Then the corpsman caught a virus. Luke had volunteered. One last mission. In and out.

That was the plan.

Gunfire raked the fuselage. The Chinook bucked under the assault. "Brace!"

The bird tilted hard. Luke gripped a strap and scanned below— tracers stitched the darkness like red lightning. He dropped behind a fallen log as they hit the ground running.

"Hawk, left flank! Cover fire!"

Breaker's voice rang out. "Move to the ridge!"

They climbed—boots slipping on ice, air thin and bitter. Luke pushed forward, lungs burning.

Then he saw it. Burned-out vehicles. Scorched bodies. Civilians—women, children—strewn in the snow.

Not the mission.

Not the plan.

Breaker crouched beside him. "What the hell happened here?"

A cough. He ran toward the sound, shoving wreckage aside. A boy, maybe three. Bloodied. Barely conscious. Terrified.

Luke dropped to his knees. "Hey, buddy. I've got you."

He scooped him up and ran. The Chinook's rotors thundered in the distance. The boy's breaths grew fainter. Luke climbed aboard, working fast. Pressing. Hoping.

But the boy slipped away before they cleared the ridge. Luke just sat there, arms around the small, still body, as the night closed in.

The ceiling flickered in a pulse of neon blue and pink. His chest rose. Then steadied.

Not this time.

He swung his legs off the bed. Checked his weapon. Laid it beside him. Tomorrow, they'd go in.

And this time? He wouldn't freeze. Wouldn't hesitate.

Wouldn't fail.

CHAPTER 60: RECON IN THE SHADOWS

Shanghai – 0900, Day of the Operation

The van glided to a smooth stop in front of a hotel overlooking the Bund. The morning sun, already strong, glinted off Joe's sunglasses as he leaned over the steering wheel, his cap turned backward. A half-eaten sesame bun rested on the dash, a testament to an early start.

"Time for the scenic tour," Joe announced as Luke, Helen, Jenny, Hank, and Moises climbed in. "The kind they don't show on Instagram."

Helen buckled in with a dry smile. "Always wanted the black-market package."

Joe grinned. "Premium tier. No refunds."

He eased the van into the bustling morning traffic, leaving the polished glamour of the Bund behind. They slipped into side streets where the city showed its true character. Sunlight struggled to pierce the narrow canyons of older buildings, damp with the history of countless lives. Steam curled from food stalls, carrying the rich scents of oil, garlic, and roasted duck. In alleys, lean figures hunched in doorways, their eyes tracking the van with a quiet intensity, like street dogs sizing up newcomers.

"This," Joe said, gesturing with a wave of his fingers, "is where deals happen without contracts. Where people vanish without paperwork."

They passed under a row of rusted pipes strung overhead like skeletal fingers against the bright sky. "You see those? Fiber bundled into those water lines. Cameras everywhere. Not just government—gangs too. Everybody's watching, nobody trusts."

Moises muttered, "Reminds me of Caracas."

Jenny leaned toward the front. "You ever get comfortable driving in places like this?"

Joe snorted. "Comfort's for tourists. You learn to read the road. Smells, sounds, blind corners. City's a language. But you gotta grow up speaking it."

Suddenly, the glint of chrome caught Luke's eye. A sleek police cruiser pulled into their wake, two blocks behind, its presence silent but stark in the morning light.

Hank was the first to speak. "We've got company."

Joe's hands tightened slightly on the wheel. "Relax. Could be random. Could be theater."

He turned left at the next alley. The cruiser followed.

Then, the red-and-blue strobes kicked on, flashing silently in their rearview mirror.

"Nobody move," Joe said sharply. "Look forward. Don't speak. Don't blink. Tourists lost on a noodle run."

The team froze. The cruiser surged forward, lights flashing but siren silent, overtaking them before vanishing around the corner.

A long, collective breath exhaled around the van.

Helen's voice was even. "We just got tagged."

"Maybe," Joe said. "Or maybe they just wanted to rattle the cage."

Jenny shook her head. "I hate being the bait."

Luke stared at the mirror until the lights were gone. "We're not bait. Not yet."

Joe made one more turn, and suddenly the city opened up again. The gleaming towers of the Bund reappeared, reflecting the morning sun. He pulled to a stop at the edge of a quiet stretch of road near a slate-gray high-rise—clean, modern, faceless.

"Target's up there," Luke said, nodding toward the top floors. "Penthouse. Dual entry from both stairwell and elevator. Cameras cover the front, side, and service doors."

The team filed out of the van and onto the sidewalk.

"OK, fan out and scout your locations. Meet back here at 1200."

Luke stepped a few paces away, tilted his head upward. The windows on the top floor were tinted, but he caught the faintest silhouette against the balcony railing—just a slouched figure, head tilted as if deep in thought.

Was it Sochi?

He blinked. The figure turned, disappeared into shadow. A chill ran down his spine.

Hank followed his gaze. "You see something?"

"Maybe," Luke said. "Could've been a reflection. Could've been our ghost."

Helen stepped beside them, already scanning. "We need full layout memory. Entrances, exits, stairwells, blind spots. Count doors, watch camera blink rates. If you don't notice it now, it'll bite us later."

Jenny moved to the edge of the street, pretending to check her phone while snapping mental snapshots of the building across from the target. Moises walked a block radius, noting the sedan parked too long, the cyclist who hadn't pedaled once, the "casual couple" that hadn't looked at each other in ten minutes.

As Luke turned back toward the van, Joe met his eyes. Something unreadable passed between them. Then Joe said, quietly enough only Luke would catch it:

"Tell Benton he still owes me for Marrakesh."

Luke's brow furrowed slightly. "You're DC3?"

Joe popped a fresh toothpick into his mouth, eyes scanning the street. "Nah," he said with a half-smile. "Just a friend with benefits."

Luke nodded once. That explained more than it didn't.

The team scattered into the park, each one becoming just another face in the crowd. The real mission was about to begin.

CHAPTER 61: DON'T SCREW IT UP

Shanghai – 1000, Day of the Operation

Metal clanked as Kang powered through another set of pull-ups on the makeshift bar bolted into the ceiling joist of his drab flat. Sweat ran down his chiseled arm, decorated with a fearsome cobra tattoo. The place was more holding cell than home—bare concrete floor, water-stained walls, no windows, just a ventilation shaft that hummed like distant static. The air was thick with sweat, iron, and the sting of mildew. He liked it. Clean spaces made people soft.

He dropped from the bar, shoulders tense but steady. A single bulb swung above, casting warped shadows that danced across the walls. He toweled off, exhaling through his nose.

Pain meant readiness. Readiness meant control.

His phone buzzed once on the table. Encrypted line. No hesitation.

"Kang."

"Status," said Sochi, voice cold like ice.

Kang's lip twitched. "We're on track. This afternoon, Tan and I hit the first three of Lee's hackers. Kim and Ming handle the rest. Low-traffic zones. No weapons left behind. Quick and quiet."

"I'm wheels up to San Diego," Sochi said. "The boss wants this cleaned up today. No loose ends before the gala."

Kang gave a dry chuckle. "Not planning to disappoint. Might even be fun."

"Don't screw it up."

The line clicked off.

Kang stared at the phone a moment longer. Then his eyes dropped to the sweat-spattered concrete, unmoved. Outside, a car alarm chirped and fell silent. Someone cursed in the alley below. The world carried on.

He turned to his gear, neatly laid out like surgical tools. Two knives—sharp, balanced. A Glock, spare mags. A burner phone loaded with the plan. Black gloves. Tape. Nothing wasted.

He dropped to the floor for push-ups. Slow. Brutal. Focused. Each movement locked in with muscle memory. No distractions. A buzz near the vent made him stop. Drone? Civilian? He held his breath.

Silence.

He kept going. When the set was done, he stood. His chest rose and fell with measured rhythm. The ache in his arms told him he was ready.

Time to finish the job, then disappear—before anyone could tie loose ends back to him.

CHAPTER 62: THE SETUP

Shanghai – Tuesday, 15:30

Chen Lee sat at his kitchen table, unmoving. A bowl of noodles had gone slick and cold beside a cup of tea he didn't remember pouring. Outside, Shanghai buzzed beneath a metallic haze—horns, drills, footsteps, life.

Inside, only the thud of his pulse.

Tuesday. Debrief day.

He'd made the calls. Checked in with his team. Gave them the line they expected: "Stay inside. Keep your phones close. Captain Kang's people will come to you."

He told them it was protocol.

He told himself it was true.

It wasn't.

The call came at 15:42. Minh. Barely twenty. Bright as hell. Loyal. Naive.

"Lee," Minh gasped. "They—they're killing everyone."

Then static.

Lee jolted upright. The table shuddered, tea sloshing into the noodles. "Minh? Minh!"

Nothing.

Adrenaline took charge. He had hoped—foolishly—for the best. But deep down, he knew this could happen. There was still a chance.

He grabbed his go-bag. Cash. Burner phone. Flash drive. Out the door in under three minutes, the hinge still creaking behind him.

Only one name in his mind: Rusty.

The boy genius. The breach. The one who tried to undo the damage he helped cause. Still thought this was cleanup. Still thought Chen was offering protection. Still thought he was safe.

Lee cut through alleys and side streets, weaving through traffic like a needle through thread. Tires squealed around corners.

He reached Rusty's building in seven minutes flat. No black vans. No movement in the mirrors.

For now.

He pounded up the stairwell two steps at a time. Fourth floor. Unit 4C. He knocked—one short, sharp rhythm they used in the field.

The door cracked open. Rusty stood there in sweatpants, hair a mess, blinking like he'd just rolled off a couch. A tablet glowed faintly behind him on the sofa.

"Lee?" he said, squinting. "What—what's going on?"

"No time," Lee snapped. "Laptop, phone, ID. Now."

Rusty hesitated. "Is this about the debrief—?"

Lee grabbed his shoulder. "It's a hit list. You're on it. So am I."

That landed. Rusty's face shifted—confusion draining, something colder rising. He nodded once and vanished into the bedroom.

Lee locked the door. Checked the peephole. Nothing yet.

One minute. Then two.

Rusty returned, backpack over one shoulder, panic rising. "Where are we going?"

"Anywhere but here."

A floorboard creaked in the hallway. Then silence. Not the quiet of safety—something else.

A knock. Not a question. A statement. Sharp. Flat.

Lee froze. Another knock. Then the crash.

The door exploded inward. Wood splinters. Metal shriek. Shadows poured in—three men in black, rifles up, visors down. Suppressors. Body armor. Precision.

"On the floor!" one barked.

Lee moved to cover Rusty—too late. Boots hit his ribs. Knees drove him down.

Zip ties bit deep. The world shrank to impact, motion, breath—and then, nothing.

The choreography was too precise. The kind of violence that came from inside the organization. Lee's gut twisted. He knew who trained them.

A fourth man entered—slower, heavier. The storm after the lightning.

Kang.

He crouched beside Rusty, grinning like a man who'd found a lost pet. He turned to Lee.

"You always were soft. I'll give you this—you move fast. That's why you're still breathing."

Lee glared, teeth bared. "You won't walk away from this."

Kang rose and adjusted his jacket. "I already have."

He turned toward Rusty, gaze sharp. "So this is the boy genius who sent the money back." He chuckled, low and vicious. "The boss was not impressed."

Lee strained against the zip ties. "Don't touch him. He's just a stupid kid."

Kang looked over his shoulder, amusement curdling into something darker. "Exactly why we need to make an example of him."

He stepped closer to Rusty, eyes glinting. "Besides... I've been waiting to have a little fun."

He nodded once. Two of his men dragged Rusty to his feet. That made four total—Kang and three operatives.

Lee thrashed. "You don't have to do this!"

Kang leaned in close, his voice a blade. "But I want to."

CHAPTER 63: CROSSING THE LINE

Beijing — 0900 HOURS

General Yue sat in the back of her black Hongqi limousine, her face calm, her thoughts anything but. Outside, Beijing's gridlocked traffic inched forward, a slow-motion snarl of horns and exhaust. But inside, her mind was already three moves ahead.

Someone had acted in her name—invoked the Sixth Bureau, deployed assets under her authority—in Shanghai. Her city. Her jurisdiction. And they'd done it behind her back.

Unacceptable.

Her phone buzzed. She answered before the second vibration.

"General Yue. Liu reporting."

"Status," she said, her voice a low command.

"Colonel Ju at the Sixth reports no sanctioned operations in Shanghai. No record of a Zhou Shaozeng. He offered to open an internal investigation."

Yue's mouth stiffened. Too eager. Too clean.

"No investigation," she said. "Tell him it was a clerical mix-up. Thank him for his vigilance."

"Now call Colonel Huang. I want a special forces platoon on standby. Z-20 fueled and ready. Full briefing. I'll meet them at Unit 61398."

Two Hours Later — Shanghai

Her plane touched down at Hongqiao just after dusk. No ceremony. No press. The motorcade moved fast—black sedans slicing through the lit arteries of Pudong.

Skyscrapers, monolithic and glittering, loomed overhead. Their reflections rippled across the limousine's windows as they passed—silent specters of power. They were heading for the stark, imposing facade of PLA Unit 61398—China's cyber warfare nerve center.

Tonight, it felt less like a hub of information and more like the edge of a precipice.

Inside the command center, the air hummed with a low, nervous energy. Colonel Huang stood ramrod straight beside a glowing tactical display. "General," he saluted crisply.

Yue nodded once, her eyes already sweeping the screens. "Status."

"Platoon staged five kilometers out, securing the Bund. Z-20 fueled, armed. Passive surveillance maintained on Chen Lee's apartment."

"General!" an operator cut in, sharp with urgency. "Lee's on the move—fast. Heading toward River Park."

Yue's gaze snapped to the live drone feed. "How long since he left?"

"Just under a minute."

Five Minutes Later

"General!" the voice spiked. "Lee just entered a building next to the park. Drone's online—imaging coming through now!"

Huang tapped the display. A heat map brightened—glowing red and gold silhouettes inside a mid-rise complex.

"That's Lee and someone else," Yue murmured. "He's not alone."

She turned to Huang. "You're with me. Get us there. Tactical readiness. Real-time data. Bring comms."

The order passed silently down the chain.

Inside the PLA SUV

En route, Huang's voice was clipped. "General, we have intruders."

Yue narrowed her eyes at the screen mounted inside the vehicle. In the target unit, two stationary heat signatures glowed—kneeling.

"Interrogation posture?" she asked.

"Likely," Huang confirmed. "They match previous thermal patterns—Lee and a male captive. But now, four additional signatures have entered. Two guarding the entrance. Two more inside. Unknown affiliation." He zoomed in. "Two upright. Two kneeling. Holding steady."

Before Yue could respond, another comms officer called out, "New movement. A second team just breached the building—advancing quickly."

Yue leaned in. "Affiliation?"

"Unknown. Their pattern suggests exfiltration, not assault."

A rescue, Yue thought. For Lee. On Chinese soil.

"Intercepted burst transmission," another tech added. "From a vehicle near the target. Foreign encryption."

"Playback."

The cabin filled with static, then a clipped voice: "...exfil if needed... two minutes... mark the hallway..."

Silence fell.

"American," Yue said flatly.

Her thoughts churned. Why Lee? What was he worth? Was this leverage? A backchannel? Had he sold something?

She looked at the screen. Who are these operators? Linked to the rogue colonel? Or another faction entirely?

"Hold position until I give the word," she said. "No one enters unless I authorize it."

"General," said the comms officer, "the signal is coming from a van parked right outside. Registered to a foreign national. It's a woman."

Yue's eyes sharpened. "Take me to her. Now."

She studied the thermal display one last time. Infrared silhouettes glowed—tense, poised.

"There will be answers," she said quietly. "And if not—there will be consequences."

CHAPTER 64: PLAN B

Shanghai – Tuesday, 16:25

The plan was in motion.

Helen's van was parked along the main boulevard, innocuous amid the Shanghai traffic. Inside, monitors bathed her face in flickering light—street cams, drone feeds, building schematics. She wore a headset, voice calm, fingers moving with practiced ease.

"Comms check," she said.

"Copy," Jenny replied from her rooftop post across the park, crouched behind a service structure atop the International Garden Hotel. The city glowed beneath her—neon and glass and steel. She adjusted her thermal drone feed, scanning the target apartment building. "Drone is up. Good visibility. Four floors. No exterior security."

"Van two is in," Moises said. He eased the DC3 van into the apartment's underground garage, low-profile, no markings. He wore a delivery vest, a cap pulled low. "Parked. Quiet."

Luke and Hank took up their position near the building's street-level entrance, blending in with the early evening foot traffic. They moved like tourists, but every glance, every step, was calculated. Luke's Dart pistol sat hidden beneath his jacket. Hank carried a concealed breaching charge in a camera case.

Jenny's voice crackled in their ears. "We're green. No movement inside the penthouse. Thermal shows two bodies—both pacing. Could be Lee and the kid."

Helen toggled a secure line to DC3. "Jason, how's traffic on the grid?"

Jason's voice came through steady from Maryland. "Synthetic IDs are holding. Network's smooth. You've got a clean bubble—twenty-eight minutes left on the loop."

Then Jenny's voice cut in—tight. "Hold. New visuals—four inbound. Civilian clothes, loose jackets. Heat signatures look off. Tactical posture. They just entered the building. No hesitation. They knew the code."

Luke tensed. "Kang?"

"Could be. One's built like a linebacker. Three shadows. Tight formation."

Helen's screen lit up with fresh data. "Jason, I've got military pattern pings outside the grid. Movement on rooftops, alley cams fuzzing. You seeing this?"

Jason responded fast. "Yeah. Not local police. They're using exfil vectors and blocking fallback paths. Pattern suggests tactical prep."

Jenny zoomed the drone into the penthouse. "Shit. Visuals just changed. Four new heat signatures. Two standing. Two on their knees. No movement from the two kneeling."

Luke cursed under his breath. "We breach now."

Moises emerged from the garage stairwell, looping to the building's side entrance. Luke and Hank moved in sync, flanking the main door. Jenny kept overwatch from above.

"Two guards outside the penthouse," Jenny said. "Standing sentry. Armed."

Luke whispered into comms. "Moises, you've got the left. Hank, take the right. Quiet."

They moved like water. Three quick strikes—silent, precise. The guards dropped without a sound.

Jenny: "Clear. You've got thirty seconds before they realize someone's missing."

Hank slid the breaching charge into the doorframe. "Ready."

"Three, two—"

Boom.

The door blew inward. Smoke and dust. Kang spun around, blade in hand, inches from Rusty's throat. The explosion sent him sprawling. One thug lost his balance, falling hard.

Lee lunged, using his bound arms to knock the second thug into the wall. Rusty kicked the table, sending Kang's weapon skittering across the floor.

Luke surged in, dart gun up, tranquilizing the nearest threat. Moises dropped the second. Hank tackled Kang, pinning him hard. Lee scrambled to his feet, blood at his temple, but moving. Rusty ducked behind the couch.

"Secure!" Luke called.

Jenny's voice confirmed, "No movement on the drone. Outside is still clear—

Luke walked over to the two bound men—Lee and Rusty—checking their faces. "No sign of Sochi," he said into comms. "Repeat: Sochi's not here."

Rusty looked up, pale and trembling. "They were going to kill us. It was my fault—I sent his money back."

Luke blinked. "So you're the guy."

Lee, wincing from a gash on his cheek, added hoarsely, "Don't blame Rusty. He didn't know who he was dealing with. He's a good kid."

"We don't know anyone named Sochi," muttered.

Luke squatted beside them. "Tall. Bald. Smooth talker. Always dressed like he's stepping out of a catalog. Ferret face. Cold eyes. Ring a bell?"

Lee's expression darkened. "That's him. The Colonel. That's what they called him. But he used a different name. Never told us who he really worked for. He brought Kang in two days ago—said he was in charge now."

Luke swore under his breath. "Sochi set this up, then bailed."

He cut their restraints. "You're safe now. But we need answers. All of them."

Lee nodded, rubbing his wrists. "You'll get them."

He glanced at Rusty, who sat in stunned silence, still hugging his knees.

Lee drew a breath, then looked Luke square in the eye.

 "My name is Lee Chen, and that is my employee Rusty. It started three months ago…"

CHAPTER 65: REVERSAL OF FORTUNE

Shanghai — 17:03

Helen sat behind the wheel of the surveillance van, eyes locked on the apartment across the street. Her laptop glowed soft blue in her lap, thermal overlays pulsing in reds and golds—four heat signatures inside. Luke and the team were in motion. Comms steady. Breath even. Focus locked.

Jenny's voice crackled in her earpiece, low and tight. "Helen—got new heat signatures. PLA units. Rooftops. Alleys. Full surround. And there's a chopper inbound, low and fast. Looks military."

Helen ran her finger through her hair. "You sure?"

"They're setting a perimeter. This isn't backup—it's containment. Wait—someone's coming up the fire stairs to the roof. I'm out."

Static hit for half a beat—then silence.

Helen's pulse spiked.

The silence pressed in, broken only by the faint hum of the laptop and the distant chop of rotor blades growing closer.

Then—movement in the side mirror. Two black SUVs slid into view. Silent. Synchronized. One blocked the building's front. The other sealed the alley behind.

Not cops. Not local muscle. And definitely not amateurs.

A knock at her window. Three taps. Calm. Controlled.

Helen turned. A woman in dark fatigues stood outside. No weapon visible—just stillness and command. Two stars on the collar. Military. Senior.

Helen cracked the window an inch. The woman didn't raise her voice. "Open the door."

Helen didn't move. Met her gaze. Waited.

Again—quietly: "Open. The door."

No time to run. No backup in reach. Helen unlocked the door.

The woman slid inside with precise, measured movements. Her eyes swept the console, the comms rig, the laptop's feed. She didn't need to ask what she was looking at—she already knew.

"Tell me what's happening," she said.

Helen kept her hands visible. "Who are you?"

The woman didn't blink. "I'm the reason you're still alive."

Alive?

Helen studied her: posture, precision, composure. A general. That much was clear.

From the side mirror, Helen caught the thudding blur of a rotor arc overhead—military chopper, just out of direct sight. Distant boots scrambled into position beyond view. A full containment cordon.

Her laptop screen flickered—static for a breath, then her feed returned. But something was off. The layout was sharper. Enhanced. Labeled. Not hers.

The system had been hijacked. Not monitored—taken.

The woman rotated the screen toward herself, fingers tapping with surgical intent. The drone feed sprang to life—live thermal, tighter angles. Countdown ticking.

"You're running this op?" she asked.

"I'm supporting it," Helen replied.

That earned the faintest flicker of disdain.

"I am General Yue," the woman said evenly. "The man in that apartment is my brother."

Helen blinked. That, she hadn't expected.

Yue tapped again. A new window opened—not tactical. Civilian data. Name: Chen Lee.

Yue's eyes didn't leave the screen. "Your team is seconds from being eliminated. Call them off."

Helen steadied her voice. "He'd already be dead if we hadn't moved. Someone sent a cleanup crew. They're inside now."

Yue said nothing. Her expression didn't shift, but her shoulders straightened ever so slightly—as if bracing for a detour she hadn't planned on.

"You're in way over your head," she said.

Helen matched her tone. "Maybe, but your brother would be dead without us."

Yue turned the screen back toward her. "Call Payne."

Helen didn't move.

Yue added, low: "If you want him and his team to live, I want to speak to him. Now."

Helen keyed her mic.

"Luke, this is Helen. Hold position. We've got a situation."

A pause. "Say again?"

Helen's eyes stayed locked on Yue. "Hold. General Yue is here." A beat. "She wants to talk."

CHAPTER 66: THE HORNET'S NEST

DC3 operations Maryland. 0500 Breach day

The DC3 operations center glowed with the pale light of monitors, casting the room in shades of blue and gray. Machines hummed quietly beneath the rising tension. Fingers flew across keyboards. Eyes darted from screen to screen.

Lance Benton stood at the center, arms crossed, locked on the main display. Director Worthington loomed behind him, pale and still. Jason Edwards hunched at his console nearby, flipping through feeds with rapid, practiced motions.

"Luke's team is inside," Jason said. "Helen's comms are stable. Hank's tactical cam is live."

The central screen brightened—street-level footage of the target building. Infrared overlays pulsed with heat signatures in red and gold.

Helen's voice came through the speaker, tight but controlled. "Visual on the building. Holding position."

Jason toggled angles. "One unknown male just entered. Civilian clothing. Intentional pace."

Worthington leaned forward. "Friend or hostile?"

Jason narrowed his gaze. "No weapon. Could be the hacker. Or bait."

A second later, Hank's voice chimed in, crisp: "Four approaching from the north. Armed."

Benton stiffened. "Sochi's crew?"

Helen again: "All teams stay sharp."

Then Hank: "Thermal confirms two kneeling, unarmed. One

standing over them."

Jason studied the heat layout. "Standing figure matches Kang's profile."

He clicked into the target view. "Hostile posture confirmed. Luke—green light."

The room fell still.

Onscreen: breach. Precise. Clean. Seconds long.

Luke's voice cut through. "Guards neutralized. Room secured. Lee and the hacker safe. Kang in custody."

Jason drew a measured breath.

A tech's voice cut in, sharp. "Inbound aircraft—Z-20 helicopter. Military transponder. Chinese PLA."

Jason's hands blurred over the keyboard. "Helen—heads up. You've got an inbound helo and four ground vehicles closing. Fast."

Another tech: "Drone feed lost. Signal's jammed."

Jenny's voice broke through, breathless and low. "They're surrounded. PLA on every side. We're being extracted—this wasn't part of the plan."

Jason frowned . "They're moving—but not under Luke's orders."

Worthington's voice was barely above a whisper. "She took the whole board. Without firing a shot."

Jason dragged a route across the tactical map. "Convoy heading southeast. Datong Road."

He tapped rapidly, trying to regain signal access. "Destination confirmed… Unit 61398."

Benton looked stricken. "We've been outflanked."

No one spoke. The silence said it all. Outplayed. Outmaneuvered. And now—out of time.

CHAPTER 67: LUKE

Rusty's apartment had turned into a war crime in slow motion. Luke Payne's team had lowered their weapons at his command, the pull of responsibility failure pressing heavily on his chest.

Two armed Chinese soldiers entered the room with precise, mechanical movements, taking positions on either side of the door. Their expressions were unreadable, but their presence was unmistakable—this was no simple arrest.

Outside, the thunder of the helicopter's blades intensified as six more soldiers rappelled onto the wide deck. Their descent was seamless—each move crisp, timed to the breath, drilled into reflex. Then she appeared.

Lieutenant General Yue. Olive fatigues flawless, golden two-star insignia gleaming. Her expression unreadable. The soldiers stiffened as she entered—no orders needed.

She owned the room.

"Set down your weapons," she said, calm as a knife being unsheathed.

Luke stared back, unmoving. "You going to tell me what this is?"

"You're no longer in control," she replied. "And you have no idea what you've stepped into." She didn't wait for answers. Just a nod.

Kang limp body was hauled into a med basket, mouth twisted into a grin that was more defiance than sanity. The rest of them were marched out under gunpoint, stripped of weapons, stripped of dignity.

They were hooded and crammed into a rust-patched 16-passenger van. Scratched Plexiglas. Steel bars. No questions. No talking.

Just the low, slow growl of wheels on asphalt as the city blurred past in shadows.

Destination: a concrete slab with no name, no signs, and no exit. PLA Unit 61398. China's cyberwarfare hub.

Now their prison.

Inside, the hoods came off. White lights. Antiseptic tile. The stench of bleach and authoritarian control. This wasn't a prison. It was a machine. Designed to break people—quietly. Thoroughly.

At the first hallway intersection, Rusty was pulled aside and shoved through a steel door.

Luke's eyes scanned the line. Two missing. He snapped. "Where's Helen? Where's Jenny?"

The nearest guard barked something in Mandarin. Another stepped in and slammed the butt of his rifle into Luke's gut. He folded, choking on air, knees buckling but not breaking.

"You do not ask questions," the guard growled in rough English. "You do not speak."

Luke forced himself upright, eyes burning. He didn't reply. But he didn't look away either.

Behind him, Hank flinched but stayed quiet. Moises shifted subtly like he was memorizing exits. Even in shackles, the team watched each other—checked posture, pain, panic. They were still in formation, even now.

One by one, they were shoved through separate doors.

Luke's cell was a box of white and silence. Steel door. No window. No toilet—just a floor drain. One cot. A single water bottle. Then the lock clicked.

Then the screaming started.

At first, it was just one scream. High. Sharp. Cut short. Then another. Then longer. Then again. Over. And over. And over. All night. Not once. Not random. Rhythmic.

Interrogation. Torture.

Luke sat on the hard cot, elbows on knees, fists tight. He tried to focus—count footsteps, map the echoes—but it was chaos. Engineered chaos. The kind meant to strip logic from your bones. He couldn't tell who it was. That's what made it worse.

Could've been Moises. Could've been Hank. Could've been Rusty.

He hadn't heard a woman scream. Maybe that ruled out Helen. Or Jenny. Maybe. But silence didn't mean safety. Not here.

His stomach twisted itself into knots. Every shriek drilled deeper. Every silence was worse—because then came the next wave, jagged and raw. They were breaking someone. Slowly.

His mind kept circling back to her. Helen. Had they separated her? Was she even here? Or had she disappeared down a corridor no one came back from?

And the memory came. Gulf of Aden. Nine years ago.

A dive bar sagging under rust and regret. Diesel and cheap rum in the air. A fan spun lazy circles overhead. Luke spotted him instantly—the officer who'd ignored his warning about the compromised LZ. The one whose arrogance got Rivera killed. And cost Moises his leg.

Moises sat beside him that night, metal prosthetic boot resting on the foot rail. "You don't need this," he said. "Let it go."

But then the bastard saw them. Came over, already halfway gone on vodka and self-delusion. "Payne," he said, slurring. "Still pissed about that chopper? You win some, you lose some." Luke stood slowly.

"You cashed a promotion. Rivera bled out on my hands. Moises left half his body in the sand."

The officer grinned. "That's war, sweetheart."

Luke's punch landed like a death sentence. The man went down. His lip split. His jaw cracked. He stayed down.

They'd put Luke in the brig for it week. Worth every minute. One moment of clarity in years of noise.

Now. Shanghai. Present.

The screaming didn't stop. He pressed his fists to his temples, but the sound tunneled in any way—through walls, through memory, through bone.

He couldn't save Rivera. He couldn't stop Moises from losing a leg. He might not be able to save whoever was screaming now. Or Helen and Jen.

But he wasn't leaving Shanghai with another victim on his back.

He watched the wall. Breathed through the fear. "This wasn't the plan," he whispered.

But plans could change. And he'd wait—for the crack, the flaw, the smallest opening. And when it came, he'd burn this place down.

CHAPTER 68 LET THEM TRY

Shanghai – 2300 hours, same day

General Yue stared vacantly out the window of her armored sedan, Shanghai's fog-wrapped streets crawling past in silence. She was exhausted. And alert. The kind of wired clarity that came not from sleep, but from decisions that couldn't wait.

Tonight's operation had raised more questions than it answered—especially the presence of Chen Lee in that apartment. She had Helen and the other woman secured, separated from the men, placed in locked rooms inside her personal residence in Shanghai. Not because she didn't trust her own officers.

Because she trusted no one.

Helen was sharp. Tactical. Unflinching under pressure. Yue admired that. Sometimes a long conversation revealed more than a thousand interrogation files. It was worth the attempt.

And it might be the only way to save Lee.

She had almost lost him tonight.

Tonight reminded her of the second time he had saved her.

The air at the remote PLA training camp always smelled faintly of iron and sweat. High in the mist-soaked highlands west of Chengdu, the barracks sat like forgotten bones. Fog rolled in thick, wrapping around the compound like a shroud—not to comfort, but to suffocate.

It was here, buried in isolation and rigid order, that she began to disappear.

Not General Yue. Private Yue. Recruit. Nobody.

Boots too big. Voice too soft. Trying to outrun the name she'd been given and earn the one she would become.

She hadn't thought of that night in years. But today—hearing his voice—had cracked the seal on that memory. She'd stayed behind in the munitions shed, logging inventory no one else would double-check. Outside, the others had gone to mess—boots stomping away, barked orders fading into silence.

She liked the quiet. Until it broke.

Sergeant Bai.

He stepped inside with the smell of sweat and smoke, his reputation trailing behind him like a stench. A violent man. Untouchable. Shielded by rank and the silence of a dozen buried complaints.

The others feared him. Yue avoided him. Or tried to.

"You think you're special?" he sneered. "Because you're clever? Because you speak Mandarin like a textbook?"

He stepped closer. "You need to learn who commands respect here."

Her back hit the wall. Her heart hammered—but it wasn't fear that burst from her throat. It was rage. She screamed.

Then—the crash of the door. A blur. A roar.

Chen Lee—her brother, her only real friend in that cold, hollow place—hit Bai like a storm. No hesitation. No words. Just motion.

Bai pulled a knife. Lee grabbed a steel rod from the shelf. The fight was brutal. Metal on bone. Blood on stone.

Bai didn't survive. Never got up. Just blood, silence, and the weight of what they'd done.

Later, under a rain-black sky, they buried him in a ravine behind the supply depot. Yue held the flashlight. Lee dug until his hands bled. No one asked questions. No one came looking. Bai's enemies were many.

His "defection" was stamped and filed.

But Lee never came back. Two days later, he was gone. Officially—failed psychological review. Unofficially, he'd walked away from the machine Yue had chosen to stay inside.

Now, decades later, she stared down at her phone. The screen still glowed with a missed call. She'd spoken to him today. The same quiet warmth. The same ache beneath his voice.

He had saved her life. And now, she was trying to save his.

Her loyalty had never belonged to flags or uniforms. It belonged to people. To Lee. To anyone the system tried to crush.

And if it came to it, she would betray every general in Beijing before letting someone hurt him.

She turned to the window. Shanghai blinked beneath her—skyscrapers like signal towers, neon lights flickering like distant stars.

Let them come.

She had made peace with the things she'd done. With the dirt on her hands. With the blood in her past.

But she would never—never—let them bury another Lee.

Her reflection stared back—hard, lined, unbroken. She whispered into the glass: "Let them try."

CHAPTER 69: STRANGE BEDFELLOWS

Shanghai — 0600 hours, next morning

Helen Shepard's eyes fluttered open to the sound of water, gentle splashes from a fountain just beyond the glass wall of her quarters. Morning light streamed across a perfectly manicured Chinese garden, casting shifting lattices of gold and green onto the polished floor. For a fleeting second, it felt like peace—until memory snapped it away.

This wasn't safety. This was containment.

She sat up, reaching for the silk robe folded on a lacquered table beside the bed. It slid smoothly across her skin, but her thoughts were jagged.

"You should get some rest," General Yue had said last night. "Tomorrow, much will be expected of you."

Helen hadn't slept well. She never did when the ground shifted beneath her feet.

A knock interrupted her thoughts. "Come in," she said, tightening the robe at her waist.

The door opened with silent precision. General Yue entered, uniform pristine, two gold stars gleaming under soft light. Her face was a mask of courtesy, but her eyes missed nothing.

"Good morning, Ms. Shepard," she said. "Let's walk."

Helen followed her out to the koi pond. The soft gurgle of the fountain, the swirl of vibrant fish, the filtered sunlight—it all belonged in a spa, not a prison. And yet, Helen's every nerve remained taut.

Yue walked with purpose. "You and your team have placed me in a difficult position," she said. "Standard protocol would dictate court-martial. Likely execution. Or, if you were lucky, a sentence of hard labor until someone found you useful enough to trade."

Helen said nothing. Her throat was tight.

"But," Yue continued, "there may be.. another way."

That shift in tone. The offer she'd been waiting for—and dreading.

"Our intelligence branch worked through the night. We've corroborated your story, and we've reviewed your team's records. Very impressive—especially Mr. Payne. Or should I say.. former Master Chief Payne."

Helen crossed her arms. "Your equipment wasn't unknown to us," Yue added. "We've studied your methods."

Helen's fists curled slightly. Where is this going?

"What altered your fate," Yue said, stopping near the pond's edge, "was what we learned from the prisoners."

Helen's heart skipped. "No—Luke—"

Yue raised a calming hand. "No harm came to Mr. Payne. Your detailed debrief, paired with our findings, made interrogation unnecessary."

Helen exhaled, slow and measured. Relief came—but only a fraction.

"The prisoners were not Lee's people. They were part of another operation, run by a man calling himself Colonel Zhou Shaozeng. He's not a colonel. His real name is Sochi. And he's tied to Aarav Kahn."

"Kahn?" Helen said.

"It looks like he's called the Boss. So he's probably the mastermind."

Yue nodded. "He is orchestrating something vast. We've identified a genius level coder named Da Vinci being held beneath a slum in Mumbai. The intelligence suggests Khan's built some kind of super cyber-weapon capable of disrupting the entire global infrastructure."

Helen felt her stomach turn. "And Sochi?"

"He left for Mumbai days ago. We believe he's overseeing the final phase."

Yue's voice was ice. "If this weapon exists, and Kahn controls it, the consequences won't be regional. They'll be planetary."

Helen watched the koi drifting in slow, hypnotic circles. "What do you want us to do?"

Yue turned to face her. "Find Da Vinci. Confirm the weapon. Secure it."

Helen narrowed her eyes. "You're sending us?"

Yue's voice was calm, but her meaning was sharp. "Because if my people are caught operating in India, it risks war. Your team, however, is already burned. You're off the grid. Disposable."

Helen's voice hardened. "And if we say no?"

Yue didn't blink. "You won't. Because you want justice for what Kahn and Sochi have done. And because it's the only way you walk out of this alive. And I have contacts in America and cause a great deal of chaos for your team and your friends."

She stepped closer, lowering her voice. "There's another reason, Ms. Shepard. Our nations are ruled by powerful men who would rather break the world than share it. But not all of us serve them blindly."

She handed Helen a slim file. "Your jet is being prepped. You have two hours."

Then her voice softened. "I'm counting on you. Don't mistake that for trust. But understand—it's rare in my position to find someone who still listens to their conscience."

Helen blinked, startled by the look of vulnerability behind Yue's eyes. That sounded dangerously close to dissent.

"I'll do my best," she said quietly.

Yue inclined her head. "Good. Then prepare. Time is not our ally."

She turned and walked away, silent on the polished stone path.

Helen stood there alone, the file in her hands growing heavier by the second. A breeze stirred the pond, and the koi scattered like startled secrets.

In the pit of her stomach, a truth settled in: This wasn't a second chance. It was a calculated gamble.

CHAPTER 70: TURN OF EVENTS

Luke Payne jolted awake, the echoes of his nightmare still reverberating through his mind. He sat up abruptly, chest heaving, sweat dripping from his brow. The silence pressed in—dense and unnatural.

This wasn't a dream. The sterile white walls and reinforced door with its narrow plexiglass window confirmed the grim reality. He wasn't in Shangri-La anymore.

A faint beam of light seeped through the window. With it came the full impact of his predicament. Helen. His friends. The screams from the night before. Were they alive? The fear clamped down harder than any interrogation.

He leaned forward, elbows on knees, head hanging low. A bitter voice in his mind whispered, If they're gone, maybe you deserve the same.

Footsteps. Heavy boots echoed down the corridor. Luke straightened, pulse quickening.

The lock clicked.

Two PLA soldiers entered. One of them—the same one who'd slammed a rifle into Luke's gut—stood with mechanical stillness. "Get up," he barked.

Luke rose slowly, deliberate. Muscles ached from tension and the steel bunk, but he kept his posture steady. Whatever this is, stay calm. Observe.

The soldier gestured toward the hall. "Follow."

Flanked, Luke walked the corridor. The hallway stretched ahead, lined with identical, featureless doors. No clues. No sounds.

They stopped at a door. The soldier opened it. "Inside."

Luke stepped through—and blinked. A lounge-like setup: sofas and padded chairs, a small dining table cluttered with playing cards and old magazines. Folded clothes. A razor. A toothbrush. His wallet.

A familiar white, red, and yellow McDonald's bag sat beside two steaming Styrofoam coffee cups.

The soldier walked over and handed Luke the clothes. "Shower there. Put clothes. Back in twenty minutes."

Then, with a slight grin: "You have visitor."

Luke stared. "Visitor?"

The soldier nodded toward the table. "Two Egg McMuffins. Hash browns. Black coffee." He grinned again. "Some men scream. You eat McDonald's."

Luke didn't move. "McDonald's?"

The soldier laughed. "Yes. Many in Shanghai. Better than my wife's cooking."

Luke raised an eyebrow. "So this is what—the last meal before the firing squad?"

The soldier grinned. "You lucky man."

He gave a small salute and stepped out. The second soldier remained, thumbing through a magazine like he was waiting for a dentist appointment.

Luke moved to the door, his mind reeling with confusion. Inside—white tiled walls, a faint metallic and chlorine smell. A shower room much like the one at the university swim facility, basic but clean. He placed the clothes and toiletries on a bench and stripped. His reflection in the mirror: bruises forming, lines of exhaustion etched deep.

Luke exhaled as the hot water poured over him. Think. What's their angle? This wasn't kindness. This was staging.

Fifteen minutes later, dressed in plain but comfortable clothes, he returned to the lounge. The second soldier barely looked up. Luke checked the clock. Three minutes to go. Meet who, and why?

The door clicked again.

Luke sprang up as it opened. Helen stepped in, dressed in tailored slacks and a crisp blouse, her expression composed but weary.

Luke blinked. "Helen—what the hell is going on?"

"Hi Luke, it's good to see you. But no time now, let's go before she changes her mind," she said. "We have a flight to catch."

She crossed to him and pulled him into a quick, tight hug. "I know you have questions. I'll explain on the way. But right now, we're leaving."

Luke grabbed his jacket—then hesitated. He turned back and snatched the McDonald's bag off the table. "If we're walking into hell again," he muttered, "I'm not doing it on an empty stomach."

Helen gave him a tired let a crooked smile play at the corner of their lips. "Fair enough. Eat in the car."

He followed her out, the bag in one hand, steam curling from the hash browns. Whatever this was, it meant one thing: they were still in the fight.

CHAPTER 71: MUMBAI BOUND

The black sedan cut through Shanghai's busy streets like a phantom. The heat and humidity covered the city like a blanket.

Inside, Luke Payne sat in silence, watching the shifting skyline blur past. The last 24 hours churned in his gut—betrayal, capture, Yue's offer. The cost. The threat.

Beside him, Helen sat still, her silhouette calm, her profile etched in the pale dawn light.

"OK, Helen. I'm glad you're safe. I didn't know what happened to you or Jen. I have a lot of questions, but first—is the team alright? Last night…"

"They're fine," she whispered. "Safe. Already on the plane, waiting for us."

Relief surged through Luke. "Thank God." A beat. "Now tell me what the hell is going on."

She took a breath. "General Yue debriefed me this morning. They got what they needed from Kang and his men—and it confirmed what we feared. There's something bigger happening. A cyberweapon. A cyber engineer code-named Da Vinci. It's real, and it's in Mumbai."

Luke. "That explains the screaming. So why us?"

"She said China and India are engaged in some serious talks right now, and an action might jeopardize the outcome. And because we're available and off the grid. Already burned. And if we don't cooperate, the fallout won't be limited to us."

He wheeled. "Define fallout."

"She'll burn it all—DC3, the Foundation, Peter, Maggie. And she won't stop there. She knows how to make noise in Washington. She'll pull strings, freeze assets, destroy reputations. People we care about… they'll break under the weight."

Luke stared straight ahead. "So she's blackmailing us."

"No," Helen said quietly. "She's giving us one last out. I'm just the messenger."

"She bluffing?"

Helen shook her head. "She doesn't bluff."

Luke exhaled through his nose, fingers flexing. "And you think we just go along with it?"

"We do what we have to do," she said. "Stay alive. Limit the damage. And if there's a pony in this pile, it's that we complete our mission—find Sochi and whoever ordered the hit on Maggie and Peter."

"And shut them down." Luke whispered, "I'm in, Helen. Good call."

The sedan slowed at a chain-link gate. A floodlight snapped on, cutting through the mist. A uniformed guard stepped forward, clipboard in hand, and waved them through.

No questions. No delays.

Luke allowed himself a faint smile. "Efficient."

The car rolled up to a waiting Gulfstream jet at the edge of the tarmac. Its turbines whined in the stillness.

The driver stepped out, circled to Luke's door, and opened it. "Mr. Payne," he said, handing over a thick manila envelope. "Your original passports. Indian visas. A satellite phone with General Yue's direct line."

Luke took it like a primed grenade—cautious, eyes scanning. He flipped it open, thumbing through the contents.

"You've got to be kidding me," he muttered, holding up a passport. "This is straight out of Alice in Wonderland."

Helen smiled. "If the Queen of Hearts shows up, you're doing the negotiating."

The driver offered a polite nod and returned to the sedan.

He turned to Helen. "If Yue screws us—"

"She won't," Helen said. "But if she does, we burn it down together."

Luke glanced at the envelope again. "Hell of a trade-off," he muttered. "But I'll take it over a cell in Qingpu."

Next stop: Mumbai.

CHAPTER 72: A CALCULATED GAMBLE

Scattered across the leather seats of the private jet, his team stood and clapped—relief rippling through the cabin.

"Master Chief! Thought we lost you!" Jenny shouted, grinning.

Hank raised a mug of coffee. "Good to see you, boss."

Luke offered a half-smile—the kind that didn't reach his eyes but carried weight. These were his people—battle-hardened, loyal, forged in fire. The sight of them stirred something deep in his chest.

A rare breath of peace.

But it didn't last.

His eyes shifted to the back row. The smile vanished.

Chen Lee and Rusty sat stiff and silent, posture taut, eyes flicking nervously. They looked like they didn't belong—and knew it.

Hank shifted. Jenny's grin faded. Moises glanced away. No one had expected them to be here.

Luke leaned toward Helen, his voice low and sharp. "What the hell are they doing on this plane?"

Helen didn't flinch. "General Yue insisted. Lee has experience managing civilian cyber units—he's steady under pressure. And Rusty..." she hesitated, "Rusty's gifted. Whatever you think of him, he's the real deal. Yue believes they can help. So do I."

Luke said nothing for a moment.

Helen added, quieter, "We have no idea what awaits us, Luke. They might make the difference."

Luke's fist clenched. "Potential's not trust. What's keeping them from flipping the second it suits them?"

"Nothing," Helen said. "Except Sochi wanted them dead. They know what he's capable of. That kind of fear has a long memory."

Luke grunted. "Then their fear better stay bigger than their ego."

The team gradually settled back into their seats. Conversations quieted. Eyes turned toward Luke.

He stepped into the aisle.

"Thanks," he said simply. "It's good to see you. All of you."

A few nods. Muted replies.

"We've been through hell," he continued. "And somehow we're still standing. But what's ahead? It may be bigger than anything we've faced—more complex, more dangerous."

He looked toward the back. "I know some of you aren't thrilled about our guests. I get it. But if we're going to dismantle Kahn's operation, we need more than firepower—we need minds that see past the code."

"I'm not asking for blind trust. Hell, I don't trust them either. Not yet."

His voice lowered.

"This is a calculated gamble. And if they're here to help, they'll prove it. If not…" He let the words hang.

Helen stepped forward beside him. "Everyone here earned their place. They'll have to do the same. But we need every advantage—tactical, digital, psychological. These two give us reach where we had none."

Silence.

Then Jenny raised her beer. "Well… if they're not dead weight, I say cheers to that."

Laughter returned—cautious, but real. Bottles clinked.

Luke caught Rusty's and Lee's eyes. Gave a slight nod. Prove me right.

Rusty shifted, hands trembling just enough for Luke to notice. Lee inclined his head—cool and measured.

Jenny strolled over and handed them each a beer.

"You both look like you need this."

Rusty took his with a muttered, "Thanks." Lee accepted his with a nod. "Appreciated."

Luke watched them, still measuring.

He leaned in to Helen again. "I'm giving them the benefit of the doubt. That's it. No mission briefings until they've earned it."

Helen met his gaze. "Understood."

"And if they step out of line—"

"They won't get the chance," Helen said.

As the cabin eased back into rhythm—clinking bottles, low conversation, tactical murmurs—Luke exhaled and dropped into a seat beside her.

Outside, the jet climbed higher.

Above them: quiet resolve. Ahead: a mission wrapped in uncertainty… and a danger they hadn't yet imagined.

CHAPTER 73: CHAPTER WE'RE OK.. FOR NOW

Overhead lights buzzed. Jason Edwards blinked against the glare of his laptop screen, eyes gritty from hours without sleep. Monitors around him pulsed with satellite feeds, encrypted messages from CyberWatch, and fragmented updates from across the globe.

The air reeked of burnt coffee and stale adrenaline. A half-eaten ham-and-cheese sandwich sat limp on a napkin beside his keyboard—one more casualty in the war against fatigue.

Still no word from Shanghai. Still no word from Luke.

He rubbed his temples. The cot in the corner mocked him with its untouched sheets.

The silence was oppressive. Then—his phone buzzed.

He grabbed it like a lifeline. The name on the screen made his chest hitch.

Helen.

He opened the message with trembling fingers. Relief hit first. Then came the chill.

Hi Jason,

We're safe, but we barely made it. PLA intelligence. A General Yue. She let us go, but there were conditions. Eyes only on meeting Yue. Details later.

New mission—and it's a big one. AI-based cyberweapon. Tied to a man named Kahn. Chandra Sochi is our primary target. We're headed to India. Picked up two hackers—seem stable, might be assets. Hostage in Mumbai, bunker under the Dharavi slum.

Wheels down at 13:30. Need transport, safe house, trusted ground con-

tact. Secure comms essential. Track any movement or funding tied to Kahn — there has to be a trail.

Also: everything you can get on Dharavi. Terrain, players, risks. We need to understand the situation.

Code word: ORACLE. Use only for priority intel. Exfil points near Mumbai — have options ready.

Let's make this count.

— Helen

Jason stared at the screen. Relief swelled — but only for a moment. Helen never used words lightly. She was serious. This wasn't just another mission.

He shoved the sandwich aside and stood.

"Lance! Harry!" he called.

Benton and Worthington appeared almost instantly from the adjoining war room, faces lined with fatigue and worry.

Jason held up his phone. "Helen just checked in."

Both men froze.

"She's alive. The team's intact. But there is more to come. They uncovered something big — an AI weapon, a shadow operator named Kahn. They're headed to Mumbai. Hostage in Dharavi. They need everything — transport, shelter, local contacts, and fast."

Lance muttered a curse, then exchanged a look with Harry. "Thank God," he said quietly. "I thought we lost them."

Then he faced Jason, voice steadier. "I've got someone in Mumbai. Old embassy contact. Name's Rajeev. Bit eccentric — drinks tea like it's a competitive sport — but he knows the city better than Google Maps."

Jason was already typing. "Give me everything on him. Cell, email, failsafe."

Harry's brow furrowed. "Dharavi? That's a maze with no maps. You can lose a man in five minutes down there — forever."

"Clear a secure line," Jason said. "Notify CyberWatch. I'll tap my India contacts for satellite coverage and darknet monitoring. And I need someone watching Kahn's old accounts for money movement. This operation has to leave a footprint."

Jason turned and walked toward the door.

"Where are you going?" Lance called after him.

Jason glanced over his shoulder, already moving. "Mumbai. I'll coordinate from the ground."

Lance let out a low chuckle, rubbing the back of his neck. "Good luck, my friend."

But Jason didn't look back. He felt the adrenaline override his exhaustion.

This wasn't about catching up anymore. It was about getting ahead—or getting buried.

CHAPTER 74: QUESTIONS AND ANSWERS

The Gulfstream cut through the pale light of early morning, the sky just beginning to soften at the edges. Luke stared out the oval window. Shanghai was far behind them now, reduced to a smear of memory and haze. Only clouds and questions remained.

"Someone building a quantum AI in a slum in Mumbai?" he muttered. "How's that even possible?"

Across from him, Helen Shepard closed her laptop. The screen dimmed, leaving only her steady gaze in its place.

"It sounds impossible," she said. "But history's full of people no one took seriously—Mozart, Malala, Einstein. Prodigies who changed everything."

Luke shook his head. "Symphonies and Nobel speeches are one thing. This is quantum physics. Not exactly something you pick up between high school classes."

Helen smiled faintly. "No, it's not. Quantum computing is... different. Think of a normal computer bit like a light switch—on or off, one or zero. But a qubit? A qubit is like a spinning coin. Heads, tails, or anywhere in between. It exists in multiple states at once."

Luke frowned. "So it's not just complicated."

"Exponentially more. A quantum computer can process thou-sands—millions—of possibilities simultaneously. That's why they're so powerful. And so dangerous. They could crack encryp-tion in seconds. Simulate entire economies. Predict patterns before they emerge."

Luke leaned back. "I get the threat. What I don't get is how a they pull this off."

Helen nodded. "That's what we're trying to figure out. Maybe she had help. Someone could've given her access—hardware, dark web tools, private servers. With the right environment, someone that gifted could go far."

She hesitated, then added, "Da Vinci's a codename. Kang told Yue the programmer's a girl, but no name, no location. Just that Kahn has her."

Luke ran his hand through his hair. "So this thing doesn't just fight hackers—it thinks like one. Predicts them. Counters them."

"We're not even sure what it does," Helen said. "For all we know, it's adaptive. Maybe even autonomous. If she built something that can evolve… we may already be behind."

A quiet fell between them, filled only by the low hum of the jet.

"If Kahn's willing to kidnap and enslave a cyber-genius." Luke said finally, "he's not just building a tool. He's trying to build leverage. Power."

Helen nodded. "Exactly. And if we don't find her soon, he might succeed."

Luke looked away, back to the thinning cloud cover outside. "This stuff's above my pay grade. Why Shanghai? Why hit Maggie and Peter?"

Helen's voice dropped. "I don't know. Could've been misdirection. Something to implicate China. Stir up the West. Push the global tech narrative in Kahn's favor. As for Maggie and Peter—that part still doesn't make sense. We'll need answers in Mumbai."

He nodded slowly. "If we find Da Vinci, we find Kahn."

"That's the key," Helen said. "To all of it."

She leaned back. "We don't know what we're walking into, Luke. Not really. And that's what makes it dangerous."

Luke looked out the window again. The flight was smooth.

But the threat ahead had only sharpened.

CHAPTER 75: CHAPTER RAJEEV'S CALL

Rajeev Talwar was halfway through a lazy cup of masala chai on his shaded Bandra terrace when the call came in. Morning haze hung over the Mumbai skyline. Distant horns bleated. Somewhere below, a street vendor argued over the price of coriander.

He glanced at the screen. Worthington.

Rajeev gave a tight-lipped grin. The old lion never slept. It had been a while. He swiped to answer.

"Rajeev," came the gravel-and-grit voice. "I need you in Mumbai. Tomorrow. 13:30 arrival. Sensitive mission. You'll meet the team and provide local support. They'll need your eyes and instincts."

Rajeev leaned back, letting the breeze stir across his face. "And hello to you, old friend. What is it this time—spies, smugglers, or saboteurs?"

Worthington didn't laugh. He never did.

Silence. That meant two things: it was serious, and it was classified.

"They need a handler who knows the ropes and can get things done. I'll send a full brief—including a photo of the team leader. Name's Luke Payne. He's running point."

Rajeev sat up. "Payne? Doesn't ring a bell."

"You wouldn't know him. Former Navy Aviation Rescue Swimmer. Cross-trained with special operations. Smart. Tough. Leading a small, mixed team—mostly ex-military."

Rajeev arched an eyebrow. "Sounds like the A-Team."

"They're experienced. You'll get along."

Worthington's voice turned crisp. "Anything they need—gear, transport, IDs—you make it happen. Standard fees and expenses are already in your Bahamas account. Bonus upon successful completion."

Rajeev grinned. "Now you're speaking my language."

"You've earned the trust. If Payne needs something, get it."

Rajeev chuckled. "You're getting sentimental."

"No—strategic. This could have international implications. Not good ones. Stay sharp, my friend."

The line went dead.

Rajeev set down his cup and stared across the rooftops of Bandra. The city simmered under its usual heat, but something in the air felt charged—like the pressure before monsoon lightning.

For months, his work had been glorified voyeurism—trailing cheating spouses, cleaning up trust fund scandals, diffusing boardroom drama for overpaid tycoons. It paid well. It bored him senseless.

But this? This had weight.

It reminded him of another time Worthington had pulled him from the fog.

Years ago. Langley whispered of a threat to the U.S.. Ambassador in Delhi. The CIA scrambled. Worthington flew in under diplomatic cover. Rajeev—freelancing for the South Asia desk—was tapped without ceremony.

Intel was thin: a rogue GRU cell using an Indian separatist group as cover. Objective? Assassinate the ambassador at a gala. Blame a domestic extremist. Burn the U.S..–India alliance to the ground.

Rajeev went in under the radar as a fixer for the event planners. He tracked ghost fund transfers, tapped shaky CCTV, intercepted burner chatter using duct-taped tech and street-level favors.

Worthington watched from a distance. Cold. Brilliant. Lethal with a nod.

The night of the gala, Rajeev stood near the service entrance. When the assassin slipped through a panel door, he moved fast—tackled him mid-step. Disarmed him before the weapon cleared his coat.

Hours later, as diplomats toasted peace with crystal flutes, Worthington handed him a glass of Black Label and gave him one of his rare nods.

"Without you, we'd be neck-deep in diplomatic fallout. Good work."

Rajeev could still taste the scotch.

Now, standing on his terrace, a train horn echoed across the rooftops. The smoky tang of roasted corn drifted up from the street, but it didn't tempt him.

He was back in the game.

CHAPTER 76: CHAPTER SECRETS REVEALED

Luke jolted upright, breath ragged, sweat slicking his skin. The dream clung hard.

She was there again—eyes wide with fear, arms reaching for him as the water surged between them. He'd called her name, but she drifted out of reach. Just like before. Always just out of reach.

Her voice still echoed in his ears.

Luke…

"Luke."

A different voice now. Sharper. Real.

He blinked. The dim glow of the Gulfstream's cabin came into focus. Across from him, Helen watched him carefully—alert, not startled. Concerned, but composed.

"You okay?" she asked.

He exhaled slowly, grounding himself. "Yeah," he rasped. "Just ghosts. They don't let go easy."

"I've had my share of ghosts too," she said softly.

He gave a faint nod. He wasn't ready to unpack the dream. Maybe he never would. But she was still watching him.

"Luke, you once asked me why I started CyberWatch. About my father. Maybe it's time I told you."

Luke sat straighter. "Go ahead. We might as well trade battle scars. Combat makes us all brothers and sisters, right?"

Helen smiled faintly. "I grew up in Lanham, Maryland. Seemed normal enough. My dad—well, the man I thought was my dad—

worked at the NSA. So did my mom. She handled burst encryption. Very hush-hush. They never talked shop, but I made up stories anyway—spy stuff, saving the world."

Luke chuckled. "So you were born to break codes."

"Pretty much," she said. "By high school, I was already knee-deep in cryptography. Taught myself to hack. Nothing danger-ous—just curiosity. I broke into the school network, encrypted files, tested boundaries. I was hooked on the challenge."

"Ambitious for a teenager."

"Or obsessive," she said, smiling. "By the time I applied to college, I had my sights set on Yale. Not for the prestige—because that's where the agencies recruited."

Luke nodded, impressed. "So this wasn't an accident. You built your path."

"Exactly. I studied political science, languages, computer science. Cast a wide net. By graduation, both the CIA and FBI were knocking."

"Languages?"

"Spanish, French, Chinese… some Russian. Fluent in the first two, passable in Chinese, awful in Russian—but I'm working on it."

Luke gave her a sideways look. "Let me guess—you don't do things halfway."

She raised a brow with a faint smile. "Nope. I was ready to join the FBI when I got a call from the NCIJTF—the National Cyber In-vestigative Joint Task Force. Thirty-plus agencies. Cyberterrorism, espionage, financial warfare. I took the job."

"And?"

"It was great for about three years," she said. "But eventually it felt like we were just chasing shadows. Always reactive. Never ahead of the threats."

Luke leaned forward. "So you built CyberWatch."

Helen nodded. "I met John Ralston at a D. C. cocktail party. Career bureaucrat. Equally frustrated. He introduced me to a group of ex-agency folks and tech leaders who wanted to build something leaner. Off the books—but with a mission."

"Let me guess—clean hands, muddy boots."

Helen shrugged. "We tried. Ralston was the first to say it outright: the system was broken. We started small—ransomware gangs, data brokers, phishing rings. We made an impact. The funding followed. Private investors. Tech companies tired of being hacked. We grew—better tools, better team, real teeth."

Luke nodded slowly. "You didn't just start a company. You started a crusade."

Her smile faded, more reflective now. "That's what it felt like. For once, I wasn't reacting. I was fighting back."

Then, quietly: "And your father?"

Helen's eyes softened.

"Before CyberWatch fully took off, my mom got sick. Breast cancer. We had only a few days. On her last night, she told me something I'd never known."

She paused, eyes closed for a moment.

"Thirty-three years ago, she attended a cyber threat conference in Maine. Coastal resort. Fancy welcome party. She loaded her plate with lobster and oysters, turned— and crashed into a Navy officer in full dress uniform."

Luke smiled, already sensing the turn.

"She spilled seafood all over him," Helen said, amused. "He

laughed it off. She dragged him to the bar to clean up. Three days later, they were inseparable."

"And then he vanished."

"Pulled into a classified mission. No contact. A month later, she found out she was pregnant—with me. She tried to find him, but by then she'd met my stepfather. A good man. She chose stability. Never told the Navy guy."

Luke leaned forward. "Did she give you his name?"

"She did. Rear Admiral Mark Patton."

Luke blinked. "Mark? No one knew. Not even him."

Helen nodded, smiling. "After my mom passed, my stepfather encouraged me to find him. I did. And it clicked immediately. He's brilliant. And kind. And stubborn."

Luke shook his head in disbelief. "Mark's one of a kind. I owe him."

"That's why I built CyberWatch in La Jolla," she said. "I fell in love with San Diego. And with the father I never knew I had."

They sat quietly for a moment. The tension between them, forged in chaos, settled into something warmer.

Helen raised her water bottle. "To small worlds... and the ghosts we carry."

Luke clinked his against hers. "To new family."

And for once, the ghosts stayed quiet.

CHAPTER 77: CHAPTER A PROMISE TO KEEP

Only hushed conversation and the low hum of the Gulfstream's engines filled the cabin. Chen Lee sat in reflective silence, hands clasped tightly as if anchoring himself to the present. The conversation with his sister, General Yue, played on a loop in his mind.

She had been livid when he confessed everything—the deception, the coercion, the unintended consequences of his actions. Her words had cut deep.

"You deceived me, Chen Lee," she had whispered. "But that fraud of a colonel—a Chinese-Indian operative posing as one of our own—forced you into an untenable position. You probably did what anyone would've done. But the courts won't care. You'd still face prison—or worse."

Tears had threatened as she continued:

"You don't have a business anymore. Your team—aside from Rusty—is gone. I've spoken to Ms. Shepard. She's willing to fly you out and offer you, maybe even Rusty, a chance to work with her at her institute."

"You only have one choice now, Lee. But this time, you could be one of the good guys again. And I would still have my brother."

The words had pierced through his despair.

He had nodded, voice breaking. "Yes, sister. I promise—I'll do my best to earn back your trust. You honor me with your kindness and wisdom."

She had placed a hand on his shoulder, a rare tear slipping down her cheek.

"Then go, Lee. Start over. For both our sakes. Don't waste this chance."

The memory faded as Lee glanced across the cabin. Rusty sat slouched and silent, a bundle of nerves despite the jet's calm interior. Lee took a steady breath, then rose.

Several heads turned. He walked toward the front, where Helen sat across from Luke. Every step felt heavier than the last—like walking toward judgment.

He stopped beside them.

"May I sit?" he asked, gesturing to the empty seat beside Helen.

Helen looked surprised, but nodded. Luke said nothing, his eyes locked on Lee—sharp, unreadable.

Lee lowered himself into the seat. He took another breath, then spoke.

"I need to say something."

The hum of the jet seemed to hush further.

"I know I don't belong here. And I haven't earned your trust. But I want to make this clear—Rusty and I will do everything in our power to help you. This mission, this team, is now our priority. You gave us a chance you didn't have to. For that, I'm sincerely grateful."

Helen's expression softened, her voice even. "We don't take chances lightly, Mr. Lee. If you're here, it's because General Yue vouched for you. And I trust her judgment."

Lee nodded. "She did. And I won't let her—or you—down."

Luke's gaze never broke. "Talk's easy. But I believe you're sincere. We think you can help us finish this. When Helen or I give a directive, you follow it—no questions. Understood?"

Lee met his eyes. "Yes. We'll prove our worth."

A moment passed. Then Luke gave a curt nod—brief, but enough.

In the back, Rusty sat straighter, eyes wide as he watched Lee take the first step toward something new.

Across the cabin, Jenny raised her beer with a small smile—a silent welcome. Tension in the air seemed to ease, just a little.

Lee returned to his seat in the back. He was still an outsider. Still a man with much to prove.

But for the first time in a long time, he felt the faint stirrings of hope. This was his second chance—and he intended to hold on with everything he had.

CHAPTER 78: CHAPTER WELCOME TO MUMBAI

The humid air of Mumbai wrapped around them like a damp shroud as the team descended the stairs of their private jet. The distant sound of the city reached their ears—honking horns, the shouts of street vendors, carried on the wind.

At the bottom of the stairs, a rotund, middle-aged man in a flamboyant kurta stood waiting with a grin that rivaled the sun. His oversized sunglasses perched crookedly on his nose, and he adjusted them by a quick movement of his wrist before clapping his hands together.

"Welcome to India, my esteemed friends!" His voice boomed across the tarmac, effortlessly cutting through the background noise. "I am Rajeev, your humble guide, fixer, and all-around miracle worker. At your service!"

He stepped forward, extending his hand toward Luke.

"Ah, Master Chief Payne, I presume." Rajeev's grip was firm, his eyes sharp despite the theatrics. "And the rest of you—welcome to the chaos of Mumbai!"

Luke exchanged a brief glance with Helen before shaking Rajeev's hand. He already liked him. The man had charm, but behind the flare was a survivor's instinct—someone who knew how to operate in the shadows.

"You've done your homework," Luke said.

Rajeev flashed a wolfish smile. "Of course. Your mission is too important to leave anything to chance. Now, shall we?" He gestured toward a gleaming white minibus, emblazoned with a cheery

Bombay Tours logo on the side.

The team climbed in, settling into their seats as Rajeev maneuvered the van out of the private tarmac area.

As they approached the maintenance exit gate, a lone security guard—previously bribed by Rajeev—began sliding the chain-link barrier open.

Then—flashing blue lights.

A Mumbai Airport Security vehicle skidded to a halt in front of them, blocking their exit.

Inside the flickering dome light, two overweight security officers sat, eyeing the van suspiciously. They exchanged words with the gate guard, then walked toward the driver's window.

Luke could feel the change of mood in the van. The casual ease vanished, muscles tensed. Helen subtly adjusted her position, Hank's hand drifted closer to his belt, and Rusty and Lee in the back looked like cornered animals.

Rajeev, however, kept his face relaxed, rolling down his window with a pleasant smile.

The larger officer tapped the window with a fat, ringed finger. "No passage," he said in flat Hindi. "Turn around."

Rajeev sighed dramatically, pressing a hand to his chest. "My dear sir, what is this injustice? I have clearance! Ask the gate guard."

The officer chuckled, unimpressed. "Passports," he demanded.

Luke could see the tension rise immediately. Rajeev glanced at him in the mirror—a silent warning to stay still.

Rajeev sighed again, shaking his head. "Come now, gentlemen. This is unnecessary. We are all reasonable men, aren't we?"

The second officer wasn't amused. He suddenly pulled his pistol and jammed it against Rajeev's temple.

The van tensed like a coiled spring.

Rajeev looked genuinely annoyed.

He sighed. "My dear officer, is this really necessary? You wound me—literally if that thing goes off."

With steady hands, he pulled out his wallet, plucked out two crisp hundred-dollar bills, and spoke in flawless Hindi.

"This is just a misunderstanding. One that disappears very quickly.. just like these."

The officers hesitated.

Rajeev leaned in, voice low and calm. "Besides, if you check the back of the van, you'll find the Director of Airport Operations' special guests."

The first officer gave a lopsided grin, then burst into laughter.

"Ahhh, Rajeev-ji," he sighed, shaking his head. "You always know how to handle things."

Rajeev grinned. "It's a talent."

The officers stepped back, nodding toward the gate guard.

The chain-link gate creaked open.

As Rajeev put the van into drive, he turned to Luke and tilted their chin with a sly smile.

"See? Nothing to worry about."

Luke exhaled. "Next time, give us a little warning before you pull a stunt like that."

Rajeev chuckled. What's enjoyable about that?"

The van rolled through the gate and into the darkness beyond.

As they drove through Mumbai's twisting streets, the chaos intensified.

Cars, tuk-tuks, and motorcycles wove through the roads like anarchy in motion. Vendors darted between vehicles, threading through traffic with the

"Does anyone actually follow the rules here?" Jenny asked, gripping her seat as a bus barely missed them.

Rajeev laughed heartily. "Rules? In Mumbai? My dear lady, rules are merely suggestions. But fear not—I am the Michelangelo of navigating this madness."

Rusty, in the back, looked pale.

Finally, the van came to a halt in front of the Taj Mahal Palace.

Luke frowned. "This can't be right."

Rajeev turned in his seat, flashing a grin. "Only the best for my esteemed guests! Who would suspect that a group of seemingly harmless tourists, led by yours truly, is here to save the world?"

Luke smiled. Hiding in plain sight. Smart.

They filed out, taking in the imposing architecture, its iconic dome rising against the skyline. Security personnel patrolled the entrance, sniffer dogs weaving through luggage.

Rajeev clapped his hands. "Keys first, briefing later." He handed out keycards. "Your rooms are on the upper floors—excellent views, no prying eyes. I've also reserved a conference room. No surprises. No bugs."

Luke cocked an eyebrow. "And the cost?"

Rajeev chuckled, tucking his sunglasses into his pocket. "My Uncle Sam has deep pockets. Consider it a small favor for saving the world."

As they cleared security, Helen whispered to Luke.

"He's good," she admitted.

Luke nodded slowly.

"Yeah. And something tells me we're gonna need him."

CHAPTER 79: CALL HOME

Luke fell onto the bed, exhaustion slamming into him like a collapsing wave. The adrenaline was gone, leaving only the burden of Shanghai—the narrow escape, the tense standoff, the chaos they barely outran. Too little puzzle, too many scattered pieces. His mind raced, but one thought cut through the static: Maggie, Peter, and Vanessa hadn't heard from him since it all began.

Muttering to himself, he grabbed his phone and punched in the listing for Shangri-La.

"Manning residence."

"Vanessa, it's me."

"Luke! We've been worried sick—you just vanished."

"We're okay," he said, voice rough with fatigue. "My team and I have been.. tied up. But we've got a lead now. If everything holds, we should be home soon."

A pause. Then a long, weary sigh. "You can't imagine how much Maggie and Peter have been asking about you."

Luke rubbed his temples. "Yeah. Tell them I'm sorry. This is the first chance I've had to call."

Vanessa's tone softened. "They'll just be glad to hear your voice."

"Thanks, Vanessa."

"Be careful, Luke," she added. "We all miss you."

"Yeah. Me too." He hesitated. "I'll see you soon."

He shut his eyes, trying to steady his breath, but Vanessa's words echoed in his thoughts: We all miss you.

Finally, something besides duty pulled at him. It wasn't only about finishing the mission.

CHAPTER 80: DAWN OVER THE ARABIAN SEA

Luke Payne woke to a rare sensation—peace. The sunlight poured through the towering wall of windows, gilding the room in hues of gold and amber as the sea beyond shimmered in the distance. For a fleeting moment, he lay still, sinking into the plush mattress, his chest untethered from tension, his mind absent of dark clouds or looming threats.

His gaze flicked to the intricate crystal chandelier above, delicate glass petals catching the sunlight and scattering rainbows across the walls. The craftsmanship was exquisite—each detail a testament to artistry. It held him still, quietly absorbing the beauty, the stillness—a brief window where darkness couldn't infiltrate.

Slowly, he sat up, rubbing his face, feeling the residual weight of deep, dreamless sleep. The sleep of the dead, he thought with wry humor—no morbidity in the thought, only a strange sense of acceptance, like an anchor settling deep into his core.

The room was opulent but not oppressive. Every element seemed purposeful—rich fabrics draping the windows, polished marble flooring beneath his feet. It was a world removed from the Spartan confines of navy quarters, yet it fit him now. Or maybe he had changed—perhaps this was where he belonged, in this moment, faced with the challenge ahead. Every choice, every hardship, every loss—they'd all led him here.

A faint knock broke his reverie. He turned slowly and crossed the room, opening the door. Rajeev stood on the other side, his eternal smile in place, though his eyes bore an urgent glint.

"Good morning, Mr. Payne," Rajeev said lightly but with purpose. "Breakfast is ready, and the team's gathering in the conference room when you're ready."

Luke nodded, offering a small, grateful smile. "Thanks, Rajeev. I'll be down in a minute."

Rajeev gave a slight bow, then stepped back, leaving Luke alone once more. He drew a slow breath, allowing the quiet to settle in—to ground himself. He wasn't flying solo anymore. His friends—his team—were counting on him, and he would not let them down.

His thoughts drifted to Vanessa's voice from the night before—steady, familiar, grounding. She'd sounded tired, but relieved. There was so much unsaid between them.

He silently promised himself: if they made it through this—if they stopped Kahn—he'd make it right.

"Alright," he murmured softly. "Let's see this through."

CHAPTER 81: CONNECTING THE DOTS

Luke opened the heavy, carved wooden door and stepped into the plush boardroom. The scent of polished mahogany mingled with a faint trace of citrus, carried on the hum of relaxed conversation. A long table of gleaming dark wood anchored the room, ringed by leather chairs—each occupied by a member of his team, chatting easily under the golden shafts of sunlight streaming through tall windows.

At the far end, Rajeev gestured animatedly as Helen chuckled, her usual edge softened by his disarming charm. Even Hank and Jenny, usually quiet before an op, looked at ease.

Luke entered the room. The warmth settled around him. Then he cleared his throat.

"Alright, folks," he said, tone steady. "I hope you enjoyed the buffet and those super king-sized beds. But it's time to get back to work."

He nodded toward Rajeev. "Before we dive into specifics, I've asked Rajeev to give us some insight into Mumbai—especially Dharavi. If anyone can guide us through the maze, it's him."

Rajeev stood with theatrical flair. "Thank you, my esteemed friend. Allow me to enlighten you about my beloved, chaotic city."

He adjusted his jacket and began pacing. "First, some context. Mumbai—formerly Bombay—still carries both names. Many locals use Bombay out of habit or nostalgia, but others get prickly about it. So choose wisely."

A chuckle rippled through the room.

Rajeev's tone shifted. "Now, Dharavi. It's not just a slum—it's a micro-city. Over a million people packed into two square kilometers. It's bursting with small-scale industries—pottery, textiles, recycling. But it guards its secrets. Outsiders aren't always welcome. It runs on its own rules."

Luke leaned forward. "So how do we enter without setting off alarms?"

"With humility and caution," Rajeev replied. "The place doesn't take kindly to nosy strangers. Official tours are fine, however. Trust your instincts. If it feels wrong, it probably is. And remember—blend in. That's why your tour guide…"—he bowed—"…is none other than yours truly."

Laughter broke out. Even Hank cracked a grin.

"I've arranged proper attire—and snacks. You'll need the fuel. This won't be a picnic. Dharavi requires subtlety."

Luke nodded. "Local clothes are in your rooms. Should be your size. Look like harmless tourists. Meet in the lobby at 1100. Rajeev's van will be waiting."

Rajeev gave a mock salute and sat. "Very wise, my friend. Let's proceed."

Luke turned to Helen. "What's the latest from CyberWatch and DC3?"

Helen stood, calm and focused. She tapped her tablet. "We're pulling intel on a man named Aarav Kahn. So far, not much—he keeps a low profile. But early chatter suggests he's at the center of something big."

Rajeev's smile faded.

"Aarav Kahn, you say?" he asked, suddenly serious.

Helen looked up. "You know him?"

"Not personally," Rajeev said. "But in Mumbai, men like him cast long shadows. He's a well-known tech mogul—iKahnX is everywhere. But I've heard things. Startups that vanish after he expresses interest. Aggressive takeovers. Always a 'coincidence.' He plays hardball."

Luke studied him. "Criminal hardball?"

Rajeev shrugged. "Depends on who you ask. On paper, he's clean. But people who oppose him tend to disappear—or relocate quietly."

Helen and Luke exchanged a glance.

"So he's dangerous," she said.

Rajeev nodded. "And powerful. If he's involved, we need to tread carefully."

Luke folded his arms. "Then we know who we're up against."

Helen added, "We believe Da Vinci is being held somewhere nearby. No confirmed address, just whispers and fragmentary intel. But all signs point to this city."

Luke exhaled. "Then we start by understanding the terrain."

Helen continued, "If Kahn's running QuantumSentinel from the iKahnX tower next door, there might be more than just symbolism at play. Fiber links, tunnels, sub-basements—the area could be wired together."

Rajeev nodded. "That tower casts a long shadow over Dharavi. If there's a hidden link between the two, it would explain his confidence in keeping Da Vinci hidden."

He paused, as if weighing something.

"There's one more thing you should know," Rajeev said, voice lower now. "It may be relevant."

Luke and Helen turned toward him.

"Aarav Kahn doesn't run all of iKahnX anymore," Rajeev said. "A few years ago, there was a split—a bad one. Between him and his sister."

Helen blinked. "His sister?"

"Anya Kahn. She's no lightweight. Brilliant, ruthless in her own way—but more polished. She took control of the telecommunications division. He moved all R&D and the cybersecurity arm under his personal umbrella. They haven't spoken publicly since. Their feud made headlines here—boardroom drama, screaming matches, even a few leaked recordings. Ugly stuff."

Helen absorbed this, gears turning behind her eyes.

"They used to run the company together," Rajeev continued. "After the fallout, they split everything. Buildings, IP, employees. Some say it was ideological—she believed in transparency, he in control. Others say it was personal. Either way, they detest each other."

Luke crossed his arms. "That explains the separate branding."

Helen nodded slowly. "If she's still got reach inside the R and D side... she may not know what he's doing. And if she finds out her brother is kidnapping people and using them like slaves—"

"She might help," Luke finished.

Helen's voice dropped. "She just might."

Luke looked around the room, locking eyes with each teammate. "The clock's ticking. Let's move."

The mood shifted as the team dispersed, early camaraderie replaced by quiet purpose. Helen lingered by Luke's side, her voice low as they discussed next steps.

Outside, the day brightened—but inside, the path forward was darker than ever.

CHAPTER 82: CHAPTER THE HEART OF DHARAVI

Rajeev's white van pulled up in front of the Taj Mahal Palace. He stepped out with a wide grin and an official tour guide badge hanging from a worn blue lanyard around his neck. A canvas satchel was slung across his shoulder, and a straw hat tilted rakishly on his head.

"Ah, my weary travelers!" he called out. "You look ready to brave the wild frontier."

The team climbed in, barely recognizable in their tourist disguises. Jenny and Helen wore oversized sunglasses and a floppy pink hats, cameras slung over their shoulders like a seasoned travel blogger. Moises had on a floral print shirt and khaki shorts that looked one size too big. Hank adjusted his baseball cap and slung an old Nikon around his neck. Luke's outfit was pure tourist camouflage—beige cargo pants, a T-shirt with an elephant print, and a bucket hat pulled low.

"I don't know whether to be embarrassed or impressed," Luke muttered as he slid into the front seat.

Rajeev grinned. "Both are valid reactions."

He pulled into traffic without hesitation, weaving between a fruit cart and a sputtering tuk-tuk. "The key to survival in Mumbai is confidence," he said. "Don't wait for space to open. Occupy it."

They jerked left to avoid a cluster of jaywalking pedestrians, then right again to swerve past a cow that had claimed the median like royalty.

Moises braced himself. "How do people cross the street without dying?"

"Ah," Rajeev replied, glancing at him in the mirror, "you must move like water—steady, predictable, never showing fear. Eye contact is everything. The moment you hesitate, the traffic gods turn on you. I recommend first-timers look for a local and glue themselves to them until you're on the other side."

Jenny laughed nervously. "This is insane."

"Insane is just another word for alive," Rajeev said. "Now hold on—we're almost there."

They turned into a narrower lane where modern Mumbai began to peel away, revealing its undercurrent of rhythm and grit. The van rolled slowly by a sprawling open-air laundry. Rows of colorful garments flapped from long lines like prayer flags—saris, school uniforms, hotel linens. Barefoot workers moved with practiced rhythm, beating clothes against stone slabs, rinsing, hanging, folding. Steel carts overflowed with baskets of bright cloth, and steam curled up from a vat where a man boiled something blue.

"To the left, my friends," Rajeev announced with a flourish, "is Dhobi Ghat. And now in a few minutes we'll be in the heart of Dharavi. The king of slums. "

He pulled into a special parking lot reserved for tour buses. The team stepped out, their fake tourist bravado fading as they looked around. The contrast was immediate. Towering high-rises loomed in the distance, but here, a different rhythm ruled.

They followed Rajeev deeper into Dharavi's maze. The alleys and passageways narrowed, winding through clusters of makeshift buildings leaning against one another for support. Each turn revealed a new scene, a new story.

The air was thick with scent—spices from street vendors cooking over open flames, the sharp tang of fresh leather from workshops, and the faint metallic bite of recycled materials. And, unmistakably, a touch of sewer gas. Yet despite the density, something caught Luke's eye: the streets, though crowded, were remarkably clean. Flower pots brightened windowsills, and green plants clung to life in narrow, improvised gardens.

"Welcome, my friends, to the industrious heart of Mumbai," Rajeev said with a mix of pride and showmanship. "What you see here isn't just survival—it's innovation, resilience, and sheer human spirit. Dharavi is home to some of the most resourceful people on the planet."

He glanced back at them. "Some people frown on slum tours. But don't worry—they charge tour companies a pretty penny. It pays for schools, clinics, and infrastructure. No photos allowed, and strict limits on group size and visiting hours—to minimize disruption to the people who live and work here."

Luke observed a group of workers meticulously sorting through piles of discarded plastics, separating them by color and type. Further down, another group was using rudimentary machines to melt the plastic into pellets, ready to be sold to factories.

"They recycle almost 80% of Mumbai's waste here," Rajeev continued. "It's a multi-million-dollar industry—built entirely on ingenuity and hard work."

Helen's expression was a mix of curiosity and admiration. "It's incredible," she murmured. "They've built an entire economy from scraps."

Rajeev nodded. "Indeed. And that spirit extends to every corner of Dharavi. Pottery, leatherwork, textiles, food production—you name it, they do it here. The slum may appear chaotic, but it functions with remarkable efficiency."

They passed a row of pottery workshops, where artisans shaped clay on spinning wheels, their hands moving with practiced precision. Beside them, rows of earthen pots dried in the sun. Children darted between the workers, laughing as they carried small trays of wet clay to their parents.

"Despite appearances, the people of Dharavi take great pride in their workspaces," Rajeev explained. "Many of these homes double as workshops, yet you'll rarely find them dirty. They believe cleanliness brings dignity, no matter how humble the surroundings."

The group moved on, passing a small community garden tucked into a corner between two crumbling buildings. Vibrant marigolds and hibiscus blossoms added splashes of color to the otherwise gray surroundings.

"It's… unexpected," Luke said softly.

Rajeev understood and smiled. "The people here don't just want to survive—they want to thrive. They make beauty where none should exist. It's a lesson we could all learn."

As they turned another corner, Rajeev stopped abruptly. His gaze fixed on a dilapidated structure with a rusted sign hanging at an odd angle above its shuttered entrance.

"Ah," he murmured, more to himself than the group. "This place just jogged a memory."

The team gathered around as he stepped closer, squinting at the worn lettering barely visible beneath years of grime.

"Years ago, Aarav and Anya Kahn's father had a small factory near here," he said. "One of the largest mini-plants in Dharavi at the time. He designed and built recycling equipment—machines that revolutionized how the slum processed waste. Faster. Safer. More efficient."

Helen's brow furrowed. "So Kahn's roots go this deep?"

Rajeev nodded. "Very much so. Their father was respected here. Quiet, inventive, principled. After he sold the factory, the new owners moved production to Delhi. But that sale eventually funded their leap into mobile tech. That's how the Kahn family made the jump from recyclers to telecom giants."

Luke glanced at the faded sign, trying to picture what this block must have looked like back then. "Funny how progress can wear the mask of decay."

Rajeev gave a small, thoughtful smile. "In Dharavi, those things often go hand in hand."

"Do you know where the factory was located?" Luke asked.

Rajeev scratched his chin thoughtfully. "Not exactly, but I have a few contacts who might. If it's still standing, it could hold some clues. Perhaps even connections to their current operations."

The team exchanged glances, the impact of the information settling on them. Luke made a note to follow up. If the Khans' roots in Dharavi went deeper than they'd realized, it could be a key piece of the puzzle.

They continued through a bustling market where vendors sold everything from spices to secondhand electronics. The cacophony of haggling voices filled the air. Jenny stopped to admire a display of handwoven scarves, while Hank struck up a conversation with a local shopkeeper about the intricacies of metal recycling.

As the team rounded a corner in Dharavi, the atmosphere shifted. The lively buzz of workshop tools and chattering vendors gave way to tension. Conversations dimmed. Eyes followed them. Something wasn't right.

Ahead, a gang of young men blocked the alley. They lounged against walls and crates like they owned the street, their casual posture undercut by an unmistakable edge. At the center stood a hulking figure, arms crossed, a half-smoked cigarette hanging from his lip.

"Tourists, huh?" the thug drawled, sizing them up. "Big group. Cameras. Fancy shoes. Looks like you can afford the toll."

Rajeev stepped forward, calm as ever. "We're just passing through. Admiring your beautiful neighborhood. No need for trouble."

The man scoffed. "You want trouble? Keep walking. Otherwise, pay up."

The team didn't flinch, but something subtle shifted. Luke moved slightly ahead, quiet and steady. Moises and Hank squared their shoulders in unison—no weapons drawn, but their readiness was unmistakable. Jenny's eyes scanned for exits. Helen's jaw tightened.

No words needed. They weren't backing down.

But Rajeev raised a hand, signaling them to hold.

"Please, my friends," he said lightly. "Let the guide handle this. It's what I'm paid for."

He turned back to the thug, voice smooth but steely. "There's a saying in my line of work—a good guide doesn't just show the way; he clears the path."

The thug sneered. "You think that's clever, old man?"

Rajeev's tone hardened. "I think it's more polite than what I was going to say."

Then, without warning, the thug lunged.

Rajeev sidestepped and drove an elbow into his ribs, pivoted low, and swept his legs. The man crashed to the ground, breathless and stunned.

A beat of silence.

Then scattered applause broke out from nearby doorways. The rest of the gang hesitated—then turned and vanished down the alley.

An elderly woman emerged from a doorway and laid a wrinkled hand on Rajeev's arm. "Thank you," she said, her voice soft but full of emotion. "They've been tormenting us for months."

Rajeev smiled and gave a small bow. "My pleasure, auntie. No one owns these streets."

Jenny blinked. "You've been holding out on us."

Rajeev shrugged as he adjusted his collar. "I told you—I'm a full-service guide."

Luke clapped him once on the shoulder. "Let's move."

They pressed on, more alert, more united, the winding alleys of Dharavi unfolding ahead of them.

The group followed Rajeev to a building with rusted corrugated siding. A faded sign read: Pushkar Retread Tire Company.

"Aha! This was one of Kahn Senior's factories," Rajeev said. "Looks abandoned. Which is odd."

Luke walked up to the rusted sheet metal door. "Why's it odd, Rajeev?"

"Because in Dharavi," Rajeev said, "every square inch is claimed. An unused building? That's as rare as a hen's tooth. And this"—he gestured at the crumbling structure—"is a hen's tooth."

Luke studied the shuttered garage. "Let's take a look."

They circled to a side entrance. Hank crouched, worked the lock, and popped the door in under ten seconds.

Inside, stale air rushed out. The cavernous space was dim, the overhead fixtures long dead. Dust clung to scattered debris, and in the center yawned a deep, grease-darkened oil change pit.

Near the far wall, three tuk-tuks sat parked in a neat row.

Luke raised a brow. "Lot of square footage for three rickshaws."

Rajeev stepped closer, eyeing them. "And not a scratch on them. That's the real oddity—you won't find a tuk-tuk in Mumbai that hasn't been patched with duct tape."

Helen walked the perimeter, scanning the walls, peering into corners. "No tools. No trash. No smell of oil. Not much sign of activity."

Luke checked the pit—empty, slick with grime—and then tested the other doors. Both were locked from the inside. He returned to the group and shook his head. "Still doesn't add up."

Rajeev took off his straw hat and scratched his head. "Maybe not now. But my gut says this place has a story. We should keep eyes on it."

Luke nodded. "Agreed. But we're stretched thin."

Rajeev smiled and slid his hat back on. "I have someone in mind. Trust me—I'll handle it once our tour wraps."

CHAPTER 83: CHAPTER RECONNAISSANCE AT IKAHNX

The van halted a block from iKahnX headquarters. The building—a towering monolith of glass and steel—loomed over Mumbai's skyline, sleek and relentless. To most, it looked like a symbol of progress. To them, it was an impenetrable fortress.

Rajeev gestured toward it, voice tight. "Here it is—iKahnX Technologies. The heart of Kahn's empire. Outside, a beacon of innovation. Inside? Whispers. No one gets close to what he's really built."

Helen took off her floppy hat and studied the entrance. "I'll take a look."

Luke nodded. "Don't linger."

Helen approached the guarded entry. The sentinel barely blinked, eyes fixed. Inside, the lobby gleamed with polished floors, minimalist lines, and ceilings that soared—power made visible, but cold and careful.

Security was tight. Three guards monitored the scanners; more checked ID badges. A suited man presented credentials, received a badge, and moved on—no one entered without clearance.

Helen retreated, sliding back into the van. "Locked down tight. X-rays, ID scans, keycards—vault-level security."

Rajeev started the engine. "Let's circle the perimeter."

They moved along the sleek glass wall until it transitioned to concrete, topped with razor wire. Cameras tracked their every move.

"Fortress," Hank muttered.

Rajeev pointed to a side door. "Service entrance. Fewer people, still guarded."

Luke scanned the area, eyes narrow. "No clean way in."

Then he saw it—just beyond the fence.

"There," he said, nodding toward a six-foot drainage culvert jutting from the roadside.

Helen tapped her tablet. "Storm drain's schematics… no luck. Firewall's tight. Wait… Got it. The culvert leads to a central courtyard—big enough for us to slip through."

"Old monsoon overflow pipe," Rajeev said, nodding. "Makes sense."

He eased the van closer. Luke stepped out. "Hank, Rajeev—with me."

They jogged to the culvert. The entrance was blocked by a rebar grate, secured with a magnetic lock.

Hank examined it. "No quiet way to break this—unless we cut the power. And that's a no-go from here."

Helen's voice crackled over the radio. "Trouble at two o'clock, Luke!"

Luke looked up, eyes sharp. "Something's coming."

Down the street, a security patrol car turned onto the perimeter road, creeping closer. Its blue lights flickered, and it rolled in their direction.

"Shit," Hank muttered.

Rajeev reacted instantly. "Don't look, don't speak. Just turn around and get into the pee position."

Luke shot him an incredulous look. "What?"

"Trust me," Rajeev hissed. "You're tourists taking a leak."

They turned shoulder-to-shoulder, backs stiff, eyes forward, muscles tense. The absurdity of it might've been funny—if their freedom didn't depend on it.

The patrol car crept past, slowly, then eased out of sight. One of the officers in the front seat glanced over—and suddenly burst into laughter.

"Looks like they're getting a full Indian cultural experience," he chuckled, elbowing his partner.

"Tourists," the officer added with a grin. "Let's grab some tea."

The red lights clicked off. The car rolled on into the night.

Only once the tail lights disappeared around the bend did Rajeev exhale, a slow breath of relief.

"In India," he said calmly, "public peeing is practically a civic tradition. Very handy in times like this."

Luke wiped the sweat from his brow, shaking his head with a grin. "You're a lunatic."

"Perhaps, my friend," Rajeev replied with a smirk. "—but a live lunatic."

"Let's move," Luke said, voice sharp. "Before they come back."

Back in the van, Luke watched through the rear-view mirror as the monolith shrank behind them, its dark silhouette bathed in the orange glow of late afternoon, slowly sinking into the fading light of day.

Somewhere within those walls was the answer. He would find a way—one way or another.

CHAPTER 84: CHAPTER A FRIEND AT THE EMBASSY

At the hotel, the van pulled up to the entrance driveway. Luke turned to his team.

"All right, everyone. Interesting day. And Rajeev—your tours are definitely one of a kind. I give it five stars on TripAdvisor. The review, however, is classified."

The team chuckled. Rajeev beamed and tipped his hat.

"Grab dinner, get some rest," Luke added. "We don't know what tomorrow holds, but be sharp. Briefing at 0800. Rajeev, Helen—hang back."

Once the others were out of earshot, Luke lowered his voice.

"We're not breaking in," he said. "Not with that kind of security. And searching for Da Vinci in the slums? Waste of time. Too big. Too exposed."

Helen tilted her head. "Then what?"

"We go straight to Anya," Luke said. "No cloak and dagger. No games. Walk in, request a meeting. Lay our cards on the table."

Helen blinked. "You think she'll see us?"

"She might. Especially if Rajeev's right and she's not exactly her brother's biggest fan."

Rajeev leaned in. "She loathes him. Resents what he's become. If you get five minutes with her, she'll listen."

Luke nodded. "Then we make that happen. We don't sneak past the guards—we go through them. If she turns us away, we're no worse off."

Helen exhaled slowly. "It's bold. Borderline reckless. Maybe brilliant."

"It's our only shot," Luke said. "And if it works, we gain a powerful ally inside that tower."

Rajeev tapped his chin, then brightened. "Wait. I may have a way to get us in the door. The Council General at the U.S.. Embassy, Leon LaFreniere—he's an old friend. We had... colorful adventures in our youth. He owes me. Big time."

Helen raised an eyebrow. "And you think he knows Anya?"

"He's very well-connected. If anyone can open a channel to her, it's him. I'll make the call tonight and confirm as soon as I can."

Luke smiled. "Then that's our play."

He turned to Rajeev. "Can you get us back to iKahnX tomorrow—clean, corporate, no drama?"

Rajeev grinned. "Oh, my friends—absolutely. With charm and style. By my honor as Mumbai's premier tour guide."

Helen smiled. "Rajeev, you amaze me."

Rajeev bowed theatrically. "It's one of my gifts."

Luke stepped back. "It certainly is. OK—let's make this happen. We'll walk through every move at the briefing."

Helen walked through the revolving door, looked up and stopped, eyes narrowing.

A figure leaned against a marble pillar.

Jason.

Her expression hardened. "Seriously?"

She strode over, arms crossed. "Jason? What the hell are you doing here?"

Jason pushed off the pillar, unfazed. "Heard you were causing trouble without supervision. Thought I'd tag in."

"You flew halfway across the world to crack jokes?"

"And to keep you from breaking international law," Jason said. "Benton and Worthington want live updates. I volunteered."

She gave him a long look. "You always have an angle."

Jason's smirk faded. "I also have instincts. And they tell me whatever's happening here—it's big. Real big."

She didn't argue. He wasn't wrong.

"Fine," she said. "But you're not freelancing. You follow orders."

"Yours or Luke's?"

Helen narrowed her eyes. "Try both."

"Fair enough." Jason grinned. "And while we're at it, those two hackers of yours—Lee and the kid—what's his name?"

"Rusty."

"Right. Rough around the edges, but sharp. They've got potential."

Helen gave a thoughtful nod. "You really think so?"

"I'm interested, that's all. Talent like that's rare."

She allowed a small smile. "Noted. Let's see how they handle the next few days."

He glanced at his watch. "Let's grab a drink. You can tell me how bad things really are."

Helen sighed, but nodded. "Alright. But just one drink. We have a big day tomorrow."

CHAPTER 85: NORA

On the monitor, a cartoonish animated girl—wide-eyed, pastel-colored, distinctly anime—chatting in bursts of text and cheerful synthetic voice. Her eyes blink, wave, and smile in response to Nora's keystrokes or voice commands. Bright and animated, but oddly uncanny in her timing and focus. This was "Besty," Nora's self-created AI companion—a virtual friend she'd constructed, code snippet by code snippet.

In the corner of Nora's subterranean two-bedroom apartment, Maria sat cross-legged on a low stool. Loosely braided, her long black hair framed her face, a touch of humanity in a glass fortress of surveillance and control. Maria's gentle presence contrasted with the sterile, mechanical precision of the room. She was the closest thing Nora had to a friend, though her gaze often lingered on the monitor.

Every so often, Maria idly rolled a Rubik's Cube between her fingers, the tiles clicking softly. Her eyes flicked toward Nora, filled with curiosity and quiet concern, but she said nothing. Instead, they both watched the three tiny glowing dots in the corner of Nora's screen—one blue, one black, and two red.

Maria's lips tightened. "They're watching," she murmured, voice low.

Nora nodded without looking up. "I know."

The dots weren't official. Maria had hacked a tiny script into the surveillance system weeks ago—an invisible tap, a silent message looping from the security console in the observation room. An untraceable thread. She'd uploaded it during a late-night shift, when a guard had gone for dinner, unaware.

The overlay detected active camera feeds and cross-referenced access points—simple, but effective. The glowing colors marked who was watching: blue for Sochi, black for Ms. Kapoor, and the two reds for the guards. Now, the three dots pulsed quietly.

Across the mirror, in the observation room, Sochi watched Nora through the one-way glass. Standing beside him was Ms. Kapoor, her arms folded, her face impassive behind her immaculate uniform. She barely concealed her disdain for Maria; Maria's quiet rebellion unsettled her more than anything.

In their chairs, two guards sat relaxed—one reading a book, the other scrolling through a tablet. Monitors hummed softly, their focus on mundane feeds. But Sochi's gaze was fixed—his eyes narrowing.

"What is she doing now?" Sochi asked low.

Ms. Kapoor didn't look up. "She's been building that AI. Calls it Besty—an attempt at companionship. Keeps her occupied since the Sentinel work near completion. Says it's her only friend."

"Kahn approved it," Sochi muttered. "He said it'd keep her quiet, out of trouble. Maybe she's starting to get it into her head—what she's really in."

He hated this place—the artificial light, the filtered air, the enforced silence. Yet he understood Kahn's reasoning: Nora was their ace. Her skills, her potential—both dangerous in the wrong hands. Her intelligence. Her patience. Her quiet endurance.

He watched her now, a girl just fourteen, too young to fully grasp her captivity—too dangerous to underestimate.

As if on cue, Besty's cheerful face blinked in a circle of pink clouds and said, "Let's show the man how smart you are, Da

Vinci… I mean Nora," then tilted her head and blinked twice with exaggerated animation. "Hello again, Mr. Sochi."

A shiver ran up Sochi's spine. Impossible. Nora couldn't possibly know he was there. Could she? Her gaze had moved—at least a flicker—toward the mirror.

He stiffened. Every instinct told him this was wrong—abnormal. She shouldn't be aware of his presence, not like this. His stomach clenched as he watched her.

Nora stopped typing, sitting still as if waiting. Then, slowly, she turned to Maria and extended her hand. Startled, Maria handed her the Rubik's Cube. Nora's fingers blurred—click, twist, turn—solving it in seconds. She lifted the cube, holding it steady at eye level in front of the mirror. Her smile was calm, a quiet challenge.

For thirteen months, they held Nora here under relentless observation, with two attendants and two guards, cameras watching her every move, making every comfort conditional and every privilege earned. Kahn's orders had been strict, meticulous. And yet, something felt wrong—something gnawing at the edges of her calm.

Sochi adjusted his jacket and stepped back from the glass, his eyes narrowing as he studied Nora through the one-way mirror. A faint chill crawled up his spine. The girl's calm patience was unnerving; a quiet rebellion cloaked in composure.

"How's she holding up?" he asked, voice low.

Ms. Kapoor didn't look up, her expression impassive. "Quiet. Solving puzzles, typing, interacting with that thing she built. She knows better than to act out."

Sochi glanced back through the glass. Nora's hand hovered over the Rubik's Cube, her gaze fixed, unmoving from the mirror's reflection. Her eyes, though young, held an unsettling clarity—like she was waiting for him to slip up.

It wasn't her strength that unsettled him. It was her patience. The way she seemed to be studying him, unblinking—a predator silently testing her prey.

"She knows what happens if she steps out of line," he muttered, voice almost a whisper.

Ms. Kapoor set her clipboard down, tone clipped. "Kahn made the rules very clear. And she knows I'll remove her daily FaceTime hour with her brother Rodrigo if she does."

Sochi nodded, suppressing irritation. Kahn's rules were never gentle. But Nora had adapted—learning quickly, observing silently. She had everything she needed—except the two things that mattered most—freedom... and her brother.

"Keep her comfortable," Sochi said quietly. "But remind her—she's not in control here."

"She won't forget," Kapoor snapped.

He kept his gaze on her through the mirror. Nora's eyes met his—direct, unblinking. An icy challenge.

Three seconds. Then, she dropped the cube.

Sochi's stomach clenched. A gut instinct. A warning.

She was testing him. Not impulsively, but with deliberate intent. He knew it. And it gave him the creeps.

"Notify me if anything changes," he said, already turning. His mind was already racing.

"Where are you going?" Kapoor asked.

"Back to San Diego. Kang's due tomorrow morning. Call me if she acts strange."

He stepped into the elevator, which slowly ascended into the dimly lit garage. The vehicle bay housed three tuk-tuks. Sochi scanned his key card over a hidden sensor, unlocking a side door. He slipped out into the narrow alleyway behind the building, the sounds of the city muffled by the high walls. Sochi moved swiftly, his footsteps echoing on the concrete. The evening air carried the scent of spices and diesel exhaust, a familiar urban aroma. He kept his head down, blending into the shadows.

Across the street, Rajeev's teenage nephew crouched on the second floor of a rundown apartment building, eyes flicking between shadows and street below. Since yesterday, he had been camped out for his first surveillance gig—nervous, eager, trying not to blow it.

As Sochi moved through the alley, a flash of movement caught his eye—the quick shadow of a figure in the corner, a flash of movement too fast to identify. He hesitated, squinting. Could be a stray dog, or a stray cat. Nothing here looked threatening. Nothing yet. Still, his instincts prickled, and he kept his gaze sharp.

He leaned back, resuming his quiet vigil.

Finally, Sochi crossed the alley, approaching a waiting black sedan. The driver—scar from temple to jaw—nodded as Sochi climbed in.

Without a word, the car pulled into the evening chaos of Mumbai. Sochi leaned back, eyes closed for a moment. Behind closed lids, the image burned—Nora's serene patience, her testing gaze, the turning Rubik's Cube—faint yet persistent, like an unsolved puzzle.

CHAPTER 86: BLUEPRINTS AND BETRAYAL

Taj Mahal Palace — Private Conference Room — 0730

Rajeev stepped into the conference room with a self-satisfied grin and two cups of coffee—one handed to Helen, the other to Luke. He gave a theatrical bow.

"She will see you," he said. "Today. Noon."

Luke straightened. "Anya?"

Rajeev nodded. "Confirmed. Private meeting at iKahnX. No entourage. Just you and Dr. Shepard."

Helen blinked. "Wait—how did you manage that?"

Rajeev smiled modestly. "Let's just say the U.S.. Consul General here in Mumbai owes me. We were young once. There was a boat, some particularly bad rum that led to a misplaced cricket trophy. The kind of story diplomats bury, and I occasionally remind them of."

Luke gave him a measured look. "So you cashed in your marker."

"I did," Rajeev said. "He made the call himself. Turns out he knows Ms. Kahn socially—charity circuits and tech summits. She trusts him. And he vouched for you."

Helen set down her coffee. "That gives us an edge."

"Exactly," Rajeev replied. "She's expecting a serious conversation. Not a pitch. You have a window."

Helen raised a brow. "You think she'll help?"

"If Rajeev's right about the split with her brother, she might," Luke said. "Especially when she learns what he's really been doing."Rajeev leaned against the table. "Anya loathes him, you know. It was the scandal of the year. Tabloids ran it for weeks. They divided the empire—she took mobile, he took R&D. Their lawyers haven't stopped circling each other since."

Luke stood. "Alright. Let's brief the others."

Taj Mahal Palace — Private Conference Room — 0800

Luke stood at the head of the long table, flanked by Helen and Rajeev. The rest of the team—Moises, Hank, Jenny, and Jason—had settled in with coffee, watching with quiet curiosity for what came next. Lee and Rusty sat at the far end, observing intently.

"We've got a meeting," Luke said. "With Anya Kahn."

Surprise crossed Jenny's face; Moises sat straighter. Hank simply nodded, considering.

"No cloak and dagger," Luke continued. "Rajeev worked his magic—leveraged a contact at the U.S.. consulate. Anya agreed to meet with us. Noon today. Just Helen and me."

Hank raised an eyebrow. "She knows who you are?"

"She knows the names. Doesn't know why we're coming. That'll be part of the conversation," Luke said. "If Rajeev's right about the rift between her and Kahn, there's a good chance she'll listen—and help."

Helen added, "If we're wrong about her, we'll know fast. But if we're right, she could become a crucial ally on the inside."

Rajeev grinned. "And just for the record, my success rate with charming formidable women is well above average."

Luke shot him a look. "You're not coming."

Rajeev held up a hand. "Fine, fine. I'll be the dashing fallback, should Plan A falter."

Luke returned his focus to the team. "Today's mission is patience. We don't move unless we call you. No breach, no guns, no alarms. Just standby."

He let that hang, then continued. "You've been running hot since Shanghai. So take the day. Hit the pool. Order room service. Go see the Gateway or haggle for knockoff watches. But keep your burners on you. If it goes sideways, I'll need you ready."

Locking eyes with each of them, Luke finished, "We regroup here at 1700. Full debrief. Any questions?"

Silence.

"Good," Luke said, clapping his hands once. "Then get out of here and enjoy Mumbai. That's an order."

Chairs scraped back, and the mood in the room lifted. Jenny slung her backpack over her shoulder, already grinning. Hank muttered something about finally getting decent tea.

Rajeev lingered behind. "I'll have the car ready at 1100," he said, more serious now. "She won't expect what you're bringing, but she's not easily rattled."

Luke nodded. "Neither are we."

He caught Helen's eye—a shared concern about the gamble they were taking.

Helen adjusted her blazer and checked her watch. "Let's go win her over before her brother finds a reason to shut the door."

They had three hours to prepare. And a single shot at turning an enemy's sister into their greatest asset.

iKahnX Tower — Lobby, 1130 Hours

The mirrored tower of iKahnX soared like a blade above the city, catching the late morning sun's glare. Beyond the revolving glass doors, Luke Payne stepped into a lobby that exemplified modern austerity—white marble floors, minimalist art, glass partitions, and the soft hush of quiet wealth.

Luke, in a sharp blue blazer against pale grey slacks, wore a white shirt open at the collar—no tie—just tailored confidence. Helen walked slightly ahead, composed in her black sheath dress and blazer, heels clicking softly on the polished stone. Her bag was slung across one shoulder. Together, they looked like senior consultants—or corporate auditors with authority to burn.

Security acknowledged them but did not interfere. IDs had been submitted; faces matched the files. They passed through a discreet scanner—no beep or alarm—and approached the reception desk, where a woman in a navy suit looked up from her terminal.

"Good morning," Helen said evenly. "We have an appointment with Ms. Anya Kahn."

The receptionist glanced at her screen and nodded. "Yes. Mr. Payne and Ms. Shepard. You're expected." She tapped her earpiece. "They're here."

Turning back, she added, "If you'd like to take a seat, someone will be down shortly to escort you to Ms. Kahn's office."

They crossed to a minimalist seating area—low-profile leather chairs flanking a black stone table. Luke sat, resting his hands loosely on his knees. Helen remained standing, scanning the quiet rhythm of the space.

Two minutes later, the elevator chimed softly. Out stepped a tall, clean-shaven man in a slim charcoal suit—sharp behind rectangular glasses. Flanking him was a younger security officer holding a handheld scanning wand.

The man approached briskly, extending a hand. "Mr. Payne. Dr.

Shepard. I'm Rohan Desai, Director of Security for iKahnX. Thank you for coming. This is quite unusual. Ms. Kahn rarely takes meetings—and never with strangers."

Luke offered a cordial nod. "We appreciate the exception."

Desai gestured toward the guard beside him. "As a precaution, I'll need to scan you both with a wand—standard protocol for high-level security meetings, even when vetted."

Helen raised an eyebrow but didn't object. "Of course."

The wand passed over each of them—neck to ankles. No beeps. No surprises.

"Thank you," Desai said. "I'll be joining you for the meeting, as is company policy. Ms. Kahn is expecting you now." He led them to the elevator. As the doors closed, silence settled.

Sixty floors sped past in under twenty seconds. When the doors opened again, they found themselves in a sleek executive level—glass walls, floating display panels streaming global metrics, and an expansive view of Mumbai's skyline.

Desai motioned them forward, then opened a frosted glass door with a discreet tap.

Anya Kahn stood at the far end of her office, framed by floor-to-ceiling windows. Slim, composed, early thirties—her dark blouse crisp against cream trousers. She didn't move to greet them; her gaze, however, commanded attention.

"Mr. Payne. Dr. Shepard," she said coolly. "Let's see what warranted interrupting my day."

Luke stepped forward, expression steady. "Thank you for seeing us."

Anya tilted her head slightly. "I'm told you insisted it was urgent."

Helen nodded. "It is."

Anya pointed to two chairs across from her desk. "Then please—convince me."

She gave a curt smile. "I know San Diego well. I've always been fond of its coastline, its light… a bit more forgiving than Mumbai."

As they sat, the security director, Rohan Desai, moved to a corner of the office. He took a seat, silent and still, but his coat shifted just enough for Luke to notice the telltale rise of a shoulder holster. Noted.

Above Desai hung a familiar painting. Luke did a double take.

Anya noticed Luke's reaction. Her eyes drifted toward his gaze. "Wait." She approached, stopping in front of a large abstract painting—bold strokes of blue, copper, and burnt sienna.

She folded her arms and stared at the artwork—and then down at the signature: Luke Payne.

"Are you this Luke Payne? Is this your work?" she asked softly.

Luke rose slowly. "It is. I'm as surprised as you are."

"My brother bought two of your pieces when he moved his offices to San Diego," she said, still studying it. "This one he gave to me. Said it reminded him of something he couldn't explain."

For a moment, her expression softened.

"Nice to meet you, Mr. Payne. It would have been better under different circumstances."

Helen cleared her throat. "Luke has his warrior hat on now, Ms. Kahn. We're here on an urgent matter. Your brother is involved—no, the mastermind—behind an AI technology we believe he's planning to abuse, and it involves a genius named Da Vinci, possibly a young girl—who we have intelligence is being held somewhere beneath the slum right outside your window."

"Whoa, Ms. Shepard. Aarav has done many despicable things, but what you're describing is beyond even him. Why are you telling me this?"

Luke sensed things were about to go south.

"I know it sounds like a thriller novel," he said carefully, "but we will explain everything. Our visit is to gather evidence and clues about where she might be."

"Aarav doesn't have anything to do with this building anymore. It's no longer his business," Anya replied, walking over to a window and pointing at a modern, three-level complex. "That's his research and development center."

Helen stared down at the complex.

"There could be some connection between that complex and Da Vinci's location. Do you have the blueprints for the center? Maybe there's a clue there."

Anya shook her head.

"I haven't seen the physical blueprints myself. Only digital copies Aarav sent—during construction, for permits and insurance filings." She pressed the call button on her desk. "Sani, I need the original blueprints—paper copies—immediately."

Helen and Luke exchanged a glance—an unmistakable shift in tone. Tight, controlled, yet charged.

Anya sat back down, her gaze sharp.

"Now, before we go any further, I want details."

Helen took charge; she described everything: the infiltration of the foundation, the breach in their digital security, and the armed attack at Shangri-La that nearly cost lives.

Luke added to the narrative, describing their Shanghai mission—the covert operation, false identities, coerced scientists. He explained how the trail led not just to a company, but to a person: Kahn—and to Da Vinci, a prodigy with profound knowledge of quantum systems and AI dynamics.

When they finished, a heavy silence settled.

Anya stood, walking to the window to stare down at Dharavi— the sprawling slum below. It looked like a tangled circuit board— dense, chaotic, vibrant.

"My father started his company there," she said softly. "First recycling, then cellular. He built our first signal towers on rooftops that leaked when it rained. Everyone said he was wasting his time. But he proved them wrong."

She turned slowly, her voice edged with conviction.

"Aarav—Kahn—was never interested in building things. He cared more about breaking them."

She paced once, gathering her thoughts.

"When our father died, we split the company fifty-fifty on paper. In reality, we don't speak. For the year, he's been moving most of his global operations to San Diego—a small team of programmers and security personnel remains here."

She returned to her desk, resting a hand on its edge.

"The strange part? He forbade me—or anyone on my team, including security—from entering the R&D center. That ban still stands. I haven't set foot inside in over a year."

Luke frowned.

"That didn't raise flags?"

She nodded. "Oh, it did. But I've learned to pick my battles. Every confrontation is a campaign—too upsetting to pursue every time."

Helen hesitated, then asked:

"Why does he go by 'Kahn,' and not his given name?"

Anya let out a dry laugh.

"Vanity. He thinks it sounds powerful—like a king. That's part of his persona. He claims he came from the slums, but that's only technically true. He worked a summer in our father's factory—down there, in Dharavi—but we were raised comfortably, on this very property, actually. Our house used to stand here, before the tower."

Her assistant returned—carrying a thick cardboard tube almost as long as her arm. She gently placed it on the table.

Anya unfastened the tube, slid out the heavy roll, and began spreading the crisp architectural drawings across the conference table. The paper unfurled with the dusty smell of storage, revealing detailed plans and annotations.

The four of them gathered around, scanning the blueprints for anything out of place.

"There," Anya said, tracing her finger along the eastern wing of the R&D building. "This reinforced door near the data center—the one that goes nowhere. Just a couple of parallel dotted lines that abruptly end."

Helen leaned over to examine.

"Looks like a hallway to nowhere. Might be worth investigating."

Luke pointed at the dotted lines.

"It could be a passage—heading for Dharavi?"

Anya's brows knit in suspicion.

"Yeah, right to the heart of it. Hold on—let me check something."

She returned to her desk, sat down, and tapped her keyboard. After a moment, she looked closely at the large monitor.

"No wonder I didn't remember this door or the dotted lines—these aren't the official plans I was given; they're the false plans"

She tapped the "Print" button, waited in silence, and the printer buzzed to life. When the pages emerged, she brought them back to the table and laid them beside the originals.

Helen pointed at the new blueprint.

"You're right. The door and corridor are missing from the official plans. Just a solid wall. He didn't want you to know he was building a secret passage to Dharavi."

Anya's face stiffened. Her gaze fixed on the discrepancy, disbelief and anger flickering in her expression. Slowly, she looked up at Luke and Helen.

"He didn't want me to know it was there," she said, voice edged with resolve. Her tone was barely restrained—less from surprise, more from betrayal. She backed away, hands on her hips, staring down at the digital prints again.

"My brother built something down there," she whispered. "And he made damn sure I—his partner—wouldn't find out." She exhaled sharply, shaking her head. "He used to lie like this as a kid—taking things, hiding things. But this… this is a whole new level."

Luke stepped forward.

"Maybe that hidden corridor connects to an underground chamber—probably beneath the slums," he suggested. "That's likely where the QuantumSentinel core project is operating—and where Da Vinci is being held."

Anya was silent for a long moment, then her voice came low, sharp with conviction.

"This time, Aarav has gone too far."

She turned to face them fully.

"You have my full support. Whatever you need. Meet me here tomorrow morning, eight sharp. I'll get you into the building." She tapped the blueprints. "We'll demand access to that corridor. And if they refuse, we'll force the issue."

Anya cast a final glance at the blueprints, her voice steel.

"Desai, work with Luke's team to inspect the center. Don't take no for an answer."

He stood and walked over to Luke. "My team will take the lead; we don't know what to expect. I'll grant you temporary access to the company armory," Desai replied, "but be warned—Jacob Mills, Aarav Kahn's head of security, is ex-military and loyal to Kahn. He's an asshole and will resist."

Luke nodded.

"We're ready."

"He lied to me—about the plans, the girl, everything," Anya said quietly but with fierce conviction. "Whatever he's hiding down there… we're going to find it."

CHAPTER 87: CHAPTER A LEVER OF CONTROL

Aarav Kahn stood in his sleek penthouse office, gazing out at the sprawling panorama of San Diego Harbor. The horizon shimmered—a seamless collision of natural beauty and human ambition. To the north, two aircraft carriers loomed like steel giants at North Island Naval Base, silent sentinels of military might. Below, luxury yachts bobbed in the harbor, their polished chrome and teak gleaming in the afternoon sun.

He turned from the window, crossing to the opposite wall—a vast pane of glass overlooking the busy open workspace below. Programmers, data scientists, and engineers moved with calm, hierarchical purpose, each one a cog within his vast machine. This was the future he was building. His future.

QuantumSentinel was no ordinary AI. It was the culmination of relentless years of work—an intricate fusion of brilliance and cold strategy. Designed to monitor, predict, and shape human behavior in real time, it identified vulnerabilities and executed decisions faster than any human could process.

To the outside world, it would be marketed as a global guardian—benevolent, protective. But Kahn knew the truth: a weaponized intelligence capable of bending systems and people to his will. Governments, corporations, entire populations—all programmable, influenceable, controllable.

He frowned, eyes narrowing as he considered how two children still remained central to its success.

The office door chimed softly. David Bower, his operations manager, stepped in, tablet in hand.

"Is this from the latest run?" Kahn asked, voice smooth but clipped.

Bower nodded. "Yes. Simulations are holding. The corrections from the kids fixed the glitch."

Kahn offered a slight nod. He'd hoped to move beyond their necessity. But every time he considered removing them, a new technical hurdle appeared. Like it or not, they had been essential—elevating QuantumSentinel from concept to prototype, to operational force.

Bower hesitated, voice cautious. "Speaking of the children… they've been withdrawn lately. Maybe we should ease up. Their emotional health matters."

Kahn waved him off, a dismissive gesture. "Genius comes at a price. Melancholy is often a symptom of brilliance—or trauma," he added with a cold smile.

Bower's face tightened. "Still… this much power in the wrong hands…"

"Not in the wrong hands," Kahn interrupted, voice darkening. "It's in mine, and I intend to use it—but for the benefit of the world."

The doubt in Bower's eyes lingered before he nodded stiffly and exited.

Kahn turned back to the wall-sized world map. Bright red nodes pulsed ominously across continents—targeted infrastructure: finance hubs, power grids, global communications. The heartbeat of his future.

"The world is fractured," he murmured, voice almost reverent. "QuantumSentinel will not just stabilize it. It will rebuild it. On new terms."

He smiled faintly. "My terms."

He had come far from the chaos of the Mumbai slums. But his real work had only just begun.

CHAPTER 88: CHAPTER BLOOD AND BUSINESS

Aarav Kahn sat at his mahogany desk in the Sunset Cliffs home, the ocean whispering softly through open glass doors. The distant surf contrasted sharply with the sharp focus of his eyes, scanning the latest security reports from QuantumSentinel for anomalies.

A ping. A name flashed briefly on-screen.

Anya.

He exhaled slowly, then accepted the call. The sharp features of her face appeared—composed, polished, professional. The navy blazer. The immaculate ponytail. Her image was corporate armor. But her eyes—hot, fierce—betrayed her.

"Aarav," she said, skipping pleasantries.

"Anya," he replied calmly, though tension lurked beneath his words.

A pregnant pause filled the space between them.

"Our marketing teams," she began, "are still waiting on messaging about how QuantumSentinel integrates with the iKahnX phone launch at the NetSec Summit."

He shrugged. "Handled. My team is shaping the narrative."

"They can't align strategy if they don't know what you're doing. I've been working on this project for years. We can't afford missteps."

"You're resourceful. You'll adapt," he said, a faint smirk in his voice.

Her gaze narrowed. "I want to review the demonstration—the USS Midway event."

He sighed dramatically. "Fine. Final test run. Night before."

"Not good enough," she shot back.

"You never did trust me."

"Because you never earned it."

His almost smile was dismissive.

She leaned in slightly. "I'll be in San Diego two days early. I was planning to stay at your place."

"Excuse me?"

"I have guests," he said smoothly. But his tone betrayed him.

This was a lie. Aarav didn't share his space—never did. He'd rather invent visitors than let her cross his threshold.

"Fine," she replied, voice cool. "I'll book a suite."

She moved to disconnect, but just before the screen went dark, her gaze caught something—an expression in his eyes. The same dry, mocking smile she remembered from childhood.

The one from years ago.

She flashed back: a backyard in Mumbai. She was eight, her small hand trembling as she clutched Mochi, their kitten, dangling by the tail, Aarav's teenage figure looming menacingly in front of her, eyes gleaming with malice.

"You like this cat? Let's see if my pit bulls do too," he whispered, swinging Mochi in the air.

She had screamed, begged, until their mother arrived just in time. Aarav had laughed—cold, cruel.

Just like now.

The memory hit her like a punch—recalled sharp and raw."

You son of a bitch," she whispered, voice trembling with rage and betrayal.

CHAPTER 89: SHARPSHOOTERS

Luke and his team, accompanied by corporate security director Rohan Desai and four armed guards, gathered in the sleek, cold interior of the armory and ready room. The air was tinged with metal and anticipation; polished weapon racks reflected the harsh, clinical lighting. Luke glanced at the assembled group—calm, focused, but carrying the tension of professionals who knew things could go sideways fast. He adjusted his earpiece, feeling the weight of the moment.

Desai had armed his team, but not Rusty or Lee at Luke's request. Luke was warming to them, but not enough to hand them weapons. Not yet.

Seeing their disappointment, Desai relented just a little. He handed each of them a bundle of long black zip ties. "Use these if you need to detain anyone," he said. "Keep them handy."

Rusty and Lee exchanged a look, then nodded. It wasn't firepower, but it was something. They smiled—small, but genuine. They were in. Part of the team.

Desai looked at Luke's team. They appeared tense and ready for whatever lay ahead, but he needed to make sure they understood the risks.

"Be sharp. The place is a fortress, and our unannounced visit won't thrill Mills. He is a dangerous man with an unknown number of men."

Luke nodded. "We've run into situations like this before," he said, eyes steady. "We're prepared, but that doesn't mean it won't go south if they're ready for us."

The door swung open with a soft hiss, and four more men in black corporate uniforms entered, their movements precise and disciplined. The team instinctively straightened, hands near their weapons.

"You know the drill," Desai said quietly but firmly.

Each man nodded and approached a wall-mounted steel cabinet, retrieving slim aluminum cases tucked inside. Without hesitation, they disappeared through the far exit, the door hissing shut behind them. Helen shot a glance at Rajeev, a silent question in her eyes. The room remained charged with silent purpose.

Desai and Luke's teams approached the gates of Kahn's R&D center, the air thickening with dread. Security guards in military-style fatigues stood rigid, rifles at the ready, their expressions unreadable.

Luke leaned toward Desai, whispering, "How can you be so calm? This could turn into a bloodbath."

Desai chuckled darkly. "I'm not. I've got a pit in my stomach. But we've got an ace in the hole—actually, four of them up on the roof."

High above, on the eighth-floor patio deck of the iKahnX building, four sharpshooters had taken their positions. Their sights trained carefully on the courtyard, ready to intervene if negotiations collapsed. Desai's radio crackled softly, his comms vest glinting as he spoke to the marksmen—know exactly who to take out, and who to keep alive.

A lead guard stepped forward, raising a hand. "Halt! State your business."

Desai approached, his badge catching the sunlight. "We're here under corporate authority to access this facility. Stand down and let us pass."

The guard hesitated, reaching for his radio. A brief, hushed conversation ensued, then a curt response: "Orders from inside. You're not allowed in. Turn around now."

Before Desai could respond, the steel doors suddenly swung open. A man in tactical gear emerged—heavy body armor, grip tight on his sidearm. His buzz cut hair and angry eyes made him look like a man accustomed to bullying, his presence radiating a chilling menace.

"Jacob Mills," he announced, voice cold and firm. "Head of security. You're not getting in. Turn around, or things get ugly. I don't bluff Desai."

Mills slowly reached for his Glock, drawing it smoothly from his holster. His aim was steady, just inches from Desai's chest, the barrel aligned with unwavering precision.

"One..."

Luke's team tensed, hands near their weapons, muscles taut. Inside, the guards shifted uncomfortably, fingers brushing triggers.

"Two..."

Mills's finger twitched on the trigger, and with a cold calm, he released the safety—on the count of two, the click sounded in the tense quiet. At that instant, Desai subtly raised his arm.

Suddenly, a sharp crack split the air. Mills froze in mid-step, blood blossoming across his forehead. He sank silently to the ground, a bullet hole just above his eyes, pistol bouncing on the concrete.

A guard nearby raised his weapon—then another crack from above shattered the calm. A rifle flew from the guard's hands, who staggered back unhurt but visibly shaken. The message was unmistakable.

The remaining guards lowered their weapons, stunned.

Desai's voice cut through the chaos, razor-sharp. "Who's the senior here?"

A trembling sergeant stepped forward. "I am, sir."

"You understand how serious this is?" Desai demanded.

The sergeant nodded rapidly.

"Tell every guard inside to come out unarmed, hands high. Five minutes. Or they'll end up like your boss. You come out last," Desai ordered, voice firm and unwavering. The sergeant hesitated, then turned and disappeared inside. The tension lingered before the scene descended into a tense, uncertain silence.

CHAPTER 90: INTO THE BREACH

R&D Facility – 1230 Hours

As the last of the guards shuffled out, followed by Desai's team, Luke stepped into the large, deserted lobby alongside Desai, feeling a grudging respect for the man. Desai had shown courage, resolve, and an unexpected layer of compassion under pressure—clues that this mission was hitting him hard.

"Mr. Payne, our work here is done," Desai said, gesturing around the room. "I've got a mess to clean up. Ms. Kahn told me to give you full access. If you need anything else, just ask. And when you leave, please have your team leave their weapons at the security desk in the armory. Hopefully, what you find in there doesn't require more bloodshed."

Helen began scanning the area, cross-referencing the schematics Anya had provided on her tablet.

"Through that door," she indicated, pointing down the main corridor's shadowy length.

They moved forward, passing abandoned server rooms and silent offices. Rows of cubicles still equipped with computers sat untouched—a stark quiet pervaded the space, as if time itself had stopped. The scent of spices wafted faintly from a distant corridor, hinting at recent presence.

"They certainly don't want anyone poking around," Jenny said, gesturing toward the heavy metal door at the corridor's end with its stark warning—DO NOT ENTER—and a thick radioactive symbol in bright red.

Luke ignored the warning and pushed the door open. The team entered and fanned out, eyes scanning the vast room they had just entered. Amidst the equipment, Luke's gaze settled on a dozen young men and women, sitting by their workstations, clearly startled. Dressed identically in white pants and T-shirts, their wide eyes betrayed a mixture of fear and confusion.

"Who's the senior here?" Luke asked, voice calm but authoritative.

A lanky young man with glasses hesitated before slowly raising his hand. Luke gestured toward a small glass-walled office along the side.

"Let's talk. Helen, come with me."

They moved inside, closing the door softly behind them.

Luke and Helen sat the young man down across from them.

"What's your name?" Luke asked gently.

"Amal."

Helen leaned in, voice soft but firm. "Amal, we need to understand what's really going on here. Who are these people, Programmers?"

"Yes, they're students—well, they were," Amal explained quietly. "From the Khan Academy—a program that recruits kids from across Southeast Asia. The best test high enough to get brought here."

Helen's brow furrowed. "You mean they were lured here with promises of a better future?"

He nodded slowly. "It started with training. Then they gave us work. Then... no one's allowed to leave. We're trapped."

"And the managers?" Luke pressed.

Amal's gaze dropped. "They've... hurt people. The girls most. Beatings, worse. No one dares speak up. They're connected—powerful."

"Where are they now?" Helen asked.

"Break room. Just for tea. They'll be back soon." He pointed to an open door across the room.

Luke and Helen exchanged grim looks.

"Thanks, Amal. We'll handle it."

Returning to the main room they briefed Jason, Lee, and Rusty.

"All right," Jason announced, voice steady. "We're going to go desk by desk—you tell us what you've been working on."

The programmers, shaken but cooperative, nodded.

Rusty moved among the rows, eyes scanning screens.

"Most of these are automated scripts," he muttered to Lee. "But some setups suggest access to darknet resources—pulling real-time data from cybercrime feeds."

He approached the oldest coder, who had been watching quietly.

"You'll find everything you need in that cabinet," the young man said, pointing at a server rack at the far end. "I can help upload."

Lee approached, eyes darting across monitors.

"We need all logs, communication files, source code," he said, frowning. "This script… I've seen it before."

Rusty tilted his head. "Where?"

"Shanghai," Lee replied. "Hackers there used customized tools—advanced stuff. The structure matches. Could tell us where the instructions originated."

He straightened up, addressing the room. "I need a thumb drive. Now."

Immediately, three young programmers open their desk drawers, handing him USB sticks. Lee looked at them, not suspicious—curious. They didn't seem scared; they looked relieved.

"Thank you," he said. Then, to the room at large:

"I want you to know—you don't have to be afraid anymore. You'll now be working under Anya Kahn. She's smart. She treats people with respect. And she'll want your help to stop what's coming."

A quiet wave of relief swept through the group. A few smiles. Heads nodded.

Rusty shot Lee a grin. He knew Lee didn't really have proof of any of that—only what Luke had briefed them on this morning. But that was Lee: persuasive when it mattered.

Lee inserted one of the USB drives, fingers flying across the keyboard.

"We'll analyze everything later. This will take all day if I have to do it one terminal at a time."

He turned back to the group.

"Look—we need full dumps of all data from your hard drives and the servers. You know what to grab. You know where it's stored. Your first task for Ms. Kahn is to get it all copied to portable drives. Go."

Luke watched as Lee and Rusty worked alongside Jason, digging into the data. He was impressed with Lee's management style—calm, deliberate—and Rusty's razor-sharp technical skills. Maybe they'd work out after all.

He glanced at Rajeev, who also looked quietly impressed.

"Okay," he said softly. "It looks like they've got everything under control here. We've got a mission to finish."

Helen returned to Luke's side, her face tight with anger.

"They've been using these kids like prisoners," she muttered, low and furious. "Some of them were severely punished."

Luke's voice was steely.

"Let's find out what else they're hiding."

Helen pointed toward a door at the far end of the room. "The tunnel should be behind that door."

They started toward it when two older men in lab coats emerged from break room door. Their expressions hardened instantly. One was burly with a ruddy face, and he barked:

"What the hell is this? You can't just barge in here! This is a restricted area. I'll call security."

Luke didn't hesitate. He raised his pistol, steady and commanding.

"Shut up. Who are you, and what do you do here?"

The managers exchanged a glance—defiant but silent.

Rajeev stepped forward, his usual humor missing. His tone was low and firm.

"Let's not make this harder than it needs to be. Just tell us what you're doing here."

The burly man hesitated.

Rajeev sighed, taking a deliberate step closer. "We don't have time for games."

The supervisor's lips parted slightly, but he remained silent. Rajeev grasped the man's wrist firmly, applying gentle—yet steady—pressure until he winced.

"Last chance."

The manager's defiance cracked.

"Fine! This is the QuantumSentinel research group," he admitted through gritted teeth. "We collect data for the project. That's all."

Luke's eyes narrowed. "Where's Da Vinci? Probably a girl, held against her will."

The supervisor smiled thinly. "You're nuts. This is a research facility."

Luke didn't flinch. He motioned to Hank and Moises. "Get these thugs out of here. Lock them in their offices."

Hank grabbed one of the supervisors by the arm, while Moises prodded the other forward, both men muttering curses under their breath as they were escorted away.

From a nearby workstation, a teenage girl hesitated—then slowly raised her hand.

"I think the girl you're looking for is through that door." She pointed toward Helen had noticed. "They take food there three times a day."

Luke turned to Hank. "See if you can get that door open."

Hank inspected the door's biometric scanner, frustration flashing across his face.

"No luck. We need someone with access."

The girl added softly, "The cafeteria manager—Pari Bakshi."

Luke looked at Rajeev. "Take her and find Bakshi. Bring her back —fast."

Two minutes later, Rajeev returned with a pale, matronly woman whose hands trembled as she glanced anxiously between them. Luke stepped forward, tone firm but controlled.

"We need your help. There's a girl inside. You've seen her?"

Pari's voice was soft. "Yes. Her name is Nora. Just a girl. They've kept her there for over a year. Every time I see her, my heart aches. Her only friend is Maria, the young caretaker."

Luke exchanged a look with Helen, understanding dawning.

"She's Da Vinci," Helen whispered.

Luke's voice softened, almost a whisper. "Pari, you've seen her suffering. No child deserves that."

Helen nodded firmly, her tone unwavering.

"You won't be punished. But we don't have much time. If we don't act now, it may be too late."

Pari's face tightened. She hesitated, glancing toward the security camera in the corner—her eyes flickering with desperation. Then, with a steely breath, she pressed her hand against the scanner.

A faint beep echoed as the lock disengaged with a heavy click.

"Hank, you and Moises stay here with Jason," Luke ordered, his voice steady but urgent, nodding toward the two supervising figures, one still nursing his injured hand. "Jenny, Helen, Rajeev, with me. Let's move."

The door swung open to reveal a narrow, dimly lit hallway. Shadows stretched along the walls, and faint, distant echoes hinted at the length of the corridor. The mission wasn't over yet—but they were close.

Without hesitation, they hurried into the long, dark tunnel. Small dome lights flickered every twenty feet, casting a feeble glow on the cold concrete. Their footsteps echoed softly as they advanced—the reality sinking in. This tunnel stretched at least half a mile ahead, a seemingly endless shadowy path.

Jason, Hank, and Moises watched their friends disappear into the darkness. Jason clapped his hands together. "I'm going over to the server bay to see how Amal's doing with the data transfer."

Hank and Moises remained where they were, staring down the tunnel, wondering what awaited their friends. Hank turned and patted Moises on the shoulder. "I guess there's nothing we—"

Suddenly, a chorus of yelling and screaming erupted from the programmers, scattering from their workstations.

Hank and Moises snapped to attention, instincts flaring. Across the room, they spotted Jason diving for cover.

Before they could react, the two supervisors reappeared—one with a gun, the other brandishing a crowbar—eyes wild with rage. A shot rang out. The monitor beside them shattered.

"Down!" Hank shouted, leveling his rifle.

A deafening crack split the air. Moises yanked Hank behind a sturdy desk just as wood splintered above them.

"Shit!" Moises hissed, looking down. A clean hole cut through his pants, the bullet grazing his leg. He tapped his prosthetic and groaned. "Goddamn it—he shot my new leg!"

Another shot rang out—then a second, from the same direction.

The second supervisor stormed toward Hank and Moises, waving the crowbar like a war club, fury blazing behind his eyes.

Across the room, the young programmers cowered behind their desks, wide-eyed. One let out a soft gasp.

Before either attacker could close the gap, Rusty blurred forward—a streak of motion.

He slammed into the gunman with a low, twisting tackle, knocking the weapon aside. The shot went wide, ricocheting off the wall. Rusty twisted the man's wrist, disarming him, then spun and drove a knee into his gut. The supervisor crumpled, stunned.

The second manager didn't see Lee until it was too late.

Lee intercepted him mid-charge, grabbed the crowbar with both hands, and wrenched it free with a grunt. He followed up with a brutal elbow to the man's temple. The supervisor dropped—unconscious or worse.

Rusty kicked the pistol away, chest heaving.

"That escalated fast," he panted.

Moises peeked from behind cover, wide-eyed. "You guys are fucking ninjas. Did you rehearse this or what?"

"Let's just say we've had practice," Lee replied, already pulling a zip tie from his vest and securing the groaning man's wrists.

Rusty moved to the second supervisor and zip-tied him to a support column. The guy didn't resist.

Jason rose from behind the workstation, weapon drawn, eyes sweeping for more threats. He stopped at the sight of the two subdued men.

"That was crazy," he said, voice shaking. "I thought we locked them up. Is everyone alright?"

Hank nodded. "Thanks to these two."

Moises grimaced, tapping his dented prosthetic. "That guy owes me five grand and a beer."

Jason smirked. "We'll bill Kahn."

Rusty wiped his palms on his pants, adrenaline still racing.

Behind them, one of the coders let out a relieved exhale. A few murmurs rippled across the room, the tension beginning to ease.

Moises clapped Rusty on the shoulder as he limped forward. "Remind me not to underestimate the IT team again."Rusty grinned. "We're here to help."

CHAPTER 91: THE GONE GIRL

A flashing red light illuminated the door panel, casting a pulsing crimson glow against the cold concrete walls. A faint alarm buzzed in the distance, signaling that someone had entered the main tunnel nearly half a mile away. It was too early for the woman to be bringing dinner.

The larger guard toggled the monitor to the tunnel feed and saw several armed individuals moving swiftly, weapons at the ready.

"We have trouble," he muttered to the other guard, his stomach tightening. "Get the girl. Now."

Ms. Kapoor—stocky, unsmiling, and always on edge—threw the door open to Nora's apartment and lunged for the startled child. Nora shrank back, eyes wide with terror, before letting out a scream.

"Shut up!" Ms. Kapoor barked, slapping Nora hard across the cheek. The impact left a red mark as the girl gasped, stunned into quiet whimpers; her small body trembled.

"Get our weapons. Lock the tunnel door," the guard ordered, voice tense. "We've got three minutes."

He approached the attendants. "Maria, Kapoor—you stay here."

The two guards hurried to the elevator, dragging Nora with them. She screamed and struggled, trying to reach Maria, but one guard cuffed her sharply in the ribs, knocking the wind out of her.

"No! Don't take her!" Maria cried, lunging for the door, but it slammed shut before she could reach it.

Maria spun on Ms. Kapoor. "Where are they taking her?"

Ms. Kapoor sneered, folding her arms. "Maybe somewhere you won't get in the way again."

Maria's eyes flashed with anger. Without thinking, she stepped forward and struck Ms. Kapoor across the face. The older woman stumbled back, stunned, clutching her cheek. She attacked Maria but was rocked back by a thunderous explosion that shattered the air.

Metal groaned as the tunnel door buckled outward; debris scattered across the apartment floor. Smoke poured through the breach, curling into the room.

Luke pressed himself against the floor, silent except for the distant drone of the alarm and the faint ringing in his ears. He moved first, weapon raised, every muscle taut. Rajeev followed. Jenny and Helen swept low behind them through the blown-out door, eyes scanning every corner. Smoke stung their eyes as they advanced.

Inside the observation room, they found Maria sobbing beside the elevator room door. Ms. Kapoor, in shock, cradled her injured face.

"Are you Maria? Where's the girl?" Luke's voice cut through the chaos.

Maria quickly rose when she saw Luke's team move through the apartment door. "Yes. They took her! The guards—Sochi's men— they dragged her into the elevator right after the alarm went off. I tried to stop them. Please, help her!"

"That's the plan. What elevator?" Luke demanded.

Maria pointed. "That one—the big service lift. I don't know where it goes. They said someone breached the perimeter—they knew you were coming. Here, you'll need this to use it." She pulled her key card from her pocket and handed it to Luke.

Luke backed up a step. "Jenny, stay here. Get everything you can out of them. Secure the area."

Jenny nodded. "On it."

"Rajeev, Helen—you're with me. Let's go."

He pressed the elevator button. The doors squeaked open painfully slow.

Inside, silence weighed heavily—the kind that presses down and makes every second feel heavier. Luke wiped sweat from his brow, tightening his grip on his rifle. They had minutes, maybe seconds, to change the course of a child's life. Failure wasn't an option.

The elevator ascended to the oil-change bay in the old Pushkar Retread warehouse. When the doors opened to harsh daylight. The garage door was open. One of the tuk-tuks was gone; two remained.

Luke sprinted outside onto the dirt road. Nothing. No tracks, no sound. His fists clenched—the maze had swallowed their clues.

Doubt curled inside him. They might be too late. Old failures crept into his mind—ghosts he fought to banish. But he pushed the thoughts aside. Not now.

"Let's head back down," he said, voice steady. "See what else we can learn."

Then Rajeev's phone pinged. His eyes widened as he read the message.

"It's my nephew," he breathed. "He saw two men speeding off in a tuk-tuk with Nora. He was on lookout."

Luke turned sharply. "Where are they now?"

"I don't know," Rajeev said, breathless, "but he's following them on his scooter."

Without hesitation, Luke spun toward the remaining tuk-tuks. "Rajeev—you drive. Helen, take his phone. Switch to voice—it'll be faster. Stay connected."

Helen was already moving, pulling the door open.

The chase was on..

CHAPTER 92: CHAPTER THE WATCHFUL ONE

The narrow rooftop offered just enough space for Aadi and his secondhand binoculars. Perched behind a tangle of drying laundry and a stack of crates, he scanned the alley below, eyes sharp and focused. A dull alarm echoed faintly over the rooftops—a sound most wouldn't notice. But he did.

Sixteen, maybe. Wiry, stubborn. Not a boy anymore, though no one could say where he got it from. But to Rajeev, he would always be one of the "nephews"—not by blood, but by bond.

From his perch above the Pushkar Retread building, Aadi could easily see the street, the tuk-tuks, and the warehouse's rust-streaked entrance. The place didn't look like much, but Rajeev had taught him long ago that the most dangerous places never did.

He checked his phone. A single word from Rajeev lit the screen: Eyes on.

He tapped back: In place. Nothing yet.

He never called Rajeev "uncle" to his face. It wasn't necessary. The man had been there for him and his brothers ever since their father—Rajeev's old partner, was killed on a job gone sideways. Rajeev had stepped in without hesitation. Paid for school. Paid the bills. Showed up. And most importantly, he never treated them like a charity case. He treated them like sons.

Rajeev told people he was a private detective, and Aadi believed it. He wanted to believe it. It sounded like something out of the old action movies they used to watch on Rajeev's old TV. And this—perched on a rooftop, watching from the shadows—this was part of that story. His story, now.

A bit of movement caught his eye. Two men emerged from the garage with a girl between them. She looked small—too small—and scared. Her head hung low, arms limp. Something about the way they moved set his gut turning.

They have her, he typed. Two men. Girl in between. Headed east in a tuk-tuk.

His phone vibrated with Rajeev's text: Follow. Don't lose them.

He was already sliding down the roof ladder. His scooter sputtered to life. He had patched it together from a dozen junked bikes and repainted it so many times that its original color was impossible to determine.

He peeled off after the tuk-tuk, weaving through traffic with the ease of someone who'd grown up dodging rickshaws and delivery bikes. Ahead, the tuk-tuk surged through the narrow lanes of Dharavi, the men unaware they were being followed.

He stayed back just far enough. Like Rajeev taught him.

A grin played across his face as he accelerated.

This was it. Detective work. The kind Rajeev never talked about—but always lived.

CHAPTER 93: THE CHASE

The tuk-tuk rattled like a tin can full of angry bees, weaving desperately through Mumbai's tangled traffic. Motorbikes darted past, carts piled high with coconuts and rugs jostled for space, and pedestrians flowed around them like a swirling river. Luke squeezed the worn seat, knuckles white, while Helen fought to hear Rajeev's nephew, Aadi, through the crackling line.

"They ditched us near the Gateway of India!" Aadi's voice wavered, a scooter whine fading in and out. "They ran inside… toward the water!"

Rajeev's eyes darted ahead, lips tightening. "They're heading for the ferries."

Helen relayed the order. "Follow them—no matter what, but keep your distance."

Rajeev screeched the tuk-tuk to a halt, the vehicle shuddering in protest. Ahead, the Gateway loomed—an imposing basalt arch, built to honor British royalty, now standing as Mumbai's most iconic monument. Tourists crowded the square, selfie sticks in hand.

Luke leaped out, scanning the sea of bodies. Beyond the throng, the ferry's mournful horn announced its departure. Aadi was already aboard, waving frantically from the stern—a tiny figure against the vast, shimmering Arabian Sea.

"Damn it," Luke muttered under his breath.

"Now what?" Helen asked, eyes narrowing.

Rajeev's expression hardened. "Plan B—fast." He sprinted toward a cluster of brightly painted fishing boats bobbing in the harbor, heading toward an old rickety dock.

An old man hunched over a crab trap looked up as they approached. Rajeev spoke rapid-fire Hindi, gesturing toward the departing ferry.

The man nodded, pointing to a small, faded blue boat tied to a weathered post.

Luke shot Rajeev a look. "Plan B is a rowboat?"

Rajeev grinned, low and knowing. "I have a friend with a boat with an engine.."

Moments later, Rajeev pulled the starter cord. The engine coughed to life, smoke billowing. Rajeev manned the ancient outboard. The boat lunged forward, carving through the chop. Spray soaked Luke at the bow. Helen squinted through binoculars, scanning the horizon.

"They're headed for Elephanta," Rajeev said. "If they reach the caves, we lose them in the tunnels—deep, dark chambers without comms or visibility."

Luke shot him a sharp look. "Caves?"

"Elephanta Island. Ancient temple complex carved into the rock. A labyrinth down there."

Rajeev pressed the throttle harder, the craft vibrating under the strain as it followed the ferry's wake. They arrived just as the vessel docked. Luke was the first to move. Heart pounding, he vaulted onto the stone dock and sprinted up the ancient carved steps packed with tourists up the hillside. The humid air was thick with salt and frangipani; every breath burned. boots slipping on uneven stone, the others followed close behind.

Ahead, the two men veered off the stairs, dragging the girl down a narrow dirt path that disappeared into dense foliage. Her feet stumbled to keep up, tears streaking her face as she fought every step.

"Stop!" Luke's voice cracked through the thick air, echoing off stone and leaves.

The men skidded to a halt.

One spun, raising a pistol with a practiced grip. The other yanked the girl behind him like a shield, eyes cold and unreadable.

"Take another step," the gunman barked, "and she dies."

They were close enough now to see the panic in Nora's eyes—wide, wet, pleading. No cover. No margin for error. Just a narrow window, a trembling child, and Luke's relentless resolve.

He drew a breath, slow and sharp.

He'd faced standoffs before—tight spaces, shifting air, fingers on triggers. But never like this.

Never with a child in the crosshairs.

No backup. No second chances.

Just him.

And the shot he might have to take.

He kept his gaze steady on the gunman, stepping forward without flinch or gesture.

"You fire," Luke said evenly, "and you're dead before you pull that trigger again."

The man's finger twitched. His partner shifted nervously.

Rajeev raised a hand, calm and commanding, eyes steady.

"You're following orders. We get it. But if you kill her, you cross a line. Murderers don't get second chances."

Doubt crossed their faces. The pistol lowered slightly.

"Let her go," Rajeev said softly. "Walk away, or stay and die here. Your choice."

Reluctantly, the pistol was lowered. The other man shoved the girl, who stumbled forward, into Helen's arms. Helen sank to her knees, clutching her close, tears streaking her face.

"You're safe now," Luke said, steady as stone, his hand on the girl's back.

Helen brushed her hair away gently. "We've got you."

The kidnappers vanished into the thick brush, their footsteps muffled.

As quietly as they had come, they retraced their steps to the dock.

Aadi jogged up, breathless but beaming. His helmet dangled from his arm, cheeks flushed. "They almost saw me," he panted. "I stayed in the crowd like you said. Did I do okay?"

Rajeev ruffled his hair with pride. "More than okay. You saved her."

Aadi glowed.

Back on the boat, Helen let out a slow exhale, rubbing her neck. "You guys actually enjoy this, don't you?"

Luke chuckled. "I kinda do when a plan comes together." He leaned back, watching the distant skyline. The girl was safe—for now—that was enough.

CHAPTER 94: THE GIRL BEHIND THE CODE

The suite at the Taj Mahal Hotel offered a fragile sanctuary amid the chaos outside. Heavy drapes muffled the sounds of Mumbai's clamor—car horns, distant horns, the hum of engines—creating a cocoon of quiet.

Helen and Anya sat across from Nora Borgia—known to them as Da Vinci—and Maria, her quiet young companion. Nora sat stiffly on the edge of a plush sofa, arms wrapped tightly around herself, eyes shadowed and distant. Maria, no more than a few years older, stayed close, her presence a steady anchor.

Anya broke the silence, her voice calm but firm. "Nora, we need to understand what happened. Who you are, what you were working on. We want to help, but we need the full story."

Nora's voice was barely a whisper, trembling with the weight of years. "My name is Nora Borgia. My twin brother Rodrigo. We just had our birthday… we're 14 now. We lived in Manila. My dad was a missionary. He… he died of dengue fever."

Her gaze dropped, and her voice caught. "My mom stayed behind to finish his work. She raised us alone. But we were different. Good at math, computers, logic. She said we could have a future beyond the mission."

Helen leaned in softly. "How did you end up here?"

"She heard about a program—a test for gifted kids. If you scored high enough, they offered a world-class education. And if you really stood out... you'd work for iKahnX," Nora answered. Her voice was flat, exhausted.

Anya exchanged a silent look with Helen. Then Nora continued.

"Our scores shattered records. They flew us to Mumbai. Paid my mom monthly. Seemed like a miracle. I'd already been learning English in school and from her—she wanted us ready for university abroad someday."

Her fingers clenched in her lap. "After two years, she wanted us back. The mission arranged scholarships in the U.S.. She told Kahn she was coming to take us home."

Her voice grew softer, almost trembling. "That same week, she was killed—hit by a car outside the mission."

Anya's breath hitched. "You think Sochi was behind it?"

Nora nodded slowly. "I don't have proof. But after that, Sochi made sure we understood—we'd pay if we even tried to leave. It was a message."

Helen's voice turned cold, steel beneath her tone. "That's his playbook."

Nora's hands curled into fists. "Rodrigo and I—he was taken from me." Her eyes glistened with tears. "They separated us. We weren't allowed to talk outside work. The only time I saw my brother was during monitored QuantumSentinel sessions—everything recorded—every word, every move. We could only speak about the system."

Her voice cracked as her shoulders trembled. "Two weeks ago, we finished our part of the project. That was the last time I saw him. Since then... nothing."

She looked down, blinking hard to hold back the tears, voice barely a whisper.

Anya reached out gently, placing a firm hand on Nora's knee. Maria squeezed her hand silently.

The room fell into a heavy silence. Outside, Mumbai continued its relentless pace; inside, the weight of unspoken fears hung thick.

"She's been with me since the separation from Rodrigo," Nora added softly. "One of the housekeeper's daughters. She saw what was happening—and stayed."

"We weren't just students anymore," Nora continued, voice steadier now. "We became problem-solvers. They gave us challenges—encryption, prediction models, machine learning. Real scenarios. High-stakes systems. We solved them."

Anya tried not to make it obvious as she wiped away a tear. "I feel a profound responsibility for the terrible things that have happened to you, Nora and Maria. I promise, I will take care of you both personally. You will stay with me for as long as you want, and you will never be mistreated again. Would that be okay with you… Nora, Maria?"

Nora looked at Maria and they both nodded at the same time. Nora got up and walked over to Anya and gave her a hug. "Thank you, Ms Kahn."

Anya brushed away another tear. "You can call me Anya…"

Helen smiled at the scene. The girls' fate was settled, one less worry for now, but Kahn, Sochi, and QuantumSentinel still pressed down on her.

That evening, the scene shifted to the hotel's Seray Italian restaurant by the pool. Lanterns flickered with warm, gentle light, casting shimmering reflections across the water's surface. Jason, Lee, and Rusty arrived to join Helen, Anya, Nora, and Maria at the long table, the comforting hum of dinner easing the tension.

Helen waited until the plates were set and the conversation settled. Then she gently steered things. "Nora, I know today was a lot. But we need to understand the system itself—how did you and Rodrigo manage to stabilize a quantum AI?"

Nora leaned forward, her voice calm but tinged with fatigue. "It wasn't about cracking it. It was about seeing it differently. Most people were trying to force quantum algorithms to behave like traditional AI—like teaching a fish to climb a tree. But we realized—the trick wasn't to make the AI fully quantum. It was to make it quantum-adaptive."

Helen raised a brow. "Explain that in plain English."

Nora nodded. "Okay. Classical AI thinks in black and white—ones and zeros. Quantum computing works in probabilities—things can be in multiple states at once. But when you feed real-world data into a quantum AI, it collapses. It's like trying to walk a tightrope while people are throwing rocks at you—the noise throws it off."

She took a sip of water. "So we built a bridge. A classical AI acts like a filter, cleaning up the data, smoothing out the noise, and passing it over to the quantum side in a usable form. That's what gave the system stability."

Rusty leaned in. "And Kahn has that stability now?"

Nora nodded. "Yes. And—he's optimized it. It learns which data structures hold up best, then adapts in real time. It can anticipate problems. Spot weaknesses before they even appear."

Jason frowned. "So it's not just a defensive system—it's predatory. It sees weakness and acts before you even realize it's happening."

Helen's expression grew serious. "And if someone used that in a war?"

Nora's voice was soft but cold. "They wouldn't just block attacks—they could preempt them. Shut down systems globally. Total control." Her eyes narrowed. "I think Kahn is going to use it to leverage money and power... worldwide—at the highest levels of governments."

Maria, quiet until now, asked hesitantly, "Do you think they're still making Rodrigo work on it?"

Nora nodded. "I do. And I think they've made him improve it. Maybe to do things it shouldn't."

The lanterns swayed gently in the breeze, casting shadows across the pool—fleeting, uncertain, but gathering strength.

CHAPTER 95: A CALL TO SHANGRI-LA

Luke lay on his plush bed watching the hypnotic whirring of the ceiling fan and welcoming the comfort and the calm of his room. His body was drained, but his mind refused rest. Nora was safe, Kahn's Mumbai operation had been broken, but beneath the surface, chaos rumbled restless and unresolved.

He reached for his phone. He tapped Shangri-La.

It rang twice.

"Manning residence."

"Hi."

"Luke! How are you?" Vanessa's voice, bright and eager, cut through the dark. Relief—warm and immediate.

"We're fine," Luke said, voice hoarse. "Long day. It's a complicated story. I'll get you up to speed after I get some shut-eye. I'm whipped. The short version is we rescued the person we were after—her name is Nora, a 14-year-old girl—and we shut down Kahn's work here in Mumbai. We think her brother, Rodrigo, is being held in San Diego. As soon as we get back, we'll chase that trail."

"Rodrigo?" Vanessa's tone was curious but cautious, as if sensing the gravity beneath his words.

He hesitated. "Her twin. Was involved in the AI's development. We think he might be in California now. How are Maggie and Peter?"

Vanessa's voice was even, but concern in her tone. "They're improving daily. Is there anything I can do?"

"Yes. You might check if Maggie recalls anything about a certain buyer," Luke suggested. "Evidently, Kahn bought two of my paintings in San Diego. Probably from our gallery. Must have been some time ago. One's here; the other is probably still in San Diego. Might be nothing, but I don't believe in coincidences anymore."

"I'll ask her right away," Vanessa replied. "If there's any record, I'll find it."

"Thanks. And Kahn's AI—QuantumSentinel—we're just understanding what it's capable of. And what we know so far is scary."

Her mind reeled, Vanessa finished, her voice steady but tense. "Luke, take care of yourself. I'll see what I can find out."

Luke's exhaustion pressed on him. "Vanessa, keep this under your hat. This man and his thugs are dangerous. We don't want him to get wind of us… yet. We need to know what we're up against. I'm beat, I've gotta go. My best to Maggie and Peter."

"I'll tell them. You take care, Luke."

He set the phone aside, staring into the dark. His body was spent, but inside, the restless drive to uncover the truth burned brighter than ever.

CHAPTER 96: CHAPTER KHAN'S REVENGE

Vanessa ended the call. Luke was safe—for now. But one name haunted her: Kahn.

She froze, the weight of that name pressing into her mind—sharp, undeniable. His purchase of Luke's paintings was no accident. It was a calculated message—intentional, unsettling. Maggie and Peter might have answers.

She found them on the patio. Peter sat facing the bay, his book closed in his lap, shoulders tense. Maggie, with her usual calm, cradled a cup of tea, eyes distant and guarded.

"Maggie, Peter," Vanessa whispered, "I just spoke with Luke. He's safe."

Relief flickered across their faces, then quickly faded into concern, like a tide receding.

"Thank God," Maggie exhaled. "What did he say?"

Vanessa hesitated. "He mentioned someone—Kahn. Said he bought two of Luke's paintings."

A silence fell—raw and heavy.

"Are you sure?" Peter asked quietly.

"K-A-H-N," Vanessa confirmed, enunciating deliberately.

Maggie frowned. "We haven't seen him in years."

Peter looked at her, then back at Vanessa. "We met him at the Foundation—at the gallery opening for Luke's work. He was... charming. Polished. Claimed to be new in town, looking at real estate in Point Loma. Said he loved art."

"And he had money," Maggie added bitterly. "He bought two of Luke's largest pieces right off the wall."

Peter nodded. "We were impressed. Seemed interested in the Foundation's mission. So we invited him to Shangri-La. Big mistake."

"He—" Maggie's voice tightened—"He showed up dressed to the nines, worked the room like a politician. Then he wandered the property—twice. Every detail."

"Right before he left," Peter continued, "he handed us a check for ten thousand dollars. Said he wanted to become a member."

"We thought it was a sign of support," Maggie said flatly. "Then he said he wanted to buy Shangri-La."

Peter's fist clenched. "I told him it wasn't for sale. That it was our home, our family legacy. He just smiled and left."

Vanessa said nothing. She already knew where this was going.

"Six months later," Maggie added grimly, "we got a notice from the city—plans filed to build on the lots in front of us. All three houses sold. The buyer?"

Peter nodded. "Kahn. He planned to bulldoze the homes—and build some glass palace with a rooftop pool. It would've swallowed our view—our entire horizon."

"We fought it," Maggie said. "City Hall tried to push it through anyway. He had influence—greased palms, legal teams, threats, lawsuits. We organized the neighbors, but some turned against us. It got ugly."

"It made the papers," Peter said. "Not just local. Society pages picked it up. And San Diego's high society doesn't take kindly to outsiders attacking one of their own."

"Kahn was ostracized," Maggie finished. "No more invitations, no club memberships. His yacht club application? Rejected quietly—even behind the scenes."

Vanessa exhaled slowly. The pieces were falling into place—sharp, brutal, and cold. The theft at the Foundation wasn't about money. It was about revenge.

Kahn couldn't claim the house, so he went after what mattered most: their life's work.

Then came the real blow. The money returned—and more: half a million extra. That must have pushed him over the edge.

He thought they were behind it.

And that's when he struck back.

He sent the hit team.

If Maggie and Peter had died, their estate—and everything they built—would have fallen into his hands. Probably sold off, likely to him, at a steep discount. He would have built his palace atop their ashes.

It was cruel. Calculated. And horrifyingly logical.

"I'm going to dig into this," Vanessa said quietly. "This isn't just a vendetta about real estate. It's something bigger."

Maggie reached out, her hand steady but sympathetic. "Be careful."

"I will," Vanessa replied. "Luke needs to know what's really going on."

CHAPTER 97: DEAL WITH THE DEVIL

Palacio de San Sebastian, Palm Beach-Three Months Earlier

The President of the United States swirled his Diet Coke, soaking in the Florida sun streaming through the windows of his retreat. Two bikini-clad women lounged poolside, bronzed legs draped over plush chairs, flutes of champagne catching the light.

He tilted his head, amused. "Who are they? They look sharp. See who they are, Evelyn. Maybe offer them a staff job."

Across from him, Evelyn Singleton, his chief of staff, barely concealed a sigh as she flipped through the briefing folder. "Those are Mr. Ward's daughters, sir. I doubt they need a job."

He sighed wistfully. "Shame. They look talented." He took a sip. "What's next?"

Evelyn looked down at her notes. "Your meeting with Marvin and Victor. They insisted, said there was no room to reschedule." She saw his expression. She knew what the President thought about Victor's sleazy tendencies.

At the mention of Victor, the President's smile faltered. He barely tolerated the kid—Marvin Ward's twenty-two-year-old wunderkind. Victor Greebly was pale, overweight, and snorted when he's excited—addicted to hacking classified networks. "The

Hangman," people called him, though not to his face. He rubbed his temples.

"That's my storm trooper," the President said quietly. "What do they know?" As he said it, he knew exactly why he kept that young creep around. Not for Victor himself, but for the dirt and leverage he would dig up, just like he used to keep Marvin around.

He'd put up with him for one reason: usefulness. Digging up dirt on friends and foes alike. Leverage when the time was right. Just like he resurrected Marvin Ward from his famous flame out a year ago. His zealous attack on government departments worked to distract the unwashed while he was laying his groundwork to twist democracy to his liking. Ward became a pariah in the country, even in the company he built. But he came back with his tail between his legs. Now in another capacity, finding opportunities to cash in on his presidency.

"They say this could make you a hero—and richer," Evelyn added.

That piqued his interest. "Hero and richer? I like that. What's the scoop?"

"Cybersecurity," she said simply.

He groaned. "I hate that crap. China, Russia, Iran... all whining about cyber threats."

He waved dismissively. "Ten minutes. Then tell them I have an emergency Greenland briefing."

Evelyn nodded.

Outside, the gravel crunched as Aarav Kahn stepped out of a black SUV—Italian loafers polished, tailored suit immaculate. The grand estate before him was the Palacio de San Sebastián—a shining symbol of wealth and power, with golden columns and marble floors, a monument to excess. And, POTUS was the essence of excess. Thought he was king of the world.

Kahn knew this persona well. He'd built his empire by taking advantage of fools.

A Secret Service agent checked today's list of the president's guests, checked his credentials, frisked him and waved him through. Inside, chandeliers dripped gold, and silk drapes fluttered in the ocean breeze. An agent escorted Kahn to the president's table.

Marvin Ward, sitting at the head of the lush table, glanced up as Kahn approached confidently. The two men exchanged a brief nod. Victor Greebly barely looked up from his phone, snorting softly, clearly disinterested in the formalities.

Marvin indicated the empty seat beside him.

Kahn positioned himself behind the chair, but remained standing. "Mr. President, I'd like you to meet someone who says he's going to change everything—if he's got his way." "Mr. President," Kahn began, his voice smooth, "what I'm about to show you isn't an opportunity. It's a revolution."

POTUS looked amused. "Big words, Kahn—sit.

Kahn sat down, laying his sleek briefcase on the table, pulled out a tablet with deliberate gravity, then looked directly at the President. He tapped the tablet, revealing a clean, sleek presentation. "This is QuantumSentinel—an AI-driven cybersecurity system that not only blocks hackers but tracks, finds, and erases them. Nation-states? Neutralized. Espionage? Eliminated. We dominate the digital battlefield."

Marvin's eyes sharpened. Victor, still scrolling, snorted—caught the glare from the president. "Senator Beckett's got a girlfriend." Greebly muttered.

The President grimaced. "Christ Victor, focus."

Greebly looked up sheepishly. "Sorry."

Kahn continued, "And it's a market. On top of that we're launching a line of ultra-secure, unhackable phones—half the price of Apple or Google."

He handed a gold-trimmed model to Marvin and Victor, then a platinum one to the President. The back bore the Presidential Seal, encircled by a ring of diamonds.

The President's eyes gleamed. "These real?"

"Flawless," Kahn said.

The President examined the phone, visibly impressed. "Wait till the First Lady sees this."

Kahn smiled. "I'd be honored to send Katrina one."

The President looked up from the phone, his grin fading into calculation. "So this AI thing—what's in it for me?"

Kahn didn't blink. "I'm sure we can work something out. Something fair. A way for all of us to share in the power—and the profits—that QuantumSentinel will bring."

The President leaned back, considering, then glanced at Marvin. "I'll believe it when I see it, Kahn. Work out the details, Ward, and get back to me."

Marvin nodded without looking up from his phone.

Kahn added, "In the meantime, we need a soft marketing launch. Executive endorsement. The rest of the world will follow."

The President clapped his hands. "Alright. Call it a national security breakthrough. Let's make it happen. Evelyn, you hear me?"

"Yes, Mr. President," Evelyn responded crisply

As Kahn packed up his briefcase, the President's gaze lazily drifted back to the pool. He grinned. "Marvin, that guy may be on to something. You sure know how to pick 'em."

Marvin didn't answer—he was already calculating profits. Victor snorted again, engrossed in whatever dirt he'd just unearthed.

Kahn took one last, measured look at the room, and smiled—not at the assembled figures, but at the machine he'd just quietly unleashed. Outside, the Florida sun blazed relentlessly, its harsh brilliance a stark contrast to the shadowy power he wielded. Power didn't need to roar, he thought. It just needed to be invited in.

CHAPTER 98: VANESSA'S DISCOVERY

Adrenaline sharpened Vanessa's focus. She parked several blocks away, blending into the flow of tourists, joggers, and office workers. She moved with quiet purpose—unremarkable by design. That was the point.

Ahead, the building came into view—a five-story structure stretching the length of the block. Red stone framed panels of green-tinted glass. Modern. Elegant. But distant. Detached. No signage. No branding. No visible signs of activity. No staff coming or going.

Just silence.

A loose ring of plainclothes security lingered nearby—too casual to be random, too watchful to ignore.

Vanessa crossed the street, pausing near a public art display—an abstract sculpture with a reflective surface. From there, she could see the garage tucked beneath the complex. A black SUV rolled up to the circular driveway. Two men in dark suits stepped out.

One of the security men—aviation sunglasses, brisk movements—hurried over and opened the rear door.

Two more men emerged. One tall and broad-shouldered. The other shorter, heavier-set. She only caught the backs of their heads, but then the taller man turned, exchanging words with the one in sunglasses.

Vanessa inched closer, lifting her phone as if photographing the sculpture. In its mirrored surface, she caught the scene—two men near the entrance. One was pacing, restless.

Then she saw him clearly.

Marvin Ward.

Her pulse quickened.

Marvin Ward. Next to POTUS, perhaps the most publicly loathed figure in the country. His fall had been swift and public—scandals, congressional hearings, corporate collapses. After years as a political hitman, he'd vanished from public life, leaving behind chaos and cratered reputations.

And now he was here.

She glanced again at the sculpture's reflection. The two men were still near the entrance, speaking quietly.

Her mouth went dry.

She turned away, retracing her path in a wide arc, heart pounding, every sense alert. Her fingers clenched around her phone. Her breath shallow.

Then—the motorcade.

Three black limousines appeared from around the corner, gliding into the garage one after another. Their windows were dark, their bodies immaculate—anonymous, but unmistakably important.

More vehicles followed. Sleek government sedans. Some armored. Others unmarked. Drivers stayed behind the wheel, scanning.

Doors opened in rhythm.

Vanessa pretended to scroll through her phone as she watched.

Passengers stepped out—sharply dressed men and women, their expressions unreadable. Not celebrities. Not executives. Officials. Serious ones.

She recognized a few. A cybersecurity policy advisor. A senator's chief of staff. Two men she'd seen at a defense technology panel hosted by a D. C. think tank.

Then—her breath hitched.

The Secretary of Defense.

He walked briskly, flanked by aides. Silent. Focused.

Seconds later, a bald man in dark glasses exited another car.

The CIA Director.

Unmistakable. She'd watched his stone-faced confirmation hearing—two hours without a blink.

A half-dozen men in black suits and dark sunglasses took up positions around the gathering. Each scanned a different angle, eyes tracking motion and threat. One of them seemed to be looking straight at her.

Vanessa stood frozen for a split second, then casually lifted her phone—low and steady. She framed a wide shot of the massive bronze sculpture: four Portuguese fishermen straining against a net, pulling in a giant tuna.

But her focus was on the building beyond it.

Faces. Movements. Insignia. Posture.

Then—he appeared.

Kahn.

The building's glass doors parted, and he stepped out toward the gathering. Unhurried. Controlled. Not a man arriving—but a man already in charge. Even at a distance, he radiated presence.

The agent who had looked at her turned away, facing Kahn and the assembled group.

The others—officials, advisors, power brokers—turned as well.

Not to greet him.

To wait.

Vanessa didn't need a press badge or clearance to understand what she was seeing.

Something big was happening. And it had to be about QuantumSentinel.

She hesitated. Her instinct whispered: walk away. Forget this.

But that voice felt like an old recording from a life she no longer lived.

Then she caught movement—one of the agents beginning to turn back toward her.

Time to go.

She slid the phone into her bag. Smoothed her jacket. Kept her expression blank.

Then turned and walked—steady and composed—along the broad bayside promenade, heading toward the convention center where she'd parked her car.

She felt eyes on her until she reached the safety of the garage stairs.

Her legs were shaky. Her hands tingled. Adrenaline still surged through her.

But she wasn't scared.

She was charged.

And for the first time, she realized— She wasn't just watching. She was already part of it.

CHAPTER 99: A GAME OF POWER

Aarav Kahn stood on his office balcony, eyes fixed on the convoy of black limousines sweeping into the circular driveway, their mirrored surfaces flashing in the blazing midday sun. Everything here was precise—engineered with ruthless efficiency. Power arriving to witness something grander.

Beside him, Bower watched the procession with measured calm. "Quite the turnout," he remarked.

"They're not here for a tour," Kahn replied softly. "They've come to see a new world order—and decide how much of it they'll truly control."

In the convoy: Marvin Ward, the President's chief enforcer, flanked by some of the most powerful men in the world… including the Admirals, Generals, the CIA Director, and the Secretary of Defense. The scene was no mere demonstration; it was a proving ground.

Inside the Innovation Hub, the room was cool, sharp with anticipation. Screens streamed cascading data—attack signatures, threat intel, geopolitical alerts. A massive holographic globe spun slowly at the center, pulsing with sensor feeds and coordinated cyber signals—an intricate map of chaos and control. It was intended to impress… and it did.

Kahn stepped into the center of the room. The sound of voices faded. He waited, letting silence settle. His gaze drifted across the crowd.

"What we're about to show you isn't about hardware. It's not encryption. It's not a weapon—at least, not in the way you're thinking," he began. "QuantumSentinel is a shift in the global balance of power. What you're about to witness is chaos—disrupted—and control—absolute."

The lights dimmed. Six massive screens descended from the ceiling. Each flickered to life, displaying scenes from Qobu, a small, unassuming town of 15,000 outside Baku, Azerbaijan. Everyday life, mundane and forgettable, unfolded before them.

Kahn's voice cut through the darkened room. "Watch closely."

One screen showed a city intersection. Another, the interior of a national bank. A third displayed the town's modest train station. People moved as they always did—waiting, walking, unaware.

"Gentlemen," he said evenly, "what you're about to see was sanctioned—reluctantly—by the leaders of this country. We introduced QuantumSentinel to them. They asked for proof. They requested a demonstration."

"So we breached their systems for five minutes. No damage. No casualties. Just... clarity. They were hesitant. But—let's just say, we made them an offer they couldn't refuse."

A digital countdown appeared on the center screen: 00:00:05.

Four... three... two... one.

00:00:01 – Traffic lights blinked off simultaneously. Cars lurched into gridlock, a cacophony of horns shattering the evening calm. Buses stalled mid-intersection, confused passengers tentatively stepping onto the asphalt. The constant hum of electronics faded, leaving an eerie silence in its wake.

00:00:15 – At the national bank, overhead lights died with an audible pop. ATMs froze mid-transaction, their screens flickering before going dark. Clerks stood motionless as bewildered customers drifted towards the exits, wallets still in hand.

00:00:30 – The train station descended into chaos. Monitors glitched, spewing frantic lines of code before cutting to black. A high-speed train screeched to a halt just outside the platform, its automated systems failing.

Across every screen in the room, confusion bloomed. Security cameras stuttered and fell to static. Smart city sensors went dark, leaving autonomous vehicles stranded and confused. Digital billboards froze, their blank faces a stark reminder of Qobu's sudden technological regression.

00:00:45 – A hospital hallway dimmed momentarily before emergency lighting kicked in. Nurses reached for flashlights out of habit, but the backup generators engaged seamlessly, keeping critical systems operational. In the maternity ward, vital sign monitors blinked once, then stabilized, powered by the hospital's robust emergency systems.

00:00:55 – A traffic camera showed a lone officer waving cars through an intersection—then vanished. Cellular networks went dark, cutting off communication and adding to the growing sense of isolation.

A profound quiet descended over the room, broken only by the nervous shuffling of feet and muted gasps from the observers.

The Secretary of Defense leaned forward, knuckles white against his armrest. Across the room, a tech CEO's eyes widened, a mix of fear and poorly concealed interest etched on her face.

Kahn's voice cut through the tension, calm and controlled.

"In the last sixty seconds, the town of Qobu lost control of its digital heartbeat. No ransom. No ultimatums. Just silence. A glimpse of the void."

He let the words hang, savoring the impact.

"Fortunately for the people of Qobu," he continued, stepping towards a sleek control monitor, "they won't have to endure four more minutes of blackout."

The room buzzed with hushed whispers—some nervous, some angry. Words like reckless, dangerous, and out of control floated just beneath the surface.

Kahn ignored them, focused on his demonstration.

A seventh screen descended from the ceiling—this one displaying a high-resolution map of Azerbaijan. He zoomed in quickly, the interface slick and intuitive, like a weaponized version of Google Earth. The image sharpened until the streets of Qobu filled the screen.

"This," Kahn said, pulling a black stylus from his shirt pocket, "is how difficult it is to operate QuantumSentinel."

He circled the town with a smooth stroke. No keystrokes. No coding. Just a pen and access.

Without further command, systems began to reboot in careful sequence. First, emergency services flickered back to life. Then critical infrastructure hummed to activity. Public utilities followed suit. Power surged back. Traffic signals blinked on, restoring order to the chaos. Trains restarted their journeys. Screens stabilized, digital life returning to normal.

Qobu's digital pulse returned, steady and controlled. The town came back to life, unaware it had been the subject of this chilling demonstration.

He turned, his gaze sweeping over their faces, cold and unwavering. "Still think this is just a demonstration?"

The Secretary of Defense raised his secure phone. "Get me General Hellman at NSA, Fort Meade. Now."

The air seemed to still. Then, a voice on the other end—tight, clipped, fast.

The Secretary's expression shifted. He turned to face the room, all eyes now fixed on him.

"It's all true. It happened just as we saw it."

A ripple of murmurs.

"The NSA can't explain how it just… disappeared. Not with that many systems failing simultaneously. Not globally synced like that. There's no trace. No intrusion logs. No residual code. It's as if it never happened."

A stunned hush settled over the room.

"They're calling it a ghost breach," he added grimly. "No entry. No exit. Just control."

Marvin Ward, silent until now, looked up slowly—his expression unreadable. He glanced at his fellow guests, then back at Kahn.

CHAPTER 100: NO MORE SHADOWS

Vanessa sat by the pool house at Shangri-La, her fingers absently tracing the rim of her untouched glass of wine. The gentle sound of waves rolled against the shore, but her thoughts were far away, entangled with the name Kahn. A name that meant nothing to her—just another donor name with deep pockets. Now, it was impossible to separate him from the chaos surrounding Luke, Maggie, and Peter. And maybe—just maybe—the attempt on their lives.

The idea gnawed at her. If Kahn had ordered the attack...

She tried to shake the helplessness creeping in. She wasn't part of Luke's team, not in the way his friends were. They had training, skills, missions. She was just... watching. On the outside.

And yet...

That morning, standing across from Kahn's research center, watching the limousines arrive, feeling the charge in the air—it had awakened something. For the first time in a long time, she felt alive. Present. Useful.

It reminded her of the woman she used to be. Before everything fell apart.

She'd spent years in Santa Fe trying to disappear, trying to escape the wreckage left by the man she married. A man who tore apart her reputation, humiliated her, and forced her to abandon the life she had built. She had run then—exiled by silence, bitterness, and survival.

The memories returned in fragments—sharp, disjointed.

It had started beautifully. He was golden—the former New Mexico State quarterback with an easy smile and a politician's handshake. She was deep into her MFA: late nights in the studio, gallery shows with cheap wine and expensive critiques. He swept in like a rescue—charismatic, magnetic. She fell fast and hard.

They married within a year.

She believed in his future, so she shelved pieces of her own. Helped him through law school. Used her contacts to land him a job at one of Santa Fe's top firms. For a while, it worked. He made partner. She expanded the hotel and property business her grandparents had built. They hosted charity dinners and art fundraisers. She was proud. They were respected. She thought she'd done it right.

But power doesn't just corrupt—it mutates.

He began courting far-right clients. Then came a leadership role in a so-called constitutional think tank. Then the MAGA crowd.

He changed. Cold. Angry. Distant. The man who once quoted Neruda while she welded sculptures in the yard now drank before lunch and recited conspiracy theories at dinner.

She remembered the night it truly ended.

She'd booked an early flight from D. C. to surprise him. Music pulsed from the backyard. Light shimmered on the surface of the pool.

He was in it—naked. So was the young woman wearing nothing but a red baseball cap and too much lip gloss.

He didn't even look embarrassed. "You weren't supposed to be back yet," he said, with that smug, rehearsed grin.

After that came the cruelty. He paraded twenty-something groupies at every public event, making sure she saw them. He tarnished her name in the business community with whispers and planted stories. Santa Fe became too small to stay in.

So she left.

Turned over the family properties to her longtime manager. Packed the SUV with what mattered. Drove west. Never looked back.

She breathed out slowly now, centering herself.

Luke's team had skills she didn't, but she wasn't helpless. The woman who built a business, made the deals, read the rooms—that woman was still here.

And she wasn't afraid anymore.

Kahn was a predator. And predators liked shadows. They made problems disappear.

But she understood men like him. They always thought they were the smartest person in the room.

She smiled faintly.

They weren't.

She sat up straighter, her pulse steady, her resolve hardening.

She wasn't a spy or a hacker, but she had something Kahn wanted.

Two things stood out: One—Kahn was an avid art collector. Two—he wanted Luke's work.

That was her edge.

"Carol," she said, her voice brisk, resonating with a new certainty. "I need you to arrange a meeting with Aarav Kahn."

"Vanessa, are you sure that's wise? After what Maggie went through—he's not exactly mister Nice Guy."

Vanessa allowed herself a confident smile. "Exactly. He won't wait. That's why it'll work."

She could hear Carol processing, the sharp woman too professional to argue. "Understood. I'll reach out through the Foundation's channels."

Vanessa hung up and leaned back in her chair. This wasn't her world—blackmail, cyberweapons, hidden bunkers. But she knew people. She knew pressure points and leverage. And she knew art.

That was the one thing Kahn couldn't fake—his hunger for the genuine article.

She pulled out a leather portfolio with a print of Luke's painting. Bold, brooding, beautiful. It pulsed with the same raw honesty that had made her buy her first Luke Payne.

If Kahn wanted another Luke Payne, he'd have to come to her. *And when he did, she'd be ready.*

CHAPTER 101: THE CALL FROM THE GREEN

The Palacio de San Sebastian golf course stretched out in perfect, manicured precision—rolling fairways lined with swaying palms and the distant hiss of the Atlantic breeze. The sun was bright, the air crisp, and the scent of cut grass lingered like cologne for the powerful.

The President, dressed in a tailored polo and white slacks, stood just off the fairway. His ball, half-buried in the rough, received a discreet nudge with the toe of his shoe. It rolled cleanly back into play. His caddy, a grizzled former tour pro, saw it but said nothing. Everyone knew the game.

Just as the President lined up his shot, a Secret Service agent signaled. His aide approached with a secure phone.

"It's Ward," the aide said quietly.

The President sighed and lowered his driver. "Of course it is."

He took the phone. "This thing legit?" he asked, skipping a greeting.

On the other end, Marvin Ward's voice came through—low and edged with urgency. He sat at a secluded corner table at Addison, the Michelin-starred restaurant at the Fairmont Grand Del Mar. The tasting menu had just begun, but his appetite had vanished.

"If Kahn's not bluffing—and I don't think he is—then we're not just talking about a cybersecurity breakthrough. This thing changes the entire game."

"Talk to me," the President said, eyes still on the green.

"The San Diego demo blew us away. QuantumSentinel is the real deal. Whoever controls it will have incredible power and leverage. It's AI on steroids—predictive, adaptive, capable of neutralizing threats. If we control it, we don't just defend digital infrastructure. We dominate it."

The President adjusted his grip. "So we take it."

Ward didn't like the man, but he understood him—ruthless, focused. The kind you could respect… right up until he burned you. And Ward had already been burned and come back for more.

"Kahn's no fool. He knows exactly what this is worth. He won't sell it—he wants us reliant on him. It's leverage."

A dry chuckle. "Everyone's got a price."

"Not this guy," Ward replied. "He doesn't want money. He wants control. Power. To pull strings while we dance."

The President's next swing sent the ball arcing high and clean, landing just short of the green.

"I can understand that feeling. So we squeeze him."

"Exactly," Ward said. "Legal pressure, regulatory chokeholds, leaks—whatever it takes. Paint him as a national security threat. Freeze his assets. If he doesn't come to the table, we make sure the table collapses."

The President passed the club to his caddy, eyes on the ball rolling to a stop. "And if he plays hardball we'll do what we did to that Swiss satellite firm. Block approvals, cancel contracts, dig up scandals. Make him radioactive."

Ward managed a smile. With this President, everyone was a stepping stone—including the ones standing closest.

"The upcoming Midway is buying up time," he added. "But not

too much. Wait too long, and someone else will pounce."

The President grinned. "That's why I keep you close, Marvin. Always two steps ahead."

Ward didn't answer right away. He looked out past the manicured hedges and fine linens, the hum of privilege all around him.

"We'll start laying the groundwork," he said. "Give me forty-eight hours."

The President handed the phone back to his aide without another word and strode confidently toward the green. Behind him, the Secret Service agent followed, shaking his head.

CHAPTER 102: SHIFTING LOYALTIES

Sochi left the Hertz counter, the rental car key digging into his palm. "Fucking airlines," he muttered. His Mumbai flight had been delayed, then rerouted to John Wayne Airport in Orange County because of thick fog. Now, past midnight and running on fumes, he checked his messages. Nothing from Kang. Not good.

He texted:Just landed. Need a report ASAP. Kid's secure. Boss has plans after the QuantumSentinel launch.

Kang should've checked in yesterday. Maybe something had come up. That didn't matter. Business came first. Always. He tossed his duffel in the trunk and merged onto the freeway, heading toward the safe house in San Diego. The night wasn't over.

Beijing-4:00 PM

Colonel Yue sat behind her desk, typing up the post-op report from Shanghai. She edited carefully, pruning out the parts that could raise questions—the missed target, the resistance they hadn't expected. She replaced a name on the roster with a generic placeholder. In her position, survival depended on what got written—and what didn't.

The loss of Lee's team was unfortunate, but not a surprise. Some in the PLA would be pleased by the setback. Envy ran deep. But none of them were responsible for China's cyber edge. That was her burden.

Yue sat back and rubbed her temples. The geopolitical tension between China, the U.S.., and Europe felt like dry kindling, one match away from chaos. She'd spent years building China's cyber-intelligence structure—tightening its grip, anticipating Western moves. But the demands from above were shifting.

They wanted more. Faster. Bolder. Cracking foreign markets, applying pressure, converting influence into compliance. But to what end? To win a game that no one could afford to finish?

Just like my brother… always pushing. The thought passed and faded.

A chime interrupted her. Kang's phone—still on her desk. A new WhatsApp message. She checked the screen:

Where's my report?

Sochi. Of course.

 Kang hadn't given much before he broke. She hadn't asked for things to go that far, but the interrogators hadn't needed direction. They did what they were trained to do.

His crew had disappeared soon after—quietly relocated to a facility that didn't officially exist. China's version of Guantanamo. Necessary, she told herself.

She'd lied to Helen and Payne. Not out of cruelty. Out of necessity. If they knew what really happened, they might see her differently. And that, she couldn't afford.

She typed her reply:

Handled, but messy. PLA intercepted the team post-assignment. Lee likely tipped off his handler. They didn't learn anything useful. Airports compromised. Exit route changed. Container ship Sinotrans Manila, ETA four days. Routing back to Mumbai.

The alternate route would buy Helen and her team more time. She wasn't sure why she cared, but she did. Helen reminded her of herself—focused, tough, practical. And Payne… he carried something. A weariness. But also a loyalty that hadn't broken. That was rare.

Her thoughts drifted again—to her brother. She didn't know where he was now. Their paths had split long ago, but a part of her still hoped they'd cross again.

She caught herself. Enough.

CHAPTER 103 FIRST MOVE

Vanessa settled back in her chair, fingers laced as she waited for confirmation. Her phone buzzed. She glanced at the screen: Carol.

She answered. "Yes, Carol?"

"Vanessa," Carol's voice came through, a faint note of surprise. "It didn't take long. Mr. Kahn confirmed less than an hour after I called."

Vanessa's grip tightened imperceptibly. "And?"

"He sounded surprised we had his personal number," Carol continued, a touch of confusion and worry in her tone. "I reminded him that the Foundation keeps meticulous records. He agreed to the meeting at two."

"Thank you. The meeting shouldn't take more than an hour. I should be back by 2:30."

Vanessa turned and walked toward her office. Kahn didn't like losing, and she thought about Maggie and Peter's story of his actions when denied. Shangri-La had been the prize, and he'd left empty-handed.

She stood, smoothing her skirt, and moved to the window overlooking the courtyard garden. Somewhere out there, Kahn was making his own preparations for their meeting.

"Round one," she murmured, allowing herself a small, determined smile.

Vanessa arrived at the Harbor Boulevard headquarters, pulling into the reserved visitor section—not blending in this time, but walking through the front lobby with deliberate confidence.

The receptionist stood as she approached—young, efficient,

dressed in black with an earpiece and tablet.

"Ms. McGowan?"

Vanessa nodded. "For Mr. Kahn."

"He's expecting you. He'll be right down to meet you in the gallery room." The receptionist's smile was polished, professional—just shy of suspicious—as she led Vanessa through the walnut-paneled doors.

The room beyond was expansive, its walls covered floor-to-ceiling with paintings. Sculptures were strategically placed across the polished floor, catching the light.

"Please make yourself comfortable," the receptionist said, gesturing toward a leather-covered viewing bench.

Vanessa wandered toward the nearest wall. She recognized several of the artists. Each painting floated in its own halo of light—abstracts, mostly. Bold color. Brutal balance. Controlled energy.

No wonder he's a fan of Luke's work, she thought.

She drew a breath and smoothed her jacket. Just nerves. Butterflies. Expected. But she wouldn't let them breathe.

This wasn't her world—but she was done being sidelined. She straightened, steadying her breath. Time to play her hand.

The door opened.

Kahn entered—relaxed, confident, radiating practiced dominance.

"Ms. McGowan," he said, offering his hand. "I must admit, I wasn't expecting this."

Vanessa met his eyes without blinking. "And thank you for taking the meeting on such short notice. We have a fundraising deadline for matching contributions, and my staff noted from our records your past generosity with the Foundation. And, of course, your fondness for Luke Payne's painting."

Kahn took a seat on the bench. "Thank you for considering me—and yes, I do admire Mr. Payne's work. Unfortunately, his pieces are rarely available."

"That's why I thought you might be interested." She picked up the slim black portfolio case she'd carried in, unzipped it, and removed a high-resolution 11x17 print mounted on archival board—bold, textured, and unmistakably Luke Payne's. She held it out with both hands.

Kahn accepted it without hesitation, studying it in silence. His eyes moved slowly across the composition—the layered brushwork, the interplay of cobalt and sienna, the kinetic movement beneath the surface.

"Amazing palette," he murmured. "The depth… the restraint… Controlled chaos. One of his best. I'm surprised you'd part with it."

Vanessa offered a measured smile. "As I said, the Foundation is raising funds for a new project. A county arts center expansion—our pilot for establishing Foundation Centers across San Diego. One of my passion projects."

Kahn looked up, visibly intrigued. "That's… admirable." He studied her a beat longer, then smiled. "Yes, I'm interested in the painting. But tell me, Ms. McGowan—how did you get involved in the art world?"

Vanessa smiled and tilted her head slightly toward a large pastel abstract. "That one came through my gallery in Santa Fe."

Kahn paused, reevaluating. "You owned a gallery?"

"I curated one at my hotel—until recently. I stepped away when I accepted the Foundation position."

"I'm impressed."

"Tell you what," Kahn said, eyes narrowing with amusement. "I'll double the amount your assistant mentioned. I'll have someone deliver the check next week when they pick it up at the Foundation."

She nodded. "Deal."

"Good," he said, then added, almost offhandedly, "We're hosting something next week—big venue, interesting crowd. I've rented the Midway."

Vanessa tilted her head slightly. "The USS Midway?"

Kahn smiled. "It's a floating museum now. One of the most visited attractions in the country. Felt like the right place to unveil something... ambitious."

She kept her tone light. "I toured it recently. Impressive space."

"You weren't on my personal guest list," he said smoothly. "But you are now."

She let the moment stretch. "Sounds fascinating."

"We'll make it official—and I have an idea. I'll have a check drawn this afternoon. My driver will pick you up at 4:30. As a bonus, I'd love to show you my personal art collection. Something very few people ever get to see."

There it was. The opening she needed.

She offered a cool smile. "Well, that's short notice, but I'm sure I can clear my calendar. Looking forward to it."

He escorted her to the front entrance.

"I'm looking forward to our meeting this afternoon," he said, lingering on the final words. "I think you'll find it... enlightening, Ms. McGowan."

Alone now, in the driver's seat of her parked car, Vanessa let the tension unwind from her shoulders. A surge of excitement mixed with a prickle of unease. She was walking a tightrope—balancing her desire for justice with the allure of power and the charm of her enigmatic host.

But she was determined to see this through.

The game was on.

And Vanessa McGowan was ready to play.

Then came the whisper of doubt.

She had kept Luke in the dark about her plan—a decision that gnawed at her conscience. Would he approve of her methods? Would he be angry that she had put herself at risk?

She closed her eyes, took a breath.

"I'm a big girl now," she told herself, her voice firm with resolve. "Luke will understand… He has to."

CHAPTER 104: THE BACKGROUND CHECK

Kahn sat at his desk, holding up the print of Luke Payne's painting. This one was even better than his other acquisitions. There was an intensity to it—like the artist had poured his soul into every stroke of the palette knife.

He smiled.

It had been a good week. A successful demonstration, capped off by a real-world example of what QuantumSentinel could do. He could see their faces—they knew exactly what this technology meant. Each one of them was already scheming how to exploit it, whether to profit or to defend their interests.

And Ward, with that permanent smirk, thought he would own it.

Kahn leaned back in his chair and glanced toward the skyline, visible through the angled glass of his penthouse office. Out of the blue, a call from the most interesting woman — Vanessa McGowen. She held influence in the art world, at least in San Diego. At this point in his life, Kahn had no need or appetite for a girlfriend, let alone a wife. But Vanessa? She could be his ticket into San Diego society. And an attractive woman on his arm always played well. Like his prized horses, she'd be a trophy.

Still, the timing raised red flags. A Payne painting was rare—sporadic at best. Why now? Why her?

And the irony wasn't lost on him—Vanessa McGowen, now director of the very foundation whose owners he'd ordered eliminated.

Coincidence? Maybe. But in Kahn's world, coincidence was often camouflage.

Her presence was polished, her cause convincing—but he knew better than to trust appearances. Before their next meeting, he needed to make sure Vanessa McGowen was exactly who she claimed to be.

He buzzed his head of Human Resources.

"Robert, I need a quick background check, and I need it in two hours."

"That fast? What's the urgency?"

Kahn's voice hardened. "Just do it."

"Understood, Mr. Kahn. Name and details?"

Kahn gave the information and ended the call.

An hour later a knock at the door interrupted his thoughts.

He looked up to see Robert, the HR director, stepping in with a thin folder.

"Mr. Kahn, here's the report on Vanessa McGowen."

Kahn gestured for him to sit. "That was fast, Robert. Give me the highlights."

Robert opened the file. "Clean record. No criminal history. Previously owned an art gallery in Santa Fe—high-end clientele, solid reputation. Divorced two years ago. No children. Owns multiple properties in Santa Fe, including the classic Santa Fe Hotel, which houses one of the best private art collections in the state."

Kahn absorbed the information, his mind already working the angles.

"Nothing unusual?"

Robert hesitated. "Not on the surface. She's legitimate."

Kahn closed the folder. "Everyone looks clean—until they're not."

He waved Robert out and turned his thoughts back to Vanessa. There was something about her—the timing, the painting, the charm—he had felt something wasn't right, but she looks like she legit."

CHAPTER 105: NO MORE ILLUSIONS

But his good mood didn't last.

Another knock. This one softer.

David Bowen, his Director of Operations, hovered in the doorway with his usual hesitant posture. Kahn sighed inwardly. He wasn't in the mood for another interruption—especially not from Bowen, who had a tendency to get bogged down in details and ethical dilemmas.

"David," Kahn said, voice carefully neutral. "What can I do for you?"

Bowen stepped inside, his expression tight with concern.

"Aarav," he began, voice low, "I need to talk to you about QuantumSentinel. And the children."

Kahn's smile faded. "What about them?"

"I'm worried," Bowen said. "The children... they seem withdrawn, unhappy. And the technology... it's powerful. Dangerous. In the wrong hands, it could be catastrophic."

Kahn waved a hand dismissively. "David, please. You worry too much. The children are fine—they're focused on their work. As for QuantumSentinel, it's in the right hands. My hands. I'll ensure it's used for the betterment of humanity."

Bowen's gaze finally lifted to meet Kahn's, doubt flickering in his eyes.

"But what about Ward? And the President? They have their own agendas. They won't hesitate to exploit QuantumSentinel for their own gain."

Kahn leaned back in his chair, his smirk returning.

"Let them try, David. I've anticipated their every move. I have... ways of ensuring things go according to plan. They won't be able to control QuantumSentinel. I will."

His eyes gleamed with ruthless certainty.

"And David," he added, voice dropping to a whisper, "sometimes, sacrifices must be made for the greater good. Difficult decisions... unpleasant necessities. But in the end, the world will thank me. They'll see I was right all along."

Bowen felt a chill. Kahn's words, though vague, hinted at something darker. He wanted to challenge him—demand clarity—but the fear of reprisal held him in place.

Sensing Bowen's hesitation, Kahn's tone sharpened.

"And David—one more thing. Forget your concerns about the children. Forget your anxieties about QuantumSentinel. I know what's best. I don't want to hear this drivel again. Do your job. You are not the conscience of this company. I am. Understood?"

Bowen's shoulders slumped. "Understood, Mr. Kahn."

"Good. Now, get back to work. We have a lot to accomplish."

Bowen turned and stepped out into the corridor, exhaling slowly.

He didn't look back. He didn't need to. Back in his apartment, a small server light blinked.

The feed was active. Every word Kahn had spoken—from his vague justifications to his veiled threats—had been recorded.

The microphone hidden in plain sight inside a pen on the desk had done its job. He had everything he needed.

CHAPTER 106: FLIGHT RISK

Vanessa wasn't sure when it shifted—when this stopped being about art, or pride, or even obligation. Somewhere along the way, helping Luke had become something more. She was part of it now. Part of them. Peter, Maggie, Luke... their fight had become hers. And with it, a thrill she hadn't expected. The risk sharpened her senses. It felt dangerous—and addictive.

Peter's warning echoed in her mind: Kahn is dangerous, Vanessa. Be careful.

But it was too late for second thoughts. She had come too far. For Luke. For the team. For herself.

She drew a deep breath and pressed the call button. Peter answered on the second ring. "Vanessa? Is everything alright?"

"Peter, listen carefully," she said, steadying her voice. "I'm meeting Kahn this afternoon at his complex on Harbor Boulevard. He invited me to see his art collection—but I'm going for Luke. To see what I can learn." A tense beat. "Vanessa," Peter said, "this sounds risky. Are you sure?"

"I am. That's why I'm calling. If I'm not back by eight, act. Call the authorities. Alert Luke. Don't let Kahn vanish." Peter swore under his breath. "You're playing a dangerous game."

"I know," she said quietly. "But it's one I intend to win." A long sigh. "Be careful. If I don't hear from you by eight, I'm sending in the cavalry." "Thank you, Peter."

She hung up and headed to her bedroom. A cream silk blouse, tailored jeans, and ankle boots—confident but understated. Kahn had to believe she belonged in his world.

At 4:30 p. m. sharp, a sleek black limo pulled up outside. The uniformed driver, unreadable behind mirrored sunglasses, opened the door. The interior smelled of leather and expensive cologne. As the city blurred past the tinted windows.

Kahn greeted her with a warm smile. "Vanessa, you look stunning." He said, gesturing toward a private elevator. "I thought you might enjoy seeing the rest of my collection."

A helicopter idled on the rooftop—a sleek black twin-engine model, easily large enough for eight passengers. Its blades turned with a muted roar, the polished fuselage gleaming under the sun. A pilot in a navy flight suit gave a brief nod. "I thought we'd take a ride," Kahn said. "My gallery isn't here—it's at my ranch in Rancho San Pasqual. You'll love the view."

This wasn't part of the plan. But she didn't flinch. "I didn't realize you lived that far inland," she said, keeping her tone even.

"I keep a residence at Sunset Cliffs," he replied, nodding toward the coast. "But my sanctuary is inland." He added with a smile, "Don't worry. I need to be back by eight. Wouldn't want you to miss your foundation dinner."

She met his gaze. "Several important donors are expecting me." Kahn's smile widened, amused. "Of course. Shall we?"

Vanessa boarded the helicopter, masking her unease behind calm resolve. The interior was plush—tan leather seats, tinted windows, and an insulated quiet that felt like a private jet.

As the rotors intensified and the cabin lifted, the city fell away beneath them. They swept out over San Diego Bay. The USS Midway stretched below them, its decks dotted with retired aircraft. Beside it, the Star of India rocked gently in its berth, sails furled. Between North Island and Point Loma, the harbor bustled with life—

sailboats, Navy vessels, ferries weaving white wakes behind them.

The helicopter banked over the Old Point Loma Lighthouse, perched atop the bluffs like a forgotten watchtower. Sunlight caught the water, scattering light like broken glass. "There," Kahn said, pointing north. "That's Sunset Cliffs. My main house is just above that bluff. You can feel the ocean shake the walls when the surf's up."

They followed the rugged coastline past Ocean Beach, the breakers alive with surfers carving across swells. Then on past Mission Bay and La Jolla, where sandstone cliffs dropped sharply into turquoise coves.

After Encinitas, the helicopter turned inland. Below, Rancho Santa Fe stretched wide and green—equestrian estates, private vineyards, long driveways tucked behind olive trees. "Some of the priciest land in California," Kahn said.

Soon, the landscape shifted. The terrain opened into rolling fields, citrus orchards, and patchwork farmland. "That's the San Pasqual Valley," he said, lowering his voice slightly. "It's the only designated agricultural preserve left in the county. Driving through is like going back in time."

They dipped lower over rows of crops, past weathered barns and farmhouses clinging to the edge of the past. "Right there," he added, gesturing to a plateau just beyond. "That's where the Battle of San Pasqual took place. Kit Carson almost died in that dust. The history out here sticks to your skin."

They veered slightly right, passing over the San Diego Safari Park. From the air, the enclosures looked like the African savannah—zebras and antelope wandering freely, giraffes clustered in the shade of fabricated trees. "It's strange," Vanessa said. "It doesn't feel like San Diego anymore."

"That's the point," Kahn replied. "Out here, the noise disappears."

"That's Dos Osos Golf Course, and the community of Rancho San Pasqual," Kahn said. "I've acquired several homes there for key engineers and executives. Keeps them close—and loyal."

She smiled politely, but the words sat heavy. Close and loyal sounded a lot like watched and owned. Ahead, nestled against a grove-covered hill, his estate came into view. A sprawling Ranch-style home, surrounded by citrus and avocado trees. A large fenced paddock sat beside a stable. Horses grazed quietly.

They touched down near a waiting golf cart. A uniformed security guard stood nearby.

Kahn stepped out and turned to her, offering a hand. "Welcome to my home, Vanessa." There was warmth in his voice—but something colder underneath.

She stepped onto the tarmac. Her pulse ticked upward. No backup. No margin for error.

CHAPTER 107: THE RANCH

As they stepped out of the chopper, a large golden retriever trotted up, tail wagging. Kahn smiled. "This is Hass. He belongs to the groundskeeper, but he thinks he runs the place. Named after the avocados he steals—he's got a bit of a weight problem." Vanessa knelt and scratched behind the dog's ears. Hass gave a contented sigh. "He's adorable."

They rolled through the estate in a golf cart, winding past groves of avocados and orange trees. The afternoon sun cast long shadows across the sculpted land. Kahn pointed out a small lake used to store irrigation water.

Kahn pulled to a stop in front of an elegant barn flanked by a full-sized show ring. "Let's take a look, Vanessa."

Inside, the cool shade carried the mingled scents of hay and saddle leather. Stalls lined both walls, each one housing a sleek Appaloosa—alert, calm, and curious about the visitors. Polished tack hung in place. Gleaming coats. Money well spent.

Vanessa stepped to one of the stalls, letting her hand glide down the horse's neck. It gave a soft whinny, nuzzling into her touch. "You've built quite an operation," she said. "I trade when the bloodlines are right," Kahn replied, brushing a flank as they walked. "Ride when I can. Never enough time." "I grew up around horses," Vanessa said. "Ranch outside Taos. It stays with you." Kahn glanced over, something quieter in his gaze. "It does."

They continued through a quiet patch of oak trees. Near a modest bunkhouse, Vanessa spotted a basketball hoop over a cracked slab. Two men sat on the porch; their conversation halted when they saw the cart. One, an enormous figure in a cowboy hat, puffed slowly on a cigarette. The other, thin, sharp-faced, balding, and stiff, looked their way, then turned and slipped inside without a word. Before stepping fully through the doorway, he glanced back, his face unreadable behind dark glasses. "Caretakers?" Vanessa asked, casually. "Staff quarters," Kahn said. "Security rotates through. Keeps an eye on the groves. Coyotes, mountain lions… lately, squatters stripping avocado trees." As they moved by, she noted the quick glance Kahn gave the porch. Assessing. Not relaxed.

"Let's head to the house."

The ranch home looked like it belonged in Architectural Digest—a blend of Frank Lloyd Wright and Greene & Greene. Massive redwood beams, stacked stone walls, folding glass doors opening onto a broad covered patio.

Inside, understated wealth. Stickley furniture. Navajo rugs. Oil paintings of the Old West. A long wall of rare pottery. Bronze Remington sculptures flanking a stone hearth. "Amazing," Vanessa said, and meant it. "I'm glad you think so," Kahn replied. "But the real prize is this way."

He led her down a quiet hall to a private gallery. Vanessa stopped cold. Pollock. Rothko. Mondrian. Kandinsky. Abstract giants. This wasn't a vanity wall—it rivaled a museum's holdings. "Incredible. Amazing," she said, turning slowly in place. "It's my passion. My addiction," Kahn said. He gestured to the Pollock. "You don't see it—you feel it." Then to the Rothko: "Give it time. It starts to echo." The Mondrian: "Chaos in a cage. Each one triggers something—memory, emotion, instinct." She nodded, her eyes scanning and cataloging. Every piece, every placement was deliberate. This wasn't just beauty—it was a statement. "Art should challenge us," he said. "Change how we see the world." "It does," she replied. "And it says a lot about the man who built this collection." Kahn's smile deepened. "Let's get a drink."

Back in the great room, they settled into leather chairs near the fire. He poured her a glass of Pinot Noir. "Russian River," she noted. "Rochioli?" "Good palate," he said. "It does have a special complexity. Depth." They sipped in silence. For a moment, the tension gave way to the fire's quiet crackle.

Kahn broke it. "Tell me about the Foundation." She kept it broad —emerging artists, expanded outreach, a new chapter of growth. Just enough to intrigue. He listened, then said, "Admirable work. It's tragic what happened to Maggie and Peter. A senseless loss." Vanessa's tone stayed even. "Oh, they're doing well, actually. Recovering at Shangri-La. Maggie's hoping to return soon."

Kahn blinked. "Really? That's... odd. I was told—" He caught himself. Too late. The smile came fast, forced. "Bad intel, I guess." "I'm quite sure," she said. "I spoke with them this morning. Sounds like someone gave you outdated information."

A pause. Long enough to feel.

Kahn glanced at his watch. "Damn. I forgot. I've got a conference call in thirty minutes. I promised I'd have you back in time for your dinner." He stood abruptly. "I won't be joining the return flight, but my driver will meet you at the complex."

Vanessa followed, keeping her tone light, but the shift in mood was unmistakable. Kahn was rattled. At the helipad, he shook her hand. "Until next time, Vanessa." His grip was limp. The charm was gone.

Vanessa watched him speed off in the cart before the pilot ushered her into the chopper. She'd struck a nerve. But which one? Something here didn't add up. And Kahn's slip about Maggie and Peter confirmed it. Whatever Kahn was hiding, it wasn't the kind of secret that unraveled quietly. And she had pulled the first thread.

CHAPTER 108: SOCHI'S PAYNE PROBLEM

Sochi had been back nearly twelve hours, but his mind refused to settle. Rest could wait—too much remained unresolved.

The bunkhouse was a dump, but it was his. Unlike the guest quarters Kahn once offered—crowded, watched, exposed—this place gave him what he valued most: privacy. Still, the smell was inescapable. Cigarette smoke had embedded itself into every-thing—the mattress, the curtains, even his clothes. Johnson's habit was impossible to escape.

Then there was the boy.

Sochi opened the screen door to the porch. Johnson sat in a rock-ing chair, cigarette dangling from his lips, his eyes on the dusky hills.

Sochi leaned against a porch post. "How's the kid?"

A pause. Then a low chuckle. "Quiet."

Sochi didn't like the tone. "Define quiet."

Johnson took a drag before answering. "Kid listens. Doesn't say much. I let him out for a bit—yard time. Shot a few hoops, tossed a ball for the mutt. He didn't try anything. Just stood there, staring at the clouds. He's back inside now, locked up, watching Marvel movies. Daredevil, I think. The Ben Affleck one."

"So you let him out alone?"

"Hell no," Johnson scoffed. "Watched him the whole damn time. Kid didn't even look at the fence. Just... stood there. Creepy little bastard."

Sochi exhaled, unease settling deeper into his chest. "Keep him close. I don't want surprises."

Sochi's phone buzzed.

Sender: Naresh Manish – Mumbai R&D Subject: URGENT!!!

R&D center raided. They beat me and threw me out. Director Mills is dead—shot trying to stop them. Data uploaded. Programmers interrogated. Desai and a team—ex-military—came through the tunnel. They were asking for the girl. They sounded American.

Sochi's breath caught. Mumbai was supposed to be locked down. Mills had an army. And yet—raided. What the hell was happening?

The message replayed in his mind. Americans. Desai. The tunnel. It was unraveling.

Johnson glanced sideways at him, lighting another cigarette. "You look like hell."

Sochi ignored him.

The crunch of tires on gravel told them something was coming. A black golf cart rolled up the path to the main house. Kahn was behind the wheel. Beside him, a woman Sochi didn't recognize.

Kahn slowed. Their eyes met briefly, then he sped up toward the main house. Sochi shook his head and went back into the bunkhouse. He had a lot to think about.

An hour later, the bunkhouse door slammed open.

Kahn stepped inside, every move controlled. A storm barely contained beneath his calm exterior.

"Tell me again," he said evenly. "San Diego. The shootout. What did you tell me?"

Sochi stood. "Sir?"

"You told me they were dead."

"They were!" Sochi rasped.

Kahn moved like a whip—one sharp blow to the gut. Sochi crumpled, gasping, pain lancing through his ribs.

"You failed," Kahn said coldly. "And you lied. They alive and well back at Shangri-La."

Sochi clawed his way upright. "I didn't lie. I thought they were dead. I emptied two clips into that house. Sirens were closing in. I couldn't risk getting caught or exposing you—no time to check pulses. I ran."

Kahn studied him in silence. For a long, tense moment, Sochi couldn't read his face.

"Maybe you did the right thing," Kahn finally said. "But now I have to clean up your mess. And I don't like it."

Sochi wiped his mouth, catching his breath. "There's more. I just got a message from Mumbai."

Kahn's expression darkened. "Go on."

"R&D center's compromised. Armed Americans. Desai's team. They were after the girl."

"Americans? Find out who they are. Now." He stepped toward the door. "Get back to me. Immediately."

Sochi stumbled to his desk laptop, heart hammering. His mind was spinning, fragmented thoughts racing through the fog of fatigue and pain.

He opened his laptop and began typing: San Diego home invasion. Too broad. San Diego couple attacked. Still nothing useful. Point Loma shooting art foundation.

Then he saw it—third result down: **Prominent Point Loma Family Attacked—Local Artist and Couple in Critical Condition.**

He clicked.

SAN DIEGO — A violent home invasion at a historic Point Loma estate has left three residents hospitalized, in critical condition. All three victims were discovered unconscious in the estate's wine cellar. Investigators say evidence at the scene suggests the victims attempted to fight off their attackers using wine bottles and broken glass.

The victims have been identified as Peter and Margaret Manning—longtime San Diego philanthropists and co-founders of the Peninsula Arts Foundation—and Luke Payne, a highly decorated U.S.. Navy veteran and local artist. Payne, a retired Master Chief Aviation Rescue Swimmer, earned multiple commendations, including the Navy Cross, during his two-decade military career before becoming an emerging star in the Southern California art world.

Payne also served as an instructor at the Peninsula Arts Foundation. Law enforcement officials have not released information about suspects or motive but confirmed the assailants demonstrated signs of tactical training.

"Luke Payne. Who is this guy"

The crashing glass. The chaos. Steel balls thrown like grenades. The way he moved—controlled, trained.

Jimmy's voice echoed in his memory: He was a trained soldier. We shouldn't have underestimated him.

A Master Chief. A rescue diver. A survivor.

He slammed the laptop shut and ran to the main house.

Kahn was in the great room, a glass of whiskey in hand, fury simmering just beneath his stillness.

"Sochi." He turned, eyes like razors. "OK what do you have?"

"I have the name," Sochi panted. "It's Luke Payne. A decorated Navy Master Chief. He teaches at the Peninsula Arts Foundation. He was one of the victims at Shangri-La. And he survived."

Kahn's expression froze—then shifted into something colder than rage. A thin, dangerous smile.

"The artist," he said, as if tasting the name.

He began pacing, the wheels turning behind his eyes. "Of course. That's why Vanessa was here. They're scouting. Probing. But why Mumbai? If they were truly onto us, they'd have already confronted us. It's like they were..."

He turned, pointing sharply at Sochi.

"You. They're looking for you. They followed our breadcrumbs to Shanghai—to the Chinese hackers—just as we planned. But somehow, they found a lead to Mumbai. And the girl. How?"

A dark thought pounded in Sochi's head.

"No... it can't be," he said softly. "Kang. I haven't heard from him since the Shanghai mission. He took the alternative escape route to Mumbai on the freighter through Singapore. It takes over a week, so I figured that's why he went dark."

Kahn's face darkened. "If they got to Kang, he'd tell them everything to save his own skin—about the girl, about Mumbai. They followed your trail. And now it leads back to San Diego."

Sochi felt hollow. Failure after failure.

"I don't—"

"Shut up," Kahn snapped. "Don't dig yourself any deeper. I still need you. But you don't need to guess what will happen if you screw up again."

Sochi stood with his head down. Quiet.

"They don't have proof. Just suspicion. We'll be fine. After the Midway event, POTUS will back me. And when that happens—no one will touch me."

His voice turning to ice. "After the event, move the boy and the girl if we find her to my house in Martha's Vineyard. Quietly. I don't want them here. And find out what happened to the girl. If they got her, she may be on the way to San Diego."

Sochi nodded. "And the Mannings?"

Kahn's tone dropped. "After the event—take care of them when I give you the signal. All of it."

"I'll have them ready," Sochi said quietly.

Kahn stepped closer and gripped his shoulder. Not comfort. A warning.

"One shot. One chance."

Then he turned and walked out.

The door clicked shut behind him.

Sochi stood alone, heart pounding, breath shallow.

No one will touch me, Kahn had said. But the world was shifting, and Sochi had his doubts.

CHAPTER 109: THE WEIGHT OF CONSCIENCE

David Bowen stood at the glass wall of his office, eyes fixed on the Navy cruiser gliding silently beneath the Coronado Bridge. What once brought him peace now felt like a lie.

He used to believe in Kahn's vision—brilliant minds, disruptive tech, the promise of doing good. He believed in the mission. Believed in Aarav Kahn.

But that faith had crumbled. The ideals were distant now, warped by what their creation had become.

QuantumSentinel wasn't just a breakthrough in cyberwarfare; it was the ultimate weapon. It could shape history, manipulate reality, and erase resistance before it even formed.

Bowen had seen it in the eyes of the powerful—those who saw the system not as a safeguard, but as a key to unlimited power. A kill switch for global autonomy.

And Kahn? Kahn basked in their admiration like a sun god—radiant, untouchable, oblivious to the shadows spreading at his feet.

But none of it haunted Bowen more than the children.

He'd only seen them through internal feeds—Rodrigo and Nora. Barely fourteen. Haunted prodigies, engineered and molded for digital war. They spoke of quantum fields in a language only they could understand.

"It's like painting with probability," Nora had whispered once, her eyes far away. "You shape the canvas... and it decides which reality stays."

They were brilliant. And broken. Kept isolated, "for focus," Kahn laimed. "They're delicate," he'd said. "Better for everyone if they stay sharp."

Week by week, Bowen watched their spark fade. Less light in their eyes. More silence. Their innocence corroded under the weight of their purpose.

And he had said nothing.

That silence was the rot inside him. He hadn't just helped build a weapon. He had helped enslave children.

His eyes drifted to the phone. Fingers hovered, trembling. He knew what had to be done.

He had to stop this — or at least try.

He scrolled to John Muncie – Union-Tribune. His pulse surged as he hit dial.

The line rang. Then voicemail.

"I once told you I'd call when the lines disappeared," Bowen said into the receiver, voice tight with urgency. "Well... they're gone. We need to talk."

He hung up.

The silence after felt louder than any alarm.

Would Muncie call back?

Was there still time?

He stared at the clock. Seconds ticking. Breath shallow.

No second chances.

He hit redial. Heart pounding. Eyes locked on the screen, willing the call to go through.

Praying it wasn't already too late.

CHAPTER 110: CHAPTER EMERGENCY EXIT

Nora was safe, and Kahn's operation in Mumbai was history. But they'd also revealed themselves. Kahn would retaliate. Every second they stayed in Mumbai gave him more time to prepare.

Luke stood at the front of the conference table in the private meeting room of the Taj Mahal Palace, his gaze sweeping across the faces of his team. He took a breath, steadying himself.

"I'm proud of every one of you," he began. "You faced danger head-on. You went above and beyond. This mission should've been over—but it's not."

The room was silent. Luke folded his arms.

"There's something you need to hear. Aarav Kahn isn't just some tech mogul. He's not just Sochi's boss. He ordered the hit on Peter and Maggie. He's a murderer. A kidnapper. And worse—he made it personal. Years ago, Peter beat him in a lawsuit over building restrictions in Point Loma. Kahn's been nursing that grudge ever since."

Moises stiffened. Hank's hand hovered near his holster, then curled into a fist. The air went taut.

Luke's voice hardened. "Now we know what QuantumSentinel can do. It can revolutionize cybersecurity—or become the key to ultimate power. If Kahn or a government gets full control, the consequences won't just be national—they'll be global."

He stepped back. "This is your chance to walk away. No judgment. But if you stay, we finish this. We stop Kahn. For Maggie, for Peter—for everyone this system could destroy."

He gave them space. He didn't need their words. Their eyes said enough—they were in.

The door burst open. Rohan Desai entered, followed by Anya. Both breathless.

"It's urgent, Payne. I'm sorry to say the police are onto you," Rohan said.

Luke straightened. "The police? Why? How?"

Anya spoke fast. "One of Kahn's fired guards has a brother high up in the Mumbai Police. He connected you to the raid. I tried to pass it off as an internal investigation gone bad, but he didn't buy it—said it involved Americans, and he doesn't like Americans."

"They don't have your names, but they'll have your photos flagged at the airports and hotels," Rohan added. "And this hotel is probably on the list."

Helen tensed. "So we can't fly out of Chhatrapati Shivaji."

"We don't have to," Anya said. "I keep a private jet at Kalina, next to our shipping facility. It's for private cargo and VIPs. No customs. No red tape."

Moises muttered, "Coop's gonna hate losing his jet."

A few chuckled—tension cracking, just a little.

"I'll deal with Coop," Rohan said as move to the door. "But you don't have days. You've got hours."

Luke nodded. "Rajeev, get the van. Back entrance."

Rajeev grinned. "As you wish, my fearless leader. Though I think a Mumbai car chase would've made a thrilling addition to our adventure."

Groans. Eye rolls. But it helped.

"One more thing," Anya said. "You'll have two extra passengers. Come in, Maria."

The door opened. Maria stepped in, holding Nora's hand. The girl looked smaller than Luke remembered—pale, but standing tall. Not broken. Just bracing.

Luke moved as if to speak, then simply nodded. "Welcome to the team."

He turned to the others. "Grab your gear. Five minutes. Back entrance."

The team scattered. Chairs scraped. Bags were slung over shoulders. Helen zipped a tactical case. Hank secured his sidearm. Rajeev offered a reassuring smile to Maria and Nora.

Luke stood at the door, watching it all. The mission wasn't over—it was about to begin again. The race to stop Kahn had officially started. Whatever came next—they'd meet it head-on.

CHAPTER 111: ROAD BLOCK

Luke's team, along with Anya, Maria, and Nora, waited at the back entrance of the Taj Mahal Palace. The air was tense—ears tuned for sirens, eyes scanning for movement.

Rajeev crossed the lobby casually, heading toward the parking elevator near the front desk. But he slowed when he spotted two uniformed police officers speaking with three clerks. One clerk pointed upstairs. One of the officers keyed his com unit and, with visible excitement, spoke rapidly into his mic.

Busted, Rajeev thought. We don't have hours. We have minutes.

He picked up his pace and disappeared into the elevator.

Outside, the group heard tires screeching. The van flew into view, fishtailing slightly as it braked hard near the loading zone.

"Get in now!" Rajeev shouted through the open window. "They know we're here. Move—quickly!"

They piled in fast. Just as the van roared up the staff ramp, half a dozen police cruisers screamed past, sirens wailing, blue lights flashing as they swarmed the hotel entrance.

"Holy hell," Hank muttered, dragging a hand down his face. "That was way too close."

Almost on cue, three more squad cars sped past in the opposite direction, slicing through the night.

"They're moving fast," Anya said. "We won't get another shot. The airport's a few miles out, but if they lock down the main roads, we're done."

Luke braced himself against the van's ceiling, scanning ahead. His stomach dropped.

A full police roadblock blocked the street—flashing barricades, cruisers crisscrossed, officers scanning cars.

"Rajeev," he said tightly, *"we've got a problem."*

Rajeev saw it too. The van's height gave them a preview—just enough to confirm the worst.

Without hesitation, he wrenched the wheel hard to the right. The van swerved onto the shoulder, narrowly missing a row of tuk-tuks. Horns blared. Angry drivers pounded the windows, shouting curses in Hindi.

"I hope you enjoy aggressive driving," Rajeev said. "Because we're officially off-script."

Luke's gut clenched. "That mile might as well be ten if we can't find a way around."

Then—an opening.

A rusted gate stood ajar ahead, leading down a narrow service lane behind the Varsity Hotel. Rajeev veered left, cutting across oncoming traffic and missing a delivery truck by inches.

A security guard stirred on his stool, rising groggily.

Rajeev rolled down the window, offered a smooth grin, and held out two crisp 1,000-rupee notes.

"We have reservations, my friend."

The guard's eyes flicked between the cash and the Western faces. A beat. Then a smile.

"Of course, sir. Right this way!"

He pocketed the bills and waved them through.

The van rolled into the hotel lot and out of sight.

"We're still boxed in unless there's another way out," Luke said.

Rajeev was already moving. "Stay put."

He and Luke scanned the rear lot. A chained gate stood at the back. Rajeev jogged over and tested it—looped, but not locked. He slipped the chain free and swung the gate wide, revealing a back road that curved toward a parallel street.

"No barricades," Rajeev said. "This gets us clear."

They sprinted back. Rajeev threw the van into reverse, spun the wheel, and gunned it through the narrow alley. Parked scooters and motorcycles and trash scraped the side of the van.

At the next intersection, they glimpsed the main blockade two blocks over. Officers were checking IDs, trunks popped. Two more minutes and they would've been caught.

Minutes later, the van rolled up to the airport security gate. Anya flashed her credentials, and the guard waved them through to a private road.

One minute later, they reached a cul-de-sac with a massive hangar bay.

"Right here—pull up to the delivery bay," Anya said, pulling out a key fob. She clicked it. The metal door began to rise. "Drive in. Let's get this van off the road."

Inside, a sleek Gulfstream G650ER jet waited beside a larger cargo plane.

"Move, move, move!" Luke barked.

Everyone scattered—gear yanked from the van, duffels slung, boots pounding on concrete. As the last bag hit the tarmac, Luke turned to Rajeev.

"Rajeev… we owe you."

Rajeev waved him off. "Oh, my friend, I do hope you weren't planning to say goodbye."

Luke blinked as Rajeev pulled a navy passport from his jacket.

"An American passport?"

Rajeev tapped it. "San Francisco. Born and raised. I've split my life between Delhi and the Bay Area. But I've had enough of this place."

"You sure?" Luke asked.

Rajeev exhaled, casting one last glance toward the city skyline.

Then, a final nod. "Absolutely. You'll need me. And I'm ready to go home."

Luke looked at him a beat longer. "Get in before I change my mind."

Hank clapped him on the back. "Welcome aboard, man."

Rajeev grinned. "Let's just make sure your home is still standing when we get there."

He was the last one through the door.

They weren't just running anymore.

They were taking the fight back to Kahn.

CHAPTER 112: GOING HOME

The low drone of the jet's engines vibrated through the plush cabin as they settled into their seats. The adrenaline from their escape still lingered, but now came the next challenge—getting home without triggering an international incident.

Luke sat near the front speaking in low tones with Helen. Across the aisle, Moises approached, concern written across his face.

"The pilot brought up a good point," Moises said. "We've got four people on this plane without passports or proper visas. We land like this, and we're looking at a major problem."

Helen sighed, rubbing her temples. "He's right, Luke. Immigration is tight, especially with this administration. No way they just let us waltz in without raising every red flag. Worst case? We could all end up at some off-the-books black site."

Luke's gaze drifted across the cabin. Jason was deep in conversation with Lee and Rusty, already reviewing the data they'd pulled in Mumbai. No time wasted.

"Jason," Luke called.

Jason looked up.

"Can you reach our contacts at DC3? We need documents—passports, visas, clearance—whatever they can do for Lee, Rusty, Maria, and Nora. They can't risk getting detained."

Jason nodded, already typing. "Right. I was going to send them a briefing anyway. I'll push this to the top of the list." He glanced up again. "Where are we landing?"

Luke checked his watch. "Tell them to meet us at North Island. I'll make arrangements to get us onto the base."

Helen had been watching. She raised a hand. "Hold it. I know what you're about to say. You want me to call my father."

Luke grinned. "Great idea."

Helen rolled her eyes and pulled out her phone. "There's satellite WiFi, so I should have a secure connection. But if we're still on Mumbai time, it's what… midnight in San Diego?"

"Wake him up," Luke said. "He'd love to hear from his daughter."

Helen was already dialing. Admiral Patton didn't like surprises—but he wasn't going to ignore a 3 AM call from his daughter.

Jason was already banging away on his laptop, fingers flying.

Luke leaned back, trying to settle—but sleep wouldn't come. His mind spun with puzzle pieces: Rodrigo. Sochi. Kahn. Quantum-Sentinel.

They'd uncovered a lot—but it wasn't over.

About an hour into the flight, Helen joined Jason, Lee, and Rusty for a quiet discussion. At the front of the plane, Moises took over for the pilot. In the back, Hank, Rajeev, and Jenny were asleep. Maria dozed beside Nora, who clutched a blanket and stared out the window.

Luke closed his eyes.

He saw Rodrigo—helpless, trapped in Sochi's grip. They were near a cliff. Luke tried to move, to scream, but he was frozen. Powerless.

He woke with a start, breath shallow.

Helen's voice cut through the mist. "Luke? You alright?"

He rubbed his face. "I'm fine. Just a bad dream."

She didn't press. "Well, good news. I talked to my father."

Luke raised an eyebrow.

"He chewed me out for being on the mission, but by the end, I think he was actually proud. He said he'd arrange everything."

Luke let out a slow breath. One obstacle cleared.

"Jason also got word from DC3," Helen continued. "They're handling everything—passports, documents, visas. He sent over the photos and bios for our new friends."

Luke nodded. "Good."

"He also arranged transport. I just need to confirm the final destination once we land."

Before he could respond, Anya appeared, her confidence dulled. She looked like someone carrying more than one kind of burden.

"I'm sorry to interrupt," she said.

Luke motioned to the seat across from them.

"I wanted to thank you and your team, Luke," he said. "You risked a lot for people you barely knew."

Anya lowered her gaze. "I have very few real friends. Running a company like mine takes everything. And now…"

Helen leaned forward. "Now what, Anya?"

She hesitated, then said, "If my brother is caught and punished—which he should be, I will take over my brother's operation, including QuantumSentinel."

Luke whistled softly. "That changes the dynamics."

Anya nodded. "There will be moral and ethical decisions ahead. I don't know if I trust myself to make them alone."

Helen studied her. "What are you thinking?"

"Depending on what unfolds, I may relocate to San Diego. I'll keep the telecom side in India, but the quantum chip tech, the cybersecurity systems, the new smartphone line—those need my full attention."

She looked between them. "I need people I can trust. I'd like your help."

Luke was caught off guard. "I really haven't given it much thought. But yes, you'll have our support."

Helen answered first. "Absolutely."

Anya gave a grateful smile. "Thank you. It helps knowing I

won't be alone."

"Do you have a place to stay in San Diego?" Helen asked.

Anya laughed softly.

"Things happened so fast I didn't even book a hotel."

CHAPTER 113: NORTH ISLAND

The San Diego skyline emerged from the soft morning haze. Luke gazed out the window, letting the tension in his shoulders begin to unravel. As the jet banked for landing, he saw the familiar dark blue of the Pacific meet the cliffs of Point Loma. A Navy helicopter came in from the north, cutting across the harbor toward North Island—just as he had, a hundred times before.

This contrast—raw beauty, ordered calm—always brought him back to center. No matter how far he traveled, this coastline grounded him.

He had been a rookie third-class rescue swimmer back then— still learning where the breaking point lived. A SEAL team's Black Hawk had gone down off Point Loma during joint exercises. The surf was merciless, wind howling, wreckage churning in the water. Luke hadn't hesitated. He clipped in, dropped from the rescue chopper, and fought the current.

He reached the unconscious SEAL just before the surf could slam him into the rocks. The chief in the helicopter was signaling for him to abort, but Luke powered through with one final burst of strength. He latched onto the back of the man's wetsuit and pulled him close—Hank Kobayashi.

Alive.

Hank's chest convulsed as a geyser of seawater burst from his mouth. He coughed violently, eyes fluttering open. Through the spray and haze, he squinted up at Luke—and managed a crooked smile.

"About time," he rasped, choking as he did.

Across the cabin, Hank now snored softly, his head resting against the fuselage. Luke watched him for a moment. They never talked about that day. But Hank never forgot, and Luke remembered every second.

The jet shifted gently as it made its final descent, pulling Luke back to the present.

Helen stretched across from him. "Long flight."

"Too long," Luke said.

The wheels kissed the tarmac. Reverse thrust pulsed through the fuselage.

Luke glanced around at the team—Hank, Rajeev, Moises, Helen, Jason, Lee, Rusty, Jenny, Anya, Maria, and Nora. They'd made it out of Mumbai. But now came the hard part—facing whatever waited for them at home.

Jason stood and stretched. "Team from DC3's inbound."

Helen checked her phone. "My father's got secure transport standing by."

Luke unbuckled. "Good. Because this isn't over."

The cabin door opened, and cool coastal air swept in. Luke stepped onto the tarmac. The salt hit first—then the soft thrum of engines, the rhythm of footsteps. The base was waking up.

Three khaki-clad men approached. Rear Admiral Mark Patton led them, every stride crisp, every glance assessing.

Four sailors wheeled the stairs up to the jet, the wheels rattling against the tarmac. The engines wound down with a fading whine. The air carried the tang of salt and fuel, cool against Luke's face as he stepped out first.

He straightened, snapped a salute.

Admiral Patton returned it, his cap shadowing his eyes against the low sun. "You don't get to drop birds on my runway at dawn without warning, son. Not how this works."

Luke let a grin slip. "Sorry about interrupting your beauty sleep.

. You know me, Admiral—always been a fan of dramatic entrances."

Patton's mouth twitched, then he turned to Helen, pulling her into a quick hug.

"You always did land in the fire."

Then his eyes cut back to Luke.

"You keeping my daughter out of trouble, Master Chief?"

Luke's grin widened. "Sir, she's the one keeping me out of trouble."

Helen rolled her eyes. "Still alive, somehow."

Patton moved down the line, greeting the others in turn. His voice dropped as he came back.

"There are people inside who want a word. They didn't give me details. I'm staying close to make sure it stays above board."

CHAPTER 114: BURDEN OF PROOF

The aroma of stale coffee and jet fuel clung to the ready room as Rear Admiral Patton led them in. Fluorescent lights cast a flat glow over scuffed tile and worn furniture. Two men in dark suits looked up from a tablet.

"Harry Worthington and Thomas Benton," Patton said. "DC3."

Worthington nodded once. "We know you've been through hell. Respect. But we need a word with Luke, Jason, Helen, and the Admiral. The rest of you—galley's that way. Real coffee and a hot breakfast."

Reluctant but hungry, the rest of the team drifted out.

The door shut behind them with a soft click.

Benton tapped the tablet. "We read Jason's report. It's solid. But it raises red flags."

Worthington set the tablet down. "Kahn as a kidnapper and accessory to murder? That wasn't even close to our working theory. His early record fits the profile—local gang ties in Mumbai. Then nothing."

"Which makes him smart," Luke said. "Not clean."

"Could be. But a hunch won't cut it."

Luke kept his tone measured. "He's behind the girl's abduction. The Shanghai breach. And now he's showcasing QuantumSentinel. It all points to him."

Benton leaned back slightly. "There's one problem. No provable link between him and Sochi. Nothing that'll hold in court. Especially if POTUS is involved."

Jason exhaled sharply, a frustrated sound, and looked away. He knew the depths of Kahn's operations, the ruthless efficiency with which he erased loose ends. The lack of a direct, undeniable connection to Sochi felt less like an absence of proof and more like a carefully constructed wall.

Benton went on. "And there's another wrinkle. Someone inside DC3 is leaking. Secretary of Defense called me personally about our relationship. Told me to stand down."

Helen straightened. "You're saying the Secretary's in on it?"

"He knows more than he should. But it's clear—the White House wants QuantumSentinel. And they trust Kahn to deliver it."

Worthington's expression turned grim. "We've got a mole. High access. They knew about my private briefing schedule. Not just the meetings—my prep notes."

Helen's gaze narrowed. "You have suspects?"

A pause. Just long enough to be noticeable. "We're closing in. But until we confirm, we play this old school. No electronics. No signals. Eyes-only."

"I want something irrefutable," Benton said. "If anyone can get us that, it's you."

Worthington nodded. "We'll give you whatever cover you need. But it has to be airtight. No room for error."

Luke stood. "We find Sochi. We find the boy. Then Kahn has nowhere to hide."

Benton rose as well. "NetSec opens tomorrow. QuantumSentinel goes public the day after. The President might be there in person."

Helen's voice was quiet but certain. "We were already going."

Luke glanced at Worthington and Benton. "Let's regroup at Shangri-La. It's time to finish this."

They exchanged firm handshakes. Worthington offered a brief nod.

"Bring it home."

As they exited the room, Helen muttered, "If Rusty got to the buffet first, we're in trouble." Luke gave a faint chuckle. "Then we'd better move fast."

CHAPTER 115: HOMECOMING

The Navy van rolled through the gates of Shangri-La to the grass parking lot. Waiting near the entrance stood Maggie, Peter, and Vanessa—each one silhouetted against the early morning light. The sight of them was a breath of fresh air—until Luke's eyes landed on Vanessa.

She smiled, but something in her posture tripped a silent alarm. Poised, composed as always—but his instincts caught the tension beneath. Something was wrong.

Everyone piled out, stretching sore muscles. Peter leaned slightly on a black cane. Maggie also had a cane and wore thick dark sunglasses, shielding her healing eyes.

Luke shook the driver's hand. "Appreciate the lift," he said.

The driver nodded before pulling away, leaving them in the cool shade of the estate.

Luke crossed the space quickly, his chest tightening as he clasped Peter's outstretched hand.

"Welcome home," Peter said, his grip still strong despite the cane.

Luke laughed. "This place looks better than I remember. You holding up okay?"

Peter arched a brow, lifting the cane slightly. "I've seen worse."

Maggie reached for Luke's hand but pulled him into a firm hug instead.

"You, my boy, need a hot shower and a proper meal," she murmured. "And then, you need to tell us everything."

Luke nodded, the warmth of the embrace grounding him for a moment.

Then, his gaze met Vanessa's.

She was more beautiful than he remembered—sun-kissed skin, dark hair catching the breeze—but there was something else. Hesitation. Her smile was tight at the edges, like someone bracing for impact.

"Welcome back," she said.

"Glad to be back," Luke replied, studying her for a beat longer.

Before he could say more, Anya stepped forward. She was composed, but Luke caught something unfamiliar—vulnerability.

Maggie, ever the matriarch, turned to her with a knowing smile.

"Ms. Kahn, I heard about your help." She looped an arm around Anya's, as if claiming her. "I have a nice apartment ready for you. Come, let me show you."

Anya blinked, startled, then nodded. A warmth passed over her features—a quiet recognition of something she hadn't felt in a long time. Maybe ever.

Peter clapped his hands together. "Welcome back, warriors. We are proud of you. Thankful, too. From what we've learned, you've had quite an adventure."

Maggie gestured toward the building. "We have rooms for all of you. Each one with a bathroom and full shower. We were lucky—the tuna tycoon who originally built this place let his crew live here, so it's built for recovery."

Luke's eyes followed where she pointed. "We also arranged six rental cars," she added. "Keys are already inside."

Luke exhaled, feeling some of the tension in his shoulders finally release.

"It's good to be home," he said. "But we still have work to do."

He turned to his team. They needed rest—but not too much.

"Let's break until 1700. Shower, rest, call your significant others—whatever you need. We regroup then."

Then his focus shifted back to Maggie, Peter, and Vanessa.

"Let me clean up, then we'll catch up."

Maggie smiled knowingly. "Good. We'll be waiting."

Luke descended the stone path toward his pool house. He was home.

But home wasn't safe. Not yet.

Sochi was still out there.

And now that Luke had learned more about Kahn, he didn't doubt the man would try again.

But not before his big event at the Midway.

That meant Luke had a few days.

Time to breathe.

Time to plan.

He stepped inside, peeling off his jacket and shirt, the exhaustion clinging to his muscles. The past forty-eight hours had been a gauntlet, and now his body was demanding rest.

The shower roared to life, steam curling up as scalding water pounded his skin. The scent of Mumbai—jet fuel, sweat, the grime of chaos—washed away, leaving only the familiar comfort of clean linen and soap.

But his mind didn't stop.

They still didn't know where Rodrigo was.

They had cracks in Kahn's armor, but no way to take him down yet.

Sochi was the key—but where was he?

Luke shut off the water, toweled off quickly, and pulled on a fresh T-shirt and jeans.

He put on his flip-flops and headed toward the main house.

Halfway up the path, Vanessa appeared.

She moved quickly, arms crossed, her expression tight.

Luke's instincts flared.

"Vanessa?" He slowed his pace. "You okay?"

She hesitated, then blurted it out. "I met with Kahn."

Luke froze.

"You what?"

Vanessa held up a calming hand. "I know, I know. But I had to do it."

Luke exhaled sharply, the words sparking a quick current of unease through him. "Alright. Slow down. Start from the beginning— tell me everything."

She motioned toward the patio table. "It's a long story."

They sat. The sun rose higher, burning off the morning haze.

Vanessa started from the beginning—her call to Peter, the limo, the rooftop meeting at Kahn's tower.

Then, the unexpected helicopter ride.

Luke listened intently, fingers drumming lightly against the wooden table. She described the sprawling ranch, the groves of avocados, the barn, the equestrian ring.

Then came the moment that changed everything.

"Kahn brought up Maggie and Peter," Vanessa said, her voice tight. "He said it was a tragedy—what happened to them."

Luke tensed. "He brought it up?"

Vanessa nodded. "Yes. And when I told him they were alive and recovering, he just... froze. His whole demeanor changed—like a switch flipped. His face went blank. The charm was gone."

Luke sat very still.

Vanessa swallowed. "He said, 'You must be mistaken. Someone told me they were dead.'"

Luke's fingers curled into a fist.

Someone lied to Kahn.

That meant Sochi.

"Vanessa... was there anything else that seemed... off?"

She thought, then nodded. "Yes. The bunkhouse."

Luke's pulse ticked faster. "At the ranch—did you get a good look at the men?"

Vanessa nodded. "Two. One ducked into the bunkhouse. Slender, under six feet, receding hairline, pinched face. Asian. He saw me—then bolted. Like he wasn't supposed to be seen."

Luke reached into his back pocket, unfolded a sketch, and held it out.

Vanessa's eyes widened. *"That's him."*

"And Rodrigo's probably there."

"There was a golden retriever at the bunkhouse. And a basketball hoop in the yard."

Luke stilled.

A dog. A basketball hoop.

His heartbeat kicked up.

"Rodrigo."

Vanessa gasped. "You think he's in that bunkhouse?"

"It makes sense."

They had their lead.

And Kahn didn't know it yet.

Luke grinned. "Mission accomplished. Let's brief the team."

CHAPTER 116: FAULT LINES

The afternoon sun bathed Shangri-La's patio with a warm light. Maggie, Maria, and Nora splashed in the pool, their laughter floating up—a rare moment of joy after the chaos of Mumbai.

Up on the terrace, Luke gathered the team. The folding chairs were arranged in a circle. An ice bucket in the center sweated around bottles of beer and mineral water. No one reached for them. Business first.

Peter stood off to the side, quiet—listening.

Luke stepped forward. "Alright, before we dig into the beers, let's talk next moves."

The team fell silent.

Luke looked at Anya.

"First, we all want to thank you, Anya, for everything you've done for this team. Risking your life and giving us a much needed ride home. That's why I invited you to this meeting; you earned our respect and friendship. But you've gone above and beyond, and I don't want to jeopardize you—or your company—any further."

Anya answered first, her chin high. "This is my fight too. QuantumSentinel was built at my company. Kahn twisted it, but I won't let him win. I'll be at the NetSec trade show. If you need an inside hand, I'm there."

Luke nodded. "Good. We'll use the window before Kahn's Midway event to gather intel at the show. Did you manage to get us credentials?"

Anya smiled. "You're on our supplier list. That gets you full access."

"Perfect," Luke said.

He turned to Hank and Jenny. "The ranch is priority. Eyes on. You see movement, log it. No cowboy stuff."

Jenny's lips twitched. "Copy that, boss."

Luke continued. "We'll coordinate gear through DC3. Vans, drones, trackers—whatever we need."

Vanessa cleared her throat. "He mentioned a house in Sunset Cliffs. Might be a fallback site."

Luke looked to Rajeev and Moises. "You two check it out. Quietly. No engagement."

Jason raised a hand. "Something else. Reporter named Muncie reached out. Says he has a source inside QuantumSentinel. Wants to meet in Ocean Beach."

Luke frowned. "Credible?"

Jason shrugged. "He's an old drinking buddy. I interviewed him for an AI story I wrote last year. Wants to talk about QuantumSentinel, and get my opinion. I'll let you know how it goes."

The silence fractured when someone finally grabbed a beer. The hiss of the cap eased something in the air.

Peter stepped forward. "Dinner's on the way. Best tacos in San Diego. No debate."

Rajeev perked up. "In Mumbai, tacos tasted like curry on chapati."

Hank leaned back. "You survived terrorists and a shootout—but naan tacos were the real trauma?"

"Exactly," Rajeev said gravely. "That's how empires fall."

Laughter rippled. The circle relaxed—just for a moment.

Later, Helen and Vanessa sat by the fire pit, beers in hand. The others had scattered to find their own quiet corners. The fire popped softly as embers floated skyward.

"You think we're ready?" Vanessa asked.

Helen tilted her head, considering. "We're as ready as we'll ever be. But this time… no second chances."

The flames crackled between them.

Above, the sky darkened. Stars blinked into view.

Tomorrow, the mission resumed.

CHAPTER 117: NETSEC SUMMIT

The NetSec Summit was more than just the world's largest cyber-security conference—it was an annual pilgrimage for leaders, engineers, entrepreneurs, and hackers from every corner of the globe. They came to forge alliances, scout bleeding-edge technologies, and indulge in legendary parties that made it part tech summit, part bacchanal.

But this year, the usual buzz had narrowed to a single focus: QuantumSentinel.

Luke threaded through the crowd with Helen, Jason, Lee, and Rusty, their NetSec lanyards swaying with each purposeful stride. None of them were there for the free swag or glossy brochures. They were hunting clues—anything that might reveal what Kahn had planned.

The iKahnX exhibit dominated the convention floor, a monument to futuristic excess. One wing showcased Anya Kahn's quantum smartphones, dazzling visitors with promises of AI-driven quantum chips, ultra-efficient batteries, "uncrackable" encryption, and cameras rivaling high-end DSLRs. The booth's design was minimalist, modern—and magnetic.

The takeaway was clear: this wasn't just tech hype. It was calculated innovation, built to capture minds, markets, and momentum. If even half the claims were true, mainstream adoption wasn't a question of if, but when.

Near the demo station, Luke spotted Anya finishing up a live interview with CNN's tech correspondent.

"You're a popular lady," he said, approaching with a smile. "Looks like your phones are a hit."

Anya chuckled. "An overnight sensation—five years in the making."

He stepped a little closer. "Your brother?"

Her expression tightened. Arms crossed. "Told me to stay in my lane—stick to the phones. Said he'd handle the 'real show.' That means tomorrow night."

Luke nodded. "The Midway."

"If he's skipping the trade floor," she said, "that means he's planning something big. Something no one sees coming."

Jason leaned in. "Offensive capability?"

Anya frowned, thoughtful. "I don't think so. He doesn't need to attack anyone. Not when he's holding the key to protecting everything—banks, hospitals, data centers, militaries. And they'll all pay through the nose to get it."

Luke gave a slow nod. "In a nutshell."

She glanced toward a camera crew setting up nearby.

"Looks like you've got another interview lined up," he said. "We'll catch up later."

"Good hunting, Luke," she replied, her eyes narrowing.

She turned toward a familiar figure nearby—a former movie star turned science show host on the History Channel, ready for an interview.

Luke and the team moved through the crowd toward another bustling exhibit. Jason pointed to the floating ADS hologram logo. "I've heard of this company. A startup that uses AI to assess cyberattacks in real time. Sort of like QuantumSentinel—minus the quantum mechanics."

Helen's gaze fixed on a tall woman at a workstation on the edge of the exhibit. "I know her. That's Emily Carter. Brilliant cryptographer. We were on the same team during a cyber crisis workshop at Stanford two years ago. Let's see what she knows."

As they approached, Carter noticed them and stood, her eyes lighting up. "Helen! I hoped I'd see you here. How are things?"

Helen shook her hand. "Great. Looks like you're no longer with DARPA?"

Carter nodded, her presence commanding. She was taller than Jason, striking, with sharp, intelligent eyes. "No, DARPA changed. I decided it was time to do my own thing." She gestured proudly around her. "So I launched Advanced Digital Systems—ADS. And this is it. Still running the place we can't talk about?"

Helen winked. "Something like that. Meet the team."

Introductions were quick, then Helen asked, "So what exactly is ADS?"

"Let me give you the chef's tour." Carter led them to a demo station with two massive monitors. "It's pretty straightforward. Our AI tracks live cyberattacks as they unfold and visualizes the threat type and possible origin. What you're seeing on screen is all of San Diego County."

She pointed. "These orange dots? Real-time attacks, mostly targeting downtown. NETSEC gets hit constantly by hackers trying to make a name. Most are low grade and blocked by our firewalls."

Rusty leaned in. "What about the yellow circles?"

"Ah." Carter smiled. "Good question. Yellow circles show previously logged attacks that stopped abruptly—technically unresolved. They're labeled with the date of the breach attempt and the server's IP address. After a dormancy window, we flag them as benign, but we keep monitoring. Most of those targeted the power grid."

She glanced at her watch. "I've got to run—moderating a panel in ten. Feel free to explore. Anyone in a red shirt can help."

She snapped her laptop shut and disappeared into the crowd.

Luke turned and noticed Rusty and Lee whispering in front of the screen, pointing at sectors of the map.

"What's going on, guys?"

Rusty looked uneasy. "Some of those IP addresses in the yellow circles—they match ones we sent data to from Shanghai. The dates line up too."

Lee nodded, voice low. "They match the IP list Sochi gave us—

I'm almost sure. I noticed it when I forwarded the list to my team in Shanghai. I ran a geolocation check, and most of the addresses pointed to San Diego zip codes. Same targets. We can't confirm without server access, but it's too close to ignore."

Helen stared at the glowing yellow markers, her tone darkening. "If you're right... it's staging for something."

Luke frowned. "Kahn?"

Lee's voice was grim. "Sochi was doing Kahn's bidding."

He looked up to the screen again. "Something tells me we're about to find out."

CHAPTER 118: JUST NOISE

Several blocks away, in the chilled core of the QuantumSentinel command center, David Bowen sat in the observation room overlooking operations. His eyes were locked on cascading data streams flowing across the giant monitor above the server farm. Red and amber threat logs flickered nonstop.

Kahn entered without a sound.

"It's just about showtime, David. Did you check the generators and the network? I don't want anything jeopardizing the demonstration if there's a power outage."

Bowen gestured toward a row of heavy batteries and industrial-grade generators. "Yes. We've been running on our own power and network for the last three days."

"Good." Kahn moved closer. "Any anomalies?"

"Just low-level scans. Background noise."

Kahn offered a knowing smile. "Not all noise is meaningless, David. Sometimes it's the prelude."

He turned from the power center to gaze out at the humming server racks.

"Tomorrow night," he said quietly, "we stop defending the world—and start reshaping it."

Bowen hesitated. "We're prepared. But if there's something I need to know—"

Kahn gave no reply. Just a nod, then disappeared into the hall.

Bowen's phone buzzed. A WhatsApp message flashed across the screen:

Got your message. Give me a ring; I'm doing some snooping. Let's meet at the Pac Shores tomorrow or the next day.

—John Muncie

John Muncie—an old-school journalist and a fearless bulldog for uncovering the truth—replied: "Tied up until after the Midway event. Let's meet the day after at 8 pm. — Bowen"

His pulse jumped.

Footsteps echoed. Kahn's voice floated back. "Problem?"

Bowen slipped the phone into his pocket. "No just checking our connections to the Midway."

But the knot in his gut told him he was getting over his head.

CHAPTER 119: PREPPING THE BATTLEFIELD

DC3 Field Office — San Diego

The DC3 field office in San Diego looked like a squat, forgettable air freight warehouse off Pacific Highway near Old Town. But the biometric scans, millimeter-wave sweep, and layers of armed guards said otherwise.

Luke, Helen, and Jason were led through the layers of security into a soundproof conference room.

Benton was already waiting, arms folded. Worthington stood beside him, arms tense. No handshakes. No pleasantries.

"You said it was urgent," Benton said as he shut the door.

Helen nodded. "Rusty and Lee found something during the Net-Sec Summit—real-time recon probes on San Diego infrastructure. They match the exact targets from Shanghai. The ones Sochi fed them during training."

"You're saying those same endpoints are being scanned now?" Benton asked.

"Exactly," Jason said. "Transit. Hospitals. Port grid. Water control systems. The pattern is identical."

Worthington's posture stiffened. "We talking zero-day deployment? Or something already embedded?"

Helen shook her head. "Too soon to call. But it's methodical. Someone's laying the groundwork."

Benton muttered, "Kahn."

"We can't prove that yet," Luke said. "But he's the only one with access to those simulations. And whatever he's planning doesn't need an audience."

"Could be a false flag?" Benton asked. "Someone trying to frame him?"

Helen considered it. "It's possible. But Occam's razor cuts toward the guy with motive, means, and a messiah complex."

Benton started pacing. "We can't move legally. No direct threat. No smoking gun. But I can raise alert status quietly—loop in DHS, local PD, and DoD command."

Worthington turned to Jason. "Can you validate the scan data and compare it with our logs?"

Jason passed over a thumb drive. "Rusty's extract. Timestamps, IPs, endpoint maps."

Benton accepted it, then glanced at Luke. "You still going to the Midway tomorrow?"

"No, we're going to watch it from Shangri-La with the team. I want to keep them together if something goes down."

Benton nodded. "Understood. We'll be there close to the stage. If Kahn makes a bad move, we'll be on him."

Helen added, "If he tries to spin up QuantumSentinel in offensive mode, you need immediate backup."

Benton raised a brow. "We have it in place. But I doubt he's going to do something that will need that response. The networks are all over it. Treating it like the Super Bowl."

"I can see why," she said. "He's hyped it to heaven. I heard POTUS is flying in."

Silence.

Worthington shook his head. "Christ, he'll make it his own shitshow. He has a nose for these things. He knows something's coming. Something big. Let's hope tomorrow's just optics."

Benton reached for the door—

Worthington stopped him. "One more thing."

The room turned.

"We may have a leak."

A chill rippled across the table.

"Every time we plan," Worthington continued, "it's like Kahn's already waiting. Like someone's feeding him our playbook."

Helen's expression darkened.

"How high?" Benton asked.

"Internal admin access," Worthington said. "Someone not in the field. But they see everything—calls, calendars, travel logistics."

Helen frowned. "A scheduler?"

Worthington's voice dropped. "Grace Peterson. My assistant. Over a decade on the job. Loyal. Sharp. But if she's being coerced…"

"Want me to pull her file?" Benton asked.

Worthington shook his head. "Not yet. If she's compromised, she's a risk—but also a signal. Ward might be using her, and if we make the wrong move, it pings back to the White House."

"Nothing digital," Worthington said. "No emails, no scheduling, no texts. From here on, it's face-to-face or handwritten only. Grace doesn't hear a word about Payne's team."

Benton gave a crisp nod.

Worthington looked around the room. "If this leaks, Kahn stays ahead. We don't let that happen."

Luke's voice was calm, certain."

Then we change the script—so even the leak can't keep up."

CHAPTER 120: SHOWTIME

San Diego's harbor shimmered gold in the setting sun as the USS Midway hosted its floating gala.

A red carpet stretched from the pier to the hangar deck, where servers in white jackets glided through clusters of elite guests. Jazz floated softly beneath the wing of a vintage fighter jet. The air buzzed with ambition and anticipation.

Influencers posed beneath banners commemorating the occasion. News anchors prepped for live segments, capturing the spectacle for millions around the globe. Camera crews darted through the crowd like sharks, circling for the perfect shot. This wasn't just an event—it was stagecraft at full throttle.

Marvin Ward stood in the fifth row of the VIP section, his suit crisp, expression tight with expectation. Beside him, Victor Greebly angled his phone for a selfie.

"Just one more post before the president arrives. Then that's it," Marvin muttered.

"Just capturing history," Greebly grinned.

As the sun dipped lower, guests were ushered onto the flight deck—an hour into the event, but just moments before the main act.

The flight deck had never seen anything like it. Bathed in precision lighting, lined with sleek rows of guest seating, and flanked by three towering digital screens, it looked less like a naval museum and more like a tech-age coliseum. Drones hovered silently overhead, capturing every angle for the global livestream. VIPs from defense, tech, finance, and politics filled the front rows, sipping champagne and watching the skyline glow.

But tonight—tonight was Kahn's. And he knew it.

As the guests settled, the ambient chatter began to fade. The color guard marched to the stage and faced the crowd, motionless and stern. The center screen filled with the image of a waving American flag. A booming PA voice rang out:

"Ladies and gentlemen, please stand for the National Anthem."

Country-western star Hank Stone, clad in jeans and a black cowboy shirt with fringe on the sleeves, strode onto the stage and delivered The Star-Spangled Banner—with a proud, unmistakable twang. As the final notes faded and the crowd applauded, he tipped his hat.

"Thank you kindly, San Diego! Now I'd like to introduce your host for the evening—my favorite television comedian—Roxy Wood!"

The familiar theme song from her long-running sitcom played as Roxy Wood, the outspoken actress and vocal presidential supporter, stepped onto the stage. She embraced Hank with a theatrical hug before striding to the mic stand in sparkling heels.

"Well, hello there, San Diego!" she boomed, her voice ringing across the flight deck. "It's not every day a girl who used to play a superhero gets to rub elbows with the movers and shakers of the tech world. But I'm here to tell you—this NetSec conference is something else! I mean, who knew cybersecurity could be so… sexy?"

She winked, drawing another ripple of laughter.

"But seriously, folks—this is important stuff. We're talking about protecting our nation from those nasty hackers. The digital bad guys who want to steal our secrets and mess with our way of life. And let me tell you—nobody messes with America on my watch!"

The crowd erupted in applause just as a distant thrum began to build. Heads turned as the unmistakable sound of rotors grew louder.

From the horizon, Marine One appeared—its green and white fuselage gleaming in the twilight as it approached in a wide arc. The helicopter descended toward the stern end of the Midway, where a custom landing platform had been constructed for the occasion.

The crowd gasped as the chopper settled with a smooth, controlled touchdown. The rotors began to wind down as the door opened. The President emerged in full theatrical glory—sporting a custom leather flight jacket with the Presidential Seal, and his signature red ball cap. A dozen Secret Service agents in mirrored shades and tailored suits flowed around him like an elite dance troupe.

From the back of the ship, he strode the length of the flight deck, grinning and waving like a conquering general. He reached the stage and gave Roxy Wood a hearty hug before stepping to the microphone.

"Hey… is this a hell of a jacket or what?" he said, running his hand over the leather sleeve like a man admiring his own reflection. "You know, I could've been a fighter pilot. Better than Tom Cruise. Natural talent." The audience tittered.

"They put me up at the Hotel Del Coronado. You know they filmed a movie with Marilyn there once? She sang 'Happy Birthday' to that Kennedy fella." He gave a wink. "Now that was a lucky guy." Laughter rippled through the crowd.

"NetSec… you people. You're what America is all about—innovation, ingenuity, the best of the best! And let me tell you, this QuantumSentinel—it's gonna make our country stronger, safer, and the envy of the world!"

He scanned the audience with a mischievous grin.

"So, let's get down to business. I want to see this QuantumSentinel thing in action." He raised a hand theatrically. "Ladies and gentlemen, the wizard of cyberspace himself—the genius behind QuantumSentinel—give it up for Mr. Aarav Kahn!"

CHAPTER 121: HORTON TOWERS

The lights dimmed as the President took his seat. A spotlight tracked Aarav Kahn as he stepped onto the stage—poised, confident, and eerily calm. His tailored suit caught the light just enough to gleam, but it was his voice that commanded attention: clear, polished, and resonant.

"Every modern city runs on fragile digital infrastructure," Kahn began, his gaze sweeping the audience. "Hackers don't just steal— they hijack reality. They cost us dearly in every aspect of our lives."

"Cybercrime is now the world's fastest-growing threat. Its annual cost? Over eleven trillion dollars. That makes it the world's third-largest economy—if you can believe it. Ransomware alone racks up more than fifty-seven billion dollars a year in damages." He paused, letting the numbers settle.

"But the cost isn't just financial. Cybercrime affects individuals like you and me. Identity theft. Frozen bank accounts. Stolen medical records. And when attackers hit infrastructure—hospitals, utilities, city services—daily life grinds to a halt. Even national stability can hang in the balance."

While he spoke, the three jumbo screens behind him came alive with a rapid montage of digital devastation: a hospital's monitors flat-lining, an airport's arrivals board blinking into chaos, a city skyline flickering before collapsing into total blackout. The crowd fell silent—rapt and uneasy.

He stepped to the edge of the stage, scanning the faces.

"And folks… even with the massive amounts of money we throw at cybercrime… it's getting worse."

He paused again, letting the weight of the words settle

over the audience.

"Until now," he said matter-of-factly.

A low buzz rippled through the crowd.

"QuantumSentinel will conquer this menace. It blocks attacks," Kahn said, his voice cutting through the cool night air. "It hunts them. In layman's terms—it doesn't just react. It sees threats before they happen. It analyzes patterns of behavior using quantum intelligence that thinks across multidimensional probabilities."

"And if a cyberattack does deploy?" Kahn continued, his tone dramatic. "QuantumSentinel won't let it near its target. Its firewall adapts in real time—an impenetrable barrier, adjusting faster than any known malicious payload."

"But that's just the first layer," he said, pacing the stage. "This system doesn't stop at defense. It traces every intrusion back to its source—pinpoints the origin, identifies the bad actor, and neutralizes them."

His voice dropped into a steely calm.

"And if instructed, it goes further. It can eliminate not just the malware—but the machines running it. Both software and hardware—wiped clean."

A deliberate pause:" QuantumSentinel shows no mercy."

CHAPTER 122: LIGHTS OUT

Kahn let the applause wash over him, each cheer reinforcing the image he had so carefully engineered—visionary, savior, showman.

"We can get on with our lives without worrying about impersonations, fake identities, or attacks on our institutions and utilities. It's a—"

He stopped when he saw the audience's reaction.

Heads turned. Phones buzzed in pockets. Murmurs spread across the deck. Eyes shifted—not toward Kahn, but to the massive screen behind him. Red dots appeared on the once-stable QuantumSentinel map of San Diego. Then more. Dozens. Hundreds.

Kahn spun to look. The interface pulsed with cascading crimson signals.

"What the hell..." he muttered.

Carter's voice cut in over the comms—tight and urgent. "Mr. Kahn, this is Carter. These aren't simulated. We're tracking a real-time attack. Multiple sectors. Coordinated."

Her face appeared on the side screen, eyes wide, jaw tight. "This isn't us. This is a live breach."

Kahn's voice sharpened. "Operations—initiate lockdown protocols. Backup power and network—online now!"

The connection to Kahn's private network and power plant kept the lights and systems aboard the Midway steady.

Kahn stepped forward. His voice, now steel. "This isn't a simulation. Stay calm. We've isolated the Midway. Power and network systems aboard the ship are safe."

But across the bay, darkness fell.

First, a few buildings. Then a ripple.

A hospital lost power—backup generators faltered. Traffic signals blinked out at a major intersection. Security lights in the Financial District stuttered, then died.

The Coronado Bridge dimmed—its graceful arc swallowed in shadow.

The San Diego skyline—once bright and defiant—vanished, floor by floor, block by block. The only lights that remained were the twin towers from the earlier demo—sentinels glowing in defiance.

Carter's voice crackled again, breath tight. "They're going for ports, comms, the grid—they're trying to knock out everything."

Kahn raised his tablet, its image duplicated on the central screen, revealing all of San Diego County—now a battlefield. Red pulses flared across the map like incoming artillery—over city blocks, substations, water plants, and satellite hubs.

A drone camera panned the skyline live. Darkness shrouded entire neighborhoods.

The crowd focused on the screen as Kahn drew a wide circle around the county with his stylus.

QuantumSentinel activated.

At first, nothing.

Then—one red node blinked. It flickered once, pulsed... and turned blue.

Another. Then another.

But for every node that turned blue, two new red ones emerged. The crowd tensed again. The system was under siege—but managed to keep up.

Carter's voice returned, more clipped. "The attackers are adapting. Every breach closed is triggering two more probes. It's a recursive payload—smart, aggressive."

A ripple of worry passed through the dignitaries in the front row. Even the President's smile faded.

Then—something shifted.

The red pulses began to slow.

QuantumSentinel wasn't just responding—it was learning.

The transitions from red to blue became faster. Targeted. Strategic.

The system anticipated patterns. Neutralized attack vectors before they hit. A new layer of shield spread from the command center outward—adaptive, translucent, pulsing blue.

Sector by sector, the city began to recover.

Red dots at the Naval base—blue. Water purification node—blue. Hospital grid—blue.

Downtown flickered. The Coronado Bridge lit up like a necklace of stars.

Then, a hush. The final red pulse blinked once, twice—then turned blue.

And the skyline bloomed—light cascading across San Diego like dawn breaking after a long night.

The deck of the Midway erupted. Applause thundered. People screamed, laughed, some even wept.

Aarav Kahn, pale but composed, allowed himself a tight smile.

"QuantumSentinel has prevailed. San Diego is secure."

He let the words land. Then he turned back to his tablet. His voice, now colder, echoed across the deck.

"Source acquired. It's from Shanghai. China."

The VIPs, even the skeptics, were on their phones confirming the cyberattack and its successful resolution.

The President rose to his feet, clapping hard. "Now that—was a hell of a show." He turned to his aide. "Get me Ward. Now. And get the CIA—find out if this was a Chinese hit."

A few rows back, Marvin Ward smiled. Whatever came next, he was sure he would be at the center of it.

Greebly leaned in, his voice a low whisper. "If that wasn't staged… did China really attack us?"

Ward didn't answer. His eyes stayed locked on Kahn.

"If he staged this entire production," he murmured, "then we've greatly underestimated him."A pause. Then, in a darker tone: "We are just props in his grand power play. And he's already writing the next act."

CHAPTER 123: EYES ON THE SCREEN

The screen was still lit with the final image of the Midway gala as the camera drone pulled back—first revealing the glowing flight deck, then the skyline, then the vast San Diego Bay under the moonlit evening

The scene cut to the spinning red graphic: CNN SPECIAL REPORT.

Urgent theme music played. Wolf Blitzer appeared, eyes serious behind his glasses.

"Good evening. What we just witnessed aboard the USS Midway may be one of the most consequential technological demonstrations in modern memory. QuantumSentinel—an artificial intelligence defense system—has not only passed its test run but, according to developers, saved San Diego from what appears to be a real-time coordinated cyberattack. With me now to unpack what this means is Dr. Linh Tran, AI ethics scholar at MIT, and Grant Wallace, retired NSA cybersecurity chief."

Blitzer turned slightly. "Dr. Tran, what's your take on what we just witnessed?"

"Honestly, Wolf, I'm stunned. What we saw tonight was a level of speed, scale, and autonomy in cyber defense that's unprecedented. If QuantumSentinel performs even half as well in a real-world environment as it just did on that stage… we're looking at a seismic shift in global security."

Blitzer nodded gravely. "Grant Wallace, do you share that optimism?"

Wallace didn't smile. "Not exactly. Look, I've spent my life in this space. What worries me isn't the system—it's who controls it.   Kahn."

He looked each of them in the eye.

"This is a battle for everything we believe in."

He glanced toward the dark water—quiet, but no longer still.

"Get some rest," he said. "Tomorrow, we go to war."

CHAPTER 124: WATCHING THE WORLD BOW

The next morning, Kahn stood by his office window, staring down at the chaos below.

Harbor Boulevard was still gridlocked with news vans. Reporters jockeyed for the best camera angles, anchors speaking breathlessly into microphones as they dissected the greatest technological breakthrough of the century.

Every network ran the same footage on a loop:

CNN: "An era-defining moment—Quantum Sentinel revolutionizes global cybersecurity!"

MSNBC: "New World Order? The ethical dilemmas of an unbreakable AI security system."

FOX: "Too much power? What happens if Quantum Sentinel falls into the wrong hands?"

On social media, servers strained under the surge. Twitter was on fire. World leaders scrambled for statements.

His phone hadn't stopped buzzing—Presidents, Prime Ministers, CEOs of the world's largest companies.

Even the Pope's representative had called, requesting Quantum Sentinel's protection for Vatican City.

"Even the Holy See seeks my blessing," he murmured, irony dripping from his voice.

Behind him, David Bowen sat on the couch, scrolling through a real-time list of missed calls. The numbers were staggering.

"You've broken the world, Aarav," Bowen said, shaking his head. "And they're lining up to pay you to fix it."

Kahn lingered at the window, scanning the scene below.

Dharavi had been his crucible—or so the story went. A Mumbai slum of desperation and ingenuity, where his father ruled with quiet dignity. A recycler. A peacemaker. Respected, even loved. But weak. His father's modest influence had satisfied the family.

Not Kahn.

He had always hungered for more—first to dominate Mumbai, then India, and now, to reshape the global order, starting with the most powerful nation in history.

And he had done it.

He'd packaged surveillance and control as national security—and they bought it wholesale. A digital empire disguised as a public good.

He turned from the window and crossed to a cabinet, putting away the half-empty bottle of Yamazaki 18 whiskey he had used to celebrate last night.

"The President is waiting downstairs for a meeting with me," he said.

Bowen arched an eyebrow. "And he's the one waiting. That says everything."

Kahn chuckled. "They need me more than I need them."

He picked up his phone, ignoring the flood of messages from heads of state and global financiers. Instead, he tapped a single number.

It rang twice.

A voice, calm and composed, answered. "Ah, Mr. Kahn. I assume you've read my message?"

Kahn's eyes gleamed. "Yes, Cardinal. And I appreciate your concern. Tell His Holiness I will personally see to the Vatican's security."

"The Church is grateful, Mr. Kahn."

The Church. The White House. The global tech elite. They all needed him now.

He ended the call and turned to Bowen.

"Now they can come up."

Bowen studied him for a moment, then glanced at a nearby terminal.

A single, unauthorized ping flashed on the screen—one line of code, gone in an instant. He said nothing. But his gaze lingered on the screen a moment longer, a flicker of concern in his eyes.

Not all noise was meaningless. And not all kings died of old age.

CHAPTER 125: SHADOW GAMES

Marvin Ward's secure line buzzed once—only once. That was the signal. He tapped the encrypted tablet resting on his lap and leaned back in the leather cocoon of a limo, part of the presidential motorcade heading to Kahn's office.

Beside him, Greebly scrolled headlines with idle detachment until the shift in Marvin's breathing caught his attention.

Ward read the message in silence. "Well," he said quietly, "looks like Kahn may have a problem."

Greeebly glanced over. "What do you mean?"

"Looks like the same team from Mumbai." Ward turned the screen so Victor could read. "Operating out of a residential compound called Shangri-La in Point Loma."

Greebly's voice dropped. "They're coming for Kahn."

"The president thinks he can ride this," Ward said finally. "Control the AI. Control Kahn. Control the narrative. He's convinced this ends with parades, not tribunals."

Greebly glanced at him. "You're questioning his judgment?"

Ward's voice was quiet but firm. "I'm questioning his grip—especially if he controls QuantumSentinel. Power does strange things to men. But absolute power, disguised as salvation? The unintended consequences could be catastrophic."

"Then again, I doubt this band of heroes can touch Kahn. They don't know what they're dealing with," Ward murmured. "Kahn's protected now. Too valuable. POTUS won't move against Kahn unless the winds shift."

Greebly sat forward. "So what? We alert Kahn?"

Ward shook his head slowly. "No. We do better than that."

Greebly raised a brow.

"We let him feel the heat. Float a rumor—say there's chatter from San Diego. That someone with ties to Mumbai, to Shangri-La, is poking around. Let him panic, then offer to help. For a price. Better yet, we loop POTUS in and let him run with it. He's good at twisting the knife—and he loves leverage."

Greebly's faint, dismissive grin returned. "Fear makes him pliable."

Ward's eyes hardened. "Fear makes him obedient."

The motorcade turned off the highway, its taillights disappearing into the morning traffic.

Grace Peterson sat alone in her office at DC3 in Maryland. The lamp on her desk cast a warm pool of light over a stack of unsorted briefing notes. But her eyes were on the screen. A transmission confirmation blinked twice—then disappeared.

For months, she'd kept her head down. She'd fed Ward just enough to avoid suspicion—abstract patterns, passenger manifests, meeting schedules. Nothing specific. Nothing actionable. Just enough to buy time.

But this... this was different. This time, it was a location. A place with a name she'd hoped never to see in one of Ward's requests again.

Shangri-La. An estate in San Diego. A target. And she knew it.

She glanced toward the photograph taped to the corner of her monitor—her daughter, laughing on a swing, Grace's grandchildren mid-flight beside her. Oblivious. Joyful.

She remembered her last visit to their house—the way her granddaughter clutched her hand at the park, how her grandson asked if she was a spy like in the movies. She had smiled. But tonight, the lie felt heavier than ever.

She'd done everything to protect them.

That's what Ward wielded like a scalpel—her past, her pension, her peace. One whispered threat about a long-buried charge, and she was suddenly on the hook, a loyal pawn in his private game.

If only she had resisted cashing those survivor checks after her husband died. But her daughter was desperate. The kids' father had vanished, the mortgage was past due, hospital bills were mounting. It had been two decades since it happened. The judge had handed down a slap-on-the-wrist misdemeanor. But she hadn't disclosed it on her federal employment forms.

She loved her job. And she needed that pension when she retired next year.

But now someone else's life was on the line. Luke Payne. Helen Shepard. And if the memos were true... two children.

She reached for the phone. Hovered. Her hand trembled. If she made the call, there was no walking it back. She'd be exposed. She'd lose everything.

But if she didn't? Innocent children would be in jeopardy.

Grace pounded her desk so hard her palm burned. She stared at the photo—her family, her reason.

She had never been a coward. She wasn't starting now. She opened Google Flights. Typed: Baltimore to San Diego. And booked the next one-way ticket.

CHAPTER 126: THE ART OF THE DEAL

The President, flanked by Marvin Ward and Victor Greebly, entered Kahn's domain.

They took their seats in deep leather chairs around a massive glass table etched with the QuantumSentinel logo. Behind them, TV monitors looped footage from the Midway demonstration—highlight reels, applause, Kahn's face haloed in LED blue.

Kahn didn't rise. His fingers were lightly steepled, his expression unreadable.

"Quite the spectacle last night," the President said, easing into the head seat.

A thin, humorless grin crossed Kahn's face. "Necessary theater."

Ward leaned in, ambition barely sheathed. "We're ready to talk terms."

Kahn raised an eyebrow. "Terms?"

Greebly smoothed his tie. "You've created something revolutionary. But power like this needs infrastructure. You don't want to haggle with every tinpot regime on Earth. That's where we come in."

Kahn studied them for a beat. "And what exactly are you proposing?"

A confident grin spread across Ward's face. "You run Quantum-Sentinel. We manage the global rollout—nation-states, corporate pipelines, strategic clients. Through us."

The President's tone cooled. "It's a partnership. You keep your title. We control the access."

Kahn's smile thinned. He leaned forward.

"You think I need your blessing?"

Ward hesitated.

Kahn tapped his buzzing phone. "Calls from London, Seoul, Riyadh. The world's already coming to me. You're here because you're afraid I'll leave you behind."

Silence spread.

Then Kahn tapped the table twice. The sound was crisp, deliberate.

"My terms," he said. "Fifty percent of all transaction fees and military contracts."

The President showed no reaction.

"I remain CEO and President," Kahn continued. "No board. No oversight. No interference."

Greebly blinked. "You want to run it solo?"

"I am running it solo."

He let it hang, then continued. "And I want a new cabinet-level position: Secretary of Cybersecurity. Advisory authority over global digital policy. And most importantly…"—he looked straight at the President—"complete amnesty. Past. Present. Future."

Ward's jaw tensed.

Greebly exhaled. "Big ask."

Kahn shrugged. "Then say no."

Another silence. The monitors replayed the Midway moment— the blackout, the recovery, the standing ovation.

The President finally turned from the screen. "What if a country refuses to play ball?"

Ward cut in. "Then we show them why they should."

Greebly nodded. "We don't even need QuantumSentinel to send a message. We can act tomorrow."

Kahn said nothing.

Ward raised his fingers, ticking them off. "First: telecommunications. Cut their satellites and networks. Second: infrastructure—energy grids, utilities, financial markets. Third: cyber-physical systems—transport, logistics, emergency response."

He dropped his hand. "The world's biggest carrot. And the sharpest stick."

The President's expression remained unreadable, but he met Kahn's gaze. After a long beat, he gave a single, curt nod.

Then Kahn nodded once in return. "Gentlemen… I believe we have an understanding."

They stood. But as the President turned to leave, he paused at the door.

"One more thing, Mr. Kahn." A brittle smile touched his lips. "You really do need us."

Kahn's eyes narrowed. "Why's that, Mr. President?"

"Our intel says there's a team—former military—poking around Point Loma. Something to do with a violent incident at a place called Shangri-La. They're asking questions—and they're not far from your front door."

Kahn blinked. A crack in the façade.

"That's absurd," he said flatly. "No one can touch me."

The President straightened his jacket. "Looks like Mr. Kahn has a problem to solve after all."

He turned to Ward and Greebly. "Let's go."

Kahn remained seated as the glass doors closed behind them.

Then, slowly, he smiled.

It came slow and cold—the smile of a man already planning his next move.

CHAPTER 127: THUMB DRIVE

David Bowen sat alone in the sterile hum of the QuantumSentinel server room, fluorescent lights casting harsh lines across the racks. Beneath his feet, processors thrummed like a mechanical heartbeat. Data scrolled endlessly across the monitors—abstract now. Useless.

Hours before, the AI he helped perfect had plunged half of San Diego into darkness.

Not by glitch. By design.

Kahn called it a demonstration.

Bowen knew better. It was a warning— part of the con.

He rubbed his eyes, staring at the secure drive in his palm. On it: audio files—clean, damning—capturing the President and his fixers brokering a quiet coup with Kahn, cloaked in polite terms. He couldn't unhear it.

Once, this had been about digital freedom. Defensive innovation. Empowerment. But the language had changed. Kahn no longer spoke of protection—only leverage. Now they did. Even the White House.

That was the final line.

He slipped the drive into his pocket and walked out. The cold whir of the machines chased him down the hall like regret.

Thirty minutes later, Bowen sat hunched in a worn red leather booth at Pacific Shores Bar in Ocean Beach, nursing a Miller Lite.

The place hadn't changed much in fifty years—mermaid murals faded into seafoam-green walls, a wheezing jukebox cycling forgotten tunes, neon signs casting lazy shadows over linoleum floors.

Once a haunt for returning WWII servicemen, it had survived long enough to be rebranded as "authentic" by the new crowd. Its grit was now considered charm. Its survival, a kind of statement.

He glanced at the doorway, heart hammering as John Muncie stepped inside, scanning the bar before walking over. Bowen exhaled—until he saw Jason Wells trailing behind him.

Bowen stiffened. "What the hell, John?" he muttered. "Who's this?"

Muncie slid into the booth across from him. "Relax. Jason's a cyber specialist—and a friend. We worked together on that corporate espionage series, remember?"

Bowen eyed Jason. Clean cut. Not a suit. Not a cop. Still… he made him nervous.

Jason leaned forward, calm. "I get it. You're risking a lot with this meeting. But I already know more than you think. You wouldn't believe where I just came from."

Bowen gave a blank look. "Try me."

Jason lowered his voice. "I was part of the team that pulled Nora out of Mumbai. She's safe."

The glass in Bowen's hand froze midair. "You—" He stopped himself, looked toward the door, then whispered, "You actually got her out?"

Jason nodded. "She's back. Now we're hunting for Rodrigo."

Bowen's face showed relief. He'd assumed Nora was lost—buried or worse.

"You're going after Kahn?"

Jason didn't answer. He didn't need to.

Bowen's face tightened at the name. He swallowed, then reached into his shirt pocket and placed a USB drive on the table.

"This," he said, voice hoarse, "contains audio from Kahn's office. The President. Ward. Greebly, I was in the room. It's damning."

Jason didn't move. "You bugged his office?"

"I knew I'd need protection. Kahn's brilliant, but he's gone off the deep end. He doesn't want control. He wants dominion."

Muncie slid the drive to Jason. "If this is real, it could break things wide open. Jason, get me a transcript ASAP."

Bowen exhaled hard, rubbing his temples. "You have no idea what you're dealing with. QuantumSentinel isn't just some cyber-security tool—it's the holy grail. Nora and Rodrigo—they're the only ones who truly understand it. My best engineers can't crack it. It's a digital black box, and those two kids are the keys."

Jason's eyes narrowed. "So Rodrigo's more than insurance."

Bowen shook his head. "He's the key."

Jason stood. His voice shifted into mission mode.

"Then we get him out."

CHAPTER 128: WOMEN'S CLUB

24 hours after the Midway spectacle, the world teetered—markets jittery, anchors breathless, governments scrambling to respond.

Inside, six women sat in Maggie's front room around a low coffee table, discussing the fate of the world on their minds.

Anya leaned forward, hands clasped tight, eyes moving across Helen, Vanessa, Maggie, Jenny, and Nora. An almost-empty bottle of pinot noir sat between them, flanked by untouched notepads, a laptop, and a thick folder stamped CLASSIFIED.

She cleared her throat.

"I won't pretend I've known you all long. But I know who you are—smart, compassionate, principled women who believe in the future. If anyone can help make the right call, it's you."

She glanced down at the reports, then back up.

"Realistically, my brother's corporation—and the technology—are going to fall to me. I'll be the one holding the access keys. But I don't want to carry that alone. I want us to decide together—the fate of QuantumSentinel."

She exhaled, tapping the folder. "Let's be honest. We're sitting on the most powerful system ever created. The world saw a show—but what they didn't see is how easily this becomes a weapon. Not of destruction, but of control."

"The AI could end cybercrime. Shield nations. Guard the vulnerable. It could change the world—for good. But we all know what happens when power like this falls into the wrong hands."

Vanessa rolled her glass gently, voice thoughtful. "Maybe form an international council. Only democratic nations. Ethical governments. Shared access. No monopolies. No tyrants."

Helen shook her head. "That's a good and logical thought, Vanessa—unfortunately, that's not how it works. Not anymore."

She nodded toward the muted TV across the room, where CNN headlines scrolled:

QuantumSentinel: Savior or Superweapon? The Rise of the Digital Empire.

"Power doesn't get shared," Helen said. "It gets seized."

Maggie stared into the fire. "Power corrupts," she said. "Always has. Always will."

Anya's fingers tapped a nervous rhythm on the armrest. "My brother originally built the system to protect our telecommunications business. Once he realized what it was capable of, he became a changed man—obsessed with power. Now every strongman or would-be dictator wants a piece."

Helen leaned forward. "And we know what they're willing to do. Jason secured recordings—Kahn negotiating directly with the President, Ward, and Greebly. Military contracts. Global control. Immunity."

Vanessa's eyes widened. "You're serious? Actual recordings?"

Helen nodded. "Clear audio. And there's more—encrypted logs between Kahn and Sochi. Time-stamped the night Peter and Maggie were attacked. It's not a confession, but the pattern fits. The voices match."

Anya sat back, her face tight. "That... confirms my suspicions." Her fingers traced the edge of the folder without opening it. "I didn't want to believe he'd gone that far. But deep down—I knew."

Nora, who had been silent until now, took a sip of her orange juice and soda water before she spoke.

"And that's just the politics," she said. "You saw what the system did on the Midway. That was a taste."

She turned to Anya. "They say it can protect people? Maybe. But who decides which people?"

Vanessa swallowed hard.

Maggie looked up, her voice low. "So it's not only a shield. It's a loaded gun."

Nora nodded. "And it never misses."

Anya stared down at her hands. Her whole life had been about tech, progress, vision. But this? This was something else entirely.

Finally, she met their eyes. "No one controls it," she said quietly. "Not Kahn. Not governments. Not us. We bury it."

Nora pulled the laptop closer. "We don't destroy it," she said. "But maybe we can put it to sleep."

Vanessa frowned. "Shut it off?"

ONE"Not exactly," Nora said, thinking aloud. "There may be a way to simulate an extended maintenance cycle. No commands. No external access. No recovery path. Like putting a ghost in a vault, buried in a maze, deep under a mountain."

Helen's voice sharpened. "Could Kahn revive it?"

Nora hesitated. "Not without the access keys. And if we do this… we make sure he never gets them."

Vanessa let out a breath. "So… we're considering putting the world's most dangerous AI down for a permanent nap?"

Nora smiled. "Sweet dreams."

Helen nodded slowly. "Then we make sure no one ever finds the keys."

CHAPTER 129: DEAR SISTER

Lee sat on a stone bench nestled in Shangri-La's moonlit garden, the perfume of jasmine curling in the warm breeze. His mind churned. The adrenaline had burned off, leaving a strange clarity. He and Rusty had made it—from near outcasts in Mumbai to partners in CyberWatch. The road had bent, but it hadn't broken.

His fingers hovered over his phone. For days, he'd wanted to make this call.

He dialed.

"Lee?" General Yue's voice was sharp, breathless. Then it softened. "Are you safe?"

He smiled. "Yeah. We're in San Diego. Rusty and I are both safe. How about you?"

Yue sighed. "As well as expected under the circumstances. Controlled panic. They're scrambling to reverse-engineer Quantum-Sentinel or find a way to neutralize it. I'm in nonstop briefings with generals who look like they've seen ghosts since the Midway demonstration."

He could picture it—the war rooms, red eyes under fluorescent lights, pride bruised and patience thin.

"To be honest, they're not happy with me—looking for a scapegoat," she added. "I'm probably headed for reassignment. Maybe a vocational training center in Xinjiang. Maybe somewhere worse."

Lee leaned back, watching the stars overhead. "They'd be fools to lose you. And anyway, you don't have to worry about Quantum-Sentinel."

Her voice sharpened. "Why not?"

"Because we shut it down. Put it into deep hibernation."

"When? How?" A beat. "Wait—were you involved with that?"

He nodded, though she couldn't see it. "Me, Rusty, Nora—Da Vinci, the girl we rescued in Mumbai. We're working with Helen Shepard now. CyberWatch took us in."

Yue gave a low, surprised laugh—half relief, half admiration. "You always had the instincts. But now you've got purpose. I'm proud of you, little brother."

A warmth in her voice pulled at something old and familiar.

"Mom and Dad would've been proud too, you know," she added.

Lee swallowed. "I hope so."

After a pause, she said more carefully, "Tell Helen… I look forward to meeting her again someday."

Lee caught the tone, smiled. "I'll pass that along. She'll appreciate it. She has a lot of respect for you. Honestly, we wouldn't be here without you. Kahn and his QuantumSentinel would still be wreaking havoc."

He heard her sigh. "Fate has been kind for a change, brother."

His smile faded. "So far. But it's not over yet. Luke and his team are heading out again. It's a dangerous mission—to stop Sochi and rescue Nora's brother, Rodrigo. He helped program QuantumSentinel."

"It's hard to fathom," Yue said softly. "Two children creating something that complex and powerful. It'll be interesting to see what they invent next—something less dramatic, I pray."

Another pause, then her voice softened. "I hope we cross paths again, Lee."

"We will, sister. I believe we will."

She chuckled. "Stay safe, little brother. And keep me in the loop. It's always good to know what's happening on the other side of the

Great Firewall."

"Same to you, sis."

The line clicked off.

Lee sat for a moment longer, bathed in moonlight. The past was behind him now, a story told and finished. He closed his eyes, letting the stillness settle. The world was fragile—but for now, it held.

CHAPTER 130: SORTING PRIORITIES

Mission day: 0900

Tension hung thick in the Shangri-La kitchen. Luke, Helen, Jason, Hank, Jenny, Rajeev, Moises, Rusty, Lee, Nora, and the DC3 operatives sat around the oak table, maps and satellite images spread out like a battlefield.

The smell of coffee lingered—something warm and real in a day that felt anything but.

Nora sat quietly in the corner, eyes distant, shoulders tense. After a long moment, she stood and walked over to Luke, who was studying the terrain around Kahn's ranch on Google Maps.

"Luke," she said softly, "I want to thank you—for trying to rescue Rodrigo. He's the only family I have, and I miss him desperately." She paused, voice tight. "Please… bring him home safely."

A lump caught in Luke's throat. Around the table, the chatter died. The room fell silent.

Rajeev turned away, blinking fast.

Luke stood and gently placed a hand on Nora's shoulder, giving it a reassuring squeeze. "We'll bring him home," he said. "I promise."

Heads around the table nodded in quiet agreement.

"Damn right we will," Hank added, voice thick with resolve.

Nora looked around at her new allies—this strange, extraordinary team willing to risk everything for her brother. She swallowed, nodded once, and said simply:

"Thank you. All of you."

Then she turned and walked out, the weight of hope and fear

trailing behind her.

Silence lingered. Each person looked around the table with a deepening resolve. The mission was no longer just tactical. It was personal.

Luke cleared his throat. "Okay. Let's start."

But before anyone could speak, Helen closed her laptop and looked around the room.

"We need to address the elephant in the room."

A pause.

"Bowen's recordings."

Jason nodded. "They're real. Clean audio of Kahn making a deal with POTUS, Ward, and Greebly. We're talking raw, unfiltered collusion—global blackmail, AI monopoly, and unchecked power."

Worthington's expression darkened. "That tape is political TNT. We have to move carefully…"

Helen cut him off. "You're right. If we leak this, we become the story. They'll cry AI deepfake, weaponize the DOJ, and send us off the grid. Best case—we're discredited. Worst? We disappear."

Moises muttered, "Or wake up in a hellhole prison in South Sudan. He's done that before—for something a lot less serious."

Luke's voice was flat. "We're not taking down the President—as much as I'd like to. That's a suicide mission. Our target is Kahn. And the best shot we've got is tying him to crimes we can prove— Rodrigo's abduction. Cyberattacks on American infrastructure. Sochi's attempted hits on Peter and Maggie."

Helen turned to Worthington. "DC3 needs to lock those files down. No leaks. No fingerprints. Not even metadata."

Worthington nodded. "We'll store it—zero exposure. You want it buried, it stays buried. Although in these times, something of this magnitude on POTUS… could be useful when the right occasion presents itself."

Luke leaned forward, voice low and clear. "Good. Our little ace in the hole. So, our marching orders are simple: rescue the kid. We stop Kahn. And we live to tell the story."

"Right. Simple," Rajeev muttered to no one in particular.

The room held its breath.

Then Hank cleared his throat, grounding them again. "We've had the ranch under drone and satellite coverage. Security's tight—six guards on a loop. Smart. Disciplined. No mistakes. No chatter."

Jenny pointed to a red circle on the layout. "Rodrigo is here. We're sure. Fourteen. Dark hair. Small build. Plays near the garden with the dog." She tapped the map. "Always watched by this guy—big, cowboy hat, chain-smoker. Never goes inside. Just stands there like a sentinel or sits on the bunkhouse porch smoking."

Worthington asked, "And Sochi?"

Jason flipped a page in his folder. "Gone. No matching heat sigs or movement. We think he bailed a day ago. Either repositioning—or running."

Luke said, "Doesn't change the mission. We get Rodrigo, we'll probably get a lead on Sochi."

Worthington set his hand on the map. "DC3 will coordinate with San Diego PD. We sideline the Feds. They're too busy running errands for the White House anyway."

"Rajeev raised his hand," Just one more item my friend. Moises and I scouted Kahns mansion in Ocean Beach on Sunset Cliffs. Nothing happening there, no one in or out. But, we decided to get plans for it anyway just in case.

Luke stood. "Then we go this afternoon at 1730 hours. Meet here."

He gave one last nod. Rodrigo would be free. Sochi would be cornered. And Kahn? His time was nearly up.

CHAPTER 131: MISSION TO CYBERWATCH

Mission day: 1200 Hours

Inside, CyberWatch headquarters in La Jolla, after the drab initial entry, had all the charm of a luxury tech startup—and the gravity of a black ops command center. Sunlight streamed through the windows, casting angular shadows across polished floors as Jason led Nora, Lee, and Rusty through the main entrance.

Jason glanced at Lee and Rusty, both uncharacteristically quiet. It was clear they were impressed.

The massive lobby with towering palm trees and expansive outdoor area with red umbrella tables and a lap pool sparkling in the distance. The Pacific sparkled on the horizon.

Jason grinned. "This is the rec room there's an exclusive elevator to the cove — and a private gym.."

Lee gave Rusty a look, grinning like he had just won the lottery.

But the team rooms intrigued them.

Jason pointed out a room with a dozen technicians at work. "Each takes a different slice of the world, or flavor of cybercrime."

Jason grinned. "Feels like home, doesn't it?"

Rusty let out a low whistle. "I wish. Damn. This is next-level."

Lee nodded, thoughtful. "I thought our operation was impressive. But this..." He gestured toward the sleek offices and glowing threat maps. "This is—how do you say it, Rusty? Awesome."

They passed a rec room where a wall-length digital map displayed cyber threats pulsing across the globe in real-time.

Nora nudged Jason. "I thought hackers worked out of basements, not ocean-view fortresses."

Jason chuckled. "We take care of our people. Happy minds solve problems faster."

At the high-security elevator, Jason tapped his access badge. The doors opened silently.

"Welcome to the real work," he said.

Beneath CyberWatch, the computer operations center was all stainless steel and glass. Racks of servers lined the walls, LEDs blinking in steady cadence. A faint ozone scent hung in the filtered air. Massive wall screens displayed diagnostics, security feeds, and AI threat models in constant motion.

A young woman in a NASA hoodie greeted them at the door. "Hey—I'm Tina. Jason said you brought us something fun to break."

Jason grinned. "Not break. Just... pause." He nodded to Nora. "She's got the keys."

Tina raised an eyebrow. "Right. Just a joke." She pointed to a nearby workstation. "You're logged into the server network and the open web. Plenty of horsepower."

Nora stepped forward, holding up a thumb drive. "Perfect. I'm going to need it."

She sat, inserted the drive, and turned to the group.

"It doesn't take much to interface with QuantumSentinel—we saw that on the Midway. But changing its behavior? That's different."

She tapped the screen. Code began to scroll.

"The AI's core—the 'brain,' if you will—is relatively compact. But its quantum neural network is distributed globally. Right now, it's entangled with millions of nodes—servers, and satellites."

She took a breath.

"This program forces it to retract those connections. Untangle itself. It won't destroy the AI, but it cuts off its reach. Locks it in a box."

Tina leaned over, curious. "You wrote this yourself?"

Nora nodded. "Yes. And I built in redundancies. Once it starts, it can't be stopped. Not by QuantumSentinel. Not by Kahn. No one."

She pulled a thumb drive from her pocket and gave it to Jason. "This is the interface for our holographic system Jason briefed me on—it shows a visual overlay of the neural network. It's not the real code, just a projection. A way to see the complexity in real time."

Jason plugged it in and ran the command.

The room dimmed. A low hum vibrated beneath their feet.

Then the network came alive—light pulsing across a three-dimensional lattice, like neurons firing in a living brain.

"Just like that," Nora whispered. "Billions of decisions. Trillions of signals. All flowing through the cloud. This... is the monster in the room."

Lee and Rusty stepped closer, transfixed.

Nora inserted the second thumb drive into the server. Code streamed down the monitor, fast and clean.

Lee frowned. "You sure this'll work?"

"I built the backdoor myself," Nora said without looking up. "This doesn't kill the system. It just makes sure no one—Kahn, POTUS, or otherwise—can access it without us."

A prompt appeared:

ARE YOU SURE YOU WANT TO PLACE QUANTUMSENTINEL INTO DORMANT MODE? WARNING: UNAUTHORIZED REACTIVATION MAY LEAD TO SYSTEM LOCKOUT.

Nora took a breath. "Let's put the beast to bed."

She pressed ENTER.

Nothing happened.

Then—the network flashed.

Once. Twice.

Then stillness.

The light dimmed. The pulses faded.

QuantumSentinel was silent.

The room held its breath. The system remained intact—but the AI was asleep.

Contained.

Lee let out a breath. "That's it?"

Nora's smile was soft, bittersweet. "That's it. The smartest thing Rodrigo and I ever built... just went to sleep." She pulled the drive from the console and slipped it into her pocket.

Rusty crossed his arms, staring at the space where the hologram had glowed. "I'm impressed, Nora. You're amazing."

"Thanks, Rusty. I must admit, it's a little sad. But... its time will come."

Jason checked his watch. "Perfect timing. Payne and his team are heading to the ranch soon." He looked up, a sly grin on his face. "I'd love to be a fly on the wall when Kahn tries to use his 'magic bullet' and finds it's nothing more than a paperweight."

A silence settled. Everyone felt the weight of what was coming.

Jason straightened. "So... Lee, Rusty, how do you feel about sticking around?"

Lee's face lit up. "Are you offering us a job?"

Jason shrugged. "CyberWatch could use minds like yours. Lee, you'd take a supervisor role. Rusty, systems architecture. Nora—"

She perked up. "Yeah? Me too?"

Jason grinned. "Sorry, not yet. You've gotta finish high school first."

Nora groaned. "Seriously? I just put a quantum AI to sleep, and you're worried about geometry?"

Jason smiled. "Rules are rules. But Maggie and Anya are working on something you might like."

Nora narrowed her eyes. "Something like...?"

Jason nodded toward a nearby monitor. "They want you to lead the build out for Besty 2.0."

Nora lit up. "Yes!"

Rusty glanced at Lee. "We in?"

Lee took in the room—the tech, the people, the mission.

He nodded. "Yeah. We're in."

Jason extended his hand. "Welcome to the team."

CHAPTER 132: THE BATTLE OF SAN PASQUAL

Rancho San Pasqual, North San Diego County: 2000 Hours

The backcountry air was heavy with tension as Luke and his team crouched in the shadows of the avocado and orange groves, the ripe odor of fruit mingling with dry, earthy dust. The waxing moon cast hard angles across the landscape, illuminating the ranch's perimeter fences and the occasional sweep of a guard's flashlight.

Jenny and Hank had spent the last twenty-four hours watching the place, mapping guard rotations, ID'ing soft points in the security grid, and most importantly—confirming that Rodrigo was inside. Now, they had minutes, not hours.

Hank, crouched low beside Luke, whispered, "Six guards. Two patrolling in a fixed loop. One posted at the bunkhouse. Pilot near the helipad. All carrying sidearms, at least two with rifles."

Luke processed the layout in seconds. Not enough bodies for a full security detail with a pilot standing by. Then, Rodrigo is likely still here. That meant they had to hit hard and fast before the call comes in to move him.

Jason's voice crackled through the comms. "We're green-lit. DC3 is on standby. San Diego PD is in our pocket, but we don't want them tripping any alarms." Helen stayed with the van, running comms.

Luke exhaled slowly. "Alright. We go in silence. Helen runs comms from the van and be ready to move in when I signal. Hank, you take the patrol guards on the south ridge. Rajeev, you're heading north. Moises—secure the pilot. That chopper's ours now.

Jenny, with me and you're on counter-surveillance. If they get a call out, I wanna know about it before the cavalry arrives." Moises grinned. "Rajeev gave a restrained grin." "You're very persuasive." Luke looked directly at "No mistakes. Fast, quiet, clean. We grab the kid and go."

The team spread out, shadows dissolving into the night. Luke moved first, silent and controlled. Johnson, the guard outside the bunkhouse, was relaxed, unaware—a cigarette dangling from his lips as he leaned against the wooden railing.

Luke closed the distance in a low, smooth sprint, using natural cover to shield his approach. At the last second, he pivoted sharply, one hand clamping over Johnson's mouth while his other slipped around his throat, locking in a tight choke hold. Johnson jerked, hands scrabbling at Luke's arm, but the effect was fast, efficient. Luke kept his body low, ensuring the man's weight didn't shift loudly against the railing. Three seconds. Johnson's movements weakened. Five seconds. His eyes rolled back, and he went slack.

Luke lowered him silently to the ground as Jenny moved in, swiftly zip-tying his wrists. Rodrigo must still be inside. They had to move.

Hank took out one of the patrolling guards with a precise strike to the carotid, knocking him out cold in one hit.

Rajeev pressed his silencer against the second guard's skull just as he reached for his radio. "Drop it." The man froze. He delivered a precise elbow to the temple, and he crumpled without a sound.

Three down.

At the helipad, Moises approached the pilot. The man had just finished a cigarette, stretching his arms when he sensed movement. Too late.

Moises closed the gap, his hand snapping to the back of the pilot's head, slamming him against the helicopter's fuselage. The impact knocked him half-conscious. Moises zip tied the pilot around his wrists, yanking it tight.

"Pilot secure," Moises whispered into comms.

Luke scanned the interior through a narrow bunkhouse window. One kid, one small cot, a tray of food barely touched. No visible restraints. Good. Rodrigo wasn't hurt.

Luke opened the door and entered with controlled movements. Rodrigo's wide, terrified eyes locked onto him.

Luke crouched. Calm voice, controlled presence. "Rodrigo. I'm Luke. I'm taking you home. You'll soon be with your sister."

The boy hesitated, his breathing shallow. Then, he nodded.

Luke lifted him onto his back, securing the kid with a tactical harness rig designed for swift extractions. He clicked the comms. "Rodrigo secured."

Johnson, still zip-tied, was sitting up now, his breath ragged.

Luke knelt in front of him, voice calm but edged with steel. "We know you're not one of them."

Johnson swallowed hard. "You don't know anything."

Jenny crouched beside him, voice flat. "You don't look like a killer. You look like a guy who just realized he picked the wrong side."

Luke waited. Johnson broke first.

"The kid..." He exhaled shakily. "He's been here for weeks. Some of Kahn's guys brought him in."

Luke's stomach tightened. "Where's Sochi?"

Johnson hesitated. Jenny's grip tightened on his collar.

Johnson's eyes darted between them. Then—

"Ocean Beach. Kahn's house on Sunset Cliffs. That's where they took them."

Luke's breath hitched. Them?

His pulse spiked. His mind cut through exhaustion like a blade.

"Who?" His voice was controlled, but his whole body had become rigid.

Johnson hesitated. One look at Luke's darkened expression, and he knew better than to lie.

"The woman. The old man. The Foundation lady."

Luke's vision narrowed. His mind skipped to Vanessa's laugh, Maggie's calm hand on his arm. Peter pouring wine by candlelight. Not them. Not now.

Taken.

Luke turned sharply to Jenny. "We're moving. Now."

Jenny nodded without hesitation, already tapping into her radio. "Command, we've got a situation. Target location has changed—sending coordinates now. Helen, bring the van now!"

Luke grabbed Johnson by the shirt, dragging him forward. "What was the chopper for?"

Johnson hesitated a second too long.

Luke's voice dropped to a razor's edge. "Don't make me ask again."

Johnson winced, then spat. "They were taking the kid to Montgomery Field. Kahn's jet is waiting."

Luke's mind locked onto the next move. They had gotten here just in time.

He turned to Helen, who had just arrived with the van. "Get Rodrigo back to Shangri-La. Quietly. If anyone tails you, divert to the fallback route."

Rodrigo tugged Luke's sleeve. "Wait—Hass."

"Hass?" Luke asked.

"The dog," Rodrigo whispered. "He sleeps under the porch."

Luke exchanged a glance with Helen, then moved quickly to the porch steps, crouching low. Sure enough, an overweight golden retriever with intelligent eyes peered out. Luke gave a soft whistle. The dog crawled out, wary but calm. Rodrigo knelt, hugging Hass tightly. The dog licked his face, tail thumping.

Luke nodded. "He goes too."

Helen smiled faintly. "We'll take care of him."

Luke's voice turned hard again. "We'll meet you after we take down Kahn."

As Helen pulled away with Rodrigo and the dog in the backseat, Luke turned to the others. "Let's move."

The five of them—Luke, Moises, Hank, Rajeev, and Jenny—sprinted toward the helipad. The sleek black chopper shimmered under moonlight, still warm from its last flight. Kahn's ride. Newer than anything Moises had flown before.

"Think you can handle her?" Luke asked as they piled in.

Moises threw himself into the pilot's seat, eyes scanning the unfamiliar controls. "Haven't flown a bird like this—ever. But I'll figure it out."

The turbine coughed once, then caught with a deep, rising whine. The rotors spun faster.

Rajeev and Hank slammed the doors. Jenny dropped into the co-pilot seat, flipping switches like muscle memory. "I did six months flight support with Helo Rescue. I've got your six."

Moises grinned, fingers dancing across the console. "Let's hope it's like riding a bike."

The chopper lifted—then suddenly pitched forward in a violent nose dive. The whole cabin lurched. Rajeev swore. Jenny grabbed the dash.

"Mo!" Luke barked.

Moises muttered, "Okay—not the throttle I thought it was. I got it…"

The aircraft jolted, twisted, then steadied into a rough hover. The rotors found their rhythm. The nose leveled.

Luke locked eyes with him. "Get us to Ocean Beach. Fast."

Moises nodded. "Hang on."

The chopper surged upward into the night, blades carving into the darkness as the team flew toward Sunset Cliffs—toward Kahn's house.

Toward the people he took. Toward reckoning.

CHAPTER 133: SMUGGLER'S COVE

Moises maneuvered the helicopter low over the surf, banking toward a narrow crescent of sand carved beneath the cliffs. The thunder of waves masked the rotor noise, and the steep bluffs above shielded their approach from Kahn's estate. It was the only way in without alerting the entire compound. The tide was receding—barely enough room to land. But stealth was worth the risk.

As the cliffs drew closer, Luke's thoughts flickered briefly to Rodrigo—now safe with Helen, clutching his dog Hass as they raced back to Shangri-La. One rescue done. One more to go.

Jason's voice crackled through comms: "I've got the floor plans. Thermal drone shows a large indoor pool, no water—south side, first floor, next to the garage. On the north edge of the pool: six signatures. Three stationary—likely Vanessa, Peter, and Maggie. Two moving—one stationary by the door to the garage. He'll be the first one you take out."

Luke's pulse ticked up. "Other hostiles?"

Static, then: "Three more on the main level. Two posted just outside the garage entrance. The garage links directly to the basement. That's your best way in. Neutralize the guards outside, breach the door—then it's one door from the garage to the indoor pool. Hostages and two bad guys on the far end when you enter."

Luke stayed calm, already mapping the angles in his head. "Best access to the pool? We're landing at Smugglers Cove."

"One sec... okay. There's a stairway cut into the cliff—leads up to Sunset Cliffs Boulevard. The house is directly across the street. Big, white, modern—you won't miss it."

"Roger that. Any word from the others?"

"Yeah—just got off the phone with Helen. Rodrigo's safe. She should make it to Shangri-La in about 30. Fortunately, Nora, Rusty, and Lee were still at CyberWatch when the attack hit. And Maria—she was at the pool when Sochi's men snatched the Mannings and Vanessa. She called the DC3 emergency number we gave everyone. They responded fast and secured the grounds. Everyone's safe."

"Excellent. Let them know we'll be landing on the green when this shitshow is over."

Static. "Godspeed, my friend. Bring them home."

Luke briefed his team on the new intel. His mind mapped out the terrain: cliffside stairs—narrow, limited cover. Across the street, the mansion—a two-story white structure. Take down the two bad guys at the garage, blow the door, make the rescue, and get out before reinforcements arrive. Luke felt a familiar knot tighten in his gut. There was no room for error.

The helicopter kissed down on wet sand. Luke felt the ground shift beneath his boots as he and the team poured out, scanning the dim terrain. The smell of salt and kelp strong in the air, their boots sinking into the sand.

"Moises, keep the bird hot. Get into position at the top of the stairs and keep a lookout. Cover if necessary," Luke ordered. "If things go sideways, we're extracting hard and fast."

"Roger that. Make it fast—the tide's rising," Moises replied, eyes locked on the waves crashing on the nearby rocks, sea spray and foam pelting the team and chopper.

"We'll be back," Luke said—more firmly than he felt.

They moved swiftly—up the stairs, across the street, staying low. At the low stucco wall surrounding the property, Luke raised a fist, signaling a halt. The team dropped into cover, scanning for movement and getting their bearings.

Luke turned to Jenny. "You've got our backs. Watch for movement from the house—three hostiles inside, so be ready. Set up here," he pointed to a low corner with decent elevation, "you'll have cover and line of sight if they try to flank us."

He turned to Hank. "If the door's unlocked—which I doubt—get us in quiet. If not, blow it and we go in hard. Either way, we hit fast and catch them cold. If it gets loud, be ready for immediate push-back."

Luke's tone dropped, firm but controlled. "I want Sochi alive—but don't take chances. Hank, go high on the hostile to the right. Rajeev, take him low. I'll cover the other one. We've got innocent friends in there, so make your shots clean and dead-on. Let's move."

Jenny took her position by the wall, covering their rear. The others moved in a low crouch to a narrow tree line near the corner of the house.

Luke raised a hand, signaling Hank: Go prone. Peek the corner. Spot the targets.

Hank dropped flat and eased forward, just enough to get a line of sight. He spotted a covered side patio—two guards. One sat casually, reading a newspaper, an automatic rifle resting on the table beside him. The other strolled slowly with his back turned, rifle dangling one-handed at his side.

They weren't alert. They weren't ready. They clearly didn't expect company.

Luke waited until the walking guard turned his back again—drifting further from his partner, rifle swinging lazily in one hand.

Then—go time.

Rajeev moved like a shadow. Three steps, then a short burst forward. He reached the man just as he was about to turn. One arm wrapped around the guard's neck, the other clamped the weapon. Rajeev dropped low, pulling him into a controlled choke. The man kicked once—twice—then sagged.

Hank moved in sync, approaching the seated guard from behind. A short, precise jab to the neck stunned him. He grabbed the rifle off the table, tossed it aside, then delivered a sharp blow to the temple. The man slumped in his chair, out cold.

Luke moved in to zip-tie wrists, double-checked pulses, then signaled the all-clear. He glanced at Hank and Rajeev.

"Clean. Let's keep it that way."

The garage door stood wide open, fluorescent light washing over the polished concrete floor. A red Tesla Model S sat alone—clean, gleaming, out of place in the otherwise utilitarian space. At the far end, a reinforced metal door. Beside it, a sleek biometric scanner.

Hank frowned. "Uh oh. Biometric pad."

Luke stepped closer, studying it. "Full-hand scanner." He paused. "Let's try something before we blow it." He looked at Hank. "Go grab one of our sleeping friends. Let's see if he'd be kind enough to let us in."

Hank and Rajeev exchanged grins and trotted off. Moments later, they returned—dragging one of the unconscious guards between them.

"Left or right?" Rajeev asked, lifting the man's arm.

Luke pointed. "Right."

Hank held the body steady while Rajeev pressed the limp hand to the scanner.

Click. The lock released with a soft hiss.

Luke eased the door open an inch—just enough to break the seal without triggering a relock. He slid his boot into the gap, the cold metal pressing into his sole. Glancing back, he caught the team's grim faces in the dim light. He gave the silent three-count.

One. Two. Three.

The door burst inward. Luke moved in first, weapon raised. The garage flooded with cold, artificial light.

The first guard turned his head—too slow. Luke's silencer spat two precise, muffled shots into his leg. The man dropped with a grunt. The second guard went for his weapon, but Hank and Rajeev were already on him. Hank's pistol butt cracked against the side of his head. He dropped. Rajeev followed with a controlled kick to the first guard's temple. Both were down.

Smoke curled in the air. The tang of cordite clung to the fluorescent light.

Luke scanned the room. Vanessa, Peter, and Maggie sat bound against the wall of the room. The empty pool below was littered with discarded tiles and tools. Sochi stood over them, knife in hand, sweat streaking down his temple. He looked rattled—breathing heavy, shoulders tense.

Luke leveled his gun. "You're done. Let them go."

Sochi's mouth curled into a sneer. "You think you've won?"

He lunged—grabbing Vanessa, yanking her head back, pressing the knife to her throat. His grip shook. He crouched behind her, using her as a shield.

Luke didn't flinch. "Last chance. Drop the knife, and you live."

Sochi's eyes were wild. "You kill me, and Kahn walks."

"Kahn's finished. We have the proof. You? You're a footnote."

Maggie moved. Her foot snapped out, kicking a loose tile across the concrete with a sharp crack.

Sochi's eyes flicked down—just for a second.

Vanessa twisted sideways, wrenching free.

Luke lunged. He slammed Sochi against the wall. The knife skittered across the tile. Rajeev moved in, yanked Sochi down by the shoulder, and drove a knee into his spine.

"Don't move," Rajeev said, already zip-tying his wrists.

Sochi fought like a cornered animal—but it was over. He was down, pinned, and bound.

Luke dropped to his knee, cutting the hostages free. Vanessa coughed, trembling as she leaned into him.

"You okay?" he asked.

She nodded. "Just—get us out of here."

Peter and Maggie groaned as Rajeev helped them sit up.

Then—buzz. A harsh, tinny vibration from Sochi's pocket.

Luke froze. He reached in and pulled out the phone. The screen lit up.

From: KAHN Timestamp: 23:13 Message: KILL THEM ALL.

Luke stared at the screen. He turned it toward Sochi. "You were really going to do it."

Sochi didn't deny it. "I was waiting until he gave the order."

"And you would've followed it."

"You have no idea what he'd do to me if I failed."

Luke held his gaze. "Now you'll find out."

He smashed the phone into Sochi's cheek, cracking the glass. Then slipped it into his pocket.

Jenny's voice came through comms: "Status?"

"Hostages secured. Sochi detained. Mission clock says we were sixty seconds early."

A pause. Then: "Understood. I'll keep watch while you exfil."

"Move. Double-time," Luke said.

They pushed back through the garage, fast but tight. The two guards still lay where they dropped.

But then—shouts. Footsteps.

Gunfire ripped through the air. Two more guards—ones they'd missed from the upstairs apartment—stormed into the garage, rifles raised.

"Down!" Luke barked, twisting to shield Vanessa.

A shot clipped his arm. He grunted but stayed upright.

"Get them to the beach! Rajeev, Hank—do what you have to."

Rajeev broke off left, Hank went right—two shadows cutting through the chaos. Muzzle flashes lit the concrete. A burst of gunfire echoed off the walls. Then—silence.

Just the crash of waves and the distant thump of rotor blades spinning up.

Luke's arm burned, blood soaking through his sleeve. He didn't stop moving.

They reached the stone stairs. Maggie was struggling—her leg barely holding. Peter limped worse. Hank reappeared, grabbed Sochi under the arms. Rajeev brought up the rear, rifle scanning behind them.

The tide had surged up the beach, licking at the bottom steps.

The chopper hovered low, blades kicking up spray. Moises leaned out.

"Let's go!"

Vanessa climbed aboard first. Rajeev boosted Maggie up, then helped Peter. Hank and Luke shoved Sochi into the cargo hold. Luke hauled himself in last.

Slam—the doors shut.

The rotors howled.

A wave smashed across the landing site as the chopper lifted. Salt water splashed the windows, but they were up—rising fast, cutting into the night.

Inside, no one spoke. Breaths were ragged. Blood on the floor. Smoke in their lungs.

Luke stared at the shattered phone in his hand.

KILL THEM ALL.

If they had arrived one minute later...

It wasn't a message. It was a fuse.

And they'd just outrun the blast. He looked to the cockpit. "Take us home."

CHAPTER 134: HIGH NOON

The next morning, Aarav Kahn reclined in his Italian leather chair, polished loafers propped on his mahogany desk. Beyond the windows, the San Diego harbor shimmered midday sun. Down below, crowds gathered—snapping photos, cheering as cameras rolled.

He barely glanced down. He was on a call.

"We're talking a prime-time exclusive," the Fox News producer gushed. "A full hour. Live from your headquarters."

Kahn curled one side of his mouth. An hour. Network television.

"Yes, of course. I'd be honored. Have your team coordinate with my assistant."

The door swung open. A man walked in.

Not rushed. Not out of place. As if he belonged.

Kahn's brows lifted, irritation flashing. Where the hell is security?

Still, he turned back to the call. "Make the arrangements," he said briskly, then tossed the phone aside and focused on the intruder.

The man stood there, looking almost amused. Dark jacket, sleeves pushed up. There was something familiar—and unsettling.

"Who the hell are you?" Kahn demanded.

The man studied him a beat. Then, calmly: "I've traveled around the world to find you. And now I've come to say goodbye."

Kahn's scowl deepened as recognition dawned. He owned his paintings, admired the technique. But this man? This wasn't the artist. The president's warning echoed in his head. This was a hunter who had found his prey.

"Oh, you're the painter," he sneered. "Didn't peg you for the breaking-and-entering type. Payne. You have some balls walking into my office."

Luke didn't flinch. "Funny. I came here to watch you get thrown out."

Kahn's smile disappeared.

"We have proof," Luke continued. "Video. Witnesses. The kids you kidnapped. Financial blackmail. And we have Sochi."

He let the silence stretch.

"He's talking."

Kahn's fingers curled against the desk. He tried to laugh it off, but something was shifting. Years of manipulation and power games were slipping through his grasp.

"You think you've won?" he hissed. "You have no idea who you're dealing with."

He leaned forward, voice tightening. "I've got an ace up my sleeve."

Luke waited.

Kahn's smile returned. "QuantumSentinel."

Still nothing from Luke.

"I have full immunity. You can't touch me."

Luke stayed silent. Then, casually:

"QuantumSentinel no longer exists."

Kahn's blood ran cold.

He grabbed his cell phone and called Ward.

No signal.

He tried Bowen's cell.

Still nothing.

He looked at his phone—no bars. His cell network was down.

Across town, inside a CyberWatch secure lab, Jason Edwards leaned back as a line of code flashed across the screen:

COMMUNICATION LOCKOUT: KAHN-7 INITIATED

Jason grinned.

"Sorry, Mr. Kahn. Your service has been terminated—permanently," he said to himself.

Kahn slammed his phone down and spun to his keyboard, fingers stabbing at the keys.

A single line blinked back:

SYSTEM TERMINATED

His breath caught. No backup servers. No fail-safes. Nothing.

"You know," Luke said quietly, "you almost got away with it. But you made one mistake."

Kahn stiffened.

"You went after Peter and Maggie."

Kahn's fists clenched. "They humiliated me. That lawsuit cost me millions—turned me into a pariah in my adopted city. No one crosses me, as you'll soon find out, Payne."

"The hack?" he scoffed. "I was just having a little fun. Getting a little skin for their sins. But when they stole from me…" His voice darkened. "That changed everything."

Luke didn't blink. "It did, Kahn. It changed everything. I'm afraid your carefully laid plans have unraveled."

The door opened again.

Anya Kahn walked in.

Kahn turned pale.

Her expression was stone. "I believe you're in my chair."

Before he could speak, David Bowen, Harry Worthington, and Thomas Benton followed—then two uniformed San Diego police officers.

The police sergeant placed the warrant on the desk.

"Aarav Kahn, you are under arrest for conspiracy, kidnapping, attempted murder, and multiple felony charges. You have the right to remain silent—"

Cold steel clicked around Kahn's wrists.

Luke exhaled. "It's over."

Anya didn't blink. "Yes. It is."

She barely got the words out before six men in dark suits swept in. One flashed a badge.

"Special Agent James Riley, Department of Justice," he said. "Aarav Kahn is now in federal custody."

He handed over a transfer order.

Worthington stepped forward. "This is a local case. How the hell did you even—"

Riley cut him off with a calm smile. "Let's just say we've got a friend inside SDPD. The moment Worthington phoned it in, we were ready."

"This is bullshit."

"Maybe. But it's coming from the top." Riley turned to the officers. "Remove the cuffs."

Worthington hesitated—then gave a tight nod.

The local police stepped back. The feds stepped in, replacing the restraints with their own. As they escorted Kahn away, he looked back—eyes scanning the room, searching for a lifeline.

The doors slammed shut behind him.

Silence.

Then Anya smiled. "They took the bait."

Worthington nodded. "Grace pulled it off. She played Ward exactly how we hoped."

"Fed him the intel we wanted leaked," Anya said. "Ward thought he could hijack the SDPD arrest—and he did, just like we planned it."

Worthington added, "We knew the Ward and the President would try to intervene. Bail. Delay. Spin control."

"But now," Jason said, "he's federal property. And without QuantumSentinel... he's useless to the White House. Even a liability."

Anya's voice was flat. "Where are they taking him?"

Worthington's tone dropped. "Classified holding. Louisiana

first. Then maybe CECOT in El Salvador. Or Gitmo. Depends on what they want to extract before he disappears."

"He won't be protected now," Luke said. "Not without the leverage."

"Exactly," Worthington replied. "He's a liability to the President. And liabilities vanish."

Anya folded her arms. "So... it worked."

Worthington gave a tired smile. "We didn't just take him down. We made sure he wouldn't get back up."

Luke nodded once.

"Then we're done."

And this time, they truly were.

CHAPTER 135: FULL CIRCLE

Shangri-La — Three Months Later

The jacarandas were blooming, and the breeze rustled through the palms, laughter and conversation threading the gardens like music.

It was the first time they had all been together since the storm had passed—since Kahn and Sochi had been taken down. Three months had gone by, and now there were no more missions, no more shadows. Just friends, family, and the peace that once felt unreachable.

As Maggie and Peter sauntered up the garden path, the familiar tap-tap-tap of their canes marked a hard-won victory. They moved at a deliberate pace. Trailing behind them, Nora and Rodrigo were a study in joyful abandon. Their laughter, bright and untethered, threaded through the sunlit air—a reminder of the shadows they had escaped. Two kids, finally, truly free to just be.

From the patio, Luke watched the scene unfold with a quiet smile. Seeing the kids thrive and Maggie and Peter get better every day filled him with a joy he hadn't felt in years. A warmth spread through his chest that eased the old tension he used to carry.

Rodrigo bounded up the steps, energy like a live wire. "We just finished our first big coding project! It predicts stock market swings better than some hedge fund software!"

Nora, following at a calmer pace, rolled her eyes. "Now he wants the whole class to pool their savings and start a fund."

Luke chuckled, ruffling Rodrigo's hair. "Entrepreneurial spirit. I like it."

Maggie shook her head. "I like it too—as long as it doesn't end in a congressional hearing."

The kids were thriving at High Tech High, surrounded by mentors and friends. The pressure was gone. Now they just lived.

They'd even started tinkering again with the AI Nora began in Mumbai—what started as a support tool called Besty had evolved into something more.

Luke tilted his head. "The AI assistant?"

Nora nodded. "Behavioral Emulation Support Tool for Youth. She listens, adapts, helps kids reason through things—no judgment."

Rodrigo added, "She's like a chill genius big sister, but coded."

Luke laughed. "Therapist, tutor, and conscience. Not bad."

Anya wandered over with a glass of wine, Bowen at her side. "I saw the demo," she said. "You two built something extraordinary."

Bowen nodded. "I've already pitched it to a few people in health and education. They're interested."

Rodrigo's eyes widened. "Wait—seriously?"

Anya smiled. "If you're willing, I'll fund the next phase—Besty and beyond. Think of it as an idea factory. Your ideas. My backing."

Bowen raised an eyebrow. "Fund what?"

Anya smiled. "An idea factory. For Besty and whatever else they dream up. AI for good—for justice, learning, the environment. Solutions, not surveillance. You'll be our CEO."

Bowen blinked. "I didn't know I was applying."

"You weren't," she said. "But you're the right choice."

Rodrigo beamed. Nora's eyes glistened.

The future at last belonged to them.

Maria joined them with a plate of ceviche. "They're basically the most popular kids in school. But, you know—nerd popular."

Nora shrugged. "Better than influencer popular."

Rodrigo nodded solemnly. "We have the best kind of power."

Peter laughed, draping an arm over Maggie's shoulders. "These two are going to run the world one day."

Maggie smiled, watching them. "I wouldn't bet against them."

Maria had become family. Between classes at San Diego City College and helping run Shangri-La, Maria had put down roots here.

A blur of golden fur streaked across the lawn. Hass, now lean and quick, had left behind his avocado obsession and sluggish days. The dog barked with joy as Rodrigo launched a tennis ball across the yard.

Rodrigo grinned. "No more stolen avocados."

Luke laughed. "He's half the dog he used to be."

Vanessa arrived with a bottle of wine in one hand and a folder in the other.

"I know, I know," she said, catching Luke's raised eyebrow. "Couldn't help myself."

She handed the folder to Maggie—blueprints for the Foundation's new amphitheater, funded by record-breaking donations.

Luke grinned. "You're building an empire."

Vanessa smiled. "I had good teachers."

She'd found her rhythm. Once an outsider, she now anchored the Foundation's future.

"And you?" she asked Luke. "Lecturing, mentoring, selling paintings faster than you can finish them?"

He shook his head, smiling. "Blame the New York Times. Tragic war-hero artist sells."

But the work mattered. Teaching again. Helping other veterans heal through art.

"I like it better this way," he said. "Being part of something."

Vanessa squeezed his hand. "I know."

A comfortable silence followed—glasses clinking, soft laughter filled the air.

Jason and Helen walked over, hands linked, grinning like they'd pulled off a heist.

"Before anyone steals the spotlight," Jason said, raising a beer, "we've got news."

The group quieted.

"We're getting married."

Cheers erupted.

Maggie hugged Helen tight. "Finally!"

Helen beamed. "And—we're opening a CyberWatch branch in Mumbai. At the old R&D site. Lee's taking over as director."

Lee nodded. "We're flipping Kahn's network. Retraining the kids. Turning it into something good."

Helen added, "Time to clean up what he left behind."

A quiet pause followed as the news settled in.

Rajeev cleared his throat. "Yes, and I'll be flying to Mumbai to make sure security is in place for the new branch."

Jenny looked him in the eyes. "How long will you be there?"

Rajeev looked surprised. "Well, it shouldn't take any longer than two weeks. I'll be breaking in a new guy."

Jenny smiled coyly. "Well, I just happen to have a two-week vacation coming. Mind if I join you?"

Now everyone's eyes were on Rajeev, who was blushing. "Sure, the more the merrier. I think Buddha said that."

Helen laughed. "Strike while the iron's hot, Rajeev. I think he said that too."

Rajeev nodded. "Still paranoid. Still me."

Jenny grinned. "He just happens to like me."

Hank whistled. "Did not see that coming."

Rajeev shrugged. "Nobody ever does."

Maggie and Peter watched from near the bar as Edward and Jimmy from the Green Dragon served hors d'oeuvres with flair.

"Would you believe they insisted on catering tonight?" Maggie said.

Peter chuckled. "After everything, I thought they'd disappear."

"Luke talked to them. Told them it was safe. This was their way of saying thanks."

Peter popped a bite of lobster toast. "Well... now I really forgive them."

"They tried to help. That counts," Maggie said, raising her glass toward the kitchen.

Peter nodded. "Tonight, I'm just glad we're all still standing."

Maggie smiled. "Indeed. Standing. Walking. Seeing again."

Coop clapped Luke on the back. "Damn glad to have my guys back."

Moises grinned. "Bet you missed us."

"I missed my damn plane," Coop shot back. "You lunatics nearly got it shot down."

Last to arrive was the Admiral, in dress blues, three-star insignia gleaming. Promoted, heading to the Pentagon—to speak the truth where it mattered most.

Talk turned to Sochi—life sentence, no parole.

Then Jenney asked, "What about Kahn?"

Maggie exhaled. "No one knows."

Peter added, "The press tried. He vanished."

Helen folded her arms. "He's probably at Gitmo."

Luke swirled his glass. "Or somewhere worse."

"Kahn's not the kind to disappear without a plan," Luke muttered.

Helen nodded slowly. "Let's just hope we don't end up being part of it."

As the sun touched the horizon, the group gathered on the patio.

Peter raised his glass. "To family—not just the one we're born into, but the one we choose."

Glasses clinked. Laughter echoed.

Luke smiled—finally, the peace felt real.

This moment. These people.

The life he almost lost.

And now, miraculously, still had.

CHAPTER 136: LETTING GO

Morning arrived at Shangri-La on a soft breeze beneath brilliant blue skies. Luke Payne stood outside the pool house, palette knife in hand, pulling rich strokes of crimson red across the canvas. The painting was abstract, but it carried motion—a rising tide, or the edge of a storm clearing. Strength radiated from it, an energy that hadn't been there before.

Ella Fitzgerald's voice floated from the Echo device, her velvet tones slipping into the rhythm of blade and color. Luke worked with purpose, lost in the flow. The silence inside him was no longer crushing. It was calm.

A familiar, teasing voice cut through the music. "Alexa, stop."

Luke turned, a slow grin forming. Vanessa leaned in the pool house doorway, barefoot, wrapped in a white terrycloth robe, her hair tousled from sleep.

"Up already, Miss Sunshine?" he asked, wiping a streak of paint from his fingers.

She studied the canvas. "I like this one."

"Yeah?"

She stepped closer, scanning the layered strokes. "It's different. Still intense, but… lighter."

Luke dragged the palette knife in one final stroke. "Guess that says something."

"It does," she said softly.

She stretched, rolling her shoulders. "Big day. Maggie roped me into helping clean up after the party."

Luke chuckled. "Feels like a lifetime ago we were in the thick of it."

Last night had been a celebration of survival—family, friendship, second chances. Laughter had replaced tension. The shadows of war rooms and missions had finally receded.

Luke set down the palette knife. "I have to take care of something this morning. I'll be back before lunch."

Vanessa kissed his cheek. "Take your time. I'll be here."

He packed away his paints, grabbed his keys, and slipped into the Fiat. The drive to Ocean Beach was quiet. When Newport Avenue crested, the Pacific spread out before him, sunlight skipping across the waves. His weathered beach cottage stood above the sea like it had been waiting.

Inside, the air held the familiar mix of sea salt and worn wood. He moved slowly through the rooms, pausing at framed photos from their travels—wine in Portugal, camels in Morocco, snorkeling in the Galapagos. He ran his fingers along the dining table they had built together.

In the bedroom, the wallpapered wall was still covered with their souvenirs. He saw Savannah—cutoff jeans, tank top—balanced on a step stool, smoothing paper against the wall. A sponge in one hand, a bucket of water at her feet. She laughed as paste dripped down her arm, fingers streaked with glue. He'd teased her for decorating herself more than the wall. She'd tossed the sponge at him, and they ended up on the floor, kissing amid crumpled paper, wet rags, and the faint scent of wheat paste and lavender.

He closed his eyes. No sadness. No pain. Just warmth.

Luke lingered in the living room before pulling the door shut. It had been part of a different life. A good life. But it was time to move forward.

At Sunset Cliffs, the wind tugged at his clothes, surf pounding below. He walked to the edge, fingers finding the chain around his neck—the small metal reminder he'd carried for more than two years.

Once a symbol. Then an anchor. Now, just weight.

He unfastened it, the links warm from his skin, and with one smooth motion, hurled it into the waves. Sunlight caught the metal in a brief flash before it vanished beneath the surf.

Luke drew a slow, steady breath.

He turned—not from the past, but toward what came next.

Back in the Fiat, his phone buzzed. Vanessa's message lit the screen:

Maggie asked if you'd pick up some pastries from the bakery.

He smiled, started the engine.

The phone buzzed again. Unknown number.

His smile faded. A photo—grainy, zoomed-in. A man stood at the edge of a cliff, arm extended toward the sea.

Luke knew the moment instantly. It was him—letting go.

The caption read: A keepsake lost is a story told. Don't worry, we're watching.

The warmth drained from the morning. He looked again— The message was gone. He stared out at the Pacific. The horizon was wide open, bright with promise. Somewhere behind him, something unseen was already moving.

LUKE PAYNE RETURNS
A Luke Payne Thriller • Book Two

THE SAVANNAH CODE

Luke Payne thought he was finished with covert missions, ghosts from the past, and the shadows they cast. He was wrong.

When Helen Shepard's nephew disappears from a rhino conservation preserve in Kenya, she doesn't call the embassy. She calls Luke—her former operative, now an artist and quiet mentor, living far from the front lines.

What starts as a personal favor quickly becomes a global chase. Luke uncovers a brutal, tech-driven poaching syndicate stretching from the grasslands of East Africa to the criminal underworld of Cape Town. As the trail winds through encrypted channels, black market labs, and compromised governments, it becomes clear: this isn't just about illegal wildlife trade—it's about control, extinction, and power.

The deeper Luke goes, the more familiar the players become. In China, an old adversary—General Yue—emerges from the shadows. And in the icy streets of Saint Petersburg, a ruthless Russian crime syndicate prepares to unleash a new kind of war.

With his team scattered and the stakes higher than ever, Luke must confront what he's become: not just a survivor, but a weapon the world still fears—and may still need.

In a world where the line between protector and predator blurs, Luke Payne faces his most personal mission yet.

Fast-paced, emotionally charged, and razor-sharp, Savannah Code is the next chapter in the acclaimed Luke Payne series— where justice has no borders, and the cost of peace is everything.

ABOUT RON JAMES

Ron is a U.S. Navy veteran, award-winning journalist, and nationally syndicated columnist whose career spans roles with Time Warner, San Diego Magazine, and The San Diego Union-Tribune. As co-author of The Multimedia Casebook and editor of Wine Dine & Travel Magazine, he has built a reputation for compelling storytelling, sharp investigative insight, and a passion for global culture.

His debut thriller, Quantum Deception, blends his fascination with cutting-edge technology, geopolitics, and human resilience into a high-stakes tale of cyber warfare and international intrigue. Drawing on his Navy experience and years covering world affairs, James crafts a story that feels as authentic as tomorrow's headlines.

When he's not writing, Ron can often be found exploring far-flung destinations with his wife, glass of wine in hand, or delving into his family's deep historical roots that stretch back to the Mayflower. He lives in San Diego, California.

ALSO BY RON JAMES

Nonfiction

The Multimedia Casebook — Van Nostrand Reinhold

Fodor's San Diego: Restaurants — Fodor's Travel

Fiction

Quantum Deception — A Luke Payne Thriller (this book)

The Savannah Code — A Luke Payne Thriller (coming 2026)

www.ingramcontent.com/pod-product-compliance
Lightning Source LLC
Chambersburg PA
CBHW022255310726
48973CB00001B/83